Praise for *Crooked River*

"Exciting. Nail-biting. Quality storytelling."

—Publishers Weekly

"Preston and Child know how to craft compelling stories that are both baffling and surprising. The cast of characters feels authentic and moves the story forward in unexpected ways... The authors are masters of the procedural with a gothic flair."

—Associated Press

"[Pendergast] still remains the most charming, intelligent, cool, and creepy agent ever written... Read this. As fast as possible. Preston & Child have once again created the unimaginable and you just can't miss it!"

—Suspense Magazine

"Agent Pendergast is back and better than ever."

—The Real Book Spy

"The best mystery series going today. Preston and Child display a true master's touch. This is riveting reading entertainment of the highest order."

—Providence Journal

"Red herrings and dead ends abound in this especially intricately plotted entry in the Pendergast series, which is also noteworthy (as usual) for its finely drawn characters and its writing style, which overlays contemporary storytelling with a light ornate flavoring. Fast moving and...tense...*Crooked River* is another great entry in this series. Preston and Child keep them coming, don't they?" —*New York Journal of Books*

"*Crooked River* by Douglas Preston and Lincoln Child combines a sinister global threat, a mystery using modern medical science, and a powerful, sadistic antagonist. Who better than to combat these but unorthodox FBI Agent Aloysius Pendergast...This compelling story moves forward in unexpected ways. Readers will enjoy going on a journey with Pendergast and company." —*Crimespree*

"*Crooked River* is worth the price of admission, and Preston & Child find themselves with another surefire hit on their hands." —*Bookreporter*

"An incredible adventure." —NJ.com

Acclaim for These Novels by Preston and Child

Verses for the Dead

"Multifaceted and complex. Legendary. Working together, Preston and Child are masters at crafting a story that goes beyond a simple mystery or thriller... Readers unfamiliar with Pendergast will find this novel a fantastic launch point. He's a modern-day Sherlock Holmes, and the story reads like classic literature." —Associated Press

"Doug Preston and Lincoln Child's master detective A.X.L. Pendergast is every bit the modern equivalent of Sherlock Holmes and Hercule Poirot. And his investigative skills have never been sharper than in the altogether brilliant *Verses for the Dead* … A throwback to classic crime fiction while maintaining a sharp, postmodern edge." —*Providence Journal*

"*Verses for the Dead* is classic Preston & Child, full of complex characters, plot twists and storylines that border on supernatural or otherworldly elements […] The story is full of suspense and surprises that all converge in a jaw-dropping ending." —*Bookreporter*

The Scorpion's Tail

"Expect nice twists, hairy danger, and good old-fashioned gunplay. This one's an attention grabber. Get a copy." —*Kirkus Reviews* (starred review)

"[An] enjoyable sequel…The authors do their usual solid job of maintaining suspense throughout. Their two capable female leads are well-suited to sustain a long series." —*Publishers Weekly*

"Preston and Child have designed an intricate thriller

that takes several twists and turns, but never totally diverts from the crux of the story. This is a series that demands attention." —*New York Journal of Books*

"The authors bring the same rigorous plotting and deft characterizations to this novel as they do with their Special Agent Pendergast books…The Kelly and Swanson pairing is certainly engaging. It seems the duo might be settling in for a good, long run."

—*Booklist*

"What Preston and Child have so deftly succeeded at doing, yet again, is to combine real history with archaeological finds and forensic science to create a fascinating novel filled with the thrills of an Indiana Jones film…Buckle up because *The Scorpion's Tail* is another winner for this writing duo."

—*Bookreporter*

Old Bones

"Longtime readers of Preston and Child will love to see the beloved characters of Nora Kelly and Corrie Swanson take center stage in what is a terrific start to a new series. Their writing talent shines as this mix of history, exploration of nature, and crime will without a doubt land on the top of the bestseller lists."

—Associated Press

"*Old Bones* exceeds expectations at every juncture, a

thriller extraordinaire that turns history upside down in forming the basis of a riveting and relentless tale."

—*Providence Sunday Journal*

"A smart, satisfying read." —*Kirkus Reviews*

"This outing belongs to two dedicated women whose future adventures will be happily anticipated."

—*Booklist*

"From the thriller world's dynamic duo comes a new work of archeology, murder, and the Donner Party. This one should please longtime fans of Preston and Child, as well as new devotees drawn in by that ever-appealing setup of a past crime coming back to haunt the present." —*CrimeReads*

"Preston and Child have created a fine mix of fiction and historical fact. The story is peopled by complex and engaging characters with sometimes murky ambitions…The ending, which seems far-fetched, is definitely, disturbingly possible." —*BookTrib*

"*Old Bones* has it all: chills, thrills, and a blend of history, along with archaeological expertise you can only get from a Preston & Child novel. I loved spending time with Nora Kelly and Corrie Swanson, and look forward to seeing them in future adventures. Longtime readers will be rewarded not only by this pairing but by some other surprises leading up to the conclusion of this exciting read." —*Bookreporter*

"The two strong female protagonists [Nora Kelly and Corrie Swanson] share a dynamic reminiscent of that between Pendergast and his friend on the NYPD, Vincent D'Agosta. An intriguing series launch."

—Publishers Weekly

"Preston and Child's cast of characters spin off in their latest, starring Nora Kelly and ex-distinguished youth-turned-FBI agent Corrie Swanson. Kelly leads an expedition to excavate the Donner Party camp, while Swanson investigates a series of grave robberies. The longtime writing team yet again seamlessly merges science and suspense." *—Newsweek*

City of Endless Night

"If you'd like to know how Arthur Conan Doyle's Sherlock Holmes tales would be reviewed today, look no further than *City of Endless Night*... A typically terrific mystery laced with the gothic overtones for which this series is known... This is mystery thriller writing of the highest order, a tale as relentlessly riveting as it is sumptuously scintillating."

—Providence Sunday Journal

"Preston and Child continue to write tense and compelling tales while also invoking the feel of Sherlock Holmes or other gothic stories of the late 19th century... Marvelous." *—Associated Press*

"As always, the authors have crafted a story that is almost impossible to pull away from, and their prose is as elegant as fans have come to expect. Pendergast continues to be one of thrillerdom's most exciting and intriguing series leads, and the series remains among the most reliable in the genre." —*Booklist*

"VERDICT: Fans of the Pendergast series will be delighted with this latest romp and its careful plotting and suspense should appeal to mystery fans generally as well." —*Library Journal*

"This, yet another masterpiece by Preston & Child, will be the perfect way to start out your New Year. Just as it was when D'Agosta and Pendergast first met up in the thrilling book *Relic*, they are together once again solving a crime of mammoth proportions. Preston, Child, and their well-known characters are always sheer perfection!" —Amy Lignor, *Suspense Magazine*

"One of the best in the series—tense and tightly wound, with death relentlessly circling, stalking, lurking behind every shadow." —*Kirkus Reviews*

The Obsidian Chamber

"The latest novel in Preston & Child's Pendergast series picks up from the cliff-hanger ending of *Crimson Shore* and doesn't let up. The authors keep readers guessing…The crisp writing and exemplary stories are still in abundance in this consistently exciting and never predictable series." —Associated Press

"Rivetingly superb…great fun…thriller-writing of the highest order. A lavish, brilliantly conceived puzzle that pieces together neo-gothic plotting with splendidly rich tones."   —*Providence Journal*

"Keep[s] the excitement meter pegged…Action-adventure with a macabre, sometimes-fantastical flair."   —*Kirkus Reviews*

"As any reader of suspense knows, Douglas Preston and Lincoln Child write a series of books featuring one of the best characters in the history of suspense literature: Aloysius Pendergast. [*The Obsidian Chamber* is] an excellent story by these two unbelievably talented authors. A page-turner, a deluxe suspense, a perfect mystery—Preston & Child remain the best of the best and never let their huge fan base down!"
—*Suspense Magazine*

"A complex puzzle box of a story…stellar…most surprising."   —*Bookreporter*

Crimson Shore

"It's like Christmas for lovers of suspense when the words Preston & Child once again appear on a book cover. It's a truly great Christmas when the main character of that novel is Aloysius X. L. Pendergast. For those who have read these books voraciously, it's not a surprise to learn that this latest tale is one that will keep you riveted until the very end…Preston & Child continue to make these books the absolute best there is in the suspense realm." —*Suspense Magazine*

"Secrets and mysteries abound…the shock and twist are perfect. The unusual becomes believable and normal in the authors' capable hands."

—Associated Press

"The Pendergast novels combine elegant prose with sharp-witted storytelling, and the FBI agent continues to be one of thrillerdom's more engaging characters."

—*Booklist*

"New readers will be hooked…Die-hard fans will add this to their must-read lists."

—*Library Journal* (starred review)
LibraryReads Pick

"Douglas Preston and Lincoln Child have fashioned their most complex, ambitious entry yet in their stellar Aloysius Pendergast series…a perfect puzzle of a tale that would challenge the wits of even Sherlock Holmes. A twist-filled, tour de force of classical storytelling." —*Providence Journal*

"Douglas Preston and Lincoln Child have created one of the most distinctive—and eccentric—sleuths in the history of crime fiction. FBI Special Agent Aloysius X. L. Pendergast…solves crimes as no one else does."

—*Maine Sunday Telegram*

"One of the best thriller series of all time."

—Examiner.com

Blue Labyrinth

White Fire

"These dynamic authors' best thriller to date."

—Library Journal

"Pendergast isn't the only offbeat detective in the latest thriller by Preston and Child. With a deft hand, the pair create a new mystery for Sherlock Holmes."

—The Oklahoman

"Fans of Sherlock Holmes will devour Preston and Child's latest thriller, not only because of its connection to Conan Doyle, but because Pendergast bears a striking resemblance to the iconic detective, and has powers as eerily uncanny as Sherlock's. Readers will race toward the final page, and once there, will thirst for more."

—Bookreporter

"It has everything that has made this reader eagerly await the next book in this series: a great story, solid supporting characters, an element of the macabre (or two), and an original touch."

—TheMysterySite.com

"A remarkable plot that ties together multiple killings…a secret Sherlock Holmes story and a meeting between Oscar Wilde and Arthur Conan Doyle keep readers glued to the page."

—RT Book Reviews

Two Graves

"A good thriller forces the reader to finish the book in

one sitting. An exceptional thriller does that plus forces the reader to slow down to savor every word. With *Two Graves*, Preston and Child have delivered another exceptional book…The gothic atmosphere that oozes from the pages will envelop the reader…Pendergast is a modern-day Sherlock Holmes, quirks and all…The mystery tantalizes, and the shocks throughout the narrative are like bolts of lightning. Fans will love the conclusion to the trilogy, and newcomers will seek out the authors' earlier titles." —Associated Press

"Pendergast—an always-black-clad pale blond polymath, gaunt yet physically deadly, an FBI agent operating without supervision or reprimand—lurks at the dark, sharp edge of crime fiction protagonists." —*Kirkus Reviews*

"A lavish story and one that takes the time for some skillful vignettes and characterizations." —*The Charlotte Observer*

"Preston and Child's high-adrenaline thriller wraps up the trilogy…with a bang…[An] intelligent suspense novel." —*Publishers Weekly*

"*Two Graves* provides readers exactly what they would expect from a Preston and Child novel—thrills, high adventure, treacherous plot twists, and well-researched scientific intrigue. The story is never predictable, and Pendergast is a multi-layered personality who keeps you guessing throughout." —*Bookreporter*

"The action is constant and starts with a bang." —*RT Book Reviews*

"Another fast-paced murder mystery that crosses the country, dips into Mexico and then wallops Manhattan hotels. It's the perfect holiday gift for that thriller-genre lover in your life."   —*Asbury Park Press*

Cold Vengeance

"Before you even open the cover of a Preston and Child book, you know you're in for a good, if chilling, even thrilling time."   —*Asbury Park Press*

"[Preston and Child are] still going strong…Such is the talent of our authors that we happily follow their characters…all over the globe, from the moors of Scotland to the loony bins of New York City; the recipe is mixed well with a dash of assassins here and a soupcon of Nazis there, a couple of traitors and some really fascinating secondary characters…*Cold Vengeance* is a hot hell of a fun read."

—Examiner.com

"4½ stars! Top Pick! Preston and Child continue their dominance of the thriller genre with stellar writing and twists that come at a furious pace. Others may try to write like them, but no one can come close. The best in the business deliver another winner."

—*RT Book Reviews*

BLOODLESS

ALSO BY DOUGLAS PRESTON AND LINCOLN CHILD

AGENT PENDERGAST NOVELS

Bloodless • Crooked River • Verses for the Dead • City of Endless Night • The Obsidian Chamber • Crimson Shore • Blue Labyrinth • White Fire • Two Graves* • Cold Vengeance* • Fever Dream* • Cemetery Dance • The Wheel of Darkness • The Book of the Dead** • Dance of Death** • Brimstone** • Still Life with Crows • The Cabinet of Curiosities • Reliquary† • Relic†

*The Helen Trilogy **The Diogenes Trilogy
†*Relic* and *Reliquary* are ideally read in sequence

NORA KELLY NOVELS

Diablo Mesa • The Scorpion's Tail • Old Bones

GIDEON CREW NOVELS

The Pharaoh Key • Beyond the Ice Limit • The Lost Island • Gideon's Corpse • Gideon's Sword

OTHER NOVELS

The Ice Limit • *Thunderhead* • *Riptide* • *Mount Dragon*

BY DOUGLAS PRESTON

The Lost City of the Monkey God • *The Kraken Project* • *Impact* • *The Monster of Florence* (with Mario Spezi) • *Blasphemy* • *Tyrannosaur Canyon* • *The Codex* • *Ribbons of Time* • *The Royal Road* • *Talking to the Ground* • *Jennie* • *Cities of Gold* • *Dinosaurs in the Attic*

BY LINCOLN CHILD

Chrysalis • *Full Wolf Moon* • *The Forgotten Room* • *The Third Gate* • *Terminal Freeze* • *Deep Storm* • *Death Match* • *Lethal Velocity* (formerly *Utopia*) • *Tales of the Dark 1–3* • *Dark Banquet* • *Dark Company*

BLOODLESS

A PENDERGAST NOVEL

DOUGLAS PRESTON
& LINCOLN CHILD

GRAND
CENTRAL

New York Boston

Copyright © 2021 by Splendide Mendax, Inc. and Lincoln Child

Cover design by Flag. Cover art: statue from Getty Images © Joe Daniel Price; cemetery from Getty Images © Mark Coggins. Cover copyright © 2021 by Hachette Book Group, Inc.

Grand Central Publishing
Hachette Book Group
1290 Avenue of the Americas, New York, NY 10104
grandcentralpublishing.com
twitter.com/grandcentralpub

Originally published as hardcover and ebook in August 2021
First oversize mass market edition: January 2023

Grand Central Publishing is a division of Hachette Book Group, Inc. The Grand Central Publishing name and logo is a trademark of Hachette Book Group, Inc.

The publisher is not responsible for websites (or their content) that are not owned by the publisher.

The Hachette Speakers Bureau provides a wide range of authors for speaking events. To find out more, go to www.hachettespeakersbureau.com or call (866) 376-6591.

Grand Central Publishing books may be purchased in bulk for business, educational, or promotional use. For information, please contact your local bookseller or the Hachette Book Group Special Markets Department at special.markets@hbgusa.com.

Library of Congress Control Number: 2021939243

ISBNs: 978-1-5387-3670-8 (hardcover), 978-1-5387-3671-5 (ebook), 978-1-5387-0734-0 (int'l edition), 978-1-5387-0665-7 (Canadian edition), 978-1-5387-0608-4 (large print), 978-1-5387-0648-0 (B&N signed edition), 978-1-5387-0647-3 (signed edition), 978-1-5387-3672-2 (trade paperback), 978-1-5387-3669-2 (mass market)

Printed in the United States of America

OPM

10 9 8 7 6 5 4 3 2 1

BLOODLESS

I

Wednesday, November 24, 1971

Flo Schaffner was not at all happy with the new uniform that Northwest Orient Airlines had imposed on stewardesses, especially the dumb cap with a bill and earflaps that made her look like Donald Duck. Nevertheless, she stood at the door of Flight 305—Portland to Seattle—with a bright smile, greeting arriving passengers and checking their tickets. She was not displeased at the relatively small number of passengers on the flight; she'd thought it would be full, this being the day before Thanksgiving. But today only about a third of the main cabin was occupied, which in her experience meant a stress-free flight.

As people began to settle into their seats, she and the other stewardess, Tina Mucklow, began moving from opposite ends of the main cabin, taking drink orders. Schaffner took the rear. One of her first customers was in seat 18C of the Boeing 727: a polite, soft-spoken gentleman of early middle age, wearing a raincoat, a gray business suit, a white shirt, and a black tie. She knew his name; one of her responsibilities in checking tickets was to try to memorize the names of all the passengers and their seat assignments. It was usually impossible, but with the plane as empty as it was, today she had managed it.

"Can I get you anything to drink, Mr. Cooper?"

He politely asked her for a bourbon and Seven. When she brought it, he handed her a twenty.

"Anything smaller?"

"Nope."

She told him he'd have to wait until later for her to get him change.

The pilot, William Scott, whom everyone called Scotty, announced over the intercom for the stewardesses to secure the exits and prepare for takeoff. Schaffner raised the aft stairway and then settled in a jump seat next to it, not far from the passenger in 18C. The flight took off precisely on time, at 2:50 PM, for the thirty-minute hop to Seattle.

As the plane was leveling out and the seat belt signs were turned off, the passenger in 18C signaled to her. She came over, assuming he wanted another drink, but instead he placed an envelope in her hand. This was something that often happened to Schaffner: a lonely traveler writing her a note asking to meet for a drink, dinner, or something more. She had learned that the best way to handle such approaches was simply not to engage. She thanked the passenger warmly and slipped the envelope into her pocket, unread.

The man leaned toward her with a friendly smile and whispered, "Miss, you'd better look at that note. I have a bomb."

Schaffner wasn't sure she had heard him correctly. She removed the envelope and took out the note. It was printed in felt-tipped pen in precise capital letters, and it did indeed say he had a bomb, and that as long as everyone cooperated nothing bad would happen.

"Please sit down next to me," he said, taking the note back from her and putting it in his shirt pocket. She did as told, and he unlatched the briefcase in his lap and lifted the lid a few inches. Inside, she could see a bundle of red cylinders with wires attached, nestled next to a large battery.

He shut the briefcase and put on a pair of dark glasses. "Take this down."

Taking out her pen, she wrote down a series of instructions.

"Relay that to the cockpit," he said.

Schaffner rose, walked down the aisle, and went into the cockpit. Closing the door behind her, she told the pilot the plane was being hijacked by a man with a bomb. Then, reading from the envelope, she recited the list of his demands.

"Does he really have a bomb?" Scotty asked.

"Yes," she replied. "I saw it. It looked real."

"Oh, boy." Scotty called Northwest Orient flight operations in Minnesota. His words were summarized in a teletype.

PASSENGER HAS ADVISED THIS IS A HIJACKING. EN ROUTE TO SEATTLE. THE STEW HAS BEEN HANDED A NOTE. HE REQUESTS $200,000 IN A KNAP-SACK BY 5:00 PM. HE WANTS TWO BACK PARACHUTES, TWO FRONT PARACHUTES. HE WANTS THE MONEY IN NEGOTIABLE AMERICAN CURRENCY. DENOMINATION OF THE BILLS IS NOT IMPORTANT. HAS A BOMB IN BRIEFCASE AND WILL USE IT

IF ANYTHING IS DONE TO BLOCK HIS
REQUEST.

The hijacker also requested that a fuel truck be
waiting on the tarmac at Sea-Tac airport, to refuel
the plane for a new journey to be specified later. And
he demanded that a flight engineer board the plane
for the next leg of the journey.

He didn't say why.

2

IN THE COCKPIT OF Flight 305, Scotty and copilot Bill Rataczak discussed how to handle the situation. So far, the passengers had no idea the plane was being hijacked—and Scotty wanted to keep it that way.

After the call to Minnesota, Northwest Orient flight operations had contacted Don Nyrop, the airline's president, as well as the FBI. The FBI wanted to storm the plane, but Nyrop said he preferred to cooperate with the hijacker, that the airline had insurance and would pay the ransom. The FBI reluctantly agreed. But it would take time for the hijacker's demands to be met.

In the meantime, the 727 had reached Tacoma and begun to circle. The FBI and the airline scrambled to pull together the ransom and parachutes.

Scotty got on the intercom and told the passengers that the plane was experiencing a minor mechanical problem, there was no need for concern, and that they would be landing in an hour or so. Meanwhile, in the back of the plane, the hijacker, Dan Cooper, had been chain-smoking. He offered a cigarette to Schaffner, who took it to calm her nerves, even though she had given up smoking some time before.

Outside, a storm was developing. Soon it began to rain.

The airline contacted the Seattle National Bank, where it had done business. The bank was glad to help. It had, in fact, a store of money ready for just such a purpose: a cache of twenty-dollar bills that had been microfilmed and each serial number recorded, in case of a heist or robbery. Ten thousand twenty-dollar bills, banded in bricks of fifty, were stuffed into a satchel with a drawstring and delivered to the FBI. It weighed about twenty pounds.

The parachutes were obtained from a jump center east of the airport: two front or reserve chutes, and two rear or main parachutes. As Cooper had insisted, they were civilian parachutes, not military. They, too, were given to the FBI.

Meanwhile, the plane continued to circle Sea-Tac. Tina, the other stewardess, moved up and down the aisle, reassuring passengers. Dan Cooper explained to Schaffner how things were going to work.

"After the plane lands," he said, "I want you to go out and get the money and bring it back."

"What if it's too heavy?"

"It won't be. You'll manage. Then," he continued, "you'll get the parachutes and bring them on board." He pulled a bottle of Benzedrine pills from his pocket. "Take these to the cockpit in case the crew gets sleepy during the next flight."

She asked if he was hijacking the plane to Cuba, at the time the most common destination for sky-jackings.

"No," he said. "Not Cuba. Someplace you'll like."

She asked him why he was hijacking the plane. Did he bear a grudge against Northwest?

"I don't have a grudge against your airline, miss," he said. "I just have a grudge."

On the ground, the airport had been closed and all outgoing flights canceled. Incoming flights were either diverted or put into a holding pattern. Shortly after five, ground control radioed the plane and said the money and parachutes had been assembled and were in a car at the far end of a runway, as instructed.

The pilots brought the 727 in to land and taxied, as per the hijacker's instructions, to a remote section of runway. It was now dark and the rain persisted, accompanied by occasional flashes of lightning. The area had been illuminated with banks of floodlights.

The plane came to a halt. "Go get the money," Cooper told Schaffner.

Schaffner walked down the aisle to the exit door and descended the stairs, walking in wobbly high heels to the waiting vehicle. An FBI agent took the money from the trunk and handed it to her. Schaffner walked back to the plane, mounted the stairs, and carried the sack back to Cooper. He opened it, looked inside, grabbed a few bricks and took them out.

"For you," he said.

Schaffner was surprised. "Sorry, sir. No tips. Northwest Orient policy."

He seemed to smile faintly. "All right. Go get the parachutes."

Schaffner once again descended the stairs and, making two more trips, brought Cooper the four parachutes.

He leaned toward her. "Now, this is the important

part, Flo. Listen carefully. It's time for the captain to tell everyone on board that the plane has been hijacked. The hijacker has a bomb. He is to order everyone off the plane. They're to go straight out—not open the overhead compartments, not take their carry-on luggage or anything else they brought on board. If these instructions are not followed to the letter, or if a hero tries to come back and interfere with me, I'll detonate the bomb. Please relay that to the captain. Only the pilot, copilot, and you are to remain on board."

"Yes, sir." Schaffner got up, went to the cockpit, and relayed the demand. A moment later the captain got on the intercom.

"Listen carefully, and please remain calm," Scotty's neutral voice came over the speakers. "There is a hijacker on this plane with a bomb."

There was a scattering of expostulations, gasps, a scream or two.

"Do not panic. All passengers are to deplane immediately. Do not open the overhead bins. Do *not* take any carry-on luggage with you. You are to deplane empty-handed."

More gasps, murmurs.

"Commence deplaning now. Walk, don't run."

The passengers rose up en masse, in a babble of confusion and raised voices, and surged toward the forward stairs. Several passengers reached for the overhead compartments, and one managed to get his open.

Seeing this, Cooper rose from his seat and held up his attaché case, brandishing it like a weapon. "You!" he screamed, suddenly enraged, gesturing at the offending passenger. "Get back! I've got a bomb! I'm going to set it off if you don't follow instructions!"

The passenger, an older man, backed up, face full of terror, amid the yells and rebukes of the passengers around him. Someone gave him a shove forward; he abandoned the open bin and was pushed along with everyone else as they stumbled off the plane. In a few minutes, the cabin was empty, with the exception of Schaffner and Tina.

"You get off, too," Cooper said to Tina. "And tell the flight engineer to board." Then he grabbed the cabin phone. "How much longer for refueling?" he yelled into it.

"Almost done," the copilot told him.

The Northwest flight engineer who had been brought in came up the stairs and stood in the galley, awaiting orders.

Cooper turned to Schaffner. "Close all the shades. Both sides."

Schaffner was really frightened now. The calm, polite version of Cooper had vanished, replaced by a high-strung, angry man. "Yes, sir."

As Schaffner went around closing the shades, Cooper spoke to the flight engineer. "You. Listen carefully. As soon as refueling is done, I want you to set a course for Mexico City. Keep your altitude below ten thousand feet—no higher. Trim the flaps down to fifteen, keep the gear down, and don't pressurize the cabin. Fly at the slowest possible speed that con-figuration allows, which should be no more than one hundred knots." He paused, then said: "I intend to put the aft stairs down and take off in that configuration. Is that feasible?"

"Everything you've said is feasible," the flight

engineer said, "except it would be dangerous to attempt takeoff with the aft stairs deployed. And with the configuration you're specifying, we'll need to refuel at least once."

After a brief back-and-forth, Cooper agreed to having the aft stairs closed and making a stop in Reno for refueling.

"Now join the crew in the cockpit and shut the door," Cooper told the engineer. "And get the show on the road."

After the flight engineer had disappeared into the cockpit, the fuel truck withdrew and the jet engines began to rev up, the plane turning to taxi down the runway.

The hijacker turned to Schaffner. "Show me how to operate the aft stairs."

She showed him, then gave him a card with instructions.

"Go into the cockpit," he said. "On your way, close the first-class curtains. Make sure nobody comes out."

"Yes, sir."

She was relieved not to have to sit next to him again, but still frightened at his abrupt change of demeanor—especially now, when all his demands had been met. She went forward and turned to shut the curtain, catching a glimpse of the hijacker as she did so. He was tying the sack of money around his waist. The plane had reached the end of the taxiway and now turned onto the runway, accelerating for takeoff. The time was 7:45 PM.

3

THE MAN WHO CALLED himself Dan Cooper finished tying the bundle of money around his midriff. He then went to one of the overhead bins, the one above seat 12C—the one that had been opened by the old man. He pulled out some hand luggage, strewing it about the cabin, until he reached a battered brown briefcase. He removed it with care and placed it on his own seat. Then he opened more bins and pulled out luggage at random—bags, purses, coats, umbrellas—and tossed it around the interior. The storm had gotten worse and their course was taking them through some turbulence, the plane thumping up and down from time to time, causing additional luggage to topple out of the open bins.

Stepping over the luggage, Cooper donned a back parachute with swift and efficient movements, then put on the forward, reserve chute. He went to the aft stairs and, referring to the card of instructions Schaffner had given him, unsealed the hatch to a great roar of wind and opened the stairs into the darkness.

The sudden change in pressure alarmed the pilots in the cockpit. Copilot Rataczak got on the intercom. "Can you hear me?" he called. "Is everything okay back there?"

"Everything is okay."

The hijacker reached around and grasped his own attaché case—the one containing the fake bomb—and threw it out the hatch into the thunderous darkness. Next, he selected several pieces of luggage at random and tossed them out as well. Finally, using shroud lines cut from a parachute he wasn't planning to use, he took the brown briefcase he had removed from the overhead bin and securely tied it to his midriff opposite the money bag. He now bore a faint resemblance to the Michelin Man: parachutes on the front and back, the money tied on one side and the briefcase on the other. It may have looked comical, but it was secure.

This accomplished, he stepped carefully onto the stairs and then, a moment later, jumped into the night. In the cockpit, everyone noted the sudden lift caused by the release of weight, and the captain recorded the time: 8:13 PM. But they weren't sure what it meant. They had no way of knowing if the hijacker was still in the plane, and so they flew onward to Reno.

Cooper hurtled out into the blasting wind. He waited a moment to clear the two engines, which on the Boeing 727-100 were mounted aft; stabilized his free fall; counted a full sixty seconds—and then released the drogue. This action pulled out a ten-foot bridle, which in turn yanked the parachute out of the deployment bag. Cooper noted all these stages by feel, with satisfaction. As soon as the chute was fully open, he oriented himself, making out the faint lights of the town of Packwood, his fixed point of reference— dimmed by the storm but still visible.

Then he reached down to where he had tied the bag of money, tugged open the drawstring, and reached into the bag. With the chute open, the wind had lessened considerably and movement was easier. He grabbed a fistful of cash, yanked it out, and tossed it away. Then he began emptying the bag as quickly as possible, throwing handfuls of money off into the night.

Suddenly, he felt a jerk on the lines. Looking up, he saw that several bundles of money had been swept upward and were interfering with the main canopy, partially deflating it. At the same time, he felt his fall accelerate toward a fatal rate of descent.

He did not panic. In a practiced move, he cut away the main canopy by pulling the release handles on the shoulder straps. He now went into free fall. He quickly pulled the second handle to manually deploy the reserve chute. But when it snapped out and open, he realized there was something wrong with this, as well; it had deployed but not cleanly. Maybe it had been sabotaged or, more likely, it had simply become stiff from sitting too long without being repacked. A not uncommon problem.

But it was a dire problem for him.

Cooper felt an unfamiliar surge of panic as he dropped through the darkness, the wind tearing loose the bag with the rest of the money. Nothing he tried could correct the deployment of the reserve chute. He continued to fall, the partially collapsed reserve chute juddering in the turbulence, a final cloud of twenty-dollar bills bursting like confetti and fluttering away into the night as the struggling figure plummeted down toward the forest below, soon lost from sight in the howling storm.

4

Present Day

THE AGUSTAWESTLAND 109 GRAND shot northwest, powerful rotors humming, flying so low that its landing skids almost seemed to brush the azure-blue surface of the Atlantic. It rose as it cleared the reefs, barrier islands, and bays that led to mainland Florida.

In the luxurious cabin of the helicopter sat three people: a man in torn jeans and a plaid shirt; a young woman in a pleated white skirt and blouse, wearing dark sunglasses, with a large sun hat on her lap; and a spectral figure in a severely cut black suit, who sat looking out the cabin window with a remote expression on his sculptural features. Despite the tinting of the window, the brilliant sunshine outside turned his silver-blue eyes a strange platinum color and gave his light-blond hair the sheen of a snow leopard's fur.

This was Special Agent A. X. L. Pendergast of the Federal Bureau of Investigation. With him in the passenger cabin were his ward, Constance Greene, and his partner, Special Agent Armstrong Coldmoon. They were departing the scene of a successfully concluded case on Sanibel Island, Florida, and though relatively little conversation was taking place, there was a sense of closure in the cabin and a feeling that it was time to get on with their lives.

Now the helicopter climbed and banked right, to avoid the hotels and luxury condos of Miami Beach, glistening like an alabaster Oz against the line of sand and the blue water beyond.

"Nice of the pilot to give us a show like this," Coldmoon said. "It's like a ride at Disneyland."

"I wouldn't know," Pendergast replied in his silky, butter-and-bourbon New Orleans accent.

"You're assuming it was intentional," Constance said as she leaned forward to pick up the volume that had slipped from her hands when the helicopter banked: *Clouds without Water*, by Aleister Crowley. "Turbulent pitch and roll are often the first indications of helicopter trouble, before the stresses of a vortex ring force it into an uncontrolled descent."

This was greeted by a moment of silence broken only by the whine of the engines.

"I'm sure we have an excellent pilot," Pendergast said. "Or is that your fey sense of humor at work?"

"I find no humor in the prospect of having my person, burned and dismembered, spread across a public beach for all to see," the young woman replied.

Coldmoon couldn't see her eyes behind the Ray-Bans, but he felt sure she was looking at him, gauging the effect this morbid observation was having. Not only did this strange, beautiful, erudite, and slightly crazy woman scare the hell out of him—in the last week, she had both saved him and threatened to kill him—but she seemed to get a distinct enjoyment out of busting his balls. Perhaps, he told himself, it was a sign of interest. In which case—no thanks.

He took a deep breath. It didn't merit thinking about. Mentally, he was already thousands of miles away, at his new posting at the Denver Field Office, far from the muggy air and stifling heat of Florida.

His gaze drifted from Constance Greene to Pendergast. Another strange one. Even though he'd just completed two cases back-to-back with the senior agent, Pendergast was another reason why Coldmoon wanted to get to Colorado as quickly as possible. The guy might be a legend in the FBI and the finest sleuth since Sherlock Holmes, but he was also notorious for the number of homicide cases he'd solved in which the perp had been "killed during apprehension"…and Coldmoon had learned the hard way that anybody who partnered with the guy had only a slightly better chance of surviving than the perp.

As the confectionary beaches of the Florida coast skimmed past below him, bringing him ever closer to the plane that would take him west, Coldmoon felt a sort of release, as if from prison. He almost smiled at the thought of the incredulity on the faces of his cousins, who lived in Colorado Springs, because his assignment had been so delayed that they refused to believe he was actually coming. Cheered by this thought, he glanced out the window again. The coastline was still as built up as farther south, but the buildings were not nearly as tall now. He could see I-95 running up the coast, wall to wall with cars. That would be something else he wouldn't miss, although he'd heard that traffic in Denver had gotten crazy over the past few years. From above, it was hard to tell where they were. The flight was longer than he'd expected. Out of the corner of his eye, he could see that Pendergast and Constance had their heads together and were speaking in low tones. It was odd, though—he didn't know a lot about Miami, despite the time he'd spent there, but he was pretty sure that the airport was west of town, not north...especially not this far north. They'd passed what he thought was Miami some time ago.

He sat back in his leather seat. Were they headed for an air force base or FBI helicopter landing pad? After all, their boss, Assistant Director in Charge Walter Pickett, hadn't yet issued him a plane ticket to Denver. Maybe they were flying him in a government or military jet—it was the least the Bureau could do, given the shit he'd been through. Unlikely: now that word would soon be coming through of Pickett's promotion to Associate Deputy Director, he was probably too busy packing his own bags for D.C. to think of anything else.

"Hey, Pendergast," he said.

Pendergast glanced up.

"I thought we were headed for Miami International."

"That had been my assumption."

"Then what's going on?" He looked out the window again. "Looks like we're hell and gone from Miami."

"Indeed. It would appear that we have overshot the airport."

At these words, Coldmoon became aware of an uncomfortable tickling sensation—something like déjà vu, but distinctly more unpleasant—manifesting itself in the rear of his brain. "Overshot? You're sure we aren't coming back around for a landing?"

"If we were actually headed for Miami, I doubt we'd be over Palm Beach right now."

"Palm Beach? What the *hell*—?" Coldmoon looked down. Another narrow barrier island covered with mansions was passing below—including one particularly large and garish pseudo-Moorish compound their shadow was crossing over at present.

He sat back again, momentarily dazed by surprise and confusion. "What's going on?" he asked.

"I confess I haven't the faintest idea," said Pendergast.

"Perhaps you should ask the pilot," Constance said without looking up from her book.

Coldmoon glanced at the two with faint suspicion. Was this some kind of joke? But no—his gut, which he always trusted, told him they were as in the dark as he was.

"Good idea," Coldmoon said, unbuckling his harness and standing up. He made his way forward from the passenger compartment to the cockpit. The two pilots, with their headsets, khaki uniforms, and brown hair cut to a similar regulation length, could have been twins.

"What's up?" he asked the pilot in command in the right seat, cyclic between his knees. "We're supposed to be going to Miami."

"Not anymore," the PIC said.

"What do you mean, 'not anymore'?"

"Just after we took off, we got new orders from dispatch. We're to proceed to Savannah."

"Savannah?" Coldmoon echoed. "You mean, in Georgia? There must be some mistake."

"No mistake," said the PIC. "The orders came from ADC Pickett himself."

Pickett. That son of a bitch. Standing in the doorway of the cockpit, Coldmoon thought back to the final conversation they'd had with the assistant director before taking off. *I've just learned of the most peculiar incident that took place last night, north of Savannah*... Pickett must have waited until they'd taken off, then ordered the flight to be diverted.

Of all the backstabbing, ungrateful... Well, Coldmoon had already been suckered into taking on a second case with Pendergast and his unorthodox ways—it sure as hell wasn't going to happen again.

"Turn the chopper around," he demanded.

"Sorry, sir," the PIC replied. "I can't do that."

"You got shit in your ears? I said, turn this chopper around. We're going to Miami."

"Respectfully, sir, we have our orders," the other pilot said. "And as it happens, they're the same as yours. We're headed to Savannah." And taking his hand from the collective, he unzipped his light windbreaker just enough to display the butt of a handgun peeping out from a nylon shoulder holster.

"Agent Coldmoon?" It was Pendergast, speaking from what seemed like a long distance away. "Agent Coldmoon?"

Coldmoon wheeled around, lurching slightly with the motion of the helicopter.

"What?"

"It's obvious we can do nothing about this unexpected course of events."

"Didn't you hear?" Coldmoon blazed. "We're going to Savannah. Frigging *Savannah*, when I should be on a flight to—"

"I did indeed hear," said Pendergast. "Something

most unusual must have occurred, to say the least, for Pickett to abduct us like this."

"Yeah. He's being promoted and, as a result, has become even more of an asshole. What the hell are we going to do?"

"Under the circumstances, I would suggest nothing—except sit down and enjoy the view."

But Coldmoon wasn't about to let it go. "This is bullshit! I've got a mind to—"

"Agent Coldmoon?"

It was Constance who spoke. She said his name in her usual deep, strangely accented voice, without any particular emphasis.

Coldmoon fell silent. This woman was capable of saying, or doing, anything.

As it happened, she did nothing but gaze mildly at him. "You might find it calming to consider just how paradoxical this situation is."

"What do you mean?" Coldmoon said angrily.

"I mean, how often do you suppose an FBI agent finds himself being kidnapped by his own people? Aren't you intrigued as to why?" And with that, she returned to her reading.

5

THEY LANDED ABOUT FORTY-FIVE minutes later at a remote section of Hunter Army Airfield. No sooner had Coldmoon angrily yanked his backpack out of the rear of the helicopter's cabin than he heard the sound of a second chopper, approaching quickly. A minute later, it appeared in the sky. It was a Bell 429, government issue by the look of its tail markings, and it in fact appeared identical to the one their superior, ADC Pickett, had arrived at their private island earlier in the day. Coldmoon scoffed. Why should he be surprised?

At almost the same time, as if choreographed, an Escalade with windows tinted almost as black as its body pulled up nearby, stopped, and then waited, idling, engine on.

Coldmoon looked at Pendergast, who was removing his and Constance's luggage from the rear compartment of the chopper. Earlier, Pendergast had made it clear that he was eager—to put it mildly—to get back to New York. But he seemed to be taking this development in stride. More than that—he wasn't objecting at all.

Coldmoon turned to him. "You knew about this, didn't you?"

"I assure you I did not," Pendergast replied over the prop wash.

"Then why the hell are you acting like we're stopping for a picnic? I thought you wanted to get home."

"I very much wish to return to New York." He began walking with the bags toward the waiting SUV.

Coldmoon followed him. "Then what the—?"

"My dear Armstrong." Coldmoon hated it when Pendergast began one of his little pronouncements like that. "I fail to see what this display of agitation will accomplish. Pickett knew our wishes. There must be a good reason for him to have ignored them. Perhaps it has something to do with that Georgian senator who carries a lot of weight with the FBI. Yes…I suspect we've been diverted because of a case offering potential bad publicity."

Coldmoon looked at him. "If I didn't know better, I'd say you sound intrigued."

"I *am* intrigued." Pendergast looked around the airfield, silver-blue eyes glinting in the open air. "Savannah is lovely. Have you ever been there?"

"No, and I have no interest in going."

"It's a charming city, full of beautiful old mansions, cruel histories, and numerous ghosts. A true gem of the South. It rather reminds me of our old family plantation house, Penumbra—as it once was."

Even as Pendergast was speaking, Coldmoon turned away, muttering a long and anatomically specific Lakota curse. He honestly couldn't decide who was worse—Pickett or Pendergast. It figured the guy once had a plantation.

Now the passenger door of the Bell slid open and the trim figure of Pickett came striding toward them. "I'm very sorry about this little detour," he said before Coldmoon could object. He waved in the direction of the SUV. "If you would all please get in, I'll explain as we drive."

"Drive where?" asked Coldmoon. But Pickett was already talking to the driver. There was one furious whine from behind, then another; turning, Coldmoon saw their helicopter and Pickett's taking off in sequence, backwash blowing over them. The choppers rose, noses drooping like ungainly buzzards. He was half tempted to run toward them and cling to the skids before they were completely out of reach. In a silent fury, he tossed his backpack in the rear of the SUV and got in, sitting in the rearmost seat. Constance slipped in next to him. Pendergast took a seat in the middle along with Pickett. The driver put the Escalade in gear and stepped hard on the accelerator. Military hangars and warehouses swept past, and then they were on I-516, heading north.

Pickett closed all the windows and asked the driver to turn up the A/C, then cleared his throat.

"I want to assure you this was a last-minute development," he said. "I didn't know in advance, and I promise my visit wasn't an attempt to waylay you. The fact is, a problem has developed here that demands immediate attention. It's a cooperative investigation between the Bureau and the local authorities."

"Surely you have abundant resources here in Georgia already," Pendergast said, "that are capable of supplying that attention."

Pickett winced. "Let's just say this case is particularly suited to your strengths. It's a fast-breaking situation and we need to get on top of it and show progress right away."

"I understand. And how is Senator Drayton these days?" Pendergast asked.

"I'm going to pretend I didn't hear that," said Pickett.

"But he is an acquaintance of yours, is he not?"

"You have no idea," Pickett replied with a wintry smile. There was a brief but nevertheless uncomfortable pause. "I'm asking you to take a look, that's all."

"By all means," said Pendergast. "Although I believe those were the precise words you used a few weeks ago, when you asked me to fly to Sanibel."

Coldmoon saw his chance to jump in. "And what does this have to do with me? I'm due to report to the Denver office."

"I'm aware of that. It's the luck of the draw."

"But, sir, my arrival has been delayed once already. If you say this is Pendergast's forte, great, but I really need to get—"

"Agent Coldmoon?" Pickett said. His voice was unnaturally quiet, but the subzero tone of it shut Coldmoon up. "This is the Federal Bureau of Investigation, not a country club where you get to dictate your tee times."

In the silence that followed, the SUV took the interchange onto I-16 toward downtown Savannah. Pickett opened his briefcase and removed a slim folder.

"Three days ago," he said, "the body of a local hotel manager was found washed up on the bank of the Wilmington River. His body was completely drained of blood."

"How completely?" asked Constance.

Pickett looked up at her with an expression of surprise. "A mortician couldn't have done a better job. Initially, the local authorities thought it to be the work of a madman or a cult—or possibly a vengeance killing by a gang. But just this morning, another body was found in a courtyard of a house on Abercorn Street. It, too, was drained of every last drop of blood." He glanced at his watch. "The reason for the rush is they've been holding the new crime scene for us to examine."

Coldmoon glanced over at Pendergast. As usual, the man's face gave nothing away—except, possibly, an unnatural sparkle in his eyes. The SUV had left the freeway, and they were now driving down a narrow lane named Gaston Street. Creepy brick houses lined both sides, and the road was so bumpy it felt cobbled—perhaps it *was* cobbled. They passed a park on the right, dense with massive old trees draped so heavily with Spanish moss they appeared to be dripping. It was like something out of a horror movie. Coldmoon had grown heartily sick of Florida: the heat, the humidity, the crowds, the *southernness* of it all. But this—this spooky city with its gnarled trees and crooked houses—this was even worse.

Why wasn't Pendergast objecting? After all, he was the senior agent. A saying his Lakota grandfather was fond of came into his mind: *Beware the dog that does not bark, and the man who does not talk.*

"*Unci Maka*, Grandmother Earth, give me strength," he murmured to himself as the Escalade drove farther and farther into the heart of what seemed to him a malign and alien town.

6

THE ESCALADE EASED THROUGH a police barricade and checkpoint on Abercorn Street, coming to a stop before a magnificent mansion built of reddish stone with a pillared entryway. Coldmoon exited the SUV, getting hit by a blast of humid air, and took in the surroundings. The house faced another square of mossy oaks, with a statue of a long-forgotten man in a tricorn hat, sword drawn, standing high on a marble pedestal. Coldmoon felt awkward in his old jeans and shirt; everyone else was wearing uniforms or crisp dark suits. Pickett could at least have given him advance warning he'd be assigned another case—if, indeed, that's what this was. The thought put him in an even sourer mood.

A cop—not in uniform, but nevertheless unmistakable—was standing at the gate to the mansion's front garden, which was enclosed by a stone balustrade. Next to him was a woman in full police uniform with decorations, whom Coldmoon took to be the chief of police.

"This is homicide detective Benny Sheldrake of the Savannah PD," Pickett said as they arrived at the gate, "and Commander Alanna Delaplane of the Southwest Precinct—"

"The crime scene is waiting," Pendergast interrupted smoothly. "Perhaps we can save the introductions for later? Now, if you please, show the way."

Coldmoon felt a slight thrill at Pendergast's dismissal. The quicker he made their presence unwelcome, the sooner they might leave—he hoped.

"Of course," said Commander Delaplane. "If you'll follow me, please? The body was found in the back courtyard, next to the slave quarters."

"Slave quarters?" Pendergast asked.

"Correct. The Owens-Thomas House—this is one of Savannah's historic mansions, if you weren't aware—retains a remarkably preserved set of slave quarters. The body was found in their old work area. We have to walk through the house and gardens to get there."

"Who found the body?" Pendergast asked.

"The director of the museum, when he came in to work early. He's in the house."

"I should like to see him when we're done out here."

"Very well."

They strode through a spectacular marble entranceway and passed down a main corridor sporting richly furnished rooms on both sides before coming out on a portico at the back of the mansion. It overlooked a severely symmetrical garden with a fountain. Delaplane led them down some stairs and across the garden—Coldmoon struggling to keep up—then through a back gate and into a brick courtyard. Before them lay a plain two-story brick building with small windows, evidently the slave quarters.

The body of a young man lay in the courtyard, on its back with arms thrown out, almost as if it had dropped from the sky.

"The CSI team have finished their work," said Delaplane. "The crime scene is all yours."

"Thank you most kindly," said Pendergast in a more genteel tone. He approached the body, hands clasped behind his back.

Coldmoon wondered if he should follow, then decided not to—let Pendergast do his thing. "Where did Pickett go?" he asked, looking around. "And Constance?"

Pendergast was too absorbed to answer. He made a circuit around the body, peering down as intently as if he were examining a rare Persian rug. The victim looked to be in his thirties. Coldmoon had never seen a face so pale, or hands so white. The contrast was made more striking by the dead man's curly black hair and bright blue eyes, staring fixedly upward. The corpse made even Pendergast seem almost ruddy in comparison. The face was frozen in a contortion of horror. The right pant leg had been lacerated, as if raked by a knife or garden tool, but there was no blood to be seen in or around the wound. Not a drop.

Pendergast looked up at Commander Delaplane. "What can you tell me so far?" he asked.

"All preliminary," she said, "but it appears the blood was withdrawn from the femoral artery, in the upper thigh, where the pant leg has been torn."

"Withdrawn—how?"

"The MO appears the same as the earlier victim: a

large-bore needle, or maybe a trocar, was inserted into the inner thigh to access the femoral artery."

"How curious." Pendergast swiftly donned a pair of nitrile gloves from a dispenser on a table next to the body, knelt, and gently opened the torn pants, exposing a neat hole on the inside of the upper thigh. A single drop of dried blood clung to the edge, along with a sticky yellow substance. There were thin amber-colored threads of the same substance on the man's right shoe. They looked to Coldmoon like dried snot.

A test tube and swab appeared in Pendergast's hand, and he took a sample, then another and another in swift succession, quickly stoppering them in small glass vials that disappeared back into his black suit.

"Time of death?" he asked.

"Around three o'clock in the morning, give or take two hours, based on body temperature," said Delaplane. "The withdrawal of the blood complicates the calculation."

"And this mucus-like substance around the wound and on the shoe?"

"We've taken samples. No results yet."

Now Sheldrake spoke. "The FBI's Evidence Response Team also took extensive samples, sent them down to their lab in Atlanta."

"Excellent," said Pendergast.

Silence built as he knelt, examining various parts of the body—eyes, ears, tongue, neck, hair, shoes—occasionally employing a small hand magnifier. He moved toward the head, examining the nape of the neck.

"There was some bruising on the first victim in the thigh, torso, and abdominal region," said Delaplane, "which is also present here."

"A rather short struggle, it seems," Pendergast said, rising. "Have you established ingress and egress?"

"That's the curious thing," said Delaplane. "We haven't been able to. This is a very secure area. We've got security cameras at the entry points, of which there are only three. There was nothing on the tapes, and no gaps. Nothing, in fact, except that two of the cameras recorded unusual sounds at around three AM."

"What sort of noises?"

"Hard to characterize. Like a dog grunting or snuffling and a loud slapping sound. I'll get you a copy of the tape."

"Thank you, Commander." Pendergast turned to Coldmoon. "Come look at this."

Coldmoon ventured over to the body. Pendergast gently turned the head—rigid with rigor—slightly sideways.

Coldmoon donned a pair of gloves, then knelt as well.

"Feel the back of the head," he said.

When he followed Pendergast's instructions, he felt a lump. Pendergast parted the hair to expose what looked like an abrasion.

"Looks like he got smacked on the head around the time of death," said Coldmoon.

"Exactly. This and the many other curious issues shall have to be addressed in the postmortem."

Which curious issues Pendergast meant, exactly, Coldmoon didn't ask.

"Has the victim been ID'd?" Pendergast asked.

"Yes. His wallet was on his person. He was one of those guys who give the bike tours you see everywhere around here."

"And where is his bicycle?"

"Found on the corner of Abercorn and East Macon."

"Isn't that quite some distance from here?"

"Just a dozen blocks or so."

"Where did he live?"

"On Liberty, not far from where his bicycle was found. Chances are he was on his way home when he was accosted."

Pendergast rose, stripped off the gloves, and dropped them in a nearby trash container. Coldmoon followed suit.

"Shall we retire into the house?" Pendergast asked.

Delaplane said simply "Of course," and turned to lead the way.

7

Commander Delaplane brought them all back into the cool confines of the mansion, where Pendergast went directly into the elegant living room and took a seat in a grandly stuffed and gilded chair as easily if he were in his own home. "My partner and I have been traveling since daybreak. Would it be possible to have tea?" He threw one leg over the other and looked about inquiringly.

"Well, I don't know," said Delaplane. "This is a museum."

But a thin, unsmiling man who had been hovering in the background stepped forward. "I think that can be arranged."

"Splendid!"

"I'm Armand Cobb, director of the Owens-Thomas House museum," the man said. "Which, if you didn't know already, is this house."

Pendergast nodded languidly. "Forgive me if I don't rise. I find myself terribly fatigued from the case we just completed down in Florida."

The museum director stepped back, and Pendergast turned his eyes to the commander. "Lovely to make your acquaintance, Commander Delaplane. Thank you for your cooperation."

"Of course," said Delaplane. "And this is homicide detective Sergeant Benny Sheldrake, in charge of the case."

The detective came forward, and Pendergast took his hand. "How do you do?"

Another man, newly arrived, appeared out of the shadows. "Gordon Carracci, FBI liaison supervisor," he said. "Just seeing the evidence samples off to Atlanta."

"Very pleased to meet you," said Pendergast.

Coldmoon was amazed to see how this had developed: Pendergast sitting like some pasha on his throne, receiving obeisance as various people came forward, one after the other.

"Now, Mr. Cobb," Pendergast said. "Excuse me— or is it Doctor?"

"It's Doctor," the man said stiffly.

"Dr. Cobb, I understand you found the body."

"Yes."

"The body isn't on the way to your office, is it?" Pendergast asked. "How did you happen to come upon it?"

"I like to come in early from time to time to do work before the museum opens. I always do a quick walk-through."

"Why?"

"It's a habit. The house is beautiful. It refreshes me. Besides, this being a museum…well, it's always good to check on things."

"Naturally. So you saw the body: what then?"

"I immediately checked to see if he was still alive. He was cold to the touch. I backed away so as not to disturb anything and called the police. I then waited for them in my office."

"I see." Pendergast turned to Delaplane. "A general question, if I may, Commander: have you had any recent reports of animals being killed or mutilated, unusual signs or symbols painted on the street, or anything else that might suggest cult activity—or the presence of Satanists?"

"God, yes," said Delaplane. "Savannah draws those people like magnets. We look into them, of course, if we have good reason to think a crime has been committed. We have to be careful, though: those activities can be considered to fall under the religious freedom laws." She paused. "You think this might be something like that?"

"I refrain from thinking at the beginning of an investigation, Commander."

"What do you do in place of thinking?" Delaplane asked drily.

"I become a receptacle for information."

Delaplane gave Coldmoon a pointed glance, raising her eyebrows. Coldmoon shrugged. It was just Pendergast being Pendergast.

Pendergast stared at the floor for a long moment, and then he turned abruptly to Cobb. "Can you kindly tell us a bit about the history of this house?"

"I'd be glad to. But I'm not sure it's relevant."

"Right now, nothing is irrelevant."

Cobb launched into what was obviously a well-rehearsed lecture. "The Owens-Thomas House was built in 1819 by the English architect William Jay, in the Regency style, for Richard Richardson and his wife, Frances. Richardson had made his fortune in the slave trade. He found a profitable niche in shipping enslaved children who'd been forcibly separated from their parents or orphaned from Savannah to New Orleans, where they would be sold."

Coldmoon felt a shiver of disgust in the matter-of-fact way this was mentioned.

"This house," Cobb went on, "was built by slave labor. When it was finished, Richardson and his wife and family—along with their nine enslaved people—moved into the house. The enslaved people were housed in that old brick building in the back. Over the course of the next decade, Richardson's wife and two children died. He fell into economic difficulties and was forced to sell, moved to New Orleans, and then died at sea in 1833. The house was eventually purchased by the mayor of Savannah, George Owens, who moved into the house with his own fifteen enslaved people."

"Fifteen?" Coldmoon said in disgust. The idea of a man owning a single human being was hard enough to conceive of.

Cobb nodded. "Owens also owned some four hundred other enslaved people on various plantations in the area."

"*Zuzeca*," Coldmoon muttered under his breath.

"The family's fortunes declined after the Civil War, but they managed to retain the house up until 1951, when the last descendant died with no heir. The house then passed to the Telfair Academy of Arts and Sciences, which turned it into a museum, as you see now. It is, in fact, one of Savannah's most popular tourist attractions."

Tea was now being served, with some bland-looking

biscuits. Pendergast picked up his cup. "Tell me more about the slave quarters in the back."

"Certainly. Its two stories hold six rooms, in which the enslaved people all lived. The rooms are as barren now as they were then, and many of the residents had to sleep on the floor, with no beds and only threadbare blankets. When slavery was abolished, most of them simply became 'servants' and continued living back of the big house, doing the same work as before. But as the Owens family fell upon hard times, the servants were gradually let go. The quarters remained intact, however, until the house was turned into a museum."

"Most instructive, thank you," said Pendergast. "So one might say, Dr. Cobb—as we look about at all the beauty and wealth on display here, the erudition and elegance, the fine crystal and silver and rugs and paintings—that all of this, the house and its contents, is a physical manifestation of pure evil?"

This was greeted with a stunned silence, until Cobb finally said: "I suppose you might put it that way."

"I see no supposition in the statement," Pendergast replied.

A silence fell, and Pendergast half closed his eyes and tented his hands. "Odd, isn't it," he said languidly, "that such a crime occurred here, of all places?" And, finishing his tea, he helped himself to another cup.

8

THE CHANDLER HOUSE WAS a historic hotel on
Chatham Square, a long building with a pressed-brick
exterior and an ornate iron veranda that stretched the
length of the second and third floors, with decorative
supporting columns. To Coldmoon, it looked more
like an industrial-size southern cathouse than anything else.

"How lucky Constance was able to secure us such
an extensive suite of rooms," Pendergast said.

After their interview that morning, Pendergast had
disappeared for several hours before showing up at the
hotel. Coldmoon knew better than to ask him where
he'd been. They were now sitting in overstuffed chairs
in the hotel's ornate parlor, drinking mint juleps. The
canary-yellow room was overflowing with historical
memorabilia, in the form of silver trophy cups and
giant soup tureens, photographs, faded flags, marble
busts, clocks, framed documents, and other obscure
objects displayed behind glass, sitting on mantelpieces,
or hiding within shaded alcoves.

"Yeah, very lucky," Coldmoon said without enthusiasm. It was an "extensive suite of rooms" for sure, but his own set were separate from those of Pendergast and Constance. Not for the first time, he wondered exactly what was going on between the two of them. Pendergast called her his "ward," but Coldmoon often wondered if that was simply a title of convenience.

The julep had been pressed into his hand before he'd had a chance to order anything, and the more he sipped it, the less he liked it. He wondered if he could exchange it for a cold beer but couldn't quite work up the nerve to ask.

"Is the julep tart enough for you?" Pendergast asked.

"It's tart," Coldmoon agreed.

Pendergast looked around with satisfaction. "This is one of the more notable buildings in Savannah's historic district," he said. "That's no mean feat, when you consider that almost half the structures in town are significant architecturally or historically." His tone had taken on a faintly didactic air, and in this antique parlor, at the heart of what had once been the Old South, he seemed more in his element than Coldmoon had ever seen him. The phrase *like a pig in shit* came to mind, but he didn't voice it.

Pendergast went on. "Savannah doubled in size during the railroad boom of the mid-nineteenth century, you know, and buildings serving any number of functions quickly sprang up. This hotel, for example, was originally a hospital for yellow fever victims, and then a Confederate munitions factory, before becoming a lodging house. Like so many other structures, it fell into disrepair in the 1950s and closed in the '60s. Luckily a guardian angel came along, and she judiciously restored it to its former charm."

Coldmoon tried another sip and set the drink aside. *She?* he wondered idly. He couldn't speak to its former charm—how charming could a yellow fever hospital be?—but old: hell yes, it was old. True, the restoration had been done with care—everything was clean, there was no dust on the furniture—but the floorboards were wide and uneven and creaked and groaned with every footfall, until it felt like the whole place was griping. There were short sets of stairs everywhere, and the halls were crooked. And then there was his bedroom—large, with a four-poster bed and little frilly doilies over the chair backs and pillowcases...but no TV or internet. The bathroom was decked out like nothing he'd ever seen, with a massive porcelain tub and a marble shitter with a wooden seat. Not to mention the rows of little soaps and shampoos and body creams. A yellow fever hospital...Christ, that was perfect. What he wouldn't give for a Hampton Inn and its modern conveniences right now.

But he didn't want any more history lectures, so he changed the subject. "What happened to Constance? She left the crime scene around the same time Pickett did...and I haven't seen her since."

Pendergast's lips twitched in a brief smile. "That is no coincidence. After her previous experience with Pickett's idea of accommodations, she went along with him to make sure he booked us into a comfortable place. Good thing she did, too—he was about to get us rooms in some dreadful hotel chain on the edge of town."

Coldmoon sighed. "So Pickett left the crime scene just to arrange for our rooms? First he drags us here to Rebel Yell Central, then he vanishes. Nice way to pass the buck."

Pendergast finished his drink and set the glass on a nearby coaster. "I thought it was rather thoughtful of him."

Coldmoon looked up. "Thoughtful? He kidnaps the both of us, yanks me away from reporting to my new post—a post I was supposed to be at weeks ago—and then he dumps us in this creepy old place, to handle some damned *čheslí* case?"

"I don't speak Lakota, but I perfectly comprehend your tone of voice. And over the last several hours, I've observed your vexed attitude. So, as your partner, I'd like to make a suggestion, if I may."

Even though Coldmoon was angry, he noted Pendergast had not said *senior* partner. What was that—throwing him a bone? If so, he wasn't taking it. The agent in the opposite chair, with his pale skin, pale hair, and pale eyes, looked irritatingly complacent, if not smugly satisfied. But Pendergast so rarely offered advice that Coldmoon's instincts told him to shut up and listen.

"I know no more about this case, or the politics that brought us here, than you do. Senator Drayton is a powerful man, and perhaps his support helped Pickett achieve his promotion to the highest echelons of the Bureau. But Pickett doesn't like this case any more than you do. And he certainly isn't planning to take any credit for it, whatever the outcome might be."

"How do you know that?" Coldmoon asked suspiciously.

"Precisely because of the way he left us alone to deal with Commander Delaplane. When we examined the scene, when we spoke to potential witnesses…he was notably absent. Do you really think someone of his rank would busy himself in finding us lodging, instead of taking personal supervision of a high-profile case—one of importance to a U.S. senator?"

"What are you saying—that he's looking out for us?"

"I'm saying he understands perfectly well how we both feel, and he's signaling that he's going to let us handle this investigation *our* way—which, I must say, is a notable change." Pendergast rubbed his hands together, as if already anticipating the lack of oversight. Then he leaned forward and lowered his voice. "And the greedy Denver Field Office—may its tribe decrease!—won't deny you that empty desk, when the time comes for you to claim it."

He settled back in his chair and resumed his normal voice. "In any case, the history here is deep and strong. For example, I just took a little stroll through some of the picturesque back streets."

"Is that why you vanished? To do some sight-seeing?"

"Not at all. I was following our good Dr. Cobb."

"That museum curator? Why?"

"I had a hunch that after our conversation, he might pay a visit to someone…in rather a hurry. And indeed, he left the museum and went straight to the house of a wealthy old dowager known as Lida Mae Culpepper. She was apparently a great beauty in her time, sadly faded despite heroic surgical efforts, but well adorned in sapphires, diamonds, and gold."

Coldmoon couldn't imagine where this was going.

"The dowager Culpepper, it seems, recently invested in real estate: an old desanctified church over on Bee Road."

"And this has to do with what, exactly?"

"Random musings on the fund of secrets in this town, simply aching to be revealed. I know of a fellow calling himself an 'enigmalogist' who'd give his eye-teeth to work here." He waved his hand around the parlor. "This hotel, for instance."

"What about it?"

Pendergast looked almost hurt. "Don't you find this an intriguing establishment? Especially considering it's where the first victim was employed?"

Now Coldmoon, too, sat up. "You mean—"

"My dear Coldmoon, did you think Constance chose this place at random? The body that was found washed up on the banks of the Wilmington River had, before his death, been the manager of the Chandler. We have work to do here."

As if on cue, Constance entered the room. She glanced around with her strange eyes, then took an empty seat near Pendergast.

"I trust you found the rooms to your liking," she said to him.

"Perfect in every way. May I ask what you learned while you checked in?"

"The usual rumor and gossip. On the night the manager disappeared, he went out for a smoke, and a short time later, a distant cry was heard from the park. He never returned."

Pendergast nodded. "An excellent beginning, Constance."

"I understand the assistant manager, a Mr. Thurston Drinkman III, has taken his place."

"A charming southern name. We will need to speak with him. And the proprietress." He turned to Coldmoon. "That's the woman who restored the hotel when it was about to be razed."

Constance nodded. "Her name is Miss Felicity Winthrop Frost. She's a recluse of advanced years who occupies the entire top floor of the hotel and never leaves her rooms. She takes no calls or meetings and does not indulge in email. She is said to be very rich and, despite her age and frailty, rather fearsome."

"Constance, you are a marvel," Pendergast said. "So she's the Howard Hughes of Savannah."

Coldmoon had noticed the top floor as they'd entered. It was smaller than the lower four floors, with a cupola at its center, the tall old windows blocked with cloth.

"Anything else we should know?" Pendergast asked. "Our friend Armstrong, here, seems to feel this case might not be worthy of our talents."

Constance fixed him with her gaze. "Not worthy? Lakota belief embraces a pantheon of divinities, does it not? Han, spirit of darkness; Iktomi, the spider god who brought speech to humans; Tatankan Gnaskiyan, 'Crazy Buffalo,' the evil spirit who drives lovers to suicide and murder?"

She raised her eyebrows, as if to inquire whether this was correct, but Coldmoon was too surprised to answer.

"I would think," she continued when he did not reply, "that someone with your appreciation for spirits will find Savannah to be the most shadow-haunted place in all America."

9

W<small>ENDY</small> G<small>ANNON</small> <small>TRIED</small> <small>TO</small> tune out Betts's voice echoing down the long hallway from the editing room to the studio. She continued inventorying the lighting equipment, making a list of things she wanted to add, while Betts, reviewing the dailies, issued a loud and steady stream of expostulations, snorts of disfavor, and other sounds of disgust. As the director of photography, Gannon had initially been concerned that Betts wasn't pleased with her work, but she soon realized that most of the time he was just acting out. Even when the camera was not trained on him, Barclay Betts was stuck in performance mode.

The crew had arrived in Savannah several days ago to shoot an episode for their new, high-profile Netflix documentary mini-series, provisionally titled *America's Most Haunted Cities*. It had sounded like an interesting project when she'd signed the contract, in a town she'd always wanted to visit. Betts had a reputation for being difficult to work with, but that was true with most directors, and Gannon prided herself on getting along with just about anyone. The town was indeed fabulous. It was one of the few places left in America that had retained a special local flavor, and had resisted the numbing effect of fast-food chains, gas stations, and big-box stores. It was a DP's dream, a wonderful place to shoot, with mists rising in the early morning among the oaks draped in Spanish moss, the soft light in the evening gilding the grand old mansions, cobbled streets and charming squares—all on a bluff above a slow-moving river. The idea of the show was pretty intriguing, too. They were going to investigate the six most haunted places in Savannah with none other than Gerhard Moller, the famous medium, paranormal researcher, and founder of the Institute for Perceptual Studies. Moller was the inventor of the Percipience Camera—said to be able to capture pictures of ghosts or, as Moller called them, "spiritual turbulences"—as well as other spook-detecting devices. Each segment of the show would be devoted to investigating a single haunted locality to see if there really were ghosts and, if so, to document them using the Percipience Camera and other gadgets.

Gannon was pretty sure this was all a big steaming load of horseshit, but you never knew. She wasn't even sure whether Betts bought into it, although he seemed to. But if there really were ghosts, this was the place they'd be hanging out. She might even capture one on video. What a coup that would be.

Barclay Betts…She'd worked with egomaniacs before, but she had to admit that he was a good director and anchor. He knew what he wanted and was on top of everything. His directions to her were clear, and he had an overall vision for the look and feel of the show that meshed with her own. True, he was a narcissistic asshole with a long memory and a penchant for lawsuits. But if the truth be told, she'd rather have a guy like Betts than a nice director who didn't know what he wanted and had no clear vision. She'd worked with plenty of those, and they were far worse than a loudmouth jackass like Betts.

The annoyed noises came to an end, and a moment later Barclay Betts strolled into the studio, followed by the talent, Gerhard Moller. The two together were quite a sight, Abbott and Costello reborn. Moller was tall, silent, and handsome in a cadaverous sort of way. He looked a lot like Peter Cushing, with an expression of deep seriousness, as if pondering the end of the world. Betts, on the other hand, was round. Everything about him was rotund, from the spectacles and head to the deep, plump voice. He rarely stopped talking and moving, as restless as a large round rat in a small square box. But he had that thing all anchors must possess: charisma. Even though he wasn't physically prepossessing, when he walked into a room, you could feel it right away.

"These dailies, there's a problem with the exposure," Betts said, launching into more criticism. "Look, darling, I want you to expose half a stop lower, so that we can get more saturation and a darker feel. It's too bright. This isn't a Travel Channel informercial, this is demon-haunted Savannah. You understand what I'm saying?"

This annoyed Gannon, because she was of the philosophy that exposure manipulation was best saved for later, that it was better to give post properly exposed video. But it wasn't something worth disagreeing about—not with Betts.

"Right," she said. "Noted. Good point."

He patted her knee. "Good girl."

It was almost laughable how retrograde he was. Frankly, she didn't give a shit about being called a "girl" or having him pat her knee: Betts wasn't a harasser. In fact, his sexuality was quite mysterious—he could very well be gay, straight, bi, asexual. Which was maybe a good thing, since all his energy went into making the provocative and controversial documentary films for which he was both infamous and renowned. The critics, of course, hated him.

Barclay Betts now turned to Moller. "Don't you agree? *Demon-haunted Savannah.* I like that. Let's use that phrase tomorrow. In fact, that could be our new working title for the series."

"Mr. Betts," said Moller, his voice carrying with it a faint Teutonic accent, "may I ask when we are going to investigate a haunting? We have been here for days and have yet to inspect a single locality with spiritual turbulences."

"Don't worry, Gerhard, your star turn is coming soon. We're scheduled at the Hamilton-Turner Inn on Friday. Right now, we're shooting B-roll and background, just ironing out the kinks. We'd be further ahead if it weren't for that damned murder investigation and the blocked streets."

Moller didn't respond.

"Crazy thing. Two people with their blood stolen," Betts went on, flopping down in a chair. "Really sucks, you know what I mean?"

If he expected a laugh from Moller, he was mistaken. Gannon figured the man hadn't laughed once in his entire life. But she obliged with a chuckle.

"Thank you," said Betts. "I mean, I did overhear

somebody mention something about a 'Savannah Vampire.' You know anything about that?"

"No," said Gannon.

"Gerhard, darling?"

The man shook his head.

"This camera of yours, does it photograph vampires, too?"

"The Percipience Camera should indeed be able to capture images of vampires, werewolves, and similar phenomena involving spiritual dislocation."

Betts leaned back in his seat, rolling out a wet lower lip and placing a finger on his chin, which Gannon had learned meant he was thinking. He turned to her. "Wendy, while we're at it, we might as well grab some footage on these murders." He stared off into space. "The Savannah Vampire…who knows where it might lead?"

"Sure," said Wendy. It did make sense, "demon-haunted Savannah" and all that.

Betts turned and yelled down the hall. "Hey, Marty! Come here!"

Martin Vladimirovich was the crew's long-suffering researcher-assistant. He appeared a moment later from his cubicle down the hall. He always looked like he'd just woken up, his hair flattened along one side. Sleepy and disheveled seemed to be the style, Gannon thought, among twenty-somethings, perhaps as a way to show they didn't give a shit. But underneath that veneer, Marty was a smart and capable researcher.

"Go find out everything you can about any local vampire legends," said Betts. "You know—history, lore, victims, all that shit."

"Yes, Mr. Betts."

"And if you don't find anything, or if it's dull... well, you know what to do."

"Yes, Mr. Betts." And he shuffled back down the hall.

Betts went on. "You know, with this happening right in the middle of filming, it might even make for a great through-line. Maybe we could get a bunch of Percipience photos of ghosts or whatever at one of the murder scenes—right, Gerhard?"

"Perhaps."

"Great! Hell, maybe we could even solve the case with that camera. Think about that. This isn't some ghostly haunting that's a hundred years old—this is something going on today." He turned to Gannon. "We've got a police scanner radio, right?"

"Of course." A scanner was obligatory equipment for a film crew in a city.

"Tomorrow, let's shoot some footage of the cops and the investigation. When Marty digs up some background, we can shoot at some of those locations, too. Think about it, darling: two bodies, sucked dry of blood. You never know where this is going. It could be big, and I mean *big*."

10

Francis Wellstone Jr., slowed his brisk walk as he eyed the numbers over the stately front doors flanking West Oglethorpe Avenue. Sixty-seven, sixty-three…there it was: a neocolonial manse with just the right amount of genteel craquelure over the stone façade. It could have been a film set lifted right out of *Jezebel*.

He adjusted his tie—damn, he'd forgotten how humid Savannah was—cleared his throat, and ascended the steps. As he rang the doorbell, he caught a reflection of himself in the frosted glass: the hair with just a touch of gray, the faint patrician lines coming out at the edges of his eyes: a visage that over the years had graced so many television interviews. Odd, he thought, that he wasn't recognized more frequently on the street.

There was a bustle from inside, and then the door opened to reveal a well-preserved woman, perhaps seventy years old, makeup carefully done, white hair tinged a shade of lavender, clothes expensive enough to artfully conceal a good twenty extra pounds.

"Mr. Wellstone!" she said, her eyes running up and down his suit.

"Mrs. Fayette?"

"Please call me Daisy."

"Only if you'll call me Frank."

"It's a deal!" And with something between a curtsy and a *passé relevé*, she ushered him through the entryway, along a short hall, and into a parlor that instantly gladdened his heart. It was straight out of Tennessee Williams, down to the antimacassars, portraits of dead Confederates, and a mantle of dust. A bow window looked down over West Oglethorpe, its fringed curtains filtering the beams of morning light. An ornate bookshelf was set against the interior wall, and Wellstone gave it a habitual glance as he passed by. A moment later, as he took the proffered seat in an overstuffed wing chair, he realized he needn't have bothered: the coffee table in front of him proudly displayed four of his books. Two, he was pleased to see as he set down his briefcase, were recent, published in the last decade; *Malice Aforethought* was there as well, of course; and the other, he noticed with annoyance, bore a remainder stamp on the text block.

"It's such a pleasure to meet you!" Daisy Fayette said, blushing faintly beneath her powder. "Please, have some lemonade."

Wellstone allowed the matron to pour him a glass. "Thank you."

"Thank *you*. I was so surprised to get your letter. Bless your heart, you could have knocked me over with a feather. Imagine: Francis Wellstone, wanting to interview *me*!"

He drank this in with a smile. "Reliable sources have mentioned you're the person to talk to when it comes to Savannah's history."

"And aren't you kind to say so? I have to tell you, Mr. Wellstone—Frank—that *Malice Aforethought* was one of the most fascinating and shocking books I've ever read."

Wellstone kept his smile in place with some effort. Why was it that when people wanted to compliment him, they invariably brought up his first, and best-known, work? What exactly did they think he'd been doing in the twenty years since it was published? It was like gushing to Papa Haydn over his first damned symphony.

In college, Wellstone had planned on becoming a historiographer. However, fate intervened when, in graduate school, it became clear he didn't have the temperament necessary to pore over dusty tomes in search of insight. So he dropped out of Columbia and took an internship at *New York* magazine, doing whatever gofer work needed to be done and helping the staff writers while figuring out what to do with his life.

And it was at *New York* that Wellstone found his calling. He might not have had the disposition for analyzing ancient texts, but he had an impressive gift for research: *contemporary* research. While doing background and fact-checking for the magazine articles, he discovered a knack for teasing out secrets that the staff writers would never have found otherwise. This gift was particularly useful for smear articles on celebrities and gotcha pieces on public figures. Instinctively, Wellstone knew how to talk to doormen, nannies, and cast-off lovers; his academic background gave him insight into where to dig for information that was meant to stay buried. The articles, often reeking of snark and schadenfreude, were devoured by the magazine's readership. In short order, Wellstone stopped toiling behind the scenes and got his name among the other top-tier journalists on *New York*'s masthead.

Then lightning struck: While doing background for a piece in the magazine, he unexpectedly came across a source with a trove of gossip about the high-profile attorney Laurence Furman. Furman was beloved by all for his good works, among them saving a West Virginia town from a rapacious company eager to situate a toxic waste dump there. Furman was known everywhere for his philanthropy and willingness to fight for the benefit of the workingman.

Except this turned out to be only part of the story. Deeply buried was another Laurence Furman: a lawyer who used blackmail and political connections to crush his opponents and a man who harassed and abused his female staff and threatened them into silence. Perhaps most damningly, Wellstone discovered that Furman had worked with his opponents on the other side of several lawsuits to line his own pockets at the expense of his clients.

There was too much scandal here for an article, and the subject was too juicy a bone for Wellstone to simply toss to his employer. Instead, he wrote *Malice Aforethought*, a salacious tell-all couched in literate prose, a magnificent character assassination of Furman. Wellstone's research was so thorough, his sources so irrefutable, that—instead of challenging the scandalous allegations—Furman committed suicide two weeks after the book was published. What a triumph that had been, rocketing the book to number one on the bestseller list.

"Thank you, Daisy," he said. "This lemonade is delicious, by the way."

Malice Aforethought had been followed by several awards and a Hollywood movie. Wellstone thought he had it made. But the follow-up books hadn't sold nearly as well and, because of sloppy research, had attracted several troublesome and expensive lawsuits. Ultimately Wellstone settled into a career that more resembled Geraldo Rivera's than Upton Sinclair's, churning out dubious books of scandal based on anonymous sources as quickly as possible. Now, with twelve titles to his name, he found himself still scoring an occasional bestseller even as the reviewers trashed his work.

He glanced at his hostess, widowed a decade and living off the diminishing fortune of her late husband. She had written several pamphlets on Savannah folklore and legend and was considered a local expert, even if she taught at a dump like Savannah-Exeter. But that wasn't why he was there. He had learned something else about Mrs. Fayette—something that he sensed might be very useful.

"So, Daisy—" he said, putting down his glass and leaning forward. "Even though I didn't want to mention it in my letter, you can probably guess why I'm here."

She leaned forward. "You're going to write another *book*!"

He nodded.

"And it's going to be about Savannah!"

"Among other things, yes." He waved a hand, palm upward. "Given you're the expert on the city's history—especially its, ah, supernatural history—may I rely on you as one of my primary sources?"

"Why, of *course*!" She raised her glass to her lips, fingers trembling slightly. He couldn't help but feel flattered at her reaction to the idea of seeing her name between the covers of a Francis Wellstone book. He smiled inwardly, pleased to know he still had the touch.

"Along the same lines, I hope you'll understand that—just for the next month or two—you'll have to keep the nature of my project to yourself."

She nodded vigorously, pleased to be in on the secret.

These points established, he leaned back. "Thank you, Daisy. I don't mind telling you how glad I am for your help. It will make my work so much easier—and the final product so much better."

"A Francis Wellstone book about Savannah," Daisy said, almost to herself.

Wellstone could have told her Savannah was only going to play a minor role in his book, but his instincts were, of course, far too keen for that. The fact was, the work was almost complete. In his past two books Wellstone had focused on debunking cultural mountebanks. Those had been exposés—the first about megachurch evangelical preachers, the second about diet-hawking celebrities—and both enjoyed upticks in sales. He was taking aim in his new project at the pseudoscience of the paranormal: skewering the psychics, spiritualists, clairvoyants, mediums, and crystal-gazing charlatans who exploited the supernatural to leech money from a gullible public.

The research was basically done. However, Wellstone had found himself stumped as to the best way to lead the reader into his book. He'd considered using the first chapter to expose a "spirit communicator" employing phony equipment to contact the dead, and of course Gerhard Moller came to mind. And then he'd heard that Barclay Betts, his old nemesis, was planning to shoot a docu-series on Savannah's haunted houses, featuring Moller. At that, Wellstone knew he not only had an intro—he had found the perfect bookend for his work, at the same time settling an old and bitter score with Betts.

"So tell me, Daisy," he said as she refilled his lemonade. "How did you become Savannah's preeminent, ah, ghostly historian?"

"Well…" She paused. "My great-great-grandfather fought in the War of Northern…that is, the War between the States. One could say I was raised surrounded by ghost stories. You know, we had servants, and they loved to tell my brother and me scary bedtime stories." She giggled, as if just speaking about it was misbehaving. "And my grandfather, was he ever one for old legends! Bless my heart."

"And those old legends found their way into your books, didn't they?" He was careful to call them "books" instead of "pamphlets."

"Oh, indeed. But then, almost every old family here in Savannah could tell you stories."

"But not with the depth of knowledge you can bring to them." Wellstone shifted in his chair. "Daisy, I feel very lucky—to have met you, and to have secured your remarkable fund of knowledge all for myself."

At this, Daisy's smile faded. "Well…" she said, the pink rising in her cheeks again, "that's not *quite* the case. You see, there's a documentary being filmed, right here in town."

This was exactly what Wellstone had come for, but he pretended to be surprised. "A documentary?"

"Yes. It's called *The Most Haunted Towns in America* or something like that."

"Oh, dear," Wellstone began.

"What is it?" Daisy asked quickly.

"This documentary—who's making it?"

"That network..." Daisy glanced upward, searching for a name on the ceiling. "The big one. Netflix."

"And the director?"

"Barclay Betts."

"Barclay Betts. I think I've heard of him." Wellstone certainly had: Betts had been behind the most difficult defamation lawsuit Wellstone ever had to endure. "And I suppose he's snapped up your services. I mean, with your reputation, your knowledge, he'd be foolish not to."

"Well, he *did* approach me," Daisy said.

"I feared as much. I mean, I'm very happy for you— but what a shame for my own project," Wellstone said, giving the impression that his interest in her was now waning. He even reached for his briefcase, as if to leave.

"He came by two days ago, saying the nicest things and inviting me to the set. But when I went there, first thing this morning, they just wanted me to read some lines from one of my books to use as a voice-over."

"Is that all?" Wellstone said in mock surprise.

Daisy nodded.

"I can't understand why Betts wouldn't want you in front of the camera. I mean, with your credentials..." He shook his head in disapproval. Naturally, Betts wouldn't want this elderly, powdered creature sitting in front of his lens.

"Exactly what *I* wondered," Daisy said, a nettled tone rising in her voice.

Wellstone was still slowly shaking his head. "You'll need to be careful. It sounds to me like he wants to use your research without giving you proper credit."

Daisy froze as this unexpected possibility was introduced. "Could he do that?"

"I'm afraid these documentary filmmakers are notorious for that." Wellstone finished the sentence with a shrug. Then he brightened, as if the problematic thought had been replaced with a more attractive one, and he removed his hand from the briefcase. "But— do you know what? This could be the very thing we need."

"What do you mean?" Daisy asked. She hadn't noticed the "we"—it had come out so naturally.

"I assume you'll be spending time on the set."

Daisy nodded in assent.

"That means you'll get access behind the scenes. Now, that would be a huge benefit to *our* book. Together we'll be able to take the reader behind the curtain, show the making of a documentary. Show them trying to detect ghostly presences."

Daisy nodded—first slowly, then enthusiastically. "Yes. Yes!" Suddenly, she paused. "But they said something about me signing a nondisclosure agreement."

Wellstone raised a finger. "Not a problem at all. You would be my *secret* source. No one would ever know."

He watched as the wheels revolved in Daisy's head. Then she smiled—a cleverer, even pricklier smile than he'd believed her capable of. *God bless southern belles*, he thought.

"All right," she said, blushing as if embarking on

a liaison with a gentleman not her husband. "I might learn more about this Savannah Vampire case."

At this Wellstone started. Vampire case? This was something new. But he quickly covered up his reaction and asked smoothly, "Savannah Vampire?"

"Oh, yes. It's just like the story Miss Belinda would tell us at bedtime. The one about the Savannah Vampire. Betts thinks it's returned, you know, with these two murders."

"The Savannah Vampire," Wellstone repeated. This was pure gold. So Betts was going to spin those two murders up into some bullshit story of a vampire stalking Savannah. Of course he would. "I do believe, Daisy Fayette, that this vampire should be our very next topic of conversation. Find out all you can on your next visit, and we'll get together again soon."

And, oh, Barclay, dear, he thought with satisfaction as they clinked glasses in the gauzy parlor light, *I'm about to give you the shaft. And you—you're going to take it and love it.*

11

COMMANDER ALANNA DELAPLANE WALKED across Chatham Square with homicide detective Sergeant Benny Sheldrake by her side. It proved quicker to park on the far side of the square and walk across, instead of trying to drive around. She could see flashing lights in the park, amid teams of CSIs in monkey suits and blue gloves moving around.

Twenty minutes before, a gardener with a city subcontractor had reported the grisly find, and the whole machinery of police investigation was now clanking into operation.

In her twenty-year career with the Savannah PD, Delaplane had seen plenty of so-called paranormal stunts. There were a lot of weird people out there claiming special powers, and most of them seemed to pass through Savannah. She wondered if this was just another hustle, some joker capitalizing on the Savannah Vampire thing. On the other hand, two people were dead, their blood sucked out—and that was no stunt. Neither was the perp a fool, having left precious little evidence behind on the victims or at the crime scenes.

They approached a couple of cops stringing tape, while others were working crowd control, trying to keep people back.

"Sergeant Rollo?" she said, stopping at the tape and addressing one of the cops. "Where's the gardener who called it in?"

"Right over there, Commander."

She turned and saw a man sitting on a bench, dressed in blue work overalls, hugging himself. A uniformed cop sat next to him. Delaplane and Sheldrake walked over.

"Hello," said Delaplane to the gardener, who looked up at her. He was an older Black man with white hair, deeply wrinkled face, and frightened eyes. She was a little surprised to see how affected he seemed to be. It was, after all, only a severed finger. "I'm Commander Delaplane. Can I sit down and ask a few questions?"

The uniformed cop rose as Delaplane took a seat, Sheldrake on the other side. The detective took out a tape recorder and turned it on, setting it down on the bench.

"Do you mind?" she asked, nodding at the recorder.

The man shook his head.

"May I ask your name?"

"Gilbert Johnson."

"Thank you, Gilbert." Delaplane tried to make her voice sound kindly. She'd been told more than once that she came across as brassy and intimidating. "Tell me what happened, in your own words, starting at the beginning."

Johnson nodded. "I was working fertilizer into that

bottlebrush hedge." He nodded toward where the CSI team was clustered. "Someone had been smoking, and there were a lot of butts in there that I was picking up. Then I saw the finger. I was working fast and thought it was a cigar butt at first, because it was kind of black, but it smelled bad and then I realized what it was. So I threw it back down. And then I saw the hair."

"Hair?" This hadn't been in the brief initial report she'd received.

"Like someone was scalped. A long curl of scalp with hair. And there was blood, too." He paused, breathing hard. "A lot of blood."

"That's okay, just take a moment." She waited until he had collected himself, then asked, "And what did you do then?"

"I backed up and out of that hedge and called 911. That was about half an hour ago."

Delaplane looked past the tape. She could see the forensic team going over the hedge with a fine-tooth comb.

"What happened to the cigarette butts?" she asked.

"I put them in the garbage bag."

"Were they different brands or all the same?"

"I didn't notice."

"Where is the garbage bag?"

He pointed to a flaccid black bag lying next to the hedge.

Delaplane nodded to Sheldrake. "Make sure that's taken in as evidence."

The detective nodded back.

"Anything else you remember?"

"I've just been sitting here since."

"Thank you, Gilbert," she said, rising and looking around. It was a picture of good crime scene investigation. She wondered if the FBI was going to show up. Once again, she felt annoyed that the feds had gotten involved. There was nothing about this case that justified it. And the senior agent they'd sent down, what a strange one he was. He looked almost like a vampire himself, pale and thin and clad all in black. And when she heard him speak—in that honeyed, upper-class New Orleans accent—it made her skin crawl. She'd met his type before, and in her experience, all that southern gentility sometimes concealed a hard-core racist mindset. Maybe even a family history of slave ownership.

The other one, Coldmoon, was the opposite. Recently he'd been looking every inch the fed with his sidewall crew cut, mirrored sunglasses, blue suit, white shirt, and spit-and-polish black shoes. He, at least, had a pleasing, soft-spoken manner.

She reminded herself not to make assumptions, to keep an open mind. She'd handle the FBI intrusion by simply going forward with her investigation in the usual manner. Detective Sheldrake was the nominal head, and she'd given orders for him to liaise with Carracci and the rest of the feds on a twice-weekly basis. But she intended to lead the investigation herself. Not that she didn't have trust in Sheldrake, but this was going to be a high-profile case, and when the shit hit the fan—which she knew it would—at least she would be the one with the finger on the switch.

Delaplane turned to Sheldrake. "I'm going to look around a bit. Maybe you could circulate, make sure everyone's doing what they should be."

"Will do."

He went off and, moments later, she heard him issuing a short string of quiet orders.

She circled the perimeter and found the M.E., George McDuffie, carrying a Yeti evidence cooler to his vehicle. It was hard to believe he actually had a medical degree—he looked more like a college freshman, thin as a rail, nervous and awkward. She hadn't worked with him much and didn't know yet if he was any good.

"Hey, George," she said. "Got a minute?"

"Certainly, Commander," He placed the cooler in the back of his vehicle and turned to her.

She nodded. "Have a look?"

"Um, sure." He unhooked the Yeti and opened the lid. Delaplane peered in. In a large test tube nestled in ice was the finger. Next to it, in another tube, was a long, thin strip of bloody scalp, with the hair attached. She recognized right away that the finger must be from the first victim, found washed up on the riverbank, who was missing one. That body also had a scalp wound that was probably going to match this bloody strip. Several other test tubes contained swabs of blood, flesh, and bloody bits of clothing.

"Looks like Ellerby," she said.

"Yes, I believe so. As soon as I get this finger and piece of scalp back to the lab I'll match them to the cadaver."

"You think this is where he was killed?"

"Possibly. There was quite a lot of blood in the bushes."

"And the finger? Cut off or what?"

"Bitten, I think."

Delaplane grunted. She turned and saw Sheldrake coming over.

He peered in. "The guy from the Chandler House?"

"Yup."

Sheldrake straightened and looked around at the buildings facing the square. "Christ almighty, you'd think someone would have heard something."

"Right," said Delaplane. "Ellerby was alive at eleven, because folks at the hotel said that's when he went out and didn't come back. Pretty sure he went out for a smoke. Let's get some DNA off those cigarette butts, see if this hedge was Ellerby's habitual smoking spot." She grinned. "Sheldrake, I've got a pain-in-the-ass assignment for your team. You need to interview everyone in those buildings within earshot—say, three hundred yards on either side—about what they heard between eleven and midnight that night."

"Right. But I wonder: how the hell did Ellerby's body get from here to the river?"

"Good question. Probably dragged to the street and loaded in a car. We need dogs here, and we need 'em along the riverbank, to see where he was dumped in."

She heard a commotion at the other end of the crime scene and saw a film crew trying to push their way past the police barriers. She came striding over. It was a big crew, with two cameras—one of them a Steadicam—a sound man, and a couple of others, surrounding a little fat man holding a mic, with a tall, gloomy guy next to him carrying what looked like a big old-fashioned box camera. The videographers were obviously shooting. The tall man was taking weird gadgets out of a suitcase with foam cutouts and laying them on a piece of velvet.

"What's going on?" Delaplane boomed out.

"I've told them, Commander, that this is a crime scene," said a uniformed officer.

"Hello, I'm Barclay Betts," said the short round

man with the mic, as if she should know who he was. The cameras were still rolling. The name and face *were* sort of familiar, but Delaplane didn't give a shit enough to try to remember.

"Well, Mr. Barclay Betts, we've got a police barricade here, in case you didn't notice."

"We just need to get a *little* closer," the round man said. "We're taking some photographs with this Percipience Camera here. It's quite remarkable, Officer. You see, it can capture paranormal activity. It could be a great help to the police."

Delaplane put her fists on her hips and grinned. "Paranormal activity? Like ghosts?"

"In this case, possibly a vampire."

At this she exploded into laughter. "Oh, yeah? Well, I'll tell you what. You take one step over that barrier, and I'll confiscate your vampire camera. Could be a bomb, for all we know. We'll have to take it apart to find out, and our technicians might, you know, *oops!*, kind of break it in the process. Or you can just stay where you are and tune in to your vampire vibes from afar."

The tall man, frowning deeply, put the cover back on the camera and latched it up, while Betts yelled "*Cut!*" Delaplane could see a young lady behind a camera trying to stifle a laugh.

She walked off, shaking her head. "Vampires!"

12

I**T WAS A DOZEN** blocks from the Chandler House to the M.E.'s office, and Pendergast had insisted on walking. Humidity or not, Coldmoon didn't mind. He'd spent a restless night with no more than four hours of sleep. His huge four-poster bed might have been impressive to look at, but it was soft as a marshmallow, and he was more accustomed to sleeping on the bare ground than on a mattress like a '70s Eldorado. On top of that, he felt like those portraits and creepy black silhouettes hanging on the walls were watching him as he tried to sleep. The walk, and the heat, loosened his muscles and blew away last night's cobwebs. Best of all, Montgomery Street was a broad commercial avenue, with a quiet cluster of sober-looking buildings ahead that had to be official. No ghoulish mansions, and not a wisp of Spanish moss in sight.

Pendergast strode along beside him, a silent figure in the trademark black suit, his only concession to the sun a pair of tortoiseshell Persol sunglasses with lenses dark as his clothes. If they'd been assigned a vehicle, Coldmoon hadn't seen any sign of it. He wondered idly if Pickett would get them something, or if Pendergast would take it upon himself to go car shopping again.

Speaking of Pickett, Coldmoon hadn't gotten so much as a glimpse of their boss since the previous day, when the ADC had dropped them at the Owens-Thomas House. Was it possible he'd really left town— that he'd gone back to New York? *He's signaling that he's going to let us handle this investigation* our *way*, Pendergast had said. It would be interesting to see if his partner was right.

As they approached the complex of county offices, Coldmoon noticed the scene wasn't as quiet as it had seemed a moment earlier. Two unmarked vans and a large private bus with blacked-out windows were pulling up onto Montgomery Street. He glanced at his watch: 8:35. He wondered why Pendergast had been so insistent on leaving early.

"Appointment's at nine," he said. "Want to grab some coffee?"

"No," said Pendergast, increasing his pace ever so slightly.

As they began cutting across the plaza in front of the office complex, doors in the vans and bus opened simultaneously and a motley assemblage began pouring out: young men and women with digital tablets and earpieces, one burly guy toting a portable light, and another unspooling what looked like an audio snake. From somewhere came the low growl of a generator starting up. And then a truly peculiar figure emerged from the bus: a man no taller than five feet, with round black glasses, a silk shirt of pale maroon, and an expensive-looking straw hat with an enormous brim. He took off the hat for a moment and looked around, and when he did Coldmoon saw a perfectly bald head that gleamed in the morning sun.

The man's slow reconnaissance of the plaza stopped when he saw Pendergast and Coldmoon. Putting the hat back on his head, he started toward them, at an angle designed to cut them off before they reached the buildings. A tall, attractive woman stepped out of the bus after him, followed by three more men, one carrying a Steadicam, another a sound box and boom mic, and the third a big video camera. It was some kind of film crew, and they were closing in.

But instead of hurrying to get past, Pendergast corrected course and slowed, with the result being that the group caught up with him just as they reached the wide brick steps in front of a closed glass door that read COUNTY CORONER'S OFFICE.

"Excuse me!" the short man said, removing his hat once again. For his size, he had a remarkably deep voice. Something about him looked familiar.

Pendergast began to ascend the steps, stopping only when the man repeated: "Excuse *me*!" Then he turned.

"Yes?"

"Are you the coroner?" the man asked.

"I rather hope not."

"Are you with the coroner's office?" the man asked, unfazed.

"No."

Coldmoon stepped forward to tell the man to go fuck himself, but a gentle, restraining hand from Pendergast stopped him. In the distance, he could see other cars and vans, some with network affiliations stenciled on their flanks, pulling up. The gaggle of people before them must have noticed this, too, because now they spread out, as if to form a protective cordon around their prey.

"Bring it in closer, darling," the round person said to a cameraman behind him. Then he turned back. "My name is Barclay Betts."

So that's who he is! Coldmoon thought. He used to chair one of those weekly news-lite shows that ran on Sunday evenings, and Coldmoon had seen him from time to time hosting scandalous documentaries and celebrity takedowns.

The faintest look of irritation passed over Betts's face when Pendergast had no reaction to his introduction. "I'm doing a docuseries on the city's strange history. 'Demon-Haunted Savannah.' May I ask your role in the murder investigation?"

Expectation now hung in the air. Coldmoon wondered what amusing brush-off Pendergast would employ to rid himself of this pest. There were few things the man hated more, he knew, than interviews with the press.

"I'm Special Agent Pendergast of the Federal Bureau of Investigation, and this is my partner, Special Agent Coldmoon." In case anyone doubted his statement, Pendergast followed it by removing his ID and shield and displaying them to the camera.

Much to Coldmoon's annoyance, Betts's face turned into a mask of delight. His eyes sparkled behind the round glasses. "Is that so? An FBI agent? So the feds have taken an interest in the recent murders?"

Pendergast nodded with a combination of gravity and reserve. "Indeed we have."

Coldmoon looked at his watch. What the hell was this? They'd arrived early, when the office was still locked, allowing themselves to be cornered, and now Pendergast was stopping to talk to this jackass. He began to step forward again, but once more he felt a restraining hand.

"Splendid!" Betts said, almost rubbing his hands together with glee. No doubt he'd come in hopes of catching the coroner—but in Pendergast, he'd found a prize at least as tasty. "May we ask you a few questions?"

"On the record?"

"Yes. Certainly. For the documentary."

Coldmoon watched as Pendergast glanced in the direction of the camera, as if to see if it was on. It was. He cleared his throat and crossed his arms in front of his severe suit.

"I am at your disposal, Mr. Betts," he said.

13

Wendy Gannon, director of photography, stood back slightly from the rest of the crew, monitoring their camera feeds, watching the FBI agent talk. This was an unexpected find—they'd been planning to beard the M.E., George McSomebodyorother, in his den. If she'd expected a premature encounter like this, she would have been on the lead camera herself. But she knew Craig could be trusted to get good footage, without a lot of amateurish panning and zooming. She looked at the sky, looked back at Betts and the FBI agent, mentally framing the shot. That black suit might throw off the white-balance, and she murmured a few directions into her headset. Craig gave her a thumbs-up and zeroed in on the agent.

"Can you tell us what your investigations have un-covered so far?" Betts asked in his most ingratiating tone—the one he reserved for movie stars and high-ranking officials.

"Certainly," the agent said. What was his name? Prendergrast? Gannon glanced at Marty, the production assistant, asking him through the head-set to get all available background on this person, ASAP—to make sure they weren't being pranked into interviewing someone masquerading as someone else. This guy looked about as far from an FBI agent as possible, but then she didn't really know much about the FBI. With the undertaker's garb, he was a strange-looking fellow, and unusually cooperative for law enforcement. But his ID had looked real enough. The younger, athletic man standing next to him, on the other hand, could have been a statue stamped right out of the Quantico mill.

She glanced around, making sure her people kept the other media away until Betts got what he wanted. He was a shrewd interviewer and could be relied on to do that quickly. Pavel was shooting B-roll with the Steadicam—simultaneously, not afterward as per usual, since this interview was unscripted—and that would give her any necessary elbow room when it came to editing the footage. She checked with the sound assistant, satisfied herself with the audio levels, then looked skyward again. The light was a little hot, but that was all right. This particular interview wasn't about mood, she knew—it was about content.

She turned her attention back to the interview already under way.

Strange—Betts, interrogator first class, didn't seem to have made any progress. "So what then, exactly, have you uncovered?"

"Nothing." The man spoke with a genteel southern lilt that, Gannon thought, would fit in perfectly with the Georgia locale.

Betts looked perplexed. "You haven't uncovered anything?"

"No."

"But there *has* been a murder, correct?"

"Certainly," the agent said, in the most agreeable manner imaginable. "Two, in fact."

"I'm sorry," Betts said. "If you're sure it was murder, then how can you not have uncovered anything?"

"The body was not covered—except by the clothes, of course, which were rather a mess. I don't know where you got the impression it was covered."

"But…that isn't…" Betts paused, uncharacteristically flummoxed. He took a deep breath. "Let's try this again." He glanced at the lead camera, as if to slap an invisible clapperboard for a fresh take. "Why has the FBI been called in?"

"Called in for what?"

"The murders."

"Which murders?"

"The ones that just took place."

"Do you mean, took place *here*?"

"Yes. Of course."

"Here in Savannah?"

"Yes."

"You'll have to be more specific."

A pause. "The murders in which the blood was sucked from the bodies, as if by a vampire. Those murders, sir!"

"I ask because more than one murder has taken place in Savannah recently. I'm delighted to help you, but I can't answer a question that's insufficiently articulated."

This was said in a tone of mild reproach, like that of a disappointed elementary school teacher speaking to a favorite student. Gannon saw a hint of red appear on the back of Betts's neck, just above his tailored silk shirt.

"Now that we've established which murders," Betts said, his voice raised, "what can you tell me about them?"

"Which one?"

"Let's start with the first murder," Betts said, after a pause to compose himself.

"The first murder?" the FBI agent repeated, in a remarkable parroting of Betts's own deep, nasal voice. "Oh, I'm afraid I can't really be of much help there. I'm so sorry."

"Why not?" Betts asked tersely.

"Because I haven't seen the first body. That's why I'm here. I don't mean in Savannah, you understand. I mean this building."

A slightly strangled noise escaped Betts's lips. "Okay. What can you tell me about the *second* murder?"

"It was a man."

"So we've been told."

"He's dead. I can verify that much for you, having examined that body. As I believe I implied already."

"Can you be more specific? How was the blood sucked out?"

"From the man?"

"Yes, yes. From the man!" Gannon could see Betts was losing his legendary temper.

"Well, the body was *not* covered. Going back to your earlier inquiry, that is."

Betts waited impatiently for more.

"I confess, Mr.—Butts, was it?"

"Betts."

"Ah. Forgive me. I confess, Mr. Butts, but I'm not sure precisely what additional information will satisfy you. The victim is a male. His body was found yesterday. The cause of death has yet to be determined.

Surely that should be enough to satisfy a member of your…profession?" And here Pendergast glanced—not, Gannon noticed, in a friendly way—over the entourage.

"It's *not* satisfactory," Betts said. "*Why* is the FBI involved?"

Pendergast's wandering eye returned to the director and he waved a hand at the cameras, mics, and other equipment. "The FBI often investigates homicides. Are you representing some local, or more likely hyperlocal, news channel?"

Betts's exasperated sigh was loud enough to spike the needles on the sound equipment. "I'm making—*directing*—a documentary. 'Demon-Haunted Savannah.' Now, Mr. Pendergast, some are saying this is the work of the Savannah Vampire. Do you have any comment on that?"

"Why do you ask?"

"As an FBI agent—if in fact you *are* an agent—you should know that what we need are details. People are frightened; they need answers. They have the right to know the *truth*."

Gannon felt this sanctimonious retort would anger the agent, and she braced herself. But if anything, it did just the opposite. The man's face assumed a thoughtful, almost philosophical expression. And when he spoke again it was once more in the most cooperative of tones.

"Mr. Butts," he said in his honeyed voice, "whether or not you realize it, you've just hit on the crux of the matter. '*What is truth?*' *said jesting Pilate, and would not stay for an answer.*' If I knew exactly *which* truth you were searching for, I would do my best to help. But it seems that—forgive my bluntness—no answer

I provide you with is satisfactory. In fact, every statement I make, every truth I impart, is simply met with another question. I appeal to my fellow agent, and the members of your own gathering, in this. Despite my best intentions in speaking with you, I find myself *auribus teneo lupum*, as Terence wrote in his imperishable and inimitable *Phormio*. Have you read *Phormio*? No? Well, I fear that is all too frequently the case today. Nevertheless, despite your lack of culture—particularly sad in a man who calls himself a journalist—as a servant of the public I'm still willing to stand on these steps, *hic manebimus optime*, until I've made it clear to you that I—"

At this point, Gannon saw the lights in the office behind the two agents go on, and a woman in a uniform come forward and unlock the front door. She glanced at her watch: nine o'clock.

Instantly, the man named Pendergast turned and—with a bound as quick as a fox—leapt up to the now-unlocked door and slipped inside. The other FBI agent followed.

Betts wheeled toward the cameras. "Cut! *Cut!*" he yelled. "I don't want any of that shit on tape!" He looked at Gannon. "Move, damn it, we need to get in there and talk to that medical examiner. *Now!*"

He jogged forward, climbing the stairs Pendergast had stood on just moments before, grasped the door, and tried to yank it open. But Agent Pendergast had turned and now held the door shut as if with a rod of iron.

"I've enjoyed the persiflage, Mr. Butts," he said through the glass, a thin smile on his lips. "But I'm afraid I have an appointment with the M.E. in"—he glanced at his watch—"sixty seconds. And members of the *press*—however broad the interpretation—are not invited." Then he gestured to the woman in uniform, who smartly relocked the door.

Beyond the glass of the door, Gannon could see the three figures receding into the office. There was a strange, almost electric moment of silence among the assembly surrounding the steps. And then Betts, outraged and outmaneuvered, began to curse until his voice filled the plaza, echoing off the buildings and pegging the sound engineer's VU meters fully in the red.

14

Hᴇʀᴇ ᴛʜᴇʏ ᴀʀᴇ, sɪʀs," said the M.E., McDuffie, leading Pendergast and Coldmoon into the lab and sweeping his arm toward the two naked cadavers, brightly illuminated on gurneys in the center of the room. In their exsanguinated state, they were both so bizarrely white that they looked like alien creatures or wax manikins. Coldmoon tried to hang back a little—this was the part of the job he disliked the most. But Pendergast moved in with all the eagerness of a hungry man at a free banquet. The guy never ceased to surprise. Coldmoon had thought he'd gone crazy, talking willingly, even eagerly, to that camera crew…until he realized he'd just been stalling for time until he could ensure that he got to the M.E. before they did. Or perhaps he was just amusing himself at their expense.

Hands clasped behind his back, Pendergast peered down at the first cadaver, leaning in so close that he almost looked like he was going to kiss it. He walked around it with additional intense scrutiny. Then he did the same thing with the second. McDuffie watched, as did his gowned assistant. At least, Coldmoon thought, the autopsies had been completed and the Y incisions sewn back up. They looked frightful, of course, but it could have been worse. Much worse.

Pendergast straightened up. "Agent Coldmoon, do you find it interesting that one victim is so much more damaged than the other?"

Now Coldmoon was forced to take closer notice of the bodies. One was in decent shape, under the circumstances, but the other—the one that had been found in the river—was bloated and torn up, with half a dozen stab or puncture wounds, cuts, scratches, a piece of his scalp ripped off, the right index finger missing.

"Strange," he murmured.

"Not strange at all," said Pendergast.

Coldmoon looked at him. "What do you mean?" *God, not another lecture.*

"This is the classic pattern. With the first victim, the killer is finding his way. He is exploring: seeking his center, so to speak. And because it is all so new, he is nervous and tentative. By the second victim, he is surer of himself, and so the killing is done with greater confidence and less, shall we say, untidiness."

"You think we have a serial killer in the making?" Coldmoon asked.

"Not with certainty, no."

"Then who is it?"

"Perhaps someone simply doing his job—and getting better at it."

Pendergast wheeled a digital magnifying scope over to the first victim and focused on one of the puncture wounds. He fiddled with the dials, took a few screenshots. He moved it to another area of lacerations, then another. Again he looked up.

"Agent Coldmoon, would you care to take a look?"

"I was just waiting for a turn." Coldmoon came over and glanced into the eyepiece. It showed an odd, pucker-like wound, washed clean by the river. There were other similar wounds, some bigger than others, and several had ripped the flesh. All had been dissected during the course of the autopsy, then stapled back up.

"Dr. McDuffie," said Pendergast, turning abruptly to the M.E., who jumped at the sudden movement. "Tell us what you found in your dissection of these wounds, if you please."

"Yes, of course. As you can see, we did a transect of each wound to map it and take samples for further lab work. What you see with the initial victim are a number of stab wounds made with a trocar-like implement. Some are deep, others shallow. I can give you a map of them if you'd care to see it. The wounds are clustered on the inside anterior upper portion of the thigh. My assumption—really, the only one that makes sense under the circumstances—is that the killer was probing for the femoral artery, but in a rather haphazard way. The final stab wound intersected the artery, and that is how the blood was drained."

"How much blood?"

"All of it. Literally every drop. The heart would have stopped pumping after about three to four liters had been removed. But the final one to two liters are gone as well, which indicates there was active suction through the hollow part of the trocar—a significant amount of suction."

"Like an embalmer?" Coldmoon asked.

"I'm glad you asked about that. Embalming sometimes uses the femoral vein—not the artery—but the blood is pushed out most frequently by pumping fluid into the aorta. They call it perfusing the body. And then embalming fluid pushes out the water the same way. This, on the other hand, required *active* suction."

"Could it be the work of someone with embalming experience?" Coldmoon asked.

"That thought crossed my mind. The same equipment might be modified to suck out the blood instead of pushing in fluids—in this case, by means of a trocar, not an incision and catheter."

"And the other wounds?" Pendergast asked.

"They're indicative of a struggle. Those deep lacerations look like they were done with a crude object, possibly a broken knife. The scalp injury is harder to categorize. It looks like something hard and thin was scraped across it with great force, peeling it up almost like you might pare an apple."

Coldmoon swallowed with some difficulty. He'd had slices of apple on his oatmeal at breakfast.

"Finally, note the missing index finger of the right hand. It was crudely severed from the body—I would say bitten off. As you probably know, it was recently recovered in the square in front of the hotel where he worked."

Pendergast nodded. "May I see it?"

"I'm sorry, it was sent off to the DNA lab. Dried saliva was found on it."

"Saliva?" Pendergast repeated. "Excellent. When will the results come in?"

"Forty-eight hours."

Another nod.

When it gets back, I'll give you the finger, Coldmoon thought to himself, still fighting the queasiness.

"I'd like to show you something else," McDuffie said. He nodded to the assistant, who came forward. Together, they gently flipped the body over.

"Note—in addition to the cracked ribs—these deep bruises, symmetrical on both sides of the spine, which contused and tore the paraspinal muscles, particularly the rhomboid major. Most unusual."

Pendergast examined the marks closely with the magnifying scope. Coldmoon waved off an invitation to look himself.

Next, the M.E. launched into a long list of other medical details noted during the autopsy, including the contents of the stomach, the small amounts of alcohol and THC present in the tissues, and so forth. Much of the rest Coldmoon couldn't follow, but none of it seemed particularly important.

"Let us move to the second victim," said Pendergast.

This body, which Coldmoon had already seen in the courtyard behind the Owens-Thomas House, was much fresher looking. He hadn't been floating in a warm river for half a day—thank God.

"Note," said McDuffie, "that there's only one puncture wound. This time, the killer went straight to the femoral artery. Again, the blood was totally drained. We recovered what looks like more saliva, or mucus, around the puncture wound—or perhaps some sort of organic lubricating agent. Again, we're running DNA and chemical tests on it."

Pendergast spent a long time examining this puncture wound.

"Note there is some bruising and scraping,"

McDuffie said, "but nothing like the first victim. This one seems to have been killed much more efficiently—at least, judging by the few signs of a struggle." He nodded to his assistant.

This body was flipped over as well. Right away, Coldmoon noted the same symmetrical bruises, equidistant from the spine.

"It looks like the body—both bodies—were gripped in some sort of vise or clamp. With such force, in fact, that the muscles underneath were contused and several ribs cracked."

Pendergast examined the bruises with the magnifying scope, moving it this way and that. Silence filled the lab. At last he straightened up and looked at the M.E. with a glittering eye. "That is one of the most curious things I've ever seen on a cadaver."

"We're baffled, too. Both bodies, as you know, were moved. The first was moved from the square to the river, over a distance of more than three miles as the crow flies."

"Would you say the injuries indicate more than one person was involved in the murder?"

"I would most definitely say so. In both the killing and the transporting. At least two, probably three or maybe more. The second victim," McDuffie went on, "was also moved, even though at this point we can only speculate about the site of the actual homicide. It almost looks like these marks were made by some sort of machine—an earthmover, forklift, or construction vehicle of some type—that picked up the bodies and carried them. Baffling."

Pendergast was silent a moment before speaking again. "I think, Dr. McDuffie, that we should keep this mutual bafflement to ourselves. Perhaps you've noticed the boisterous crowd of journalists and camerapeople outside?"

"I have."

"The less information they are given, the better. I mention this because you will no doubt be cornered by them, as I was."

McDuffie nodded, eyes widening at the thought of an unpleasant confrontation. "They won't hear anything from me. I'll let the commander do the talking."

"Most excellent." And as Pendergast's eyes returned to the corpses, Coldmoon saw that they were filled with a particularly intense and silvery gleam.

15

MᴄDᴜꜰꜰɪᴇ ʜᴀᴅ ᴘᴏɪɴᴛᴇᴅ ᴛʜᴇᴍ to an alternate exit, which deposited them in a quiet back alley. Coldmoon took a deep breath of the humid air, glad to be free of the antiseptic stink of the lab.

"Are you, perchance, a churchgoing man?" Pendergast asked.

"Not in your sense of the word."

"But perhaps you'll make an exception in this case? I'd appreciate your company."

Coldmoon sighed. "Speaking of 'case,' what does going to church have to do with anything—unless you're trying to reform me?"

"Reform? That would be impossible. Perhaps you noticed the tattoo on the wrist of our good Dr. Cobb?"

"Yes. It looked like a combat patch. I never figured that old guy as a veteran."

"It's no combat patch. It was the coat of arms of an ancient and noble family. Specifically, the Báthory family of the Transylvania region of Hungary."

"Transylvania? As in Dracula?"

Pendergast nodded. "Three horizontal teeth in a stylized pattern. The full coat of arms would be surrounded by a dragon biting its own tail."

Coldmoon could see Pendergast was enjoying prolonging this discussion as fully as possible.

"It was awarded to a fourteenth-century warrior named Vitus, who killed a swamp-dwelling dragon that had been threatening the kingdom of Ecsed."

"Bully for him. I hear those swamp-dwelling dragons are the worst."

"One of his descendants, who lived around 1600, was Countess Elizabeth Báthory de Ecsed. She has the distinction of being in the *Guinness World Records*."

"What for?"

"She was the world's most prolific female serial killer. They claim she murdered upwards of six hundred fifty women, many of them virgins, so she could bathe in their blood to retain her beauty. She was known as the Blood Countess."

"Good God."

"So, in the pleasantly cool living room of the Owens-Thomas House, I asked myself: what is the staid historian Dr. Cobb doing with a tattoo like that?"

"A Báthory descendant, perhaps?"

"No. As I told you, right after we left, he practically ran to the dowager Culpepper's house. He was obviously concerned about our visit and wanted to confer with her. I followed him there, and after he'd departed, I paid her a brief call myself."

"On what pretext?"

"As a Jehovah's Witness. Before I was insolently ejected from the house, I accomplished my goal: I noted the same tattoo on Mrs. Culpepper's wrist."

"Really? Sounds like a cult."

"Exactly."

Coldmoon paused. "A cult that might need blood for their rites—if they planned to follow in Báthory's footsteps. A lot of blood."

"Excellent."

"And you think this old church she purchased is where the shit goes down?"

"That is my hope."

"Hope?" Coldmoon had to laugh. "Really? You *hope*?"

"My dear Coldmoon, I do indeed hope to solve the case, thus sparing future victims."

"Fair enough. When do we pay them a visit?"

"Tonight, at midnight. We will surprise them. In the meantime, I will apply for a warrant and arrange a raid, because we want to catch them red-handed— no pun intended."

"How do you know they're going to be doing their thing tonight?"

"Because tomorrow is the anniversary of Elizabeth Báthory's gruesome death in a castle cell. Surely such an occasion will be marked by rites—perhaps even bloody ones."

16

Constance Greene sat in the Suwanee Room of the Chandler House, sipping bao zhong tea and gazing out at the attractive little park across West Gordon Street. The hotel's tearoom was long and narrow, one wall consisting almost entirely of old, rippled-glass windows looking over Chatham Square.

Constance was finding Savannah quite to her taste, especially after spending time in Florida: a place that was too modern, too much a clash of tropical paradise with frantic metropolis. Recent murders or not, Savannah was a genteel town that embraced its past—not the awful history of slavery and oppression, but a simpler time, of the Trollope-reading, take-a-turn-in-the-park sort, when each tree was planted with a thought for how it would improve the landscape a hundred years hence. Rather than rushing to tear things down during the architectural vandalism period of the 1950s and '60s, Savannah had preserved its link with the past, which in a personal way spoke to Constance and her own peculiar connection to distant times.

The Chandler House served breakfast from eight to ten each morning. Constance had arrived at quarter to ten and requested the table in the far corner of the room. Here, with her back to the wall, she could discreetly watch the other guests as well as the activity on the street and square. Amusingly, a couple of the clientele—tourists, obviously—had stopped her to ask for directions. They must have assumed she was a local, or perhaps even a hotel employee in period dress.

She had ordered a poached egg with remoulade and watercress, along with the bao zhong. There were two waitresses on duty, one young and one middle-aged, and—as there were now few customers—they were standing in the back. As ten o'clock neared, Constance pushed the half-eaten egg away and ordered a scone with clotted cream and blackcurrant jam. By twenty past there was only Constance, absorbed in a crossword puzzle, scone untouched, and the two waitresses nearby, relaxing and gossiping now that their shift was almost done.

Constance, gazing out the window at the passing traffic, listened intently to their conversation. The waitresses were talking in low tones, but not so low that she could not catch what they said. She casually recorded the relevant employee names and details in the squares of her crossword with an antique gold pencil. After a quarter of an hour, Constance contrived to knock the dish of clotted cream off her table.

"I'm so sorry!" she said as the waitresses rushed over to clean up the mess. While the women dabbed at the floor and tablecloth with fresh napkins, Constance rose, and in so doing jostled the rest of the spilled cream off the table—onto the black skirt of one waitress and the sleeve of the other. Constance renewed her apologies and insisted on helping clean up.

"Sit down here, across from me, and let me get you some fresh napkins," she said.

"Oh, ma'am," the middle-aged woman replied as she wiped the back of her hand across her starched serving apron, "we couldn't do any such thing."

"Nonsense," said Constance, practically steering them into the other chairs at her table. "I wouldn't think of leaving until I've made this right."

Both women sat down protesting, but with decreasing sincerity as Constance—moving with far less clumsiness than a moment before—brought over a large number of cloth napkins and a pitcher full of ice water.

"You just use all the napkins you need, now," Constance said, doing her best to parrot the speech patterns she'd heard other patrons use.

"But, ma'am," said the younger, "there'll be trouble if Mr. Drinkman—"

"If he should come in, there won't be any trouble once *I've* spoken to him."

The younger one's eyes brightened. "Oh, so you're a VIP guest?"

Constance smiled and waved a dismissive hand, saying nothing but implying everything. As the conversation continued, after a bit of shrewd name dropping, thanks to the crossword puzzle, Constance had both of them on an informal basis—Helen and Joan.

"I won't keep you," Constance said after the cleanup was finished. "I know how busy you must be, with Pat Ellerby drowned...not to mention the shock of it all. *And* everyone being questioned by the police."

"Now, that's the situation and the box it came in," said Helen, nodding vigorously.

"Just between the three of us, do you think Mr. Drinkman is up to the task?" Constance said. "Pat never said much about him."

"So you knew Mr. Ellerby?" Joan, the younger waitress, asked.

Constance nodded with a sorrowful look.

"Mr. Drinkman is trying hard," Joan said. "But he's got his work cut out for him, getting up to speed. Mr. Ellerby kept to himself, didn't explain much about how things worked around here. Especially when it came to *her*."

"Her?"

Joan cast her eyes up. "Miss Frost. He was very… protective of her."

"More like *she* was very possessive of *him*." Helen poured more water on a napkin and made a final dab at her sleeve. "It's been a hot mess, I can tell you. Some guests got so spooked they left. Others have come running like ants to a picnic, especially with that vampire talk starting up again." The waitresses exchanged a significant look. "And here's Mr. Drinkman, busier than a one-legged man at an ass-kicking contest. You'll excuse me, ma'am."

"I heard Pat Ellerby was missing for a day before they found his body," Constance said.

Both waitresses nodded. "He took his cigarette breaks in the square, but never at a set time. Often he'd disappear, just like that." Helen snapped her fingers. "One minute he'd be reading the financial pages of the paper, and the next he'd have run off and shut himself up in that room of his."

"What room?" Constance asked.

"He has a room at the foot of the basement stairs he keeps to himself," said Joan. "Uses it for stock trading and that sort of thing. 'Playing the market' is what he called it. It was his passion, that's for sure. And..." She paused a second. "Well, I think he was starting to get awful good at it."

"How do you know?" Constance asked.

"These last few months, he's bought himself some things. A new truck—a King Ranch, no less. And a fancy watch."

"Joan!" Helen said reprovingly.

"How do you know they weren't gifts from Miss Frost?"

"She isn't the kind to pass out gifts," Helen said.

"But Ellerby was one of her favorites?" Constance asked.

"He was *the* favorite," Joan said. "But that didn't make him an exception to her temper. Why, just a few nights back, she appeared out of nowhere, in the lobby—first time I'd seen her out in public in a year or two at least—and she headed on down to Ellerby's basement office when he was out. So much for her being so weak and frail she can't even leave her rooms! And, Lord sakes, you should have heard the argument upstairs later, when he came back! It sounded like an entire warehouse full of china was being smashed."

The waitresses' eyes sparkled at this schadenfreude-laced memory.

"When was this?" Constance asked casually.

"Let's see..." Joan thought a moment. "That was the night before Mr. Ellerby disappeared. No...two nights before."

Constance wondered if Frost was angry because

she'd caught Ellerby skimming from hotel profits. "But until you saw her in the lobby, you thought she was too weak to leave her rooms?"

The two waitresses exchanged glances again. "Well, that's what we've been *told*," Helen said. Despite her volubility, Constance noticed that something about this question made her choose her words more carefully. "Especially these last couple of years."

"Is she ill?"

"She's...eccentric, like. And the older she got, the more she depended on Mr. Ellerby. He arranged all her meals, her cleaning and linens, doctor's visits. He would go up there and read her poetry and listen to her play the piano. Classical."

"Despite the recent argument," Constance said.

"It might be you could chalk that up to a, well, lovers' quarrel." Joan lowered her voice. "Some folks around here had some queer ideas about the two of them. Now that he's dead, she's just stricken."

"Meals have to be left just outside her door," Helen added. "She won't let anybody in. And nobody else has the key to her back stairs."

Before Constance could ask about this, Joan added, voice still low: "Nobody *wants* to go in, either. It could be...dangerous."

Assuming this to be a joke, Constance tittered politely. She let the titter die into a slight cough behind her napkin as she saw neither of the women were smiling.

The conversation abruptly ceased at the appearance of Drinkman in the doorway. The waitresses scrambled to their feet, gathering up the soiled napkins and clearing the crockery from her table. Constance watched as they bustled out a back door and into the kitchen. Then her gaze turned back to Chatham Square, and her violet eyes—enigmatic at the best of times—closed partway, like a cat's, blinking at long intervals as she sat perfectly still in the late-morning sunlight.

17

And this," said the proprietor in a sonorous voice, "is where she was hanged." His name was Grooms, and he pointed a trembling finger at a dark wooden beam in the attic hallway. "The coachman tightened the noose around the poor maid's neck, threw it over the beam, and pulled her up while she struggled and twisted." He paused, his cadaverous face taking on a ghastly expression. "You can still see the rope burns in the wood."

Wendy Gannon, watching her two camera operators shooting the man's little act through the two screens on her console, had to admit Grooms was an ideal subject for the documentary. He had the perfect look as a guide to the supernatural, and no doubt he took pains with his appearance: the threadbare suit one size too large for his gaunt frame, his six-foot-six-inch height, the stringy gray hair and sunken eyes. She suspected a judicious touch of makeup here and there added to the Lurch effect. And he knew enough about creating atmosphere to protest while the gaffer set up camera lights in the building's dim interior. Gannon could see why the haunted Montgomerie House was one of Savannah's biggest tourist attractions.

As the guide pointed his spidery finger at the beam, Gannon murmured for the second camera to zoom in on where she could indeed see abrasions in the wood.

She glanced over at Moller, listening with his head tilted, the expression on his face unreadable, as the guide told the story of the murder: two hundred years ago, the coachman of the house became engaged to one of the servants. All was well until the coachman, who was a nasty sort, fancied that she was cheating on him and, in a fit of jealous rage, forced his way into her bedroom in the attic of the house, threw a noose around her neck, dragged her out into the hall, and hanged her from an exposed beam. He then went back to his own quarters, lay down on the bed, and cut his own throat—not just once, but twice.

"And," the man concluded, "ever since then, at the stroke of midnight, *it* happens."

He paused, dramatically drawing in his breath as he raised his bushy eyebrows. "Not every night, of course, but often enough. Dozens of witnesses can testify to the horror of *hearing the murder occur*. All the recountings match. It always starts with a muffled scream, quickly choked off; then the sound of a person being dragged against their will along the passageway; next, the sound of a heavy rope being tossed over the beam; the unmistakable sound of cord tightening and sliding as the rope is violently drawn upwards. Next comes the sound of the rope swinging, accompanied by a strangled choking. Then…" He paused. "Then, after a few minutes, you can hear slow, heavy footsteps

going back down the corridor; the opening and closing of a door; the creak of bedsprings—and then, all
of a sudden, the wet gargling of a throat being sliced
down to the neck bone with a straight razor."

Gannon captured this recitation on both cameras
perfectly, and Betts called for a cut. He seemed
thrilled, rubbing his fat hands together. "Awesome!
Awesome! Gerhard, you're up."

Moller nodded sagely. He had brought up to the
top floor a large hard-shell roller case, which he now
unlocked and opened. Inside, nested within foam cutouts, were the tools of his trade.

"Get a shot of that," said Betts.

"No," said Moller sharply. "As I already explained,
Mr. Betts, I do *not* allow photographs of my equipment
while it is inside the case. You may only photograph
the equipment in use."

"Right, okay," said Betts, irritated.

Gannon kept the cameras still as Moller removed
an old-fashioned-looking oscilloscope with a round
screen; the camera in its box; a silver wishbone-
shaped object that looked like a dowsing rod; a slab
of semitransparent stone, allegedly obsidian, smoky
and dark. He laid these things out on a sheet of
black velvet. He nodded to Betts that it was now
permissible to shoot, and Gannon nodded in turn to
the camera operators.

Betts strolled into the frame, face lit from below, his
skin pale. "It's almost midnight: when the ghosts of
the coachman and the maid are said to re-enact their
grisly ends. Dr. Gerhard Moller is setting up highly
sensitive tools and instruments—some dating back to
the medieval period, some of his own devising—that
can detect what specialists in the field call 'spiritual

turbulences'—that is, ghosts and other paranormal forces. At midnight, our watch will begin. Are we ready, Dr. Moller?"

"Yes," he said.

There was a pause. Finally, Gannon nudged Betts.

"We have with us," Betts went on, "Savannah's well-known historian of the supernatural, Mrs. Daisy Fayette."

Now the cameras turned to the heavyset woman who had been standing near Moller. Offscreen, Betts scowled. He had intended, Gannon knew, to confine this unphotogenic person to several voice-overs, but she'd convinced him that the "historian's" appearance—single, brief appearance—on film would help the documentary's credibility. And, in a weird way, she was kind of frightful herself, all powdered up like that.

"The Montgomerie House," Fayette said as she stepped forward, her voice unexpectedly musical, "is considered by historians of the supernatural to be perhaps the most haunted house in all Savannah. This, scholars believe, is due to the extreme horror and brutality of what happened. These two unfortunate souls are essentially trapped in a continuum of the afterlife: a hellish loop in which they mindlessly re-enact the murder, one as perpetrator, the other as victim. Because time as we know it does not exist in the spiritual realm, unsettled spirits can become trapped in an eddy, or whirlpool, that can go on for centuries—"

"And become vampires?" Betts asked. "As in the Savannah Vampire?"

The woman fell silent, thrown off her stride by the interruption. "Well, I don't know. The Savannah Vampire is an entirely different legend, and—"

"Okay, that's enough," Betts said. He turned to Gannon. "We can edit that down later."

Gannon made a mental note to be sure Betts didn't edit it out completely.

"On me in five." The host's features morphed once again into a smile as the cameras swiveled back in his direction. "And now," he said as they once again started rolling, without bothering to thank Mrs. Fayette, "Dr. Moller will direct the extraordinary power of his equipment on the very place of the killing, at the very time it occurred, to detect and—with any luck—photograph the spiritual disturbance."

Moller's oscilloscope was now plugged in, a green sine wave lazily tracing across the screen. He picked up the silver dowsing wand in both hands, its high polish glittering in the lights. Slowly, with the two cameras following his every move, he walked in a circle around the area below the abraded beam. Meanwhile, the grandfather clock at the far end of the hall tolled out midnight.

A hush had fallen. Even Gannon, who was almost positive this was bullshit, felt a shiver creep down her spine. Between takes, the lighting had been progressively lowered and made indirect. It was a technique as old as nitrate film stock, but it was still effective. The setting was equally atmospheric, with ugly old Victorian furniture, cracked mirrors, and worn carpets. Both Grooms and Fayette were standing in the background, looking on. Fayette, obviously displeased at having been cut off so brusquely, had her phone out and appeared to be texting someone.

The twelve strokes of the clock echoed and faded away. Silence returned. Moller paced back and forth in the hallway like a sentry. After ten minutes he stopped, laid down the dowsing rod, and took up the slab of obsidian. He held it up and peered through it, looking this way and that, for what seemed an eternity. He finally put it back down on the velvet sheet.

"What is it?" Betts asked. "What have you found? Are you going to take photos?"

Moller did not respond. Instead, he said, "Take me to the room where the coachman cut his throat."

"Right this way," Grooms said. Moller took up the wand and obsidian while the assistants moved the lights. They all followed the proprietor down the hall, cameras still rolling, to a small bedroom at the far end of the attic. Inside, it was spare and close. Moller soon had his equipment set up, and the process resumed. Again he used the silver wand, walking slowly, hovering with special attention over the bed. And then he looked everywhere with the piece of obsidian. He allowed Gannon to take a brief shot through it, which made everything dark, blurry, and rather ghostlike. *Moller's got his shtick down pat*, she thought.

Another fifteen minutes passed in silence as the cameras rolled. Gannon was eating up a hell of a lot of gigabytes, and it would be a pain to edit, but she couldn't risk missing anything.

Finally, Moller stopped. With a long sigh, he turned toward the group.

Betts moved in. "Dr. Moller, we're fascinated to hear what you found. Can you share it with us?"

Moller looked up. "Nothing."

"Nothing? What do you mean, nothing?"

"This house is not haunted," said Moller. "I detected absolutely no spiritual turbulence. There is nothing here."

"How can that be?" cried the proprietor, his voice rising. "We have witnesses, *scores* of witnesses over the years, who have experienced the haunting!"

"Perhaps it's the wrong evening?" Betts asked. "The spirits are, um, quiescent?"

"It doesn't matter the evening," said Moller gravely. "There's nothing here. Even if the spirits don't manifest themselves, the disturbance can be measured. My instruments measured no disturbance whatsoever. The spirits—if there ever were any—are long gone. This is merely an empty house—a tourist trap, perhaps, but nothing more."

"Cut, *cut*!" Betts cried, turning on Moller furiously. "What the hell do you mean, Gerhard? This is the most haunted house in the whole damn town! What am I going to do with all this useless footage?"

Grooms, red-faced, nodded his agreement. "Maybe the problem isn't with the house, but with all this hocus-pocus!" He gestured disdainfully at Moller's equipment. "The ghosts are here—*you* just didn't find them!"

At this, Moller threw him a withering look but said nothing. He moved back into the hallway and began to pack up his case. The now-superfluous historian, Daisy Fayette, tried to say something, but Betts waved her away as he would a housefly. "Get her out of here," he said to one of the assistants.

"Now look here, Gerhard," he said, turning back toward his ghost hunter and trying to modulate his voice. "We've gone to a lot of trouble and expense to set this up. This is the perfect haunted house. Couldn't you, ah, be persuaded to try it again, and make the equipment work?"

Moller drew himself up and said, in an ice-cold voice, "The equipment *did* work."

"For Chrissakes, Moller, you can make it work *better*!"

Moller stared at Betts. "What I do isn't some circus sideshow. This is real. This is *science*." He paused. "You will be glad to have that footage you just shot, Mr. Betts. Because if we do discover something elsewhere—and I expect we will—having found nothing here will make those discoveries all the more credible."

At this, Betts fell abruptly silent. Gannon noted that, after a moment, a small smile began to creep around the edges of his lips. "I see your point, Gerhard. My apologies."

Moller nodded curtly.

Betts turned to Gannon. "Action."

As Gannon began filming again, Betts turned to the camera, a serious expression on his face. "As you can see, detecting a supernatural presence is a delicate, scientific process. Ghosts can't be conjured up at will. Dr. Moller found nothing—and, given his reputation, that means nothing is here."

At this, the proprietor objected. "Nothing here?" he cried. "It's a well-known fact that this is the most haunted house in Savannah!"

Betts turned coolly to him. "What will soon be a well-known fact, Mr. Grooms, is that this place is a tourist trap and nothing more—a fake, exposed by Dr. Moller."

"How dare you!" Grooms said. "Turn off those cameras!" He gestured furiously at the cameras, which of course kept rolling, zooming in on his face. "This is defamation! I'll sue!"

But Gannon kept shooting. God, it was priceless. She was amazed at how Betts had turned this whole fiasco around. And she wondered, not for the first time, if there wasn't something to Moller's tricks after all.

18

THE CHURCH WAS A twenty-minute walk across town. Even though it was late, the streets were packed with tourists and drunk college students, bars overflowing, restaurants lit up, squares teeming with people. The church lay just outside the old pre–Civil War city limits, edging into an impoverished neighborhood of far less cheer. It was a nondescript brown brick building streaked with damp, missing some of its slate shingles. The small parking lot was full, and Coldmoon noticed the cars in it were expensive— Maseratis, BMWs, Audis. The first-floor windows had all been boarded up. Pendergast had a no-knock warrant, but Coldmoon suspected he was not going to employ the usual direct method of just busting down the front door.

They went around the corner from Bee Street— busy even at midnight—and examined the building from the rear. There was a small sacristy in the back, along with a modest rectory, its windows boarded up as well. Hopping a low iron railing, Pendergast darted up to the rectory's back door. Coldmoon followed. It was fitted with a gleaming new lock that looked out of place against the weathered oak. Pendergast reached into his suit and pulled out a set of lock picks nestled within a pouch of folded leather. A moment's fiddling released the lock.

Pendergast pressed his ear to the door for a long time and then slowly eased it open. The hinges, Coldmoon noted, were well oiled.

They slipped into a dark entryway. When Pendergast shut the door, the darkness turned to pitch black. Pendergast snapped on a small penlight and shined it around. The entryway gave onto a small, shabby parlor to the left and a dining room to the right. Straight ahead was a door leading in the direction of the church. Pendergast stepped up, placed his ear to that door as well, then gestured for Coldmoon to do the same.

When Coldmoon did, he could hear, through the door, the throbbing of voices—a monophonic, ritualistic chanting, slowly rising and falling.

They retreated from the door. "A cappella," Coldmoon murmured. "Nice."

"There are usually two doors from a rectory to a church," Pendergast whispered in return. "One for the public entrance of the minister, and one for the private entrance. Let us seek the private one."

They went into the dining room, then through it to a small kitchen. The flashlight's pencil beam illuminated a plastic jeroboam sitting on a counter, full of some unknown liquid. Pendergast swiped a glass from a shelf, held it under the container's spigot, and turned it.

A thick red stream came out.

"Holy shit," said Coldmoon, taking an involuntary step backward.

Pendergast slipped out a test tube, swabbed blood out of the glass, placed the swab in the tube, then stoppered it and returned it to his suit coat. He moved to a door at the far end of the room. Coldmoon watched as he tested the handle: unlocked.

He cracked it open ever so slightly, and the sound of chanting grew louder. A reddish light filtered through the crack. Pendergast stood there for a moment, then motioned for Coldmoon to take a look.

Beyond lay the sacristy, and beyond that the apse of the church. Where the altar would normally have been there was now a stage, and on the stage was a group of about half a dozen naked people moving in a slow circle, hands above their heads, chanting—and drenched in blood. Most were old and overweight, the men bald, the women with peroxided hair—on their heads, at least. In the middle of the circle was a pentagram with bizarre symbols chalked on its arms. Roaming about the stage was a woman, also naked and covered in blood. A macabre-looking necklace, from which dangled demonic-looking faces stamped in gold, hung from her neck. She held a brush and a copper pot, and periodically she dipped the brush into the pot, then splattered it over the dancers like a basting mop. It appeared to Coldmoon that the pot was full of blood.

Beyond the stage, in the dim crimson light, was a small audience of similar age. As the chanting grew in intensity, the audience members, too, began to shed their clothes, then gather in groups of two and three, fondling and caressing each other as they watched the ritual.

Pendergast retreated from the door and Coldmoon followed.

"Are those Satanic rites?" Coldmoon asked. He felt sick.

"Something of the sort," said Pendergast in a disgusted voice. In the reflected reddish glow, he looked disappointed, if not downright crestfallen.

"Isn't that what you were expecting?" Coldmoon asked. "Looks like the orgy's starting up any minute."

"I fear I may have miscalculated." Pendergast paused. "These people are...amateurs."

"Amateurs? Looks pretty damn serious to me."

At this point, the chanting abruptly slackened. Pendergast hurried to the door, glanced through the crack, then turned to Coldmoon. "Quick, over here. She's coming."

Pendergast and Coldmoon slipped into a dark closet, then half closed the door. A moment later, the woman with the pot came in, fiddled briefly with the spigot—having some difficulty in the dark—then left the way she had come. Obviously, she had refilled the pot with blood.

A sudden loud pounding sounded on the front door of the church, followed by a voice amplified through a megaphone: "FBI, executing a search warrant! Open up! This is the FBI!"

"Right on time," said Pendergast grimly.

A second later came the boom of a ram, then another, mingled with the screams and surprised cries of the participants and their audience. The main doors flew open, splintering on their hinges, and agents poured in.

"FBI!" yelled the man with the megaphone, whose voice Coldmoon recognized as Agent Carracci's.

"Everyone on the ground! *On the fucking ground!* Do it now! Show your hands!"

At this, Pendergast opened the door wide and strode out through the sacristy, Coldmoon following. The naked group was hastily obeying, getting down on the floor amid slicks of blood. Coldmoon watched as the agents fanned out, weapons drawn, making sure everyone was unarmed and cooperating.

"Clear!" somebody yelled.

It did not take long for the agents to complete their search. Pendergast directed them into the kitchen, where they hefted the jug of blood and confiscated it, along with other things—masks, costumes, hoods, chalices, dildos, statuettes, and additional flotsam ridiculous or uncouth. Pendergast watched, lips pursed with dissatisfaction.

No one was arrested. When the search was concluded, the FBI allowed everyone back on their feet, and—as the would-be Dionysians stood in a line, shamed, their fleshy bodies illuminated by numerous flashlights—took down names one at a time. For a bunch of Satanists, Coldmoon thought, the audience was surprisingly docile, some blubbering with fear, others pleading with the agents not to make their names public. Among the group was Dr. Cobb, who, alone among the rest, took it upon himself to argue that this was a bona fide religious service, that their religious freedom had been trampled upon, and that he would be calling his lawyer first thing in the morning. His complaints were studiously ignored. Coldmoon reflected that he'd preferred the first meeting with Cobb, when the museum director had been fully clothed.

And then Carracci said tersely: "All right. Get the

fuck out of here." In a mad rush of swaying breasts and bobbing privates, the group broke apart, ran to various corners of the church, grabbed their clothes, then headed for their cars and exited the parking lot, tires screeching. After briefly conferring with Carracci, Pendergast went out the back with Coldmoon.

"Too bad we can't hold them," said Coldmoon.

"It would be a waste of time."

"What are you talking about? You don't think the case is solved?"

"I think anything but," said Pendergast. His face looked drawn. "I fear I have made a serious miscalculation."

"Miscalculation? You saw the tattoos; you made the connection; you found the church. It looks to me like pretty fast footwork, not miscalculation."

"All too fast. I did not follow my own advice; I started thinking too early."

Coldmoon thought this was ridiculous. "Come on. You saw all that blood."

"I'd wager a great deal that it's animal blood. But more to the point: when I saw that lot full of expensive cars, and those ridiculous rites, I understood the psychological dynamic was wrong. These are dilletantes, playing at Satanism. They are guilty of animal cruelty, perhaps, but not murder. The killer or killers we are seeking are far more insidious than these...these pathetic dabblers in the occult."

Coldmoon shook his head. The case had gone from being open, to closed, to open again, so fast he felt almost dizzy.

"Let this be a lesson to you, my friend, on the dangers of drawing conclusions too early," Pendergast told him. "As H. L. Mencken once said, 'There is always a well-known solution to every human problem—neat, plausible, and wrong.' This was that neat, plausible, and wrong solution."

"If you say so. What now?"

"We must look elsewhere for answers. Specifically, Ellerby."

19

Pendergast descended the worn steps, pausing at the bottom to look around. He felt deeply chagrined at the previous evening's raid and his central role in it, but for the time being he put such thoughts aside.

The basement of the Chandler House had a distinctive smell—the smell of time, for want of a better word—that he found most interesting: wet stone, dust, and the distant odor of saltpeter, no doubt from the days when the building had functioned as a munitions factory, with a whiff of burnt rubber. Here they had processed gunpowder, lead, and brass into .54-caliber ringtail bullets for the Sharps rifles favored by Confederate cavalry. How stimulating, he thought, to have the past and the present mingling here in one's senses, like a fugue.

He also noted an additional odor: the crushed-walnut scent unique to the toxin prestrycurarine. He paused. It would seem the hotel was troubled with rat infestations. It would also seem they used a backward exterminator, because that particular rodenticide had been deemed ineffective years ago; rats, lacking the physical capacity to vomit, were by nature highly suspicious of unfamiliar odors. No matter; rats in a basement were not his concern.

The entire space exuded a feeling of desuetude and abandonment. He could see bare lightbulbs hanging from cords, stretching out into the distance, leaving gloom on either side. Even from his position at the foot of the steps, he noticed that the basement was formed out of a layering of building cycles, the stone floor rising or falling to match the periods of additional excavation. In the darker corners, away from the lights, rooms were faintly visible: pantries, a disused kitchen, what looked like a scullery. One section far to the rear was roped off with yellow tape and an official-looking sign that read STRUCTURALLY UNSOUND.

The antiquarian in him would have enjoyed exploring this underground fastness further, but he was here for a specific purpose: to investigate the room hard by the basement stairs that had been Ellerby's special office.

The room was marked by a scuffed wooden door with a pane of frosted glass set into it. Pendergast tried it, found it locked. He took out his set of lock-picking tools and, with a quick movement of his nimble fingers, the door opened noiselessly.

The room was small and boxy. One of the fluorescent lights affixed to the ceiling had a malfunctioning baffle. Three computer monitors arrayed along one wall were dark, but he could see the computers connected to them were still running, albeit asleep. They were placed upon a long table, a printer at one end. A shorter table was pushed against the opposite wall, its stacks of paper, arranged into folders of various colors. This was where the late Patrick Ellerby had moonlighted as a stock trader.

As he closed the door and walked into the room, Pendergast reminded himself that *moonlighting* was misleading: from what the staff had said, Ellerby would drift down here at random times of the day or night. Which was odd, because most traders worked by the clock.

Pendergast had already examined Ellerby's rooms, located on the third floor of the hotel. There had been nothing unusual, incriminating, or particularly interesting; the books, magazines, clothing, and electronics were typical of the life of a middle-aged bachelor. Based on what Constance had told him, Pendergast had hoped to uncover something that might shed light on the nature of Ellerby's relationship with the hotel's ancient and reclusive proprietress—who had refused to speak to anyone, including the police—but he had found nothing.

As he scanned the desk, two items caught his eye. One was a set of purchase papers for an F-250 truck, loaded, that had cost just over $70,000, and the other was the receipt for a self-winding Vacheron Constantin watch from a Miami boutique, with a price tag of $30,000.

While Pendergast did not much care for Ellerby's choice of vehicle, he certainly approved of his taste in timepieces.

Both purchases had been made within the last month. Pendergast briefly conjured up the image of somebody wearing that peerless example of *haute horlogerie*...while driving a pickup. It was ridiculous—but then, his mother had always told him people in Savannah had their own peculiar ways. He had witnessed a few of those ways himself, firsthand, the night before. He riffled through the colored folders, then placed them back on the worktable.

Constance had taken a peculiar interest in the proprietress, Miss Frost, and had gathered a store of gossip about her. Two days before Ellerby's death, she had come down here, seeming not at all a frail old recluse...not to mention later that evening when they'd had a ferocious argument in her rooms. Odd indeed.

He turned toward the computers. Pendergast surveyed the long table for a moment, and then he pulled a penlight out of his jacket pocket, knelt, and examined the closest CPU, feeling its flank with the backs of his knuckles. The whining noise of the fan and the heavy accumulation of dust in its rear grill indicated these machines were turned off rarely, if at all.

He rose and walked past each computer in turn, wriggling their mice to wake them up. A password field popped up on one of the screens—not surprising, given the financial transactions it presumably controlled. The password provided access to all three machines.

These computers would be dealt with by the FBI's digital forensics lab. He glanced at them for a few seconds before his attention turned to a thick, well-scuffed ledger book covered in green cloth, sitting on the desk before the three monitors. He picked it up and began paging through it. It appeared to be a list of transactions, all handwritten in a fanatically neat hand, with each entry containing a date, a cash amount, and a variety of abbreviations and symbols. It went back several years, and had obviously been meticulously kept. With any luck, it would prove to be

Ellerby's magnum opus: the logbook that chronicled all his doings in the market. It seemed odd he didn't have a safe to put all these papers in, but then again, no one had any interest in his doings until after he was murdered. But it did strike Pendergast as significant that there was no air of secrecy, illicit trading, or deception here. Even the lock on the door was of the most ordinary nature.

Pendergast flipped through the ledger until he reached the final entries. The most recent had been made eight days before.

Eight days. Two days before Ellerby died.

Pendergast ran through the dozen-odd pages leading up to these final entries. A cursory scan indicated that the hotel manager had been actively trading every day of the week, including weekends. There appeared to be no missed days, gaps, or lacunae of any sort...until the trades abruptly ended. He looked at the final entries once again, but there was nothing about them that indicated anything was amiss. The lines of text simply stopped—and forty-eight hours later, Ellerby was dead.

Putting down the ledger and taking out his penlight, Pendergast got on his hands and knees and did a painstaking search of the entire floor of the room. This was followed by the undersides of the desks, the chairs, the walls, the single filing cabinet. He took the occasional sample, but he could see nothing of special interest: no traces of blood, no signs of violence or a struggle. It looked as if Ellerby had last come down here on one of his breaks, done some work, then walked out, closing the door behind him...and gone to meet his death.

Pendergast walked toward the door, opened it,

snapped off the light, and stepped into the basement hallway. As he closed the door, his gaze once more turned toward the array of bare bulbs, leading off tantalizingly into the darkness. Then he turned away and began ascending the stairs, pulling out his phone as he did so to arrange for the FBI's Evidence Response Team to come and take away all traces of Patrick Ellerby's lucrative hobby.

20

As they were finishing breakfast the morning after the raid, Pendergast's cell phone rang. While he answered it, Coldmoon stirred his coffee moodily and took a sip. It was terrible, of course. He noticed that Pendergast was listening for a long time to someone on the other end of the line, without saying a word, and wondered idly who it was. Constance—whose breakfast had consisted only of tea—was reading the latest issue of *The Lancet*. This seemed like odd breakfast reading material, but nothing Constance did would surprise Coldmoon anymore.

Pendergast finally said, simply, "Yes," and hung up.

"Who was that?" Coldmoon asked.

"Our old friend, Squire Pickett. The senator has asked him to ask us to participate in a press conference."

"Press conference? Good God, why?"

Pendergast smiled wanly. "To discuss the Savannah Vampire, of course."

"You're kidding, right?"

"The senator is a canny fellow," Pendergast said. "He doesn't want this blowing up in his face, and so he's getting in front of the situation by leveraging his relationship with Pickett. Rumors are running rampant about a vampire, and he wants to put some solid information in front of the public to squelch speculation. Commander Delaplane will be running the conference. The mayor will be there, and we'll be backing them up."

"But we don't have solid information to give them," said Coldmoon. "Except for the raid on the church of crazy naked blood-drinking Satanists, who have all lawyered up by now."

"True. But we have enough to fashion a small bone from, which we can toss them."

Coldmoon grunted. "And when is this conference taking place?"

"Two hours."

Coldmoon nearly choked on his coffee. "Two *hours*?"

"As I said, the senator wants to get in front of this."

Constance peeped over the top of her journal as the two men rose. "In which case, a small bone might not be enough," she said. "You should perhaps consider a tibia. Or even better, a femur."

Coldmoon shot her a glance, but her face was already hidden once again behind the periodical.

The press conference took place in the parking lot behind the police station, where a temporary stage had been set up and the television news vans with their satellite dishes had room to park. It was obviously a hasty improvisation, but Coldmoon was impressed that Delaplane had been able to put even this together so quickly. A uniformed officer moved some cones aside to let them pass and waved them on to a restricted parking area. Pendergast took out his cell phone once again and dialed.

"Who are you calling now?" Coldmoon asked.

"Pickett," Pendergast said, putting the call on speakerphone. "He wanted me to alert him when we arrived."

The phone was picked up by Pickett's assistant. "He's on with Senator Drayton at the moment, but he's been expecting your call. One second, please."

A brief silence, and then Coldmoon heard a basso profundo voice with an unpleasant rasp come through the phone's speaker. "I'm not sure you're hearing me, Walt. I've got that outdoor rally in Savannah coming up awfully soon, and I won't tolerate any diversions. You need to get this mess cleared up quickly, because—"

"I beg your pardon?" Coldmoon heard Pendergast interrupt.

There was a silence. Pickett's voice came through, slightly breathless. "Agent Pendergast, I can't take your call now. I'll call you back."

"Yes, sir." He paused a second. "It seems we might have had a phone malfunction, because I thought for a moment that I heard another voice—"

"That will do," Pickett said, his voice tight. And the phone went dead.

Coldmoon looked at Pendergast, who had a most unusual twinkle of amusement in his eye. "Is that who I think it was? The Georgia senator, reaming out Pickett?"

"Tragic how some people seem unable to master

digital technology," Pendergast said, not sounding perturbed at all.

"I don't know how, but I think you managed that little screw-up," said Coldmoon.

"Who, me? Impossible."

That Senator Drayton certainly sounded like a first-class asshole. Coldmoon couldn't help but feel a certain grim satisfaction in knowing that Pickett might himself be on the receiving end of the stick.

Pendergast was already out of the car and walking across the parking lot, and Coldmoon hurried to join him.

He mounted the stage behind Pendergast, who took up a position on one side of the podium, with Delaplane, Detective Sheldrake, and a short, red-faced man Coldmoon assumed was the mayor on the other. The press had assembled with less jostling and chaos than Coldmoon expected. Maybe it had something to do with southern gentility. He noticed that the documentary filmmaker, Betts, must somehow have gotten wind of this conference before anyone else, because his team had parked themselves at the very front, staking out the choicest spot while the area behind had gradually filled with other journalists, cameras, and boom mics.

At eleven o'clock sharp, Delaplane stepped up to the microphone and gave it a few loud taps to silence the crowd. "I am Commander Alanna Delaplane, Savannah PD," she began, "and I welcome you all to this press conference."

She took a deep breath and went on, her powerful voice ringing off the façades of the surrounding buildings. This was one way to handle the press, Coldmoon thought: at high volume. She expressed sympathy for the two victims; assured the public that all resources were being brought to bear; praised the M.E.'s work; welcomed the help of the FBI; thanked the forensic teams and labs working on the case; and burnished the investigation to such a high gloss that it left the assembled press—who were no doubt thirsting for gore and controversy—dispirited, almost as if the case had been solved while their backs were turned. No mention was made of the raid.

Then the mayor took the podium and praised Commander Delaplane in turn, along with various officials Coldmoon had neither seen nor heard of, for their splendid work on the case. Coldmoon was beginning to feel uneasy with all this self-congratulation: from his own perspective, so far they had jack shit. But the entire press conference seemed to be having an anesthetic effect, turning an inexplicable and frightening situation into something that sounded almost boring. Perhaps that was the intention.

Finally, the mayor introduced "the highly decorated Special Agent Aloysius X. L. Pendergast of the FBI"—actually pronouncing his first name correctly which, Coldmoon guessed, might be another southern thing—and then stepped aside and yielded the podium.

Pendergast stepped up to it and spent a few moments surveying the restless crowd with gleaming eyes. As he did so, a hush fell. Coldmoon had to admit his partner had a charismatic aura so magnetic it could quiet even a crowd of reporters—at least temporarily.

"Honored ladies and gentlemen of the press," Pendergast began, his honeyed accent thicker than ever, "the FBI is naturally glad to assist Savannah law enforcement in investigating these recent homicides." He went on, his sonorous tone mesmerizing the crowd without actually imparting any information of note. He finished and stepped back, while Delaplane came forward again to call for questions. A scattering of hands shot up, including Betts's.

Delaplane pointed into the crowd. "Ms. O'Reilly, of WTOC?"

"Do you have any leads?"

"Yes, we do. I can't go into them for obvious reasons, but we're working on several promising avenues of investigation. Mr. Boojum of the *Register*?"

"Commander, is there a concern there might be more killings? And, if so, do you have any advice for the public on how to protect themselves?"

"We've quadrupled law enforcement presence in the historic area," Delaplane said. "I would ask that people not walk downtown alone at night, and please avoid inebriation, which always makes one an easier target."

There was quite a bit of snickering among the press over that last piece of advice.

"Ms. Locatelle of WHAF."

"Commander, what about the raid on that church over on Bee Street? Did anything come of that?"

At this, Delaplane pursed her lips. "If you're referring to the FBI action, the SPD had nothing to do with that. I'll turn the floor over to Special Agent Pendergast to, ah, explain."

Pendergast stepped forward. "I'm afraid that was a dead end. The rites involved animal blood, not human."

"What kind of animals?"

"Ducks, apparently."

There was a rash of snickering at this detail.

"No connection was found to the current case, and no apparent laws were broken by the, ah, worshippers, and as such their names cannot be released."

He stepped back and the commander came forward to handle more questions, pointedly ignoring Betts, who was waving his hand and becoming increasingly agitated when he was not called on. Finally, he simply shouted out a question. "Commander, what do you say to reports that these killings are remarkably similar to the legends of the Savannah Vampire?"

Delaplane fixed him with a steady eye. "Vampire, did you say?" she asked in a tone one might use to humor a child. "Mister..."

"Betts. Barclay Betts, anchor for—"

"Mr. Betts, if you're asking me if we think these killings are the work of a vampire, the answer is...wait for it...*no*."

Another titter rippled through the crowd.

"However," Delaplane continued, "it might be the work of a person, or persons, drawn for unhealthy reasons of their own to Savannah...and its legends. The Bee Street raid is a case in point."

"How was the blood drained?" Betts continued. "And to what purpose?"

"We believe a tool called a trocar, similar to a large-bore needle, was inserted into the femoral artery of the leg. As to what purpose, we have no idea yet."

When Delaplane tried to move to another questioner, Betts continued. "Is it true that all the blood was sucked out...every drop?"

She arched her eyebrows and fixed him with a steady gaze. "Every drop was taken. We're analyzing how it might have been done." Before Betts could continue, she said: "Mr. Wellstone?"

Coldmoon saw a handsome figure in an impeccable suit—gray hair at the temples, horn-rimmed glasses, every inch the professor—nod in acknowledgment. "I have a question for Special Agent Pendergast," he said in a patrician drawl. "Agent Pendergast, I understand you're one of the FBI's leading experts on deviant criminal psychology, especially as it involves serial homicide. Do you think the perpetrator is, in fact, a deviant serial killer?"

Silence fell as the crowd awaited Pendergast's answer.

"Serial killer?" Pendergast finally said. "Perhaps. Deviant? Perhaps not." He paused. "Perhaps what we are seeing is the expression of a certain kind of normative psychology, not deviant so much as a deviation from our expected standards."

"What do you mean by that?" Wellstone asked.

Amen, Coldmoon thought.

But Pendergast said nothing more, and with that Delaplane concluded the press conference.

21

Standing in the muck, Commander Alanna Delaplane slapped at a mosquito and cursed under her breath. The dog handler, Boris Strawbridge, was moving ahead of her, his boots squishing along the riverbank as he forced his way through the thick vegetation. Twist, the giant bloodhound he had brought, had the longest tongue Delaplane had ever seen on a dog. The powerful animal's leash was clipped to a belt around Strawbridge's waist to keep his hands free for pushing aside vegetation. Behind, she could hear the distant rush of traffic as it crossed the river on the Victory Drive Bridge, but the trees and bushes were so thick she couldn't see the span. Where they were—along the marshy shores of Sylvan Island— might as well be the damn Amazon jungle for all its impenetrable thickness and whining bugs. The big bloodhound was snuffling about listlessly, more interested in trash that had washed up than any scent connected with the Ellerby homicide.

The body had to have entered the river somewhere,

and while it might have been thrown off the nearby bridge, that seemed unlikely, as the roadway carried Interstate 80 traffic and was almost continuously traveled day and night. Dumping the body would have involved hoisting it over a tall cement guardrail, across a breakdown lane, and over a wall: too much time, too many opportunities to be seen. Delaplane figured the body had been dragged down to the river and left there, and judging from where it was found, it might have been anywhere along this stretch of shore. She wondered how the dog could smell anything above the stench of swamp gas and mud coming up from the river, but Strawbridge hadn't seemed to think it was a problem.

Strawbridge abruptly shouted and tried to haul the dog away from something, and Delaplane could see it had gotten into a McDonald's bag full of rotting french fries and a half-eaten burger.

"No, no, Twist! Drop it!" Strawbridge yanked on his leash while the dog strained to slop more of the disgusting mess into his mouth. Strawbridge reached over and pulled away the bag, only to have the burger spill out of it, along with a mass of writhing maggots.

"Keep that damn dog moving," said Delaplane.

This was looking more and more like a wasted idea. They had already been down the cemetery side of the river, with no luck, and were approaching the place where the body had originally been found. If they didn't pick up a scent here, there was no point in going farther, because bodies didn't float upstream.

Maybe the dog was no good. In the square, the same dog hadn't even been able to track the route of Ellerby's corpse from the spot he was killed—based on where they'd found his finger and bit of scalp—to the nearest street. She supposed the body might have been carried by two people, and thus not left a scent. That itself was a valuable piece of information.

"Find!" commanded Strawbridge yet again, kicking away the maggoty burger and waving the scent object from Ellerby at the dog's nose. Ahead the woods gave way to a small grassy marsh with a mud bank. At the far end was where the body had been found by some boaters. That was their stopping point. And thank God, because beyond the little salt marsh rose a junglelike wall of green worse than anything they had gone through so far.

"We'll turn around just before those woods," she said to Sheldrake, who was bringing up the rear.

"Can't be soon enough for me," replied Sheldrake, smacking a bug. She could already see some ugly red welts on his face and neck.

They emerged from the trees into the marsh, the grass about waist high. A breeze sprang up, sweeping the bugs away and providing some welcome relief from the stifling humidity. And now, finally, Twist latched onto a scent. It was remarkable how finding the trail changed the dog's entire demeanor; how this ungainly, clumsy animal was suddenly focused, straining at the leash, nose to the ground, eyes keen.

"Got a scent," said Strawbridge, pointing out the obvious.

"Good, good," Delaplane told him. This was more like it.

Now Twist was really straining at the leash, pulling Strawbridge along with him. Strawbridge was a small man and Twist a very big dog, so it made a ridiculous sight.

They moved quickly through the grasses, the breeze continuing to pick up. She could hear Sheldrake, an infamous cannoli eater, wheezing as he jogged behind her, trying to keep up. For the first time, Twist issued a deep baying cry, then another, the mournful sound echoing across the river.

"He really has something!" said Strawbridge breathlessly as he was dragged along by his own belt.

They came around the far side, skirting an indentation in the riverbank. A few hundred yards ahead, Delaplane could see the muddy embankment where crime scene investigators had flagged the body's location.

The dog was now bounding forward in his eagerness, jerking Strawbridge like a marionette with each lunge. "Easy, Twist!" the handler said, but the dog paid no attention and bayed again: a long, powerful sound from deep within his chest.

"Twist! Heel! *Heel!*" Strawbridge grabbed the leash with both hands and pulled. But the dog was clearly in full chase mode, and it was almost comical to see Strawbridge stumbling along behind him, shouting and trying to keep up.

"Bad dog! Heel! What the hell's wrong with you?"

Twist was frantic, baying loudly, slobber flying from his mouth, his footlong tongue swinging with each bark, straining and lunging—pulling Strawbridge toward the dense wall of vegetation just beyond where the body had been found.

"Come! *Sit!*"

No command worked—and a moment later, what Delaplane feared would happen indeed happened. Strawbridge lost his footing and fell in the tall grass, but still the dog struggled forward, dragging him along. Grabbing the leash in both hands once again, Strawbridge unclipped it from his belt and the dog took off like a shot toward the line of trees.

"Damn him," Strawbridge spluttered, standing up and brushing himself off as the dog bounded away, baying like mad. "He's never done that before."

A moment later Twist dove into the bushes and then vanished into the woods, his baying becoming muffled.

"What now?" asked Delaplane, glancing back at Sheldrake huffing and puffing his way through the grass behind them.

"We follow. I think he's due for a little refresher training, frankly."

"I'll say." Delaplane could still hear the baying, fainter now, but at a higher pitch.

Strawbridge listened for a moment as the barking reached a hysterical timbre. "He's definitely found something."

They started walking and, as they did so, the baying abruptly stopped. Strawbridge paused to listen.

"Why the silence?"

Strawbridge shook his head. "I don't know."

A few more minutes of trudging through marsh grass brought them to the edge of the forest. Pushing through a screen of bushes, they entered a dense thicket, light filtering down, the heat suddenly rising along with the insects. Strawbridge took a moment to grab his cell phone.

"Think he'll pick up?" Delaplane asked, irritated.

"Twist has a GPS unit on his collar. This just tells me where he is." He fiddled with some app on the phone, then set off: naturally, toward the densest part of the forest.

"This way," he said.

"I could sure use someone with a machete," said Delaplane, pushing through a mass of palmettos. Sheldrake's only comment was a muttered curse.

The forest was totally silent. Not even the birds were singing. Strangely, after a few minutes even the insects seemed to vanish as the palmettos gave way to a forest of live oaks, so ancient and draped in moss it was like walking through curtains.

A good ten minutes of struggle and then Delaplane could see, ahead, a shaft of sunlight penetrating the green gloom—a clearing. Strawbridge hastened his pace. "Twist!" he called, still glancing frequently at his phone. "Funny, it shows he's right up ahead. Twist! Here, boy!"

Pushing aside an especially thick screen of moss, they stumbled abruptly out into a small, sandy clearing. Delaplane halted. There was something lying in the sun, almost at their feet. It took her a moment to recognize what it was: the dog's head and long tongue.

The rest of it lay about twenty feet away, connected by a long coil of viscera from which a single french fry—rotten and undigested—could be seen protruding.

22

IT WAS QUARTER PAST ten that evening when Constance ascended the wide central staircase of the Chandler House. The hotel's carpeting was attractive—intertwining gold acanthus on a field of deep scarlet—but even if the stairs had been bare wood, her steps, from long experience, would have made no noise.

She paused on the fourth-floor landing to glance around. To her right was a short hallway that ended past half a dozen guest rooms. To her left the hall stretched on for a long way before making a jog.

Although the hotel had a fifth floor, the stairway ended here, on the fourth. She stood motionless, wondering where the fifth-floor staircase might be found.

Constance had spent the last hour in the suite of rooms she shared with Pendergast—Coldmoon having been banished to the third floor when he refused to stop brewing his rank and no doubt carcinogenic camp coffee. Constance had taken an interest in the Savannah Vampire legend, and so she had gone in search of the hotel's library. Although small, it had proven to be of interest. After noting the books they had on the subject, she had indulged in a second curiosity and made her way up the floors of the hotel, one by one, until she reached the fourth—and could go no farther.

As she looked down the hallway, she could not help but admire the care, taste, and expense that had gone into renovating and remodeling the building. The small china chandeliers, the flocked wallpaper, the sporting prints and landscapes combined to create an antebellum charm that was, somehow, also fresh. Constance sensed an obsessively careful hand at work here.

She began walking silently down the hall.

Everything she'd learned about Felicity Frost increased her curiosity. Nobody knew Miss Frost's background, or who her family was, beyond the fact that she must have come from money.

In her careful inquiries, Constance had learned a few things. When Frost first converted the building into a hotel, back in the nineties, she had run the place almost single-handedly. She affected a pearl-handled cane and wore hats with veils every Sunday, even though she never went to church. In those days she had been anything but a recluse. She had a quick tongue and was not shy in conversation. Whenever anyone inquired about her past, or her "people," she would happily enlighten them. Every time, however, the story was different, and those stories grew more elaborate and outrageous with each telling. Her great-great-grandfather had made his fortune in the fur trade, and she'd grown up on a *réserve indienne* in Quebec. She was a descendant of the only child of

Bonnie and Clyde, born in secret and, on reaching maturity, invested her parents' ill-gotten gains in a young company called IBM. In her wayward youth, she had successfully hijacked a plane to Cuba and made off with a suitcase full of smuggled gemstones. She was the granddaughter of Grand Duchess Anastasia of Russia, who, instead of being massacred by Bolsheviks in Yekaterinburg in 1918, escaped to the forests of the Carpathian Mountains, taking with her three Fabergé eggs. Eventually people tired of being made fools of and stopped asking. But the curiosity and speculation never died away.

Around ten years ago, it seemed, Miss Frost—then well into her seventies—had been struck by some kind of age-related condition. It was generally believed to affect her mind as well as her body, because her behavior, always eccentric, grew markedly more extreme. She withdrew from the day-to-day work of running the hotel and became increasingly dependent on Ellerby, the manager, to attend to details. She spent more and more time in her rooms on the fifth floor, growing increasingly reclusive, until at last she kept to them entirely. She restricted access to the top floor to just a few chosen maids and Ellerby. Now and then, despite slowly increasing enervation, she was subject to fits of sudden anger. Maids could come up twice a week, to clean and to change the linens, but they had to adhere to a strict schedule; and Miss Frost was never in those rooms while the maids were present. The only other people allowed to visit were her private physician, a Dr. Phyrum—and Patrick Ellerby, by this time the hotel's proprietor in everything but title, who brought her all her meals and visited her in the evenings. Sometimes, late at night, piano music could be heard.

This was what Constance, in careful and diligent inquiries, had been able to learn. She'd considered asking Aloysius to dig into FBI databases to find out more but found herself hesitating. The story of a woman locking herself away from the world and spending time in private pursuits struck a chord in Constance. And beyond that, the southern gothic trappings, the rumors and whispers, were too delicious to ruin with the winter wind of truth.

Naturally the talk had included speculation about the nature of the relationship between Miss Frost and Ellerby. One line of gossip was that the old lady wasn't as feeble as she made out and had killed the younger man in a lover's quarrel. It certainly seemed that the older she got, the more she disapproved of Ellerby's side interest in the stock market. But Constance dismissed the more prurient of these speculations as being too obvious to be true. What fascinated her more was the idea of Felicity Winthrop Frost, feeling her strength, health, and mental faculties begin to desert her, boarding herself up—like a modern-day Miss Havisham—in her luxurious apartments.

She had nearly reached the bend in the hallway when she stopped at a door to her right. Like the others she had passed, it was closed. But something was different—there was no number on it, and the wood seemed to be of a denser, thicker variety than the others. The knob was different as well—old-fashioned, of polished brass, with an ornate lock beneath it. It was set far apart from the normal-looking hotel doors that flanked it. As she stood silently, staring at the featureless door, she thought she detected piano music—beautifully dark and dense, perhaps Brahms—coming from above. Her hand reached for the doorknob.

"Oh, *miss!*" came a voice from down the hall.

Constance, who was rarely startled, was surprised now. Quick as a snake, she turned toward the voice, the hand that had just been reaching for the knob darting into the pocket of her skirt that held an antique Italian stiletto.

A maid had just come around the jog in the hallway, holding a large silver platter with several steel domes upon it—evidently a room service order. Constance had been so intent on the music that she had not heard the woman approach. The speed with which she'd turned, however, had so startled the maid that she stepped back, almost dropping the tray.

"You can't go in there, miss!" the maid said, voice trembling slightly. "That leads to Miss Frost's apartment."

Constance said nothing. She let her hand drop slowly to her side.

"It's past ten…she's likely to be waking up any moment now," the maid continued. "I'm very sorry, but she can't be disturbed."

"Of course not," Constance said in a calm voice. "I was merely wandering. Would you mind telling me where the hotel library is located?"

"On the first floor, room 104."

"Thank you."

The maid curtsied—a little awkwardly, given the tray she was holding—then walked past Constance. Constance watched as she knocked on a guest's door; disappeared inside the room for a minute; then came back out again, empty-handed except for the bill. She walked past Constance again with a small, nervous smile, then went out of sight past the jog in the corridor, heading for the service elevator.

Constance stood where she was for another few minutes, gazing first in the direction the maid had taken, then at the unmarked door. Finally she turned and—silent as a cat—returned along the hallway the way she'd come and disappeared down the stairs.

23

Agent Coldmoon stood at the edge of the clearing, the early-morning sun filtering down through the mist that rose among moss-draped trees. A lot of useless crime scene tape had been strung, he thought: a sign of overzealous police work, unnecessary since the area where the dog had been killed wasn't accessible to the public anyway. The local homicide team and a bevy of Georgia crime scene investigators had worked the site under lights over the course of the night. The local PD technicians had made a credible show of investigating the area: taking photos, collecting samples, scouring the ground for every clue. The M.E., McDuffie, and a forensic veterinarian had gone in next and examined the corpse in situ.

Coldmoon had made sure to position himself upwind from the dead dog. It had been a warm, humid night and he didn't want to take any chances. Even without the smell it was a pretty horrific sight.

"Curious," murmured Pendergast. "Most curious."

Coldmoon wasn't inclined to ask Pendergast what

he found curious, even if the agent would have told him—which he probably would not.

"I believe it is our turn, Agent Coldmoon," said Pendergast. "Shall we?"

Pendergast ducked under the tape and Coldmoon followed. There was no need to put on a monkey suit, thank God: it was only eight in the morning but already a scorcher. And here was his partner, wearing a damn linen suit with big green rubber Wellingtons on his feet. Somehow, he'd kept the suit immaculate even as they'd pushed through vegetation and waded through muck along the riverbank to reach this spot.

Coldmoon hung back a little. Dead dogs weren't really his area of expertise, and he was happy to let others take the lead. Pendergast, on the other hand, seemed as eager as ever when a dead body—human or otherwise—was in the vicinity. He made a beeline for the severed head and knelt next to it, slipping on a pair of nitrile gloves. He examined it with a magnifying glass.

"By Jove, Watson," Coldmoon muttered.

If Pendergast heard, he made no sign. He lifted the dog's tongue, turned it over, and swabbed something from it; then swabbed the dog's canines and put both swabs in a tube. Another tube came out and he took more rapid samples. Meanwhile, the M.E. and vet were examining the rest of the dog, twenty feet distant.

Now Pendergast was examining the dog's badly torn neck. "Agent Coldmoon?"

Coldmoon came over. Pendergast was pointing to vertebrae exposed in the neck. He waved off a few flies as they looked closer at the bloody mess.

Pendergast handed him the glass. "If you please."

It didn't please, but Coldmoon took a look anyway. He could see that the tip of one vertebra had broken off and the spinal cord was ragged and torn. "Looks like a lot of force was used."

"Exactly," said Pendergast. "One might assume the head was cut off, but when you examine the flesh, here, and here"—he poked at some muscles in the neck with a swab—"and that fractured vertebra, it looks more like it was *torn* off. Do you see?"

"Right," said Coldmoon. "Right."

Pendergast rose. "Let us look at the other section of the body."

They joined the M.E. and the vet, still crouching over the remains. Pendergast gave the carcass such a thorough examination, once again with his magnifying glass almost pressed against the fast-decaying flesh, spreading open this wound and probing into that cut, that Coldmoon had to avert his eyes. He hoped to God he wouldn't be asked to examine something.

"Well," said Pendergast as he rose, examination complete. "Dr. McDuffie, what do you make of it?"

The M.E., high-strung to begin with, seemed particularly nervous. Coldmoon understood why when he saw Commander Delaplane come striding out of the swamp, a look of displeasure on her face.

"I'll defer to my veterinary colleague, Dr. Suarez."

The vet, a young fellow with a lean frame, laid-back in comparison to McDuffie's fretfulness, said: "Well, if we weren't out in the middle of a bayou, I'd say this dog had been hit by a truck. You can see evidence of trauma, significant internal injuries, and broken bones." As he spoke, he gestured with a bloody scalpel, which he had been using to take tissue samples.

"Curious," said Pendergast.

Delaplane was now standing behind them, listening, her arms crossed.

"So, in the absence of being hit by a Peterbilt, I'd say the dog was beaten badly—perhaps with a baseball bat or crowbar—and cut or slashed. Possibly, both the butt and blade of an ax were used. We'll know more when we get the remains to the lab."

"Dr. Suarez," said Pendergast, "I fear your conclusions may require some additional thinking."

Suarez raised his eyebrows. "And why is that?"

"The abuse of the dog you just described would have taken a certain amount of time. But this dog was killed instantly."

"Agent Pendergast, even without medical training you can see how extensive these injuries are. It simply isn't possible for them to happen simultaneously—unless, as I said, the dog was hit by a truck." He spread his hands and smiled. "But...out here, in the woods?"

"I respect your observations, Dr. Suarez. Nevertheless, according to everyone interviewed, the dog was killed so quickly it made virtually no sound. It was barking hysterically—and then there was sudden silence. The dog had a GPS collar, which was found within minutes of the cessation of barking."

"That's pretty damn mystifying, then," said Suarez. "Look at the forensic evidence: This dog has numerous broken bones, multiple internal injuries, and it's been ripped apart with some sort of hook or hatchet. See these ragged cuts in the abdomen, here, and the place where the head was severed? None of that's clean—just a frenzy of ripping and tearing."

"I do see them," said Pendergast. "The witnesses, however, are quite clear in stating they reached the clearing only moments after the dog stopped barking. There was no one, or no thing, there. The attacker was gone."

The vet smiled. "I would like to hear your theory, Agent Pendergast."

But Pendergast didn't answer. Something in the direction of the river had attracted his attention. He rose and wandered off, disappearing into the trees.

Suarez shook his head. "He's an odd duck. Never met an FBI agent like him."

"And you never will again," said Coldmoon, irritated. "He's the very best."

After a short silence, Commander Delaplane said: "If you're asking about theories, I've got one. We have a person who kills two people and steals their blood. Then he disembowels a dog. There's only one explanation for this: we've got a maniac on our hands, someone big and powerful enough to tear apart a dog. The question is: why?"

Delaplane rounded on Coldmoon. "Is there anything in your criminal databases like this?"

Coldmoon rose and pulled off his gloves. "There was a situation in Russia in the 1990s," he said, "of a gang who killed homeless people passed out in parks in Moscow, and drained their blood to sell on the black market. But obviously that's not likely the case here."

Delaplane frowned. "We need a break in this case, fast. The senior senator from Georgia is on the warpath, or so I'm told." She looked around, glaring. "All right," she said. "Load the remains of the dog into evidence bags and bring them back to the lab for further analysis. We've done all we can here."

At this juncture, Coldmoon heard his radio crackle.

"Agent Coldmoon?" came Pendergast's voice. "Please come to the shore. And bring the others."

Delaplane turned. "Is that your partner?"

"Yes."

"What does he want?"

"I don't know." Coldmoon set off in the direction of the voice, with Delaplane, Sheldrake, the M.E., and the vet following. They left the clearing and headed through the trees, toward the river.

"This way," came the faint voice.

The trees gave way to an embankment covered with marsh grass, leading to a mudflat along the river. Pendergast stood ten yards out in the mud, knee deep. Amazingly, the Wellies had managed to keep his cream-colored suit still immaculate. He was taking photographs.

"Take care to preserve the marks, there, in front of me," he said, pointing to a disturbed area in the mud. "I believe they are significant."

Coldmoon peered in the indicated direction. There was a large, irregular depression in the mud, as if something had swiped across its surface, leaving an unclear, confused impression.

"What is it?" Delaplane called out, standing next to Coldmoon and peering at the smear. "Why's this significant?"

"Because," said Pendergast, "when you approach you will see, in the section closest to my left, a small plug of bloody fur—which, unless I'm very much mistaken, came from the back of our unfortunate bloodhound."

24

It's very strange," said McDuffie breathily as he led the way into a small conference room to one side of the M.E. lab. "Very strange," he repeated as Coldmoon and the others all took seats around the central table. "Dr. Kumar will explain it."

The doctor, a small man with dark skin and a lively face, opened a briefcase and passed out slim folders to everyone. Coldmoon opened his. There was a cover letter, followed by a bunch of incomprehensible lab reports replete with structural formulas. He quickly shut it but noted that Pendergast, next to him, seemed fully absorbed. Was chemistry another of the agent's unexpected talents? He decided it must be.

"Well," said McDuffie, clasping and unclasping his hands, "Dr. Kumar has something to tell us about the, ah, substance recovered from two of the victims."

Dr. Kumar nodded and cast his bright eyes around the table. "As George just said, it *is* most strange. The details are in the folder, but I'll try to explain in common English."

"Thank you, Dr. Kumar," said Pendergast.

"The substance we found on both victims is a mixture of organic molecules, all very unusual. One compound, making up over fifty percent of the sample, will serve as an example. It is a very complex and large organic polymer—a long chain molecule with a core of carbon and hydrogen—with side groups of sulfur, nitrogen, iron, and strangely enough, silver. This is not a substance we would find in any living organism."

He let this hang. Coldmoon could see Pendergast's eyes glittering. "Can you expand on that, Dr. Kumar?"

"I can, at least a little. We call this class of compounds organosilvers, which are formed when silver bonds with carbon. The reason we don't find silver incorporated into the chemistry of living organisms is because it's toxic."

"Then where did it come from?" Coldmoon asked.

"I believe it's a manufactured compound. Nothing like this would occur in nature. But to manufacture this would take a very sophisticated chemist, equipped with a high-level lab." He paused. "The fact is, I've never seen a compound like this. It's sort of crazy, to be honest."

"What's it supposed to do?" Coldmoon asked.

"I'm not sure I understand the question," Kumar said.

"I mean, it must have been made to *do* something, right? To serve a purpose? So: what's the purpose?"

"Ah," said Kumar. "That is a very good question." He paused again. "I have absolutely no idea what its purpose is."

"I believe it was kind of greasy or slick," said

Coldmoon. "And it was found around the puncture wounds in the victims. Could it have been a lubricant?"

"Possibly. But why use it as a lubricant, when much simpler compounds can be purchased at the drugstore? Really, I wish I could tell you more, but we've barely been able to analyze the compound. We're still working on its structure. A full analysis could take months."

"And the other compounds found in the sample?" Pendergast asked. "What is their chemistry?"

"Equally bizarre. All organic, complex, and unlike anything we typically see in nature or in manufacturing, medicine, or chemical synthesis. Many seem to have metals in them—organometallic, we call them. Platinum and gold, primarily."

"Gold?" Coldmoon asked incredulously. "How much?"

"Minute quantities. Gold bonded to carbon to make various gold carbide compounds. Again, this is something that doesn't occur in nature, because such compounds are toxic to life—and they're not stable."

"Any idea what company might manufacture these sorts of compounds?"

"No idea who, and no idea how. In fact, that's something that should be looked into."

"And we shall," said Pendergast quietly. He turned his gaze to McDuffie, who flinched visibly in response. "What about the fur found in the mud this morning?"

"Definitely from the dog," the M.E. said.

"And the imprint itself?"

"Our CSI lab has a cast of it. They're trying to figure

out what made the impression, but it's so smeared it's hard to tell."

Pendergast leaned back in his chair and tented his fingers, half closing his eyes. "In that case, they are focusing on the wrong problem."

"What do you mean?" McDuffie asked.

"*What* made the impression is not the question of greatest significance."

"What other question is there?"

"*How* it was made. Consider, if you will, that the mark is ten feet out on the mudflat, with no other marks leading to it."

There was a silence in the room.

Pendergast rose and picked up the file. "Thank you, Dr. Kumar, for your report. My partner and I will study this with great interest."

They took their leave.

"Fascinating," Pendergast said as they left the building. "But singularly unilluminating."

"So how *was* it made?" Coldmoon asked.

But Pendergast, lost in thought, didn't answer.

25

Francis Wellstone Jr. sat in a rear corner banquette of Lafitte's restaurant—one of Savannah's most historic eateries, situated just off Warren Square. He always ate lunch promptly at noon, and when he was on assignment, he usually ate out and was careful to make his meals brisk, without wine or cocktails, and *solus*. Writing and researching were hard work. A freelancer such as himself had no boss to motivate him, no one checking up on his whereabouts, and it was all too easy to have a few martinis and let the afternoon and evening slide away. He'd seen it happen many times to other writers, and he was determined it would never happen to him.

As luck would have it, the maître d' at Lafitte's was a voracious reader of nonfiction and happened to recognize Wellstone. While he hated to admit it to himself, this was tremendously gratifying. With great ceremony, the man ushered Wellstone to a prize table, and then—unexpectedly—returned a few minutes later with a bottle of Châteauneuf-du-Pape. Wellstone was about to refuse it until he noticed it was a Beau-castel: a princely gift, and one of his favorite reds of the Rhône Valley. Under the circumstances, there was no choice but to have one glass. One. It might well be gauche for him to take the rest of the bottle with him, but it would be even more gauche for the restaurant manager to repossess it. So he'd still be able to do a full afternoon's work, then reward himself with the rest of the bottle after a light dinner.

But it hadn't worked out that way. The sommelier, after uncorking the wine, immediately decanted it. So much for taking home the rest of the bottle. But the wine was excellent: earthy, almost leathery. As he was looking over the menu, Wellstone found that not only had he finished the glass, but a second had been poured for him. What the heck—he could take an afternoon off. He ordered an appetizer of escargots à la Bordelaise and then, feeling expansive, Lafitte's famous oysters Rockefeller. But by the time he'd finished the two courses, and three glasses of wine, an uncomfortable satiety, combined with a dismaying lunchtime buzz, made him feel both guilty and dis-composed. Not a good idea, after all.

What was he doing here, anyway? The book was almost finished, and it was an excellent piece of reportage. He had more than enough extra material to put together a prologue and an epilogue. Christ, the book was already a scathing indictment of para-normal charlatanism, and he really didn't need a final exposé to cap it.

He'd spent—wasted—nearly five days already. Even this unexpected vampire story, which had mate-rialized out of the blue, wasn't worth the candle. He might be deluding himself that this was a good

investment of his time. Learning that his old nemesis Barclay Betts would be filming a documentary
here had no doubt goaded him on—that, and Betts's
damnable libel suit against him. He shouldn't have
allowed that to cloud his judgment. He was meeting with Daisy later this afternoon; he would find
out if she had anything solid and incriminating on
Betts, and if not, he might just wrap this up, call
it quits, and head north to Boston to put the final
touches on the manuscript before turning it in to his
publisher.

As he'd been musing, he noticed the sommelier had
crept up and refilled his glass. Well, he didn't have
to drink it.

At that moment, the restaurant's front door opened
and he saw none other than Barclay Betts stroll in,
followed by his cinematographer and half a dozen or
so hangers-on. *Bloody hell*. Wellstone reached for the
dessert menu as a shield, but realized it had already
been taken away when he'd ordered an espresso. He'd
drain that and be gone.

He raised the fresh glass of wine to his lips.

Betts's loud voice and braying laugh were disturbing the restrained atmosphere of the restaurant.
Heads turned as the party made its progress. As it
did so, Wellstone realized that the only tables capable
of supporting such a large group were the banquettes
along the back wall—and the only free one was
directly next to his.

He half stood, preparing to raise his hand and ask
a waiter to forget the espresso and bring his check
instead, but at that moment—just as one waiter
was seating Betts & Co. with a cacophony of scraping and tinkling—his own waiter, accompanied by

the maître d', approached, carrying something on a platter beneath a domed silver lid.

They slipped it in front of him and, before Wellstone could protest, the maître d' whisked off the lid to reveal a white ramekin with a jiggly yellow mass spreading out above it like a miniature mushroom cloud.

"*Et voilà!*" the maître d' said as he slipped a sauce boat onto the table beside the plate. "Since Monsieur Wellstone will not order dessert, we have taken the liberty to prepare one for him. Soufflé a l'orange, with the compliments of Lafitte's!" And again, before Wellstone could protest, the man took two serving spoons, dug out a large mound of soufflé—the remainder quickly sinking back below the edges of the ramekin—placed it on the dessert plate, and drizzled some of the warm sauce artfully over it, putting the sauce boat to one side.

Both the waiter and the maître d' now stood back proudly, and there was nothing Wellstone could do but murmur thanks.

"Smells good!" said one of the goons from Betts's table. They were now all seated, whipping open napkins and picking up the oversize menus.

Wellstone ignored them. He'd eat the soufflé as quickly as decorum allowed, then leave before the laughter and conversation arising from the next table spoiled his lunch. The afternoon was shot. This whole trip was a waste of time. If he chose, he might be back in Boston as early as tomorrow, ending his book with another, more elegant flourish. But first things first— he always carried a book or two of his in his briefcase, and he made a mental note to sign one to the maître d' with an especially thoughtful inscription.

Just as he was raising a spoonful of the dessert to his mouth, the bray of Betts's nasal laughter sounded from the adjoining banquette. "Well, well!" he said. "Look who it is. Horace Greeley himself. Trip over any *lawsuits* recently, Frankie?"

The resulting laughter washed over Wellstone, his table, and his dessert. He put the spoon down and picked up his wineglass instead. "Barclay Betts," he said, the wine making his voice strangely attenuated in his own ears. "That explains the smell. And here I thought someone had tracked in dog shit from the street."

Betts laughed good-humoredly. "What are you down here for, anyway? Have New York and Boston run out of creeps and perverts with law degrees for you to blackmail?"

This, of course, was a snarky reference to his first book, *Malice Aforethought*. Wellstone took another, deeper sip of wine. Swearing at Betts had felt good. He had no reason to be polite to the man. Encouraged by the wine, he said, "Thanks, but there are quite enough creeps right here at the next table," he replied.

Betts laughed again, with a little less humor this time. "Is it possible I'm speaking to a *new* Francis Wellstone? I thought you saved all the tough talk for your books and were only timid in person. Don't tell me you've grown a pair."

Wellstone drained his wineglass. "Why don't you go back to your sycophants and toadies? At least *they* will laugh at your puerile, stunted attempts at witticism. You remind me of that charming description of S. J. Perelman: *Under a forehead roughly comparable to that of the Piltdown Man are visible a pair of tiny pig eyes, lit up alternately by greed and concupiscence.*"

"Well...!" Betts said, inhaling, temporarily stunned but preparing his next sally.

"Well, *well*!" interrupted Wellstone, mimicking Betts's pompous, theatrical voice. The wine had muzzled his internal traffic cop. "Speaking of wells, how is that well of yours? Find any corpses down there after all?"

The Well had been a pet project of Betts's two years before. Traveling through Dutchess County, he'd heard about a farmhouse that belonged to a man who—according to local lore—had killed drifters and hitchhikers and thrown the bodies down his well. Betts decided the stories were true, even though the authorities didn't think so and had never investigated. Betts leased the property and raised money for a special live television event in which the well was dug up to uncover the foul crimes. Nothing was found, Betts was embarrassed, and it set back his career a few years. Rumor was he never allowed the project to be mentioned in his presence.

"Watch it, Frankie boy," Betts said. Wellstone could see, with a rising sense of triumph, that Betts was losing his cool.

"Now who needs to grow a pair?" Wellstone replied, imperially and drunkenly disdainful from the safety of his banquette. "You can't sue me for what I say to your face, especially if it's true. But don't worry," he went on in a sarcastic voice, encouraged even more by seeing Betts's face darken with anger. "My critique of your *Well* project, which I shall shortly publish, is only three words long—brief enough for even your infantile attention span. Care to hear it?" And he leaned a little unsteadily toward the leather curve of the banquette. "*Al. Capone's. Vault.*"

At this mention of the most ridiculous special ever to air on TV, Betts put his napkin aside and stood up. He moved slowly, however, and Wellstone felt in no physical danger—until the producer plucked the sauce boat from Wellstone's table and poured warm crème anglaise all over the writer's pants, shirt, and tie, paying particularly careful attention to the crotch, which he decorated in large, inelegant loops as Wellstone sat there, momentarily thunderstruck. But only momentarily: he launched himself over the edge of the banquette toward Betts, who skipped backward with a harsh guffaw. A musclebound crew member leapt up and deflected Wellstone's charge with a shove of outstretched palms, and he half rolled, half tumbled back into his own banquette, falling across his table— which promptly collapsed. As Wellstone hit the floor, and before he could process the full indignity of what had just transpired, he became aware of two things: the unpleasant musky smell of the carpeting pressing against his nose, and the inverted plate of soufflé that now lay against the nape of his neck, its contents sliding down his back in a sticky warm stream.

26

CLIFFORD MASOLINO, FORENSIC ACCOUNTANT for the Federal Bureau of Investigation, returned from lunch to find a new assignment waiting for him, delivered from Georgia by special courier, with an attached note written by one Special Agent A. X. L. Pendergast.

As Masolino took his seat in the windowless basement office, he wiped the grease off his hands from the gyro he'd just eaten. He used a paper towel, a roll of which he kept handy, because he was large and soft and had a tendency to sweat. *Pendergast, Pendergast*...the name was familiar, and he vaguely associated it with something unpleasant. The reason suddenly came to him as he opened the note: that crazy episode years ago at the New York Museum of Natural History, where a bunch of people got killed and, if memory served, there was a cover-up. A special agent named Pendergast was involved with that, and...and now Masolino recalled a spectral image of the man. Masolino had been a rookie forensic accountant in New York at the time, just getting started with the FBI, and he'd assisted in analyzing the museum's accounts after the bloodbath, where they found significant fraud involving donated monies. It was Masolino's first case and he had done well. Very well. Those were heady times indeed.

That was years ago. Pendergast's note was written with indigo-colored ink in an elegant script:

Dear Mr. Masolino,

I hope this finds you well. On the enclosed hard drives are the records of thousands of financial transactions. Could you kindly examine them for anything unusual or illegal, including but not limited to insider trading, money laundering, and financial fraud?

This data came from the computers of a deceased hotel manager in Savannah named Ellerby, who traded equities, puts, and calls in his spare time. It appears he ultimately made a great deal of money doing it. We should like to know how.

Very truly yours,
S. A. Pendergast

The handwritten note was rather an eccentric touch—didn't the fellow have a computer?—but the project itself was straightforward enough, nothing different from what Masolino had done a thousand times over the past decade.

He plugged in the first hard drive; examined it for viruses, malware, and rootkits; found it clean; and then copied the contents to his powerful, air-gapped Mac Pro, a version ordered to his own specifications, which included a 2.5GHz 28-core Intel processor, 1.5 terabytes of RAM, two Radeon Pro Vega II Duo graphics cards, 4 terabytes of SSD storage, and an Afterburner card. The monster was brand-new and had cost the FBI more than fifty grand—a sign of his value to the organization.

As he scrolled through the files, Masolino noticed that this guy, Ellerby, hadn't encrypted them. This was a pretty good hint that what he had been doing was probably legal. Of course, that wasn't saying much: a lot of the dishonest, manipulative, sleazy shit that traders did was legal, which was the main reason why Masolino didn't personally invest in the market. The last thing he wanted to be was another chump. If small-time investors knew how they were being reamed out by the big boys every day, they'd never invest again.

He opened one trading account and looked it over, just to get a feel for it. In this account, Ellerby was trading Big Board stocks, Dow Jones Industrials. It all looked aboveboard and he was openly trading in his own name, not through some offshore entity or LLC. The first thing Masolino noticed was how small many of the trades were, and how short the duration. Almost all were in and out in less than an hour. But in the end, the guy had made a shitload of money.

Masolino went through the trades, one by one. No giant killings here on any single trade, but significant amounts that nevertheless added up. With the extra leverage in the puts and calls, he was making some nifty profits. Now that Masolino was looking more closely, he could see Ellerby had made a profit not just on most trades, but on *every single one*.

This was crazy. That simply didn't happen. So it

wasn't legal, after all: there must be a scam hidden in here somewhere.

Delving deeper into the specifics, noting dates and times, he was struck again. Going back farther, he found hundreds of even quicker trades, in and out in a minute or less. But this was not computerized high-speed trading: Ellerby was doing it online by hand. Masolino called up matching historical data for the stock price movements bracketing each trade and was further astonished. Ellerby's trades came right before a stock moved sharply upward, in such a way that the trade produced a sweet little profit. The data had all the earmarks of an algorithmic trading program...but if this was such a program, it was worth billions, because it was never wrong.

No—that obviously couldn't be it. This was something illegal, for sure. This was trading tied to some information source, an inside flow of data, probably from the trading desk of a large investment bank, which would know what time the bank would be buying or selling large blocks.

Masolino let out a slow, relieved breath. So it *was* typical insider stuff after all—and, hotel manager or not, Ellerby was playing it like some back-office IT drone...except he was too stupid to hide his dirty trades amid a lot of financial noise. Masolino had been worried for a moment there, but this was going to be easy. All he had to do was identify which investment bank happened to be trading large blocks at the time these trades were made, and go from there.

The activity he was currently examining came from a few years back, so Masolino moved his focus closer to the present. He quickly noticed that the trading pattern had changed a few weeks ago. At that point, this Ellerby started making bigger trades, for bigger profits, and held on to the trades for longer—sometimes as long as an hour.

Masolino had a number of programs that he'd coded himself, and now he ran one that compared block trading of equities by large investment banks to Ellerby's trading, looking for the match.

There was no match.

This was odd. Another thing that was odd was that the stocks were always Dow Jones Industrials listed stocks.

Now he began comparing the time stamp of each trade with stock price movements in general. Ellerby's trades usually came during periods of high volatility and took advantage of small fluctuations that occurred sometimes within seconds after the trade. How was this possible? The trades always came right before an uptick in the stock. Not huge upticks, but decent enough to make money—although the money made in the last three weeks had increased dramatically.

He couldn't get around it: this was the classic pattern of someone getting tips from an insider with access to private information, probably an influential stock picker or newsletter. Masolino had a database that aggregated the stock picks of thousands of such sources, and now he ran it against Ellerby's trades.

Nothing. No match.

Now, that was damned strange.

Perhaps the trades were based on acquiring advance news about companies, like earnings reports or drug approvals, that hadn't yet been released but that some insider was privy to. He had a program that handled that, too, comparing the trades to news reports involving the same stock.

That came up empty as well.

Masolino ran Ellerby's trades against every program in his digital toolbox that matched trades with outside events: merger announcements, lawsuit filings, earnings reports, commodity movements, political news, and a host of other things that move stocks abruptly—and still couldn't find a pattern.

Next he looked at who was buying and selling these stocks just before or after Ellerby's trades. If Ellerby knew someone who bought and sold large blocks of stock, and he acted before that person did, he could make a profit from the movement of the later, larger trades.

Again, nothing came up. No big blocks of stock were dumped or purchased, no insider selling or buying from company executives. Ellerby simply seemed to have anticipated ahead of time an uptick in the stock price and bought into it, then sold at a profit. He could have made much larger profits by buying and holding some of these stocks. But he never did. The trades were quick, simple, and unremarkable—and every single damn one made money.

As Masolino went forward in time, he again saw the break that took place three weeks before the end. He saw it in every trading account. In recent weeks, the trades got bigger, more profitable, and longer.

Four hours later, Masolino, bathed in sweat, a pile of damp paper towels on the floor behind him, hands trembling, finally shut down his system. It was only two o'clock in the afternoon, but he was going home early to have a stiff martini.

Ellerby's trading went back years and years, via every imaginable financial instrument, all over the map: those same quick little trades making modest profits. Every trade was legal, or so it seemed. Masolino could think of only one answer: Ellerby was a stock-trading genius the likes of which the world had never seen. Given the short time frames on so many of the trades, he must have developed some incredibly powerful mathematical quantitative trading algorithms that monitored markets and traded accordingly. An algorithm like that—that never made a mistake and always made a profit—would be the holy grail of Wall Street. But such programs, no matter how powerful or ingenious, could never be 100 percent accurate. It was impossible, given the random fluctuations of the market, to ever be perfectly accurate. But the hard drive held only records of transactions—no indication of how the trades were identified and executed and no algorithmic trading program.

And by the end of it all, Ellerby had amassed a paper fortune of close to $300 million. A hotel manager. *Three hundred million*. And $200 million of that had been made in just the last three weeks.

Christ, Masolino needed that martini.

27

Francis Wellstone Jr., having donned a new suit and tie, sat in the same parlor, in the same venerable wing chair, with the same view of West Oglethorpe Avenue, that he recalled from his first visit. There were, however, a few differences of note. It was not morning, but past six in the evening; he'd been served sweet tea instead of lemonade; and his hostess, Mrs. Daisy Fayette, was in a less agreeable mood than the first time they'd met.

"Do you mean to say that he actually interrupted your segment?" Wellstone asked, injecting surprise and sympathy into his voice.

Daisy nodded, her lavender-tinged hair shaking in displeasure. A tiny cloud of powder rose from it before settling again. "I was just beginning to explain why the Montgomerie House was haunted—an eddy in the spiritual ether, caused by the murder-suicide—when he cut me off. In midsentence...and in front of everybody, with the cameras still *filming*!"

"I've heard that Betts has a reputation of being

an unpleasant person to work with. But to *needlessly* humiliate someone who's helping him…!" Wellstone shook his head, at the same time finding a secret pleasure in the fact that he wasn't the only one to be recently humiliated by that bloviating dotard producer.

By now, Wellstone had taken the measure of Savannah—its history, legends, and secrets. In Daisy's circle of southern gentility and decorum, Betts's oafish behavior would have been dealt with in a different way, and old Mr. Fayette, if he hadn't been moldering in the grave, might have called Betts out, fought a duel with him, over the insult. Perhaps the old ways weren't so barbaric after all.

On the other hand, Daisy's outrage was exactly what he'd been hoping for. After his fury over his treatment at Lafitte's had cooled, his mind had begun working strategically again. Daisy was almost certainly ready to become a useful informant on Betts, his inside source, so to speak.

"I visited the Montgomerie House myself just yesterday," Wellstone said, taking a sip of iced tea. "I thought it to be one of the most fascinating spots I've ever visited. *And* spiritually disturbing," he hastily added. "Especially after reading your most informative, ah, book about it."

"Thank you," Daisy said.

Pamphlet, Wellstone had almost said; fortunately he had corrected himself in time. He'd tut-tut a little more, then get down to business. "I'm surprised, actually, to hear that Betts had so little interest in the Montgomerie ghosts. I would have thought it precisely the kind of thing he could work into his documentary."

"Oh, he was interested," Daisy said. "It was that other man who said there were no ghosts."

"That other man?" Wellstone repeated, although he knew exactly which man that was.

Daisy nodded. "Moller. The one with all the equipment."

"Moller wasn't interested?" he asked.

Daisy hesitated. "No... not exactly that. He said his instruments weren't picking up any traces of ghostly activity."

Wellstone shook his head. "That doesn't make any sense. As we both know, the house is profoundly haunted. My guess is..."

He hesitated for drama.

"What?"

"That this Moller is a quack. You must have run into them, Daisy. Someone who claims to know about the science of the paranormal but is nothing more than a showman, a fake."

"I certainly have! You run into them all the time while doing supernatural research."

"I wouldn't be surprised if this whole documentary is a ridiculous charade."

Daisy took a demure sip of her tea. "I wouldn't be surprised at all."

"But... what happened when Moller couldn't find any ghosts?"

"Betts actually told Moller to make his instruments 'work better.'" She smiled slightly—the prickly smile Wellstone recalled from his first visit. "Moller told him that finding nothing there would make it all the more believable when they *did* find something."

Wellstone shook his head sympathetically. She was going to be a gold mine of information on Betts and Moller.

At that moment, Daisy perked up. "Which reminds me!"

"What is it?"

"How foolish of me to forget! Heavens, my memory isn't what it used to be." Daisy stood up and walked out of the parlor. A moment later, with a swish of pantyhose, she returned.

"I was there, in the Montgomerie House...'on the set,' as you say," she told him as she sat down again. "I had just been interrupted by Mr. Betts. I was standing in the background—rather stunned, I *might* say—when I recalled what you said about getting a look behind the scenes."

"That's right," Wellstone replied.

"I was able to get some pictures."

"What?" Wellstone asked. This was far better than he'd expected. He had almost asked her to take a few clandestine photos, but figured it was too risky. As it turned out, she'd taken the initiative herself.

"My phone has a camera, of course." She pulled out a late-model cell phone and showed it to him. She tried to turn it on for several seconds before realizing she was holding it upside down. Rotating it, she pressed the screen here and there, until at last she gave a little chirp of triumph.

"You said you wanted information, so I took some pictures while pretending to send emails. There!" she said, handing him the phone.

Wellstone took the phone. It showed a black screen. He swiped his finger across it, revealing a blurred, dark image. And another.

"I'm not really all that good with it yet," Daisy said apologetically.

Wellstone swiped his way through a dozen more

photos blurred by movement and out of focus. Then he came to a set where the phone, apparently, had self-adjusted for the environment. He saw a darkened corridor, two cameramen, that charlatan Betts...and some kind of cloth on the floor, covered with a bizarre array of tools and other objects. Beside it was something he was very familiar with, given his years in and out of television studios: a hard case with foam cutouts of the kind photographers and sound engineers used to protect their gear. When he zoomed in on it, he could see more items still inside the foam cradles: a jagged, lightning-shaped piece of silver; a metering device of some kind; a large box camera; a battered cross; an oscilloscope; and a piece of smoked glass.

These were Moller's phony "tools."

"I took pictures of his black suitcase with his equipment," Daisy said. "Moller wouldn't let them film inside of the case—only the equipment itself, only when it was being used."

Wellstone suddenly realized he was gripping the phone so hard it hurt. "Daisy," he said, "I believe you've struck gold."

The elderly matron looked at him as if he'd just given her a pearl necklace. "Really?"

"Really. Twenty-four-karat gold. These photos of the equipment will be very useful." He paused.

The memory of his lunchtime humiliation was still all too fresh—and, he realized, it had provided him with the incentive he required to investigate and write those chapters about Betts and his phony setup after all. No way was he returning to Boston until he had the goods on that mountebank Betts.

He was going to blow up those photos and study

every little thing in that case, because he was sure that in there somewhere must be the key to exposing the quack. That large camera nestled in the suitcase, for example—he'd seen pictures of Moller wielding it in the past. "Would you be willing to go back to the set again?"

Her grateful look became a little worried. "But… why would I say I'm there?"

"Offer your services again, but not on camera—just to be a help, you know, with the research. You know so much. And of course you have an in with the local people that they don't have. I'm sure you can make a good argument why you should continue helping them. Now that they've finished with the Montgomerie House, did they talk about what they were going to do next?"

"They mentioned shooting scenes involving the Savannah Vampire."

"Perfect! Once I've made the preparations, I'll call." He paused. "You know, if you're any more helpful to me, I may just have to name you coauthor."

She blushed.

He waved the phone at her. "Would you mind if I sent these photos over to my phone?"

"Not at all," she said, standing. "And might I perhaps warm up your tea?"

For a moment, Wellstone didn't understand. Then he saw Daisy had walked over to a sideboard and was cradling a bottle of Woodford Reserve.

"Why, thank you, Daisy," he said, taking his own phone out of his pocket and sitting back in his armchair. "I'd like that. I'd like that very much."

28

T OBY MANNING SHIMMIED UP the wrought iron fence and tried to swing his leg over the spikes, but his pants got hung up and he fell to the ground on the far side with a loud ripping sound. He lay there, a little shaken but otherwise unharmed, as his pal Brock Custis looked on, laughing uproariously.

"You bust ass like that again," Brock said, "and half of the dead here are going to rise up and give you the finger."

"Help me up, fagmeat," Toby said.

Still laughing, Brock extended a hand and Toby grasped it and was hauled to his feet. He checked his jeans and found a two-inch tear along the side. "Shit."

Annoyed, he slapped away the dirt and leaves and looked around. "Creepy place." A full moon hung in the night sky. Strings of low-lying mist drifted through the twisted oaks and ghostly shapes of tombstones stretching in front of them.

Brock managed to stifle his laughter long enough

to pull a pint of Southern Comfort from his pocket. "Here, take a shot of this."

Toby grabbed the pint and sucked down a couple of mouthfuls before handing it back. He could feel the heat of the liquor spreading through his gullet, and it restored his mood. "The grave is supposed to be at the far end, by the river," he said.

"Lead the way, asswipe."

Toby pulled out his cell phone—relieved to find it intact—and turned on its light. It cast a feeble glow over the white gravel path that led off into the misty darkness of Bonaventure Cemetery. He had a momentary shiver. "Gimme another hit."

Brock handed him the bottle. Toby drained it and gave it back. Brock stared at it, frowning. "You bogarted all the Sudden Discomfort!" he said, flinging the bottle over his shoulder. Toby heard it shatter against a tomb and winced.

"Three points." With a grin, Brock slipped out another pint. "Go easy on this one." He cracked the cap and they each had another swig.

Now they walked down the path, lined on either side by massive trees hanging with moss, the gravel crunching under their feet. Toby had never seen tombs as elaborate as these: miniature Greek temples, life-size marble angels, huge obelisks and crosses and urns and slabs of marble. They passed a statue of a little girl with the saddest imaginable look on her face, seated next to an ivy-covered tree stump, all pale, glowing marble. Her name, Gracie, was carved on the base.

Brock lurched to a stop. "Will you look at that," he said. "You know why she's so sad?"

"No," said Toby.

"Because she's fucking dead!" And he howled with laughter as he continued staggering down the path.

"Jesus," Toby murmured, shaking his head as he followed. He wondered if this was such a good idea after all.

Soon they were deep in the cemetery. Toby silently went over the directions he'd been given: Go to the far end, where the river is; turn right; count three alleyways and take another right. The tomb he was looking for would be on that path, just a ways down.

Or was it four alleyways?

"What's the name of that statue we're looking for again?" Brock asked.

"Bird Girl."

"Bird Girl? What the hell does that mean?"

"Because she's holding two bird baths, one in each hand. It was on the cover of that famous book."

"What's so special about it?"

"It's interesting, that's all." He paused. "We don't have to find it. We can just wander around."

The path they were on came to a T, with a mass of trees beyond. The mists were thicker here, and Toby thought he could smell mud. They must be close to the river.

"Here's where we go right," he said.

They were moving into a more out-of-the-way section of the cemetery, where the tombstones were smaller and plots unkempt, with weeds and cheap vases of plastic flowers, some toppled over, spilling their sad contents. That was all right with Toby: less chance of coming across a caretaker or, worse, a cop.

"Sure you know where we're going?" Brock asked.

"Yeah."

They passed the bottle back and forth again. Clouds had covered the moon. Now the flashlight of the cell phone barely penetrated the murk.

"Think we'll see a *ghooooost*?" Brock said with an exaggerated moan.

Here was the third path. It was almost invisible, covered in grass, and it wandered behind a row of tombs into a still more overgrown section of the cemetery.

"This is it," Toby said with a confidence he didn't feel.

The path was hard to follow. They had to step over a few fallen tombstones. The Bird Girl was supposed to be on the right, but there was nothing like that around: just more broken tombstones.

"Admit it," said Brock. "We're lost."

Toby ignored him and kept going. The cemetery was huge and Toby hoped they could find their way out again.

They came to a marble tombstone with a winged angel striding along with one arm raised, splotched with lichen.

"Now, there's a zombie angel if I ever saw one," said Brock. "Man, this is a perfect place to drain the main vein."

"Jesus, don't do that, it's a cemetery—" said Toby, but Brock was already giving the angel a good hosing down.

"We're lost," said Brock when he was finished. "And you know it."

Toby, feeling the liquor kick in, shrugged. "Totally."

Brock laughed. "What the fuck time is it?"

Toby checked his cell phone, momentarily blinding himself with the light. "Three eleven."

Brock took another long swig of Southern Comfort, then began singing, using the bottle as a mic.

Please allow me to introduce myself
I'm a man of wealth and taste

His drunken words floated off into the darkness as he hammed it up, dancing around the graves like Mick Jagger. Suddenly he stopped. "You hear that?"

Toby said nothing. He, too, had heard something, like wind in the trees, and smelled a faint stench like burning rubber. But there was no wind. The air was deathly still. He held the light up as he looked around. Nothing. Brock resumed singing behind him.

Then Toby heard it again: or rather, *felt* it. It was a broad flutter, a stirring of air. Brock's singing abruptly ceased. Toby spun around, but Brock had vanished.

"Brock? Where are you?"

There was no answer. Toby waited, holding his breath. And then, off in the darkness, he heard the shattering of the pint bottle.

"Brock!" he called, taking a step back, blood pounding in his ears. He had a sudden and profound sense of dread. "Cut it out, man, it's not funny!" He held the cell phone light out in front of him, moving it this way and that, probing the darkness. All he could see were swirling mists.

And then he felt something warm and humid brush his face.

He stumbled back, waving the light. "Who's there?"

But nothing was there. It must have been just a warm nighttime draft, nothing solid.

"*Brock!*" he yelled.

And now he heard a wet sound, a sort of gush,

and then a hot, heavy burst of wind—no mere draft this time—struck his face. The foul smell grew much stronger: burning rubber, but now mixed with something like vomit or old socks. He screamed, stumbling backward, twisting away, and then turning to run. He felt the nightmare wind rush over him again, damp and horribly fetid, and then he tripped over a broken tombstone and fell hard, the cell phone flying out of his hand and off into the darkness. He struggled to his feet. Where was his phone? He looked around but could see no light, the darkness closing in upon him like a damp cloak. Something unlike anything he'd ever felt before suddenly brushed the side of his face and, with a scream, he broke into a blind run, clawing his way through undergrowth, stumbling and rising, choking and sobbing, the dark fastness of the old cemetery absorbing his cracked, shrill cries.

29

I︭T WAS JUST AFTER three in the morning when Constance Greene once again noiselessly ascended the stairs to the hotel's fourth floor, then paused at the landing to look down the carpeted hallway. All the doors were closed, and everyone, it seemed, was asleep.

All, that is, perhaps for one.

Constance stood utterly still, taking in the somnolence of the elegant corridor.

It had not been so long ago that she'd stood in this same spot and been warned away. She had to ask herself: why was she here again?

This question had been in the back of her mind ever since she'd decided to return—a decision that had formed almost without her realizing it.

Constance had as much self-awareness as any human on earth. Her unusually long life span had given her time to understand her own motivations and desires. She was here, she understood, for more than one reason. The first involved Pendergast. Curiously, he had made no attempt to question the old proprietress himself. He had glanced over the police interview with Miss Frost—if *interview* was the correct word, as it consisted of only six sentences, questions and responses that had passed through a locked door. The responses were of no use beyond underlining that Miss Frost had nothing to say. Normally Pendergast would find some way to charm Miss Frost into unlocking her door. She was an obvious person of interest. Although it was absurd to think she could have killed Ellerby herself, she knew him well and they had had a blazing argument two days before he died.

And yet, whenever the subject of Felicity Winthrop Frost came up, Pendergast had simply nodded...and glanced pointedly in Constance's direction. It hadn't taken long for Constance to realize the task of approaching the recluse was hers.

The old lady's mysterious past and great age intrigued Constance. So did the wild rumors beginning to surface, that Miss Frost was a vampire who revivified herself through drinking the blood of others. In poking around the web, she could find no record of the woman's existence before 1972. She had communicated all of this to Pendergast, who had drily replied that perhaps she and Miss Frost should have tea some fine evening.

Almost of their own accord, her feet had begun moving down the corridor, toward the unmarked door on the right. *Nobody wants to go in. It could be...dangerous.* Perhaps the staff members she'd spoken to also subscribed to these vampire stories. The rich and eccentric drew rumor to themselves like iron filings to a magnet.

As she came near to the door, her pace slowed. *It's past ten*, the nervous maid had told her. *She's likely to be waking up any moment now.* Another stimulant to the vampire rumor.

As she stood outside the door, Constance heard piano music once again: faint, romantic, dolorous...and echoing from above. A Chopin nocturne.

She glanced both ways along the corridor. All remained still. Moving quickly, she turned the handle. The door was unlocked, which surprised her. She opened it, slipped inside, and eased the door shut behind her.

She found herself in a steep, narrow stairway, with no light except what seeped out from beneath a door at the narrow landing above. The music was louder here. Constance, used to darkness, felt no fear; instead, she stood motionless until she could distinctly make out the stairs, covered with a beautiful old Persian carpet. As she began ascending the steps to a crescendo of piano music, she became aware of a strange mixture of scents: sandalwood, moth balls, and, beneath it all, a note of some exotic perfume.

With exquisite care, Constance noiselessly climbed another step, then another, until she reached the landing. As she did so, the music abruptly stopped.

How odd. Constance could move more quietly than most cats. Surely the old lady had not picked up her footsteps?

It could be...dangerous.

The light coming from beneath the door winked out.

As she stood in sudden, utter darkness, she thought back to the room service maid and the anxiety she had displayed at Constance standing by the door to the fifth floor. It was more than anxiety; it was terror. Was it possible the maid's fear had less to do with Constance disturbing the old lady—and more with what might happen *to* Constance should she ascend?

And it was then that the door in front of Constance swung wide with a crash, and a towering figure—black upon black—loomed menacingly over her.

30

Bᴇʀᴛʀᴀᴍ Iɴɢᴇʀꜱᴏʟʟ ᴛᴜɢɢᴇᴅ ᴀᴛ his tie, pulled the knot down about two inches, undid the top button of his shirt, and plucked the collar away from his sticky throat. He didn't bother looking at his watch, but he knew it had to be at least three in the morning. When they'd entered Chippewa Hall at 9 ᴘᴍ, he had assumed the heat and humidity would have broken by the time they left. He'd assumed wrong.

"Look, Bert," said his wife, Agnes, pointing as they crossed East Jones Street. "There's a perfect example, right on the corner. Gothic revival, with strong elements of Georgian. Just look at that hipped roof!"

Ingersoll grunted and made a show of looking up. To hear the excitement in her voice, you'd think she'd discovered some goddamn rare bird with two beaks and three assholes, instead of just another decaying mansion.

As they continued south on Habersham, she gripped his arm. "And *there*!" she said, her voice almost a whisper. "What an eccentric example of

Regency detail. Imagine: putting a frieze like *that* on top of ionic columns! I've never seen a pediment with such...hold on, dear, I've got to take a picture."

Ingersoll managed to suppress a sigh of irritation, waiting as she fished in her bag for her cell phone. *Good luck getting a decent shot at this time of night,* he thought.

He should have known what he was getting into after thirty-one years of marriage. Their interests had never been all that compatible, and they'd only diverged further with passing years. On top of that, the damn ED medication he'd started taking wasn't doing its job at all.

Years ago, they'd made a deal: all their vacations would be two weeks long, one week for him and one for her. This vacation had been no different. He'd spent a fantastic, relaxing week on Hilton Head, playing thirty-six holes of golf a day and hanging out in the evenings at the country club. Agnes had lounged by the pool reading Dorothy Sayers mysteries. They'd seen each other only at breakfast and dinner. Credit where credit is due: she hadn't complained.

But now it was payback time: a weeklong conference of the Southern Architectural Society. The society's lectures were held every night at nine, and because of the late hour, Agnes insisted on his company. These were truly hell on earth: professors and architects yammering on endlessly about the most infinitesimal details, followed by the inevitable cocktail reception that never ended before two. Or, in tonight's case, even later. Ingersoll, who'd been an actuary by profession, found architecture dry and impenetrable. In his job, he'd walked through the lobby of the Birmingham Professional Arts Building—one of the most famous examples of art deco architecture outside of New York City—for twenty years without ever looking up. Who the hell cared how the damn window frames were carved, as long as the building didn't fall down?

They went another block, Agnes jabbering the whole time, neck craned, until their progress was interrupted by a tree-lined square. "This is it," she said. "Whitefield Square. I think we turn right."

"Left," Ingersoll muttered.

As they turned left onto Taylor, he could see clouds scudding across a bloated moon. A gust of wind blew by, rustling the trees in the square behind them.

"Dear?" Agnes said. "Would you mind terribly if we stayed an extra day? After tonight's lecture, Dr. Black told me this part of Savannah has some of the most interesting buildings in the entire historical district. He even wrote out half a dozen of their addresses for me."

Ingersoll almost declared that he'd rather suck the balls of Satan than stay an extra day. But he stopped himself in time. Agnes never got angry with him, not exactly—she just went quiet for a week or two. He'd made it through six days, and he'd be a fool to blow it now.

Twisting his lips into a smile, he turned toward her. "One more day?" he said. "I think that's—"

His wife suddenly halted.

What happened next, Ingersoll couldn't exactly say, even when questioned by the police about it later, because nothing about it made sense. They were swept with another gust of wind—only it was not like any wind he'd ever experienced before, thick and deep and oddly *low*. As it washed over them, accompanied by a horrible odor, he was seized by a feeling of unutterable dread, and the sense that a hideous, invisible presence was above them. And then came a sequence of sounds: a wet, sloppy impact at his feet, Agnes's sharp scream, and an unearthly *beating* noise so alien it chilled him to the bone...and then Ingersoll fell sprawling across something soft lying on the sidewalk that, it took him several moments to realize, was a warm dead body.

31

Commander Delaplane, tired, irritated, and still covered with bug bites from the excursion the previous day, was not happy at being roused at three thirty in the morning. When she reached the scene of the incident, what a sight greeted her eyes: a body lay sprawled on the brick sidewalk, on his back— a young man in jeans and a T-shirt. The CSI team was setting up lights while McDuffie and his assistant crouched over the body. The couple who had found the body were off to one side, being questioned by Sheldrake. She could hear the husband's voice, shaky and trembling, and the wife's quiet sobbing. She felt a pang of sympathy for them, but it was overridden by her need for information, and she intended to wring what she could from them now, while the memory was still fresh.

Boom, the lights went on, and now the horrible whiteness of the body stood out: the skin like marble, the blue eyes staring upward, wide open in astonishment, limbs splayed as if on a torture rack. McDuffie stepped back while the CSI team surged in and began their work.

She waved McDuffie over. "What have we got?"

"Same deal," McDuffie said. "Trocar, or big needle, to the femoral artery; same greasy lubricant; blood totally drained. Body temperature is still almost normal—I would guess this person's been dead less than thirty minutes. His head is fractured, but the injury appears to be postmortem."

"How do you know?"

"No bleeding—because he had no blood left to bleed."

She shook her head. "Fractured how?"

"I'll have to examine the corpse more closely in the lab. But from what I could see, there's some hair and scalp on the pavement where it might have struck. Perhaps he fell."

Delaplane looked up. There was a three-story brick building rising above the street, painted gray with white trim. The windows were all closed, but the building had a flat roof with a parapet. A light had just come on in an upstairs window, and she could see the outline of a person at the curtain, peering out at all the activity.

"Jumped or thrown?" she asked.

McDuffie nodded. "If he did fall, he must have been thrown after he was dead."

"Anything else?"

"The individual was intoxicated. Strong odor of liquor, although it may be hard to get a blood alcohol reading, since there's no blood left. We have other ways."

She nodded.

"And there's a trace of fresh vomit on his shirt."

"Right. Thanks. I'm off to talk to the witnesses."

The couple looked pretty destroyed, sitting on a bench while Sheldrake asked questions and took notes. Delaplane took out her cell phone and turned on a recording app.

"Commander Delaplane, Savannah Police. Mind if I ask a few questions? I'm taping, just so you know."

The man nodded dumbly.

"Did you see what happened?" she asked.

Neither answered, so Delaplane asked the question again. "Mr. Ingersoll?"

He was a heavy middle-aged man wearing a light jacket, open collar, of completely unremarkable appearance.

He shook his head. "I can't say. I felt this…this wind, and suddenly there was something on the sidewalk, and then…I fell over it." He shuddered. "There was…" He halted.

"There was what?"

"Something brushed me, something horrible. A presence."

"A presence? Like what?"

"No idea."

"A person?" Delaplane tried to keep the impatience out of her voice.

"Not a person. A *presence*…"

"An animal?"

"I can't begin…to describe it." He put his face in his hands.

Delaplane turned to the wife. "Mrs. Ingersoll, did you see anybody?"

She shook her head wordlessly, trying to stifle a sob.

"Is it possible the body fell from above?"

More mute headshaking of uncertainty.

Neither was much help—at least not now. "Thank you," Delaplane told them. "We'll need to interview you tomorrow in more detail, so please don't go anywhere." She gave them her card. "Get some rest. Officer Rudd will see you back to your hotel."

She gestured to Sheldrake and they stepped to one side.

"Got an ID from the wallet," Sheldrake said. "Name's Brock Custis, nineteen, college student, Auburn University. He was out drinking, which means there were others with him. We need to find them."

"Christ, why don't they go to Jacksonville and puke on the beaches like everyone else?"

Delaplane saw a shadowy figure at the edge of the crime scene. The black suit he wore made him look disembodied, just a ghostly head and hands. There was someone else with him. They were standing back, motionless.

"Don't look now," she said, "but it's Gomez Addams and his sidekick."

The CSI team was now placing numbers on the sidewalk, marking where evidence was being collected. Delaplane watched for a moment, then turned back to Sheldrake. "I want to interview everyone, *everyone*, connected with this. The Ingersolls, any people the kid was drinking with, the bartender who served them drinks." She pointed up to the house and the person at the window. "And that person. Eleven AM sharp in the precinct house. Think you can pull that together for me?"

"I believe so, Commander."

She thought for a moment. "Invite the feds. I don't want any ex post facto whining."

"Will do."

And with another glance in the direction of the spectral FBI agent—who was now pointing at a large white Victorian house across Whitefield Square and telling his partner, of all things, about an excellent wine tasting he'd once enjoyed there—she left the scene, shaking her head.

32

Constance—confronted by this dark menace looming over her so abruptly—leapt back a step, instinctively drawing the antique stiletto she was never without, in the *paranza corta* stance of Italian knife fighting she'd studied. But then she realized that what confronted her was, instead of a giant, the silhouette of an old woman, her shadow magnified by the dim light thrown by a Tiffany lamp, a walking cane in one hand and a pistol in the other. The woman took a step back, the lamp throwing her shadow crazily across the pressed-tin ceiling.

For a moment, the two looked at each other. Then the old woman spoke.

"Well," she said in a cross voice, "either stab me or put it away."

"You would seem to have the upper hand of the situation," Constance replied.

"This?" And the woman turned the weapon sideways, its salt-blued barrel winking at the movement. "It's not loaded."

When Constance remained motionless, the older woman sighed, raised the slide toggle, ejected the magazine, and—most unexpectedly—tossed it casually at Constance. She caught it with her left hand and saw that it, indeed, held no rounds. She straightened up, putting her knife away and placing the magazine on a nearby console table. Now she had a chance to see the woman more clearly. She was dressed in an elegant, silk-edged *yukata* dressing gown, and she was staring at Constance with a look somewhere between annoyance and amusement.

"Part of my collection," the woman explained.

"Of deadly weapons?"

"Of industrial design. I find great beauty in the marriage of form and function. Others collect paintings; I collect fountain pens, percolators, antique cipher machines—*and* weapons. Too many, in fact, to display." She came forward, retrieved the empty magazine, slipped it back into the handle, and snapped the slide back into position. "This model," she said, holding it up for Constance to admire, "was known as the 'Black Widow,' and despite its cheap Bakelite grips I think it's the most attractive of all the Parabellums."

She moved over to a sideboard—picking up a battered paperback as she did so—and placed the pistol upon it. As she walked, Constance noted that she appeared to be moving with a degree of pain that could not be concealed. Beyond the woman, Constance could see a series of adjoining rooms, sumptuously furnished, with recessed bookshelves, old tapestries, elaborate rosewood wainscoting, and crown molding. Here and there, folding *byōbu* screens of latticed rice paper were spread open, their elaborate shoji patterns acting as partitions between sections of the apartment.

Along one wall of all the rooms ran a gallery of windows, stretching nearly from floor to ceiling; beyond was a balcony, barely visible in the gloom.

The woman turned back. "You must be Constance Greene," she said.

Constance, surprised, said nothing.

"You're staying in the Juliette Gordon Low suite with that FBI agent who's causing such a stir." The woman looked quizzically at Constance. "What—did you think that just because I'm ancient and enfeebled, I wouldn't know what's going on in my hotel?"

After a moment, Constance replied: "At this point, I think the conventional response would be: 'I believe you have me at a disadvantage, ma'am.'"

The woman laughed, coming forward again. Although there were sofas and wing chairs arranged around the room immediately behind her, she did not offer Constance a seat. "And I imagine he's sent you up here to find out, with your feminine wiles, what I know about the recent unpleasantness."

Constance shook her head. "I was merely curious. I'm not here because of Mr. Ellerby."

She'd mentioned the name intentionally, and she noticed that, upon hearing it, the old woman could not conceal a wince of sorrow. "I'm here because the rumors I heard have intrigued me."

"Which rumors are those? There are so many. That I ride out of here at midnight on a broomstick? That I drink the blood of firstborn children? That I'm a direct descendant of Gilles de Rais?"

"No. That, like me, you prefer the company of fine books to that of other people."

The old woman raised her eyebrows. "Indeed! An interesting habit in one so young. I give you credit for your courage in tiptoeing up here. No doubt you heard all the fearful rumors about me as well." She paused. "And ἀργαλέος γὰρ Ὀλύμπιος ἀντιφέρεσθαι."

Constance smiled mirthlessly. "If I am courageous, it's due in large part to something we both share. συμφερτὴ δ' ἀρετὴ πέλει ἀνδρῶν καὶ μάλα λυγρῶν."

For the first time, Miss Frost's eyes registered surprise. "Forgive me," she said after a moment. "*Regina, iubes renovare dolorem.*"

"*Quisque suos patimur Manes,*" Constance quoted in reply.

This was followed by a long silence. "If you know as much about sorrow as you know about dead languages," Miss Frost said, "then you know it is best kept private."

"The sorrow, yes," Constance said. "But not necessarily the sufferer."

"An interesting coil on sorrow, that." Miss Frost went silent for a long moment. Then her gaze, which had gone distant, fixed again on Constance. "I'm so sorry I can't offer you my hospitality," she said. "But I find myself rather busy this evening."

"Of course." Constance bowed slightly, then turned to leave.

"Miss Greene?" came the voice from behind her.

Constance turned back.

"Perhaps you would care to join me another evening. For tea."

"I'd enjoy that. Thank you."

And as Constance quietly closed the door to Miss Frost's apartments and made her way down the narrow staircase, she heard the melody of the Chopin nocturne begin to sound once more.

33

COLDMOON SAW THE EARLY-MORNING glow of a café spilling onto the sidewalk and swerved toward it, not even bothering to ask his partner's opinion. It was 6 AM and the café had apparently just opened.

"My dear Coldmoon—" began Pendergast.

"If I don't get some coffee," said Coldmoon loudly, "I'm going to die."

"Very well," said Pendergast. "I wouldn't want another corpse on my hands."

Inside, the little diner was air-conditioned, shiny and cheerful, smelling of coffee and bacon. It was a relief from the muggy night air. Coldmoon took a seat in one of the banquettes and Pendergast sat opposite him, gingerly, after inspecting the interior—and the banquette seat in particular—with a barely concealed expression of disdain. A waitress appeared immediately with plastic menus and a big pot of coffee.

"Fill 'er up, please," said Coldmoon.

"I don't suppose you have, ah, espresso…?" Pendergast asked.

"Sorry, sugar. Just this." She held up the pot with a grin.

"Tea?"

"Black or green?"

"English breakfast, if you please. Milk and sugar."

"Sure thing. Anything to eat, boys?"

"Bacon and eggs for me," Coldmoon said, "over easy, toast, hash browns."

"Hash browns?" the waitress said. "We're known for our grits here. Buttered, salted, and sugared."

"No," Coldmoon said. "Hash browns. The greasier the better."

"We don't serve greasy food," she said, offended.

"Okay, fine, whatever. But make it hash browns."

She glared at him for a moment. Then she turned toward Pendergast—having picked up on his drawl—with a considerably softer expression. "And you, sugar?" she asked. "A nice plate of chicken and waffles?"

Pendergast closed his eyes and opened them. "Nothing for me, thank you very much."

She went off and Coldmoon took a gulp of his coffee. It was, of course, not as richly burnt as he liked, but the bitter brew went down well and he quickly felt its revivifying effects.

"Sorry, Pendergast, but I can't think straight if I haven't had my coffee and breakfast." He paused. "Chicken and *waffles*?"

"Keep your voice down—you've made a bad enough impression as it is." Pendergast paused. "It's a southern thing. If you have to ask, you won't understand the explanation."

Coldmoon shook his head. "Sounds toxic."

"Then perhaps I shouldn't tell you the waffles are

slathered in butter, the fried chicken is doused with hot sauce, and then the entire concoction is drowned in maple syrup."

Coldmoon shuddered.

Pendergast paused while the waitress brought his tea. "In any case, this interregnum will give us a chance to review the forensic examination of Mr. Ellerby's day-trading hobby."

"Already?"

"I spoke to the gentleman who analyzed the computer hard drives. The results are curious, to say the least."

Coldmoon's plate of food arrived in record time, and he tucked into the hash browns.

"In the three weeks before his death," Pendergast said in the same casual voice, "Mr. Ellerby made two hundred million dollars."

Coldmoon had just forked a mess of hash browns into his mouth and now he nearly choked. He chewed and chewed, finally getting the bolus of food down. "You timed that bombshell, I know you did," he said, wiping his mouth.

"What could you mean?" said Pendergast.

"Two hundred million?" Coldmoon asked. "How?"

"Simple day trading. Exclusively limited to the thirty companies on the Dow Jones Industrial Index. All of it quite straightforward, apparently, with no sign of insider trading, manipulation, fraud, or any other illegality."

"How's that possible?"

"The forensic accountant, in whose competence I have faith, says in all his years of analyzing cooked books and unscrupulous trading, he's never seen anything like it. The hotel manager's trades, every single one, appeared to be totally legitimate and aboveboard. He never made a killing, just steady gains, one after the other, across thousands of trades of stocks and options."

"Crazy."

"And," Pendergast added, "he never, even once, lost money on a trade."

"Impossible."

"One would think so."

"Do you believe this, um, impossibility is connected with his murder?"

It was the kind of question Pendergast often didn't answer, and as Coldmoon expected, no answer was forthcoming. So Coldmoon went ahead. "Did the second victim trade in the market?"

"Never."

"And the third victim—that college kid on the sidewalk—chances are he's not an investor, either."

"I should be most surprised to learn the contrary."

Coldmoon continued eating his hash browns at a much slower pace than before. Why the hell did Pendergast need to make a ten-word statement in which nine of the words were superfluous? A simple *Right* would have sufficed.

He went on. "So the fact this hotel manager made two hundred million right before his death, and the others didn't even play the market—well, if the trading is connected with his murder, what *is* the connection?"

Pendergast said nothing.

Coldmoon plucked a miniature tray of grape jelly from the little metal rack on the table, peeled off the top, and began spreading it on his buttered toast. "Who was Ellerby's heir? Do we know who's going to get the dough?"

"His eighty-year-old widowed mother. He was an only child."

Coldmoon shook his head. "Kind of rules that out as a motive."

"I would say so."

"About this morning's killing. What happened, exactly? Was that guy tossed off the roof? Was he sideswiped by a car and thrown onto the sidewalk? Or was he just beaten to a pulp? He sure looked like a mess."

"He was lying too far from the house to have fallen," Pendergast said. "Or to have been thrown. At least by a human being."

What the hell was that supposed to mean? "But he was sucked dry of blood. Like the other two."

Pendergast simply nodded.

"You think it's a vampire," Coldmoon said after a moment, shoving a piece of bacon into his mouth. "You, along with everyone else."

Pendergast took a long, contemplative sip of tea. He placed the cup down. "Do you?"

"What? No. I mean, are you kidding? Of course not. Vampires don't exist."

"Do the Lakota have any legends about vampires?"

Coldmoon was surprised by the question. Pendergast rarely seemed to acknowledge, let alone take an interest in, his Native American heritage.

"The Lakota do have a sort of legend about a vampire. He was white, of course."

"Naturally."

"A settler moved into the Black Hills to look for gold, and he built a cabin in a sacred valley, defiling it. A year later, some Lakotas found him dead in his cabin, stone cold, with a silver knife in his heart. When they pulled out the knife, the corpse began to warm up, and they grew frightened and ran away. He later began attacking people, killing them and drinking their blood. The only way he could be stopped was to put that same knife back into his heart. And then he would get cold and still again. But he wouldn't die—not really. They say his body is up there, in that cabin, waiting for someone to pull the knife out—"

Just then, Coldmoon was interrupted by an unintelligible cry from outside. He looked out the café window to see a young man staggering up the street: filthy, covered in mud and dirt, his clothes torn almost into rags. He was jabbering in distress, evidently drunk or high.

In a flash, Pendergast was up.

"What are you doing?" Coldmoon asked as he readied his fork for a frontal attack on the fried eggs. "He's just some drunken kid."

But Pendergast ignored him and went outside. Reluctantly, Coldmoon followed a few moments later. The kid had paused just down the street and was clinging to a lamppost, steadying himself. The few pedestrians about at that early hour ignored him completely. Evidently inebriated people at dawn were not an uncommon sight in Savannah.

Pendergast approached the young man, speaking in a soothing voice, holding out his hand. The kid lurched, turned, and as he did so Pendergast grasped his muddy hand in support. "I'm here to help," Coldmoon heard him say.

The kid let go of the lamppost, letting Pendergast bear his weight. "I'm here to help," the agent repeated.

The kid turned his mud-smeared face toward

Pendergast, his lips moving, the words indistinct but repeated over and over like a mantra, his eyes widening. And then, as his cracked voice grew louder, Coldmoon understood what he was trying to say:

No help, no help, no help, no help no help no help...

34

Lᴇᴛ ᴜs ᴄᴀғғᴇɪɴᴀᴛᴇ ᴛʜɪs fellow at once," said Pendergast, steering him back toward the café. "And find out what he has to say."

"Why?" Coldmoon asked. "He's just some random student."

"Random? My dear Coldmoon," Pendergast said, in a tone somewhere between pity and exasperation, "did you not see the Auburn University tiger paw emblazoned on his shirt? It's identical to the one the recently deceased was wearing." He cocked his head at his partner.

Coldmoon could fill in the rest himself. *Surely a trained FBI agent would notice such an obvious connection.* He found himself coloring. "Sorry. So you think—?"

"I think we may have found the victim's friend and drinking partner. I believe he is more terrified than he is drunk."

Coldmoon held open the door while Pendergast eased the youth over to their table.

"Now hold on, all y'all," said the waitress, glaring at Coldmoon. "We don't serve drunks or hooligans here."

"Ma'am," Pendergast said, slipping his FBI badge out of his suit and flipping it open, "this is official business."

She didn't bat an eye. "In that case, the boy needs some coffee." She swiped a mug from an adjacent table, filled it to the brim from the pot, and placed it before the kid. "He'll need something in his stomach, too. How about some buttered toast?"

"Thank you." Pendergast turned back to the new arrival. "You're safe now. Have some coffee."

The boy took the mug in both hands, trembling, and sipped, slopping it over the rim.

"Again."

He took another sip, and another. The waitress brought over a plate of buttered toast.

"Excellent."

The boy picked up a piece of toast and bit into it hungrily. The coffee and toast seemed to steady him: his eyes looked more focused now, Coldmoon thought; less glazed with shock and fear.

"And now, young man," Pendergast said, "what is your name?"

He looked at Pendergast with frightened eyes. "Toby."

"Toby..."

"Manning."

"I am Special Agent Pendergast. And this is my partner, Special Agent Coldmoon. How do you do?"

Manning did not seem to be able to answer the question.

"He reminds me of Paul Revere's ride," the waitress

said from behind the counter. "A little light in the belfry."

Coldmoon gave her a *none of your business* glance. The waitress frowned and, curling her lip, offered him a moue in return.

"Toby," Pendergast said, "do you know a fellow named Brock Custis?"

The eyes widened. "How—?"

"Mr. Custis, I regret to say, was found dead earlier this morning."

"Oh my god…In the cemetery?"

Pendergast looked at him curiously. "No. Did something happen in the cemetery?"

"Um…" He seemed hesitant to talk.

Pendergast lowered his voice to a soothing, honeyed cadence. "You can tell me, Mr. Manning. What happened in the cemetery?"

"I don't know." He took another gulp of coffee and another, spilling some on the table. The waitress came over and wiped up the spill as she topped off the cup, then hovered in the background.

"How did you get from the cemetery to here?" Coldmoon asked.

"I ran, I guess. I don't really remember."

"I see," said Pendergast. "Now, let us go back to the cemetery. Start at the beginning. How did you get in?"

"We climbed over the gate."

"Why were you there?"

"Just…for kicks, you know. To go around at night, look at the tombs."

"To see anything in particular?"

"I wanted to see the Bird Girl."

"Ah. The famous Bird Girl. So the graveyard we're

speaking of is Bonaventure Cemetery. I suppose you hadn't heard the Bird Girl was removed from that site twenty-five years ago?"

"No."

"And then what happened?"

Manning stared at his half-eaten toast. "We got sort of lost."

Pendergast's voice grew still gentler. "And?"

"And then…I felt this weird thing, this sort of hot wind, behind me. Like something…I can't explain…" His voice began to rise. "And Brock…I heard the bottle of booze shatter and Brock disappeared and…I don't know, I just ran."

"So you were drinking?" Coldmoon asked.

Hearing this, the feisty waitress rolled her eyes.

"Yeah."

"Are you feeling better now?"

"Yeah…" He hesitated. "Am I in trouble?"

"Not yet. Finish your coffee, and then we'll go."

"Go where?"

"To the cemetery, where this incident occurred."

Manning began to tremble. "Now?"

"Naturally."

"No," said Manning. "No way…Please…I won't go…*No way!*"

Pendergast's voice abruptly shed its friendly tone and took on an icy edge. "You will take us there right now. Or I can promise one thing: you *will* be in trouble, Mr. Manning."

A moment later, Pendergast was out the door, the youth in tow. Coldmoon stood up, blinking in surprise at how quickly the impromptu questioning had ended. He began to follow them toward the door.

"Excuse *me!*"

He turned around to see the waitress staring at him. One hand was on her hip; the other was holding out a check.

"Oh." Coldmoon looked at the total: $19.80. Mutely, he handed the woman a twenty, then turned and once again headed for the exit. This time, his hand got as far as the door handle before he remembered he hadn't left any tip—except, that is, for twenty cents. But it was too late to salvage the situation: Pendergast was already halfway down the block, so Coldmoon slunk out of the café. But before the door closed behind him, the waitress got in the last word.

"It must have been tough on your mother, not having any children!" she brayed at his retreating back, shaking the twenty at him like a badge of shame.

35

Mᴏʀɴɪɴɢ ʟɪɢʜᴛ sᴛʀᴇᴀᴍᴇᴅ ᴛʜʀᴏᴜɢʜ the cemetery, illuminating the last shreds of mist as the caretaker opened the gate for them. Coldmoon did not like cemeteries. The thought of all those dead slumbering in the dirt for eternity gave him a feeling of claustrophobia, even in a graveyard as huge as this: white graveled pathways extended in all directions past hundreds of tombs.

"Now, Mr. Manning," said Pendergast. "Please take us to where the incident occurred."

"We went this way, I think," said Manning. But he didn't take another step forward until Pendergast urged him on. Then he began shuffling down one of the pathways, moving as if his feet were iron weights.

Coldmoon had never seen tombs this elaborate before. Traditionally, the Lakota placed their dead in platforms perched in trees. At Pine Ridge, where he had grown up, that practice had been replaced by scattering a person's ashes at some high point, like a mountaintop or butte, so they'd be closer to heaven. The idea of sticking the body deep in the earth when you wanted the soul to go up, not down, always seemed perverse to him. But this—these tombs were costly, large, even amazing. Did the dead think they'd find a better place in heaven by being buried in rich tombs like these? Or was it just another class thing, a way to put themselves above others, even after death?

The three continued down the lane for almost half a mile. Finally, Manning took a right, and then another right, into a far area of the cemetery, much overgrown, where the tombs were not nearly so elaborate and had in many cases fallen into disrepair. Here Manning got confused and they went down one path after another, looping back several times. It was obvious his struggle to remember was at war with his extreme unease at being back here.

"I remember this," he finally said, indicating a tomb with an angel striding forward, arm upraised, standing on a marble slab, its inscription largely eroded by time. "We stopped here. That was right before…" He paused, swallowed hard. "I think we went this way."

He moved forward again, then stopped. "Just over there was where…where it happened. And then I ran." He looked down and away. "I don't want to go any farther!"

"And you won't have to," said Pendergast. "We shall halt here and not disturb the area. We've called in the local authorities and they will be here shortly. Now, if you could tell us, in as much detail as possible, what happened, and indicate your movements and Mr. Custis's—pointing them out will be sufficient—I would be grateful."

"Okay." Manning was trembling and nervous but managed to keep it together. "Okay. I was walking in front, over by those tombs." He pointed. "And Brock was behind me. He was singing and sort of dancing, around those tombs there."

"What was he singing?"

"Um, some Stones song."

"Stones?"

"'Sympathy for the Devil.'"

Pendergast stared at Coldmoon with incomprehension. Coldmoon, who'd heard Manning croaking the same tune when they first encountered him, shrugged to indicate its lack of importance. *You can't make this shit up.*

"Brock was behind me, and I heard the singing stop. Just like it was cut off all of a sudden."

"Was there any other sound?" Pendergast asked. "A gasp, perhaps—or scream?"

"No, nothing. It went very quiet for a moment. But I felt this sort of pressure, like humid air, and…and a weird smell, like burnt rubber. And then I heard, farther away, the breaking of glass. The liquor bottle, I guess."

"How far away?"

"How would I know?" the youth said, barely maintaining a grip on himself. He took a shuddering breath. "Maybe a hundred feet? Two hundred? I wasn't paying attention, I was scared as hell. I called his name a few times, but there was no answer. And then—then there was a beating sound."

"What kind of a beating, exactly?"

"Like…someone shaking out a rug. Slow and muffled. And there was another wash or gust of humid air, with that same awful smell. I just started running."

"What direction did the sound come from?"

"Overhead."

Something about the simplicity of this answer chilled Coldmoon.

"And the feeling of pressure, of humid air? Did that come from above, as well?"

Manning nodded.

"And you ran all the way back to Savannah? That's got to be about four miles."

"I ran, I walked, I ran again. I can hardly remember. I was drunk, freaked out."

"Why not call for help on your cell phone?"

"I dropped it over there somewhere. I was using it as a flashlight. It must have broken against a tombstone or something, because the light went off."

Now Coldmoon heard distant sirens from the direction of the cemetery entrance. Pendergast pulled out his phone to give Delaplane directions, and it wasn't long before Coldmoon saw the CSI van easing its way down a pathway, with several squad cars and the M.E. van behind it. They were forced to park at some distance, and within minutes a whole mass of people were headed down the winding paths, converging on them.

Delaplane arrived first, leading the phalanx of specialists carrying their equipment.

"The area over there," Pendergast said, "is where the incident occurred. To be safe, you should cordon off that half acre of ground between those two paths."

Delaplane called for police tape to be strung around the indicated spot while the CSI team suited up and got to work. Sheldrake came over, nodded to Pendergast and Coldmoon. "Mind if I borrow your witness?"

"Be our guest."

Sheldrake and Delaplane went off with the unhappy Manning, recorder in hand. Coldmoon turned to Pendergast. "What do you think?"

"I shall ponder the mystery while I take a walk. If you could remain here in case of any untoward events, I should be grateful."

Coldmoon was used to this—the same thing had happened in a Miami cemetery. "Sure thing."

Pendergast went off, hands behind his back, almost as if he were setting out on his daily constitutional. Not long after he vanished, Coldmoon heard a fresh commotion. Turning toward it, he saw a film crew arriving, with cameras and sound gear. It was that man Betts.

The group approached the police cordon, and Coldmoon watched as Betts argued with some cops who stopped him. Betts was with the other guy Coldmoon remembered from their encounter in the county plaza: the tall, serious one. What was his name? The man had a suitcase with him and was already opening it, laying out a piece of black velvet and removing all kinds of weird contraptions. In the distance, more press were arriving.

It appeared word had gotten out, big time.

Coldmoon walked over to see what he could do to help the cops deal with the press.

The supernatural guy—now he remembered his name, Moller—had taken a silver dowsing stick out of a velvet bag. He began circling the police cordon with it, both film-crew cameras trained on him. "I sense," he was saying in a deep voice, "I sense…a strong supernatural turbulence." The silver stick was trembling, jerking, almost as if under a power of its own. "Very strong."

What a load of česlí, thought Coldmoon, although despite himself he had to admit it was a fairly impressive act. The cops along the cordon were certainly engrossed, although it was hard to tell whether they bought it or not.

"Something evil happened here," Moller said, his voice climbing a notch as the silver contraption pointed toward the center of the roped-off area. "Happened very recently. The turbulence is fierce!"

"Stay behind the line, sir," warned one of the cops.

The silver wand trembled and jerked. The man's body was starting to twitch. The cameras closed in.

"It is here!" He moved toward the police tape and was again gently blocked by the cops.

"The evil! *The evil!*" he whispered fiercely.

Other press were arriving, but the show being put on by Moller was so absorbing that they had stopped to watch. Some were even taking notes and photographs of him, as if he, and not the scene of the crime, were the news.

Suddenly the silver wand flew out of Moller's hands, as if yanked by an invisible string. It was a cute move, because to Coldmoon it really did look as if something invisible had pulled it away, instead of him throwing it through some sleight of hand. Moller, as if released from an unpleasant trance, halted, took a deep breath, seemed to slump, and then recovered, wiping his brow with a silk handkerchief. Retrieving the dowsing stick, he then retreated to his suitcase and removed a large box camera, which he set up on a tripod. He then took out a strange piece of smoked glass—upon closer look it appeared to be a slab of crystal, cut and polished—that he raised in front of his face and gazed through, peering here and there across the area being searched by the CSI squad.

"The evil, become visible," he muttered. He began to tremble. One of the camera operators followed his movement, shooting close over his shoulder.

Coldmoon noticed that Betts had disappeared. He looked around and saw him deep in the vegetation, having used the diversion to slip inside the police cordon. He was with the second camera operator, filming something else.

"Hey!" Coldmoon cried, pointing and striding in Betts's direction. "Get out of there! Back behind the tape!"

Several cops turned and began jogging over as Betts and the cameraperson scurried off into the undergrowth, ducking back under the police line.

Coldmoon walked over to where they had been filming but didn't see anything of note beyond another old mausoleum with a broken door. The abandoned part of the cemetery continued into the overgrowth, the tombstones split and lying on their sides, the pathways so poorly tended as to have disappeared.

He returned to find Pendergast approaching at a brisk walk from an unexpected direction.

"Find anything?" Coldmoon asked as he came up.

"Nothing."

"Too bad."

"On the contrary," Pendergast said as he adjusted his cuffs. "It was most edifying."

36

From behind her monitor, it looked to Gannon like half the Savannah PD had been called out to keep the crowds behind the police cordon. The loud, zoo-like atmosphere contrasted with the stateliness of the old cemetery, with its ranks of mossy tombs speckled in sunlight, slumbering beneath giant oaks. Behind the tape, the police were still working diligently, the CSI team searching the area meticulously. Despite the activity, Gannon noticed that the weird FBI agent and his sidekick had disappeared, along with that officious police commander.

Gannon had her two camera operators well-positioned to capture everything. Pavel was filming the mayhem from various directions with the Steadicam, while Craig, on camera one, was focused on Moller. The paranormal researcher was putting on quite a show, first with the silver dowsing stick and slab of obsidian, and now with the camera that could supposedly capture supernatural images. Daisy, the ditzy historian of the supernatural, was also there—

despite the fact that she had no place on the schedule—trying to insert herself whenever possible into the camera frame, with Betts sidelining her every time. The mob scene was great stuff, and it would make a fine contrast to the dark and creepy scenes Gannon hoped to get more footage of. Since Betts had changed their focus to covering the Savannah Vampire, all her shots so far had involved activity and people. What they needed to do was to come back to the cemetery at night with a couple of fog machines.

Betts came up to her. "Listen, here's the plan. Moller says he's getting amazing stuff, especially pictures. The press is all here, even some national. It's a great opportunity for free publicity, to get the word out on the doc."

She nodded.

"So Moller's going to unveil some of his pictures right here, while all these people and press are around. We want to capture it all."

"Pictures of what?"

"He won't say. You know how the old fart is. But he claims he's getting pictures of 'spiritual turbulences.'"

"So that contraption is digital?" Gannon had always assumed you needed a film camera to capture ghost images.

"You tell me."

The camera that Moller had been circling the tomb with was like none she had ever seen. It was beautiful, made of polished mahogany, gleaming brass, and chrome. Judging from the way the rubberneckers and press were following Moller around like the pied piper as he took what appeared to be long-exposure photographs, this was going to be quite a show.

"Where's all this going to happen?" she asked.

"Over in that open area. In about ten minutes."

"We'll get set up." She spoke to her camera operators over their headsets, giving them orders to set up on either side of the area: one for close-in shots, the other farther away. The press were starting to get restless. They were hungry for something, and Moller was going to give it to them. She saw Betts confer with Moller in low tones. Then he stepped up onto a marble slab—so much for respecting the dead—and clapped his hands.

"Ladies and gentlemen!" he cried out, his short arms stirring the air as Moller stood next to him, cradling his camera. "Ladies and gentlemen!"

The boisterous crowd surged forward, the press muscling ahead with their cameras, boom mics swinging around. It amazed Gannon how Betts had turned the interest of the press on himself and Moller.

"As you know," Betts continued, "we have here the famed paranormal researcher Dr. Gerhard Moller. It seems his equipment has been picking up distinct amounts of unusual supernatural activity. Dr. Moller, tell us what you've found."

Moller, with a look of modest reluctance and disinclination on his face, raised his head and looked over the crowd, letting the silence build. Gannon's camera operators were rolling. The cops, guarding the perimeter, watched them warily.

"My instruments," Moller said in a deep, resonant voice, "have registered powerful supernatural currents." He paused again. "There is a strong presence of evil here."

At this, a hush fell over the crowd. Even the noisy press were rapt.

"And I have captured proof of the presence." He brandished the large camera. "In here."

Someone shouted out, "Can we see it?"

Moller swiveled his large head toward the speaker. "Yes, indeed. That is in fact my intention: to show it to you now."

This triggered a restless stirring. *How is he going to show it to them?* Gannon wondered. *There must be three hundred people here.*

"There are some," Moller intoned, "who have doubted my work. Who have accused me of manipulating my pictures." He held up the camera. "But in here are pictures I took, just seconds ago, of these tombs and surroundings. Some of them show remarkable things not visible to the naked eye—that I've captured using my own proprietary multispectral imaging technology. The photographs are in here, raw and unretouched. You will find this to be true, because you will have a chance to examine them for yourselves."

He paused and raked the crowd with a fierce gaze. "I will make these pictures available to all, with no restrictions on their use. They will be sent from my camera directly to your cell phones. Please make sure Bluetooth is enabled on your mobiles, and select 'Percipience Camera' in your device list. In thirty seconds, I will transmit three images."

He turned and bent over the camera. Those in the crowd, with a burst of chatter, fumbled out their cell phones and began frantically poking and swiping. The atmosphere of anticipation had become almost unbearable. It was brilliant theater—more than theater, as Moller had found a way to make his audience active participants. Gannon, watching the feed from her two camera operators on her monitors, was happy to see them nailing it.

"I am now sending," said Moller as he turned back.

Total silence for a moment. Then, as the photos began hitting people's phones, a great *aaahhh*-ing and *ooohhh*-ing came up like a rising wind. Everybody, press photographers included, was staring at their phone. She could even make out a few choked-off gasps and garbled sounds of fear and horror.

What was it? Gannon was dying to see, but she couldn't break off directing to grab her own phone. She glanced at Betts. He, too, was staring into his phone, an expression of sheer delight mingled with horror on his face. She went back to covering the moment, her camera operators getting shots of people's reactions.

A moment later, she heard Betts speak loudly. "Hey, what are you doing?" She looked over to see him advance rapidly toward the woman, Daisy Fayette, who straightened up. She had been bending over Moller's equipment case, and now she dropped something back into it with a guilty look.

"What is this?" Moller yelled, spinning around. "Why are you touching those things?" He rushed over. "*Alte Drache*, how dare you touch my instruments?"

Daisy went bright red, and then recovered, saying frostily: "I was curious to see your equipment. After all, I'm *also* a supernatural researcher."

"You can't go rummaging around like that!" Betts said as Moller began rearranging his case, cheeks red with anger. "In fact, you weren't even supposed to be on the set today at all. Johnny, see Mrs. Fayette out of here."

Gannon watched as the woman was led off by one of the crew, protesting ineffectually. *Good riddance,* she thought. Fayette, the opposite of photogenic, was obviously just a busybody, angling for more camera time. Gannon had herself lobbied for engaging the woman—a local point of view was an important consideration—but as happened so often, the people you thought were going to be a bonus turned out to have no camera presence. The woman should have remained primarily a voice-over, as Betts had initially said.

Now Betts came over. "Have a look." He pulled out his cell phone and swiped through.

Gannon took up the phone with great interest. The first of Moller's photographs was of the tomb with the angel with a raised arm. A CSI worker was standing to one side, blurred from the long exposure. On the opposite side of the tomb, a cloud of mist appeared to be rising out of the grass, inside of which stood a figure. Amid the blurry swirl of mist, she could just make out a staring eye, and a bony hand reaching out in a most sinister way toward the oblivious CSI worker.

She swiped. The next photo showed another cloud of eddying mist, larger and more diffuse, in which she could just make out a giant face, four feet in diameter, indistinct and bloated, and of a tremendously evil aspect. The third photo was the best—or worst—of all, showing what appeared to be a demon climbing out of the very earth, its naked, emaciated arm emerging from the ground, along with the top of a skull covered with wispy hairs, with hollow eye sockets and grinning teeth.

"Holy shit," she murmured, "these are amazing." She could feel her heart beating like a tom-tom. They were extremely creepy, and what's more, they looked real. The photos had obviously been taken just

moments before. Could Moller have somehow manip-
ulated them inside the camera before sending them
out? It didn't seem possible, but as a photographer
Gannon knew all too well that there was an almost
infinite range of digital manipulation tricks. Anyway,
it hardly mattered: this was stupendous stuff, and how
Moller got the images was his business.

She handed the phone back to Betts. "These will
make fantastic stills for the documentary."

"Absolutely. And there'll be many more."

"But…" she asked, half facetiously, "where's the
vampire?"

Moller, coming over, answered instead of Betts.
"The vampire is not here. It may be somewhere
nearby. What you are seeing are demonic presences
excited by the recent passage of the vampire, like
buoys bobbing in the wake of a big boat."

"So you think you can get a picture of the vampire
himself?" Betts asked.

"If you put me in the right place at the right
time, yes."

"Excellent!" Betts cried, slapping Moller on the
back, much to his displeasure.

37

A<small>ND YOU CAN'T BE</small> any more specific than that?" Commander Delaplane asked.

The kid—Toby Manning—shook his head. He'd washed his face and hands since she'd first seen him in the cemetery, but his clothes were still a mess. His eyes were clearer, though, and he was relatively composed. Not all that surprising, she mused to herself—he'd been asked to go over the events leading up to his friend's death probably half a dozen times in as many hours, and now it was becoming routine.

She waited a minute or two, her gaze on Manning. Then she glanced at Benny Sheldrake and past him to where the two FBI agents were seated at a small conference table. Pendergast gave a slight nod.

"Okay," she said, snapping off her recorder. "Thanks for your help. You can go now. I'll have a car take you home. Get some rest, all right? And stick around, because we'll be calling on you again in the coming days."

Manning nodded, stood up, and—with a furtive glance at Pendergast—shuffled toward the door.

Delaplane consulted a handwritten list of names, crossed off Manning's. "That just leaves the Ingersolls. They're waiting outside."

"Excellent."

Delaplane sighed inwardly. This was a necessary procedure, interviewing potential witnesses to last night's mess. They had already spoken to a woman who lived across from the Ingersolls' B and B, the bartender at the place where the two youths, Toby and Brock, had gotten hammered, the custodian of the cemetery, and a handful of others. The interviews had been short, and—unfortunately—they hadn't contributed much in the way of hard evidence to what they'd already learned.

She picked up the phone, asked a watch officer to get a ride for Manning.

"And bring in the Ingersolls," she said.

A minute later, there was a knock on the door and the two came in, escorted by an officer. Their eyes darted around the room, taking in everyone present. Then they sat down in the chairs set before Delaplane's desk. The woman, Agnes, had an expression of stone—still in shock, no doubt, from the rush of unpleasant events—but her husband, Bertram, looked aggrieved, almost angry, like Sisyphus after being assigned a larger hill.

"Mr. Ingersoll," she said, nodding, her voice clipped, uninflected, professional. "Mrs. Ingersoll. Thank you for coming."

"Of course," the woman mumbled without thinking. Her husband said nothing.

"I'll be recording this conversation," she said,

snapping the machine on again. "Do I have your permission?"

"No problem," said Mr. Ingersoll.

After going through the preliminaries of date, time, and those present, Delaplane launched into the questioning. "I know this must be difficult, but I'd like you to please go over again with me, one more time, the events leading up to your discovery of the body. Step by step, and please take your time and mention any new details you might have remembered since making your previous statements, no matter how minor."

The couple was silent for a moment. Finally, the woman began to speak in a low, halting voice. The story she recounted was, almost word for word, the same one Delaplane had heard already: the walk through the quiet streets; the sudden rush of sound combined with an inexplicable sense of movement; and then, her husband sprawling over a body and her frantic call to 911. The husband winced as she went over certain details but otherwise remained silent.

Agnes Ingersoll's story tailed off slowly, with a few final observations sputtering out as she recalled them. Then a silence fell over the room. Delaplane followed her usual strategy of letting a witness stew a little before speaking. More often than not, under the pressure of silence, they'd remember something else. But to her surprise, it was Pendergast who spoke.

"Mrs. Ingersoll," he said. "Can you tell me how quickly you dialed 911 after your husband fell to the pavement?"

Through long practice, Delaplane managed to keep her expression neutral, despite the trivial nature of the question. She noticed, however, that Coldmoon shifted his eyes toward his partner.

The woman paused, thinking. "Um…well…Bertram fell, and as I said he cried out when he hit the pavement, and I knelt over him to make sure he was all right. It all happened so quickly, you know, it seemed everything was over within a second."

"So," Pendergast prodded, "how long would you estimate before the call? Ten seconds? Fifteen?"

The husband seemed about to object, but his wife answered first. "I saw he was moving, but it was fairly dark and I couldn't tell how badly hurt he was. I saw the—the other body. Bertram moaned—and that was when I reached into my purse." She hesitated. "Fifteen seconds."

"Fifteen," Pendergast repeated. "From the moment your husband fell over the body to when you called for assistance?"

"Yes," the woman said a little hesitantly. Then, more firmly: "yes."

"Very good. And—please forgive me if I dwell on these unpleasant events—the body your husband tripped over: did it seem to you it was already in place?"

The woman looked from Pendergast to her husband and back again. "I don't understand."

"Was the body in situ, on the ground? Or did you have any sense of motion immediately before the, ah, accident occurred? Such as a body that had fallen from above—jumped or pushed?"

"No," she blurted.

"Mr. Ingersoll?" Pendergast asked.

The man stared at the agent with red-rimmed eyes. Then he merely shook his head.

"Thank you," Pendergast said, glancing at Delaplane to signal, once again, that he had nothing more to ask.

Sheldrake asked a few perfunctory questions, and then Delaplane dismissed the couple with the usual warnings. As the door closed behind them, she turned to Pendergast. "May I ask why the interest in the timing of the 911 call?"

"Naturally. And I'd be happy to answer your question—once you've checked in with that cell phone specialist of yours."

This had been another of Pendergast's bizarre questions. "I'm not sure he'll have an answer for us yet."

"Please try him anyway, if you don't mind."

"Okay." Delaplane dialed an internal extension, then turned on the speaker of her desk phone.

"Wrigley here," came a voice over the speaker.

"Wrigley? It's Alanna."

"Oh. Hi, Commander."

"Any joy?"

"As a matter of fact, I was just about to call you," the disembodied voice replied. "It turns out I didn't need to tinker with the microcode after all. Once I knew his location, the model of his phone, and its internal GPS ID, I tried the cell towers in that area, just in case. And I got lucky. The kid has a really old phone, and it pings the network a lot more frequently than today's models when its flashlight is on or it's being used as a compass. Some proposed IEEE standard that ultimately was never implemented. Anyway, sure enough, it was pinging the network: once every sixty seconds. Of course, newer phones go dormant much faster in order to save juice, but this—"

"Fascinating, Wrigley, but can we get to the point?"

"There were thirteen pings, each exactly sixty seconds apart. The first was at 3:02, and the last was at 3:14."

"Excuse me," Pendergast said. "But what was the exact time of the last ping?"

"Like I said," the technician replied, "3:14."

"I asked for the *exact* time, if you please."

"Why didn't you *say* so?" came the sarcastic response. "Three fourteen, forty seconds, and seventy-one centiseconds. That's 3:14:40.71. I'd give you the milliseconds, but the ANI/ALI signal doesn't—"

"Okay, Wrigley," Delaplane said, trying to keep from smiling. "Good work." And she hung up. "Now," she said, turning to Pendergast, "I'm not sure what you're driving at here."

"Just one last favor, please," Pendergast said in his most honeyed tone. "Would you please call your emergency dispatcher and find out when Mrs. Ingersoll dialed 911?"

"Let me guess. Down to the second."

"If you'd be so kind."

It took two calls, and about five minutes of waiting as the records were accessed, before Delaplane hung up again. "Three eighteen," she said. "And, no, they couldn't tell me how many hundredths of a second."

"That's quite all right, thank you," said Pendergast, sliding the fingers of one hand over the nails of the other in a peculiar gesture. "We can assume both time sources are quite accurate—certainly accurate enough for our needs."

"What are those needs, exactly?" Delaplane asked. She caught Coldmoon's eye, and he grinned.

"To provide the variables for the following calculation: The Manning youth dropped his phone just as he started running away from whoever attacked his friend. That means the assault took place at 3:14 and about forty seconds. We also know that Mrs. Ingersoll dialed 911 at 3:18, less than four minutes later. Which means that was the time Brock Custis was dropped."

"What the hell?" Coldmoon said, stirring behind the conference table, suddenly seeing the craziness of the timeline.

"*Dropped?*" Delaplane asked.

"My dear colleagues, consider the facts! The injury to the body, and the accounts of the eyewitnesses, make it clear that Custis had just fallen to the sidewalk a moment before Ingersoll tripped over him. Everyone has assumed that Custis fell from a window or off the roof. But that clearly isn't the case."

"How's that?" Delaplane asked.

"Because the Bonaventure Cemetery, where Custis was accosted, is almost four miles from the location on Taylor Street where our friend Ingersoll tripped over Custis's body. Given the narrow streets, urban congestion, and geographical impediments between the two locations, it's impossible to drive that distance in less than sixteen minutes—I've checked all possible routes. But Custis, or rather his corpse, made it in just four minutes. This is why I say, Commander, that he was dropped. Because the only possible conclusion is that he flew from one spot to the other—or rather, was *flown*."

"*Flown?*" Delaplane protested in a high, incredulous voice. After a moment, comprehension dawned on her face. "Oh. Oh, *shit*."

38

Aɴᴏᴛʜᴇʀ ʙɪsᴄᴜɪᴛ?" Fᴇʟɪᴄɪᴛʏ Fʀᴏsᴛ asked, holding out the plate of chocolate digestives.

"No, thank you," replied Constance, dabbing her lips with a damask napkin.

"*Hell*," the elderly woman said with feigned annoyance. "That means I can't have one, either." And she put the plate back on a silver tray that sat on the tea table between them. The china, Constance noted, was from an antique set of Haviland Limoges, understated but exquisite. But then, she thought, that was characteristic of Frost herself: antique, discreet, and with far more depth than a superficial glimpse would suggest.

Frost had sent Constance a note earlier that day, asking if she would like to have tea that evening at nine. And so Constance, accepting, had spent over an hour in the woman's company. Miss Frost had proven to be an excellent conversationalist, knowledgeable about a number of topics—especially antiquarian. She had shown Constance three rooms of the penthouse:

a library-cum-museum, a music room, and the drawing room in which they now sat. There were clearly others, but Frost had not invited her to tour them and Constance had not asked. In any case, these three were sufficient to provide her with a sense of Frost's interests and personality. The rooms contained many beautiful things: first editions of neglected nineteenth-century novelists; a Steinway Model O from 1923, the final year of original production; and an impressive collection of art that ran the gamut from John Marin watercolors to several of Piranesi's *Carceri* etchings. True, the rugs were not the hand-knotted Kashan or Isfahan pieces of Pendergast's Riverside Drive mansion, and the Duncan Phyfe furniture was not original—but the reproductions were tasteful. Everything spoke of a woman of discernment who—though her wealth was not unlimited—had accumulated and curated many beautiful things.

In addition to the collections of firearms and pens, there was, curiously, a museum-in-miniature of cipher machines and pieces from the early history of computing. Several large display cases contained, Frost had explained, a Fialka M-125 Soviet cipher device, an Enigma machine, a set of gears of Charles Babbage's Difference Engine, a relay and rotary switch from Harvard's Mark I, and a pair of printed circuit boards from the landmark early supercomputer Cray-1. Frost's knowledge of computers was remarkable, and it struck Constance this must be a significant link to her mysterious past—whatever that was.

"It's almost eleven," Frost said, glancing at a grandfather clock on the far wall. She was sitting on a chaise longue across from Constance. A well-thumbed paperback, which Constance had noticed on her first visit, was at her side, a constant companion. "I think something stronger than tea is called for— don't you?"

Constance reminded herself that, because of the woman's nocturnal habits, cocktails were apparently served half a dozen hours later than usual. "If you'd like."

"I would like indeed. At my age, self-medication is practically the only vice left to me." She stood up with effort, then walked over to a sideboard arrayed with numerous bottles. "Would you care to, ah, smother a parrot with me?"

"No, thank you," said Constance, a little more sharply than she intended.

"In that case, name your own poison."

"Campari and soda, please, if it's at hand."

"It is. And it will be in your own in a jif." The old woman fussed around for a few minutes, then returned with two glasses—one pink within, the other a pallid, milky green.

"*A votre santé.*" And, lifting her glass, Frost toasted Constance.

They drank a moment in silence.

"Campari," Frost mused. "An interesting choice for one of your age."

"Perhaps I could say the same of you and absinthe."

"Perhaps. It was made illegal before even I was born."

"Outlawed in 1915," Constance said.

"I'll take your word for it. In any case, wormwood seems to agree with me. As someone said, 'the dose makes the poison.'"

With this, the old woman sat back, observing Constance with an arched eyebrow. Constance began to say *Paracelsus*, but decided against it. Instead, she said: "I meant to compliment you on your piano playing." She nodded in the direction of the music room. "That piece the other night is one of my favorite nocturnes."

"Mine as well," Frost said. She took a sip of her drink. "Do you play?"

Constance nodded. "But I'm partial to the harpsichord."

Frost smiled. "And very accomplished, no doubt. But I'd have thought someone of your temperament would prefer an instrument with more dynamics."

"That's what the choir stops are for," Constance said.

"No doubt." And with another smile, Frost finished her drink. "Next time, I'll have to ask you for dinner," she said. "I have a decent wine cellar up here. Not what you're used to, I imagine, but serviceable." Once again, she fixed Constance with a quizzical look. "You're used to drinking the finest wines, are you not? Just as I'm sure your harpsichord is of the highest quality. And your snickersnee is a rare antique."

"Thank you," Constance said, trying to suppress a growing annoyance. "But I doubt my blade is much rarer than the Luger you pointed at me the other evening."

Miss Frost waved this away. "I only mention wine because we were speaking of music," she said. "The older I get, the more I find myself thinking of composers in terms of wine. To me, Mozart is like a bottle of Château d'Yquem: sweet and silky, but more complex than it initially seems. Beethoven is like a petite sirah: ill-bred, brutish, chewy, but once tasted, never forgotten. And Scarlatti"—she laughed—"Scarlatti is like a cheap prosecco, full of bubbles that bother your nose."

"And Brahms?" Constance asked, irritated at the aspersion cast on her beloved Scarlatti, but not wishing to be impolite.

"Ah, Brahms! Brahms is like...one of the best Barolos."

And with this, Frost rose and, moving to the sideboard, helped herself to more absinthe. While her back was turned, Constance took the opportunity to reach out and flip through the paperback on Frost's side table.

She sat back as Frost finished diluting her drink, holding it up to examine the louche, and then turning back toward her.

"It's a curious thing, but as you get older, as I'm sure you know, you find yourself more and more stuck in an endless do-loop."

"Pardon?" This *as I'm sure you know* phrase unsettled Constance.

Frost smiled. "That's the old programmer in me talking."

This was the most direct reference yet to Frost's past. Constance realized any further dancing around was pointless. She paused to take a breath. "I'd like to hear more from the old programmer."

Frost began to laugh: a low, breathy laugh, wry but genuine. "And so we come to it at last."

"Come to what?"

"The real reason you're here."

"I'm here because you invited me."

The proprietress batted this away impatiently. "Persiflage. I'd hoped perhaps you were different."

"Different?"

"Interested in stimulating conversation, rather than my past."

"Your past is only interesting because you're so mysterious about it."

But the old lady barely seemed to hear this. Her gaze had gone past Constance to some indistinct point. She sighed. "I always thought this might happen."

When she said nothing more, Constance prompted: "What, exactly?"

"Someone **might come** along acute enough to beat me at my **own game.** Maybe ten or twenty years ago, I would have **found** such parrying amusing—even challenging. But I'm tired now...old and tired." Her gaze returned to Constance. Leaning forward, she picked up her glass, drained it, and set it back down on the tea table. "So let's finish the game."

There was an edge in her voice that put Constance on guard. The elderly woman had proven a surprise: far sharper than she'd expected.

"Here's what we'll do," Frost went on. "You're a perspicacious creature. You'll make a statement about me that you think might be true. If it's true, I will say as much and you can make another statement. But once you make a statement that's wrong, the roles are reversed...and I get to make statements about you on the same terms. Agreed?"

Constance hesitated. She had the vague feeling she'd just been outmaneuvered in a chess game. But after a moment, she nodded.

The old woman sat back. "Proceed."

"Very well." Constance considered. "You were very fond of Patrick Ellerby."

Frost tut-tutted, as if this were hardly deserving of an opening gambit. "True."

"Yet he was disobedient. He disappointed you, even betrayed you."

A shadow crossed the proprietress's face, but she nodded. "True."

Constance paused. She did not want to try Frost's patience with trivial observations, but blind guessing was even more dangerous.

"You have, at least once in your life, reinvented yourself."

Now it was Frost's turn to pause. "True."

"In some respects, you have an outlaw personality. The normal rules don't apply to you."

A hesitation and she colored slightly. "True."

"You have a deep knowledge of science: particularly mathematics, programming, physics."

"True."

Constance continued probing, using her own past as a guide. "You had a difficult childhood."

"False!" Frost laughed in triumph. "My childhood was quiet and unremarkable, thank you very much."

"Where did you grow up?"

"None of that!" Miss Frost resettled herself on the chaise longue. "It's my turn."

Again, something in the way this was said made Constance wary.

"I'll give you a handicap," Frost said. "I'll make only a *single* observation about you. If I'm wrong, you win. But if I'm right…then *you* have to explain."

Constance waited, uneasy.

"Ready?"

She nodded.

"You're older than you look," Miss Frost said. "And not just measured in weeks, or months, or years…but much, *much* older."

Constance said nothing.

"Don't care to answer?" the old lady prodded. "Or

perhaps you're wondering how I know. Because I *do* know; there's no guessing involved. At first, I thought it was some caprice of my imagination. After all, how could your knowledge be as deep as, or deeper than, my own, which I've spent eight decades acquiring? So I began salting our conversation with little traps. 'Springes to catch woodcocks,' as Shakespeare put it."

"What traps were those?" Constance asked, trying to keep her voice steady.

"You not only knew the exact year absinthe was declared illegal, but you understood what I meant by 'smothering a parrot'—an expression that hasn't been used in a hundred years. You use archaic words. The very structure of your sentences is nineteenth-century, and you knew what I meant by a 'snickersnee.' You recognized who crafted my antiques, who painted my paintings—even when you didn't voice a name, I could see it in your expression. You can run circles around me in Latin and ancient Greek." The old lady leaned in slightly. "No one can absorb so much knowledge in twenty-odd years. But what really betrayed you, my dear, were your *eyes*."

"What about them?"

"They are not the eyes of a young woman. Your eyes could be those of an old woman—they could be *mine*—except they reflect even deeper experience. They are the eyes of…a sphinx."

Constance had no answer.

"So," Miss Frost went on, "I'm fascinated. Captivated. Entranced. I want to know the mechanism. I want to know how you did it."

Quite abruptly, Constance stood up.

"Are you forfeiting, Miss Greene?" she asked.

"There's still so much we can learn—from each other."

Constance remained motionless. Then, slowly, she sat down again.

"You owe me an answer, my dear," Frost said.

"The answer is…" Constance stopped for a moment. "True."

The old woman's eyes went wide. "*Really!*"

Constance volunteered nothing else.

"Go on. As I said, I want to know the mechanism." When silence was the only reply, she said: "It's only fair—"

"My life span was unnaturally extended by a scientific experiment—one that took place over a century ago."

This was said in a completely expressionless voice. Frost's eyes went wider still. She looked like a medium who'd just discovered that her fake crystal ball did, in fact, have magical properties. "Oh, my good Lord." Then, summoning her wits again, she asked: "And were you grateful for this gift?"

"The doctor who extended my life killed my sister while perfecting his experiments. He was…more successful with me." And with that, Constance stood up again—even more abruptly—turned her back on Frost, and exited the woman's chambers.

39

W e've got a bit of a shitshow on our hands," Delaplane told the group assembled in the Savannah PD briefing room. Sheldrake was at her side, and Coldmoon sat unobtrusively with Pendergast in the back as the commander reviewed the case. "You saw, or heard about, the scene at the cemetery. And no doubt you saw the national news this morning, with those ghost photos on every news channel. We need to show some progress here, people."

They were pretty damn unsettling pictures, Coldmoon thought, and he wondered how that German guy, Moller, had pulled off that level of fakery. Assuming they were fakes. He'd caught the beginning of Moller's dog-and-pony show in the cemetery, before Pendergast had dragged him away. Now he wished they'd stuck around.

Delaplane went through a brief summary of the case so far, making notations on a whiteboard. Sheldrake spoke for a few minutes about its unusual and contradictory aspects—including a brief mention of the logistics of moving the victims from where they were attacked to where the bodies were found.

As they were finishing up, there was a stir at the door. Coldmoon glanced over. A group of men in dark suits had walked in, led by a boss man in dark glasses. *He's either a politician or mobbed up*, thought Coldmoon as the man strode toward the front of the room as if he owned the place. A camera crew also appeared in the doorway and were filming—not the jackasses doing the documentary, but another crew evidently towed in by the boss guy.

Delaplane stared at the intruders and then—in a voice that wasn't exactly warm with welcome—said: "Welcome, Senator."

"I hope I'm not interrupting," said the man, turning to the group of police officers and flashing a smile of the whitest, straightest teeth Coldmoon had ever seen. He sported an artificial tan, hair implants, and, Coldmoon guessed, a face lift. The man was built like a linebacker, his suit straining at the seams, movie-star handsome, midfifties. His only drawback was a nose with a spiderweb of veins. "I'm here in my capacity as the senior senator of the great state of Georgia to offer our assistance in getting this heinous case solved." He looked at the camera with a smile. "I'm a strong supporter of local law enforcement, one hundred percent." He turned again and addressed Delaplane. "How is the investigation going, Commander?"

"We were just finishing a briefing on new developments in the case," she said.

"*Are* there new developments?"

"We're working on a number of lines of inquiry," said Delaplane evenly.

"I'm glad to hear that, because naturally I've been concerned." He paused. "As you know, I'll be holding an outdoor campaign rally in Forsyth Park tomorrow night."

"We're well aware of that, Senator. We're providing security."

"That's the issue right there: *security*. I know you've all been working overtime on this case, but as you can see, it's now become a national story, and it isn't exactly casting a favorable light on either your city or our state. We need to see some real progress on getting this solved—*before* the rally. Am I clear, ladies and gentlemen?"

Coldmoon could see that the rank and file of the SPD were not at all happy with the senator barging into their meeting. A chilly silence filled the room.

"I just wanted to say that you've got my support," the senator went on, raising his voice. "I'm going to make sure that, up in Washington, we're going to throw all our resources into solving these heinous murders. So whatever you need, Commander, just call and let me know. We've got your back, I promise you that."

"Thank you, Senator," said Delaplane.

"Thank *you*. Ladies and gentlemen of law enforcement: God bless you all!"

He made a quick hand gesture and the cameras stopped filming. The smile instantly vanished. He turned and headed back toward the door with his entourage. But instead of leaving, the senator detoured and came up to where Pendergast and Coldmoon were sitting. "Could I see you two gentlemen outside?"

Pendergast rose without a word and Coldmoon did likewise. They exited the police station into the parking lot, baking in the heat. The senator's black SUV was parked illegally in front of the station, along with several other staff cars.

Once outside, the senator turned to Pendergast. "So you're the two agents Pickett's assigned to this case." He looked at them, one after the other. "You must be Agent Pendergast."

Pendergast inclined his head.

"They tell me you're the best. That you always solve your cases. That there's no smarter agent in the Bureau to handle this sort of thing."

Pendergast remained still, face betraying nothing.

"To be frank, all I've seen so far is a whole lot of zilch. No arrests, no leads, no nothing. Oh: except, of course, for the raid on a bunch of old swingers wallowing in duck blood. And when I woke up yesterday, what did I see on the morning news? Pictures of ghosts, and Savannah the laughingstock of the nation. 'The Savannah Vampire'—Christ. May I ask, Agent Pendergast, what you and your partner have been doing in the past ten days or so?"

"You may ask," said Pendergast.

Drayton waited, but Pendergast apparently had finished speaking.

The senator stepped closer. "Let me explain something to you, Pendergast. You heard what I said back there. I've got a rally coming up that's crucial to my re-election. I can't have anything interfering with or depressing attendance. I can't do anything to reprimand *you* about your failure to move this case forward, you or your partner here. Frankly, you're too low-level, and I can't reach down that far. But your boss, Pickett—who assured me you'd solve the case, who sang your praises, and who's been covering for you—well, he was up for promotion to associate deputy director. Note my use of the past tense."

Coldmoon felt his blood rise up. While he didn't like Pickett, he felt a loyalty to the Bureau, and he took deep offense at this political hack making threats. But Pendergast said nothing.

"You understand what I'm saying, Pendergast?"

"Naturally."

This was too much. "I'm sorry to hear, Senator," Coldmoon said, "that your re-election campaign isn't going well."

Drayton turned two small, squinty, rage-filled eyes on him. "You insolent bastard. Maybe I *can* do something about squashing a low-level bug like you."

"Go ahead," said Coldmoon.

Drayton gave a smile, exposing his rack of snowy teeth. "You're both going to find out what it means to disrespect a sitting U.S. senator, that I can tell you."

"*If* you're still sitting after the election," said Coldmoon.

"Oh, believe me, the shit's going to rain on you sooner than that, Agent—" He paused and picked up the ID hanging on his lanyard, then let it drop. "Coldmoon."

At this, Drayton snapped his fingers over his head and spun around. The gesture sent his minions rushing to the SUV, some opening the door for him while he climbed inside as the rest of the retinue swarmed into the other vehicles.

Coldmoon tried to take a few measured breaths and calm himself down. He glanced at Pendergast, but the man's face was as distant and neutral as ever.

"There goes the Lord of the Douchebags," said

Coldmoon as they watched the entourage pull out of the parking lot, light bar flashing.

"You should meet my friend Lieutenant D'Agosta of the NYPD," said Pendergast mildly. "He, too, has a remarkable store of colorful expressions."

"And here I've been holding back." Coldmoon was still watching the receding vehicles. "You know, that guy really needs to be struck by lightning."

"Patience, Agent Coldmoon."

He swiveled toward Pendergast. "What does that mean?"

"Someone with his level of hubris and narcissism almost inevitably orchestrates their own downfall."

"And if he doesn't?" Coldmoon asked.

"Then I shall have to arrange for him to be caught *in flagrante*."

"Excuse me?"

"Let me put it this way: you are named Armstrong because one of your ancestors supposedly killed General Custer. Right?"

"There's no 'supposedly' about it."

"As you wish. The point is: if Squire Drayton does not manage to disgrace *himself*, then I'll personally make sure he meets his own Little Bighorn."

He would not elaborate.

40

WELLSTONE SAT, NURSING A club soda and lime, at a window table in the bar of the newly opened Telfair Square Hotel. It was almost ten o'clock, and the bar was in the quiet period between the stampede of dinner-hour drinkers and the late-night revelers still to come. He, of course, was not staying here—his own suite was in the Marriott Riverfront—but this bar was a most convenient place to keep an eye on his target, directly across State Street.

The Ye Sleepe was a quirky hotel that cultivated a kind of seedy bohemian chic. It was clearly the latest of several generations of commercial lodging: the pentimento of a red-crowned Best Western logo could still be seen faintly, beneath the façade's paint job, and the hotel's external marquee looked suspiciously like the "Great Sign" of vintage Holiday Inns.

The waiter came up to his table. "Anything else, sir? Perhaps something with a little higher octane?"

"I'll stick to club soda, thanks." He'd put booze— especially red wine—off-limits for the time being.

He sat, gazing across the street while the waiter brought him a fresh drink. When he'd heard that Barclay Betts and his entourage were staying at the Ye Sleepe, his primary feeling had been one of disdain. Couldn't the cheap bastard afford to put his people up on the waterfront? But sitting here across the street from the hotel, he could see method in Betts's madness. The rooms—so the waiter had informed him—were old and very large, and the place catered to thirsty, horny young travelers on a budget. That meant Betts could afford a lot of room to spread out his entourage, and his donkey-like braying and yelling was not likely to elicit complaints from the management.

It had another advantage—for Wellstone, at least. Its on-site parking lot, currently being resurfaced, was barricaded off and unlighted. It took up the rest of the block on the building's western flank, and it was naturally deserted. That side of the hotel was where Betts had booked a block of rooms, all on the first floor.

And Gerhard Moller's room was the fifth window in from the street.

It had taken only a little research and surveillance for Wellstone to learn this. The layout was better than he'd hoped—in fact, it made what had initially seemed like a somewhat far-fetched scheme into something very workable. Very workable indeed.

He'd suffered nothing but setbacks in his progress to unmask Barclay Betts, most recently Daisy Fayette's eviction from the graveyard shooting set. The feral cunning he sensed beneath the southern belle's veneer had, ultimately, failed him. And now, thanks to his graveyard shenanigans, Betts was working with an even higher profile. Under normal circumstances, Wellstone would have returned to Boston and not bothered with this hack. But he could still practically feel the warm crème anglaise dribbling down his back as Betts laughed. And ironically, it was Daisy's humiliation—which he'd heard about in querulous detail—that had given him an idea that might turn everything around.

As part of her breathless litany of injustices done by Betts & Co., Daisy described how Moller had taken photos with that special camera of his and then distributed them, via Bluetooth, to the crowd of reporters and rubberneckers. After leaving Daisy's house with vague promises of retribution, Wellstone had immediately gone to the tourist ghetto along Bay Street, where most of the reporters were staying, and managed to get his hands on copies of Moller's photos. There were three of them, with normal-enough subjects: a CSI worker, a tomb with a marble angel, another broken tombstone. But each one was also overlaid with a sinister apparition, indistinct but disturbing nonetheless—an outstretched bony hand; a huge, sinister face; and a wispy-haired skull and claw emerging from the earth.

Those were the words—*overlaid, indistinct*—that convinced Wellstone he knew what Moller was up to. It was obvious these were real photographs, taken in real time; after all, the "doctor" couldn't have known in advance precisely what he'd be photographing in the cemetery. That meant there had to be some apparatus within the camera to create, in effect, a digital double exposure.

That had to be it. The camera Moller was so protective of contained a mechanism for manipulating the photos it took by overlaying on them the ghostly images. This, Wellstone speculated, could only be done if the camera *already held* a large set of supernatural images—previously created by Moller. All he'd have to do was take a "real" photo, then use whatever he'd retrofitted into the camera to add an appropriate overlay from his stock of sinister images, ready and waiting. Wellstone guessed he'd use the viewfinder to frame his double exposure in the most believable way—then, with the click of a button, he'd take a photo and some algorithm in the camera would blend the two layers into a final image—to be passed on to the credulous dupes.

But what exactly was the mechanism? Was there an SSD flash drive inside the camera, preloaded with fake ghostly images, ready to overlay? That was almost certainly the case. If Wellstone could snag that drive with its store of fake pictures, he could show Moller as the fraud he was—with Betts complicit in the whole scheme.

This meant getting his hands on the camera. And the way he planned to do that could technically be considered breaking and entering. But Wellstone brushed this aside. This could go under the heading of true investigative reporting—on the level of the Pentagon Papers or Deep Throat.

Just then, Wellstone saw movement at Ye Sleepe's main entrance. A burly-looking man—the same Cro-Magnon bastard who had pushed him away from Betts in the restaurant—came out onto the street. He was followed by the scruffy-looking young man Wellstone knew was Betts's researcher. These two were followed in quick succession by the attractive DP; Betts himself, the fartbiter—and then, *Deo gratias*, Moller. Wellstone noticed the charlatan was not carrying his case.

That meant he must have left it in his room. Exactly as Wellstone hoped.

A few more people joined the entourage; they milled around outside the lobby for a minute or two, then set off down State Street toward Barnard.

Now he rose, fresh club soda untouched; dropped a twenty on the table; and moved quickly out into the lobby and onto the street. As usual, he hadn't anticipated the heat and humidity, which wrapped him like a soggy Hudson Bay blanket. There weren't many streetlights here, especially on the far side where the parking lot was broken up and being repaved, and Wellstone could just make out Betts's group as they turned onto Barnard and disappeared.

Still moving quickly, yet careful not to arouse curiosity or suspicion, he crossed the street. He'd planned this down to the last detail—but that didn't mean he could afford to dawdle.

He walked along the façade of Ye Sleepe, ducking past the construction barricades at the far end and turning into the parking lot. It quickly grew even darker. He paused to make sure nobody was around and no security cameras were aimed his way. Except for some paving equipment, he was alone and essentially invisible in the darkness.

Hurrying along, he counted the windows until he reached Moller's room. He tried peering in, but the curtains were tightly closed. Reaching into a pocket, he pulled on a pair of latex gloves. Then he pressed his fingers against the window, feeling appraisingly along its lower edge.

It didn't open from the outside. No surprise there. But—thank God—it wasn't one of those sealed portholes one found in modern hotels that made you feel you were inside a fish tank. Reaching into his pocket, Wellstone pulled out a narrow-bladed chisel and a rubber mallet. Inserting the chisel into the gap between the window and the sill, he tapped quietly with the mallet—once, twice, three times—until the steel end of the chisel was seated firmly in the narrow channel. Then, grasping the end of the chisel, he pushed up, gently at first and then with increasing force. If he could possibly avoid it, he didn't want to break the glass—that would mean switching to the less appealing plan B, in which he'd have to overturn things and make it appear an aborted robbery. But luck remained with him: the window was unlocked and the sash slid up easily and noiselessly.

He raised the window about two feet, then turned and once more made a careful reconnoiter. He was in complete darkness, and in any case the closest person he could see was in a car waiting at a streetlight two blocks away. Quickly, hand on the sash, he hoisted one leg over, then the other, slipping between the curtains and letting them close again behind him. No point in shutting the window: he didn't plan to be here long.

He took out a flashlight and, using its low beam, looked around the room. With a rush of adrenaline, he saw Moller's unmistakable equipment case, closed and sitting on the floor at the end of the bed. Now there was no doubt: he was in the right room. Daisy's images had shown that the case was zippered and latched. Moving quickly to the door, he examined its locks. In addition to the usual hotel doorknob, it had both a chain and a hinged privacy bolt. He couldn't secure the chain—that would be a dead giveaway—but he could swing the small latch halfway across the jamb, which would buy him extra time while not arousing suspicion. This probably wouldn't be necessary, but Wellstone wasn't the kind to take chances.

Now he returned to the suitcase at the end of the bed. Leaving his flashlight on and placing it on a side table, he took out his phone and snapped several shots of Moller's case from different angles. Would it be locked? He lifted it and placed it gently on the foot of the bed. It was surprisingly heavy. He unzipped it and tried the latches, and they snapped open—unlocked! He took a brief video of its contents, plucking out one item after another and turning it this way and that for the camera. He'd seen a lot of this stuff already, thanks to Daisy, but up close the items appeared a lot more fake, especially the silver wand, which felt as light as aluminum, and the smoked glass, distressed to look like obsidian.

There it was: the camera. It was snugged into its padding in a far corner of the case. Wellstone lifted it up and, still wearing gloves, took great care when placing it on the duvet cover. This was what made the case so heavy, and this was what he'd come for: the instrument of his vengeance.

He repositioned his flashlight, then carefully felt around the edges of the device. It looked like an old Hasselblad 500C box camera, except it was larger and covered with a wooden inlay. The standard controls for focusing and exposure were visible, but there was also a row of unlabeled buttons. A small metal box had been retrofitted to the antique upper lid, most likely the Bluetooth apparatus Daisy had told him of.

But enough gawking: time to figure out just how Moller worked his scam. Wellstone slid his fingers around the flanks of the camera, trying to figure out how it opened while being careful to leave no signs of tampering. Damn, it was like a Chinese puzzle box…and then, suddenly, he heard a click and the lid sprang open. He must have accidentally pressed a hidden detent. His luck was still holding.

Now, adjusting the flashlight once again, he carefully opened the lid. The interior was even more complicated than he'd expected: a couple of circuit boards, what looked like RAM chips, and a microprocessor, in addition to the guts of a 6×6 camera. But he searched in vain for the hard disk or SSD drive he knew must be somewhere inside. In his coat pocket, he had a disk cloner that could create a bit-for-bit image in ten minutes, as well as a two-terabyte flash stick. But he couldn't copy the disk if he couldn't find the damn thing.

Muttering a curse, he picked up his flashlight and bent over the device, peering more closely. No hard disk or SSD array for storage…

It was then that Wellstone noticed, hidden under a ribbon cable, a line of identical black chips, each the size of a thumbnail and thin as a communion wafer. They had tiny labels, which bore equally tiny printing in German. What the hell were these?

He looked at some of the labels. GEISTER. HEXEN. DÄMONEN. SKELETTE.

In an epiphany, Wellstone understood. Those small, identical chips were nonvolatile memory cards, such as one would find in a home security camera. And each held phony digital images. Wellstone knew enough German to translate the handwritten labels. *Geister*—ghosts. *Hexen*—witches. *Dämonen*—demons. *Skelette*—skeletons. That bastard would snap a photograph, and then—by manipulating this camera—choose a fake from his miniature gallery to superimpose over the final. It confirmed what he thought.

There was no hard disk in the camera, after all—but this was even better. He could take one or two of the chips—he'd snag the ones at the far end—and Moller probably wouldn't even notice for a while. No need for any time-consuming copying. Pushing the ribbon cable to one side, he fished his fingers into the device, preparing to pluck out the last two chips in the array.

But it wasn't as easy as he expected. The entire row of chips was held in place by a steel rod that lay across their upper edges and snapped into place on the camera's inner body. It should be a simple matter of lifting this retaining rod and removing the chips. But the rod seemed stuck in place, and he couldn't see what was—

All of a sudden, he heard voices in the hallway outside the door.

Wellstone felt his heart freeze over as he recognized Betts's argumentative voice. "Couldn't it wait?"

"I don't wish to leave it unattended." This was Moller's voice.

Wellstone crouched over the bed, paralyzed by surprise and dismay. What should he do?

"Hurry up!" Betts shouted petulantly, not caring if he disturbed the entire wing of the hotel.

"*Eine Minute!*" Moller called back irritably. Then, in a lower voice: "*Die dumme Ames geben mir keine Ruhe.*"

The voice was now directly outside the door. Wellstone yanked at the retaining rod, first gently, then violently. It wouldn't give.

He heard the click of a lock disengaging, heard a

rattling sound as the latch he'd partially set kept the door of the room from opening. Wellstone realized he had no choice. He couldn't take the entire camera. He didn't dare break it apart. Quickly, he reached for his phone, took a series of burst shots of the camera's interior.

More rattling at the door. "*Dieser verfluchte Schlüsseloch!*" came the mutter from just outside.

Moving like lightning, Wellstone put the camera back into its foam nest; closed, latched, and zipped the case; placed it back on the floor; smoothed the end of the bed; put his phone in his pocket; made sure his tools—flashlight, mallet, chisel, drive cloner, and USB stick—were all accounted for; then walked backward until he felt the window curtains brush against him, all the while keeping an eye on the door.

"Gerhard!" he heard Betts call in an impatient travesty of a German accent. "Move your *schweinehund* ass!"

"*Halt deine Fresse!*" Moller snapped in response as he gave the door a mighty shove. This time, the privacy latch slipped out of position and the door flew open. But even as it did so, the window beyond the curtains was silently closing. And by the time Moller had snapped on the light, Wellstone was jogging through the darkened parking lot, away from State Street and heading for Broughton. Only he wasn't as silent as he'd been when approaching Moller's room. Now he was repeating something under his breath as he ran:

Shit. Shit. Shit. Shit. Shit…

41

Pendergast sat on the veranda of the Chandler House, a long balcony of ornate ironwork that ran along the second floor. Below him, groups of tourists passed by on the sidewalk. An undercurrent of traffic noise rose up from the busy streets, with the occasional honk or squeal of brakes. The round table at which he sat—made, like the veranda itself, of filigreed iron—held five items: a copy of the latest *New England Journal of Medicine*, a bottle of calvados, and three snifters, two of which were empty. The agent's gaze, like that of a statue, was fixed on the middle distance. No one else was present and, to ensure his tranquility, he had secured a large enough block of rooms so that anybody who came out onto their own patch of veranda would not disturb him with an obnoxiously close presence.

Now the room door squeaked open, and Constance emerged from their suite onto the veranda. As she closed it, Pendergast said: "*Bonsoir*."

"A sou for your thoughts?" she asked as she took a seat beside him.

"I was just observing the chiaroscuro the hotel's lights throw across this balcony of ours."

"The effect reminds me of the cut-paper doilies we used to make as children."

Pendergast roused himself, poured her out a measure of calvados, and picked up his own snifter.

"No doubt you're eager to hear the results of my second conversation with the grande dame upstairs," Constance asked, cradling her snifter.

"Above all things."

"I've spent many hours conversing with her, but I'm not sure how relevant the intelligence I've gathered is—except, perhaps, in filling in some missing corners of the triptych you're painting."

"You flatter me, my dear. My mental construct of Savannah and its crimes is a diptych at most."

Constance took a sip of calvados. "As I mentioned, Frost is a most unusual woman—but she is not the blood-sucking parasite some of the staff believe her to be. She puts on a forbidding disposition in order to be left alone. In younger days, she must have appeared to staff and guests as nothing less than a force of nature. Even now, she's not as frail as she wants people to believe, and her mind remains acute. She's lost none of her memories. Her learning and intelligence are profound." She paused a moment. "By our second meeting, in fact, she had somehow intuited that I...was rather older than my appearance would suggest."

Pendergast's eyebrows shot up. "And how did she deduce that?"

Constance hesitated. "Aloysius, she told me that—" Then she broke off, with a shake of her head sharp enough to disturb her bobbed hair.

"It's not germane, really. I shall tell you sometime when we're at leisure."

"Did you tell her your history?"

"The barest minimum, trying to draw her out. But she still refused to give me any details of her life before Savannah. What I can tell you is she's read deeply in literature, philosophy, history, and science. She's very upset by Ellerby's death. She was angry at him for defying her somehow—yet she also seems to feel responsible."

"In what way?" Pendergast murmured.

"That was obscure. All I have are my speculations."

A large delivery truck rattled down the street beneath them, causing the iron veranda to tremble slightly. "By all means, speculate," Pendergast said.

"Very well. But please don't criticize my logic or ask me to provide supporting arguments."

"I would never be so importunate."

Constance suppressed a smile and looked out over the darkness of Chatham Square. "I have three thoughts in particular. One: Although she had plenty of money when she arrived in Savannah, she did not originally come from money. I believe her childhood was happy, but poor. Two: As much as she mourns Ellerby's passing—we didn't touch on just *how* close their relationship was—I sense that she had an even deeper emotional connection somewhere else, somewhere in her past. She may have lost someone, or left someone, long ago, and now in her old age she regrets it bitterly. And three: I sense that she carries a burden of guilt that manifests itself in grief—and fear."

"Guilt about Ellerby's death?"

"No, something she did long before that. It's been

her companion a long time—and it's growing more acute."

Pendergast took a long, thoughtful sip. "Very interesting, Constance."

She hesitated. "There's one other thing."

He put down the snifter.

"She has a book, very much thumbed, that she keeps with her almost constantly. Naturally, it became an object of my interest. I took the opportunity to examine it."

Pendergast leaned forward. "And?"

"It was a copy of *Spoon River Anthology*."

"Edgar Lee Masters?" Pendergast sat back, visibly deflated.

"Not exactly Ezra Pound's *Cantos*, I know. But poetry can be loved for its sentiment rather than its quality."

Pendergast waved a hand, conceding the point.

"In any case," Constance went on, "it was the inscription on the flyleaf that I thought might interest you. It's not taken from the book itself. It reads: 'From Z.Q. to A.R. To me, you'll always be "that great social nomad who prowls on the confines of a docile, frightened order." Berry Patch, 4/22/72.'"

Pendergast asked Constance to repeat the inscription again.

"And the author of that quotation?" Pendergast asked. "I'm not familiar with it."

"I googled it and came upon the French philosopher Michel Foucault. But it's been altered. The original quotation in full is: *The lyricism of marginality may find inspiration in the image of the outlaw, the great social nomad, who prowls on the confines of a docile, frightened order.*"

Pendergast pulled the bottle of calvados toward him and began turning it slowly, round and round, lost in thought. At last, he said: "What do you think it means?"

"That this A.R. is an outlaw—and a successful one."

He put down the bottle. "And who is 'A.R.'?"

Constance gave a small, gentle laugh. "I would wager *she* is A.R. To this Z.Q., anyway."

Pendergast withdrew his fingers from the bottle. "I would agree. Also that she is the outlaw."

"An admirable outlaw—at least to Z.Q."

"Indeed. And now let me tell you something of interest. You mentioned before that you could find no trace of her existence before 1972. That intrigued me. I took a turn around the FBI's most excellent databases and discovered that Felicity Winthrop Frost died in 1956."

Constance raised an eyebrow.

"She died at twelve and was buried in a cemetery in a place called Puyallup, a suburb of Seattle."

"How very strange," Constance said. "What does it mean?"

"Quite simply, our proprietress stole somebody else's identity. In the days before the Social Security Administration computerized their records and cross-referenced them with deaths, it was not difficult. You found a dead person of about your age, got his or her social security number, and obtained a driver's license in that name. With those, you could claim to have lost your birth certificate and get a replacement copy. The birth certificate would get you a passport, bank account, any official documents you wanted."

"And that's why I could find nothing about her prior to 1972."

"Precisely. She assumed her new identity in that year, the same year she received the book. Perhaps it was a parting gift as she went off into the world as a different person." He paused. "Excellent work, Constance. I congratulate you."

"You made the most important contribution yourself."

"You trimmed the tree—I merely mounted the star."

"I'm still not sure how this information advances your case."

"Information is like electricity; it powers the light that allows us to see our way forward."

"Who said that?" Constance asked.

"I did."

Constance finished her cognac, set down the snifter, pushed back her chair, and stood up. "If you don't mind, then, I'll go spend an hour or so in my claw-footed bathtub."

Pendergast rose and—wordlessly—drew her to him, kissing her good night. As their lips parted, she hesitated a moment, then leaned in again, her arms encircling his neck. Their lips met once more—longer, this time. Then Pendergast—ever so gently—withdrew from the embrace. Constance unwound her arms from him and took a step away.

"So," she said, her voice lower and huskier than usual. "It's as I thought."

"My dearest Constance—" Pendergast began again, but she stilled him by pressing a fingertip to his lips.

"Please, Aloysius. Say no more." Then she smiled faintly, drew a few stray mahogany hairs away from her eyes with the same fingertip, and left through the French doors.

Sitting down again, Pendergast's gaze returned

to the middle distance of the veranda. For five minutes, then ten, he remained motionless. And then, with a troubled sigh, he pulled his cell phone from his jacket, activated an internet browser, and began searching.

42

Forty-five minutes later, Agent Coldmoon emerged onto the veranda via the same door through which Constance had exited. He stepped out and glanced around at the evening vista. "Nice. Very nice. How come you've got a balcony and I don't?"

"You used to," Pendergast replied. "I'm afraid your addiction to burnt, boiled coffee cost you your balcony privileges. Please—have a seat."

Coldmoon settled into one of the uncomfortable iron chairs. At least the view was pleasing and the night breeze was, for a change, dry and refreshing. He noticed the bottle of calvados, saw one glass was empty.

"Do you mind?" he said, even as he poured himself a large measure.

"Not at all, as long as you appreciate that snifter now contains about forty dollars' worth of fine calvados, and not peppermint schnapps."

Coldmoon laughed. "What's up?" he asked, taking a swig.

"I wanted to give you notice that we're leaving shortly."

"Oh?" Coldmoon had never tasted calvados before, and he liked how the faint taste of apple softened the bite of the brandy. "Did you solve the case while sitting out here?"

"We are taking up another avenue of investigation. We're flying to Portland."

Coldmoon almost coughed up his drink. "Portland? As in Oregon?"

"That is correct. We need to leave within the hour, if we're to make a connection in Atlanta for the last flight of the night."

"But—but that's on the West Coast!"

"Your knowledge of geography overwhelms me."

Before Coldmoon could reply, Pendergast continued. "I can imagine the protests you're likely to make. Let me assure you I wouldn't suggest this trip if I didn't think it *absolutely* necessary. We'll only be gone one day."

"What about the investigation here?" Coldmoon said. "We're at a critical point. And that son of a bitch Drayton? He's already raising hell about our failure to apprehend a suspect."

"He will say what he will say."

"And what about the *vampire*?" Coldmoon asked with a hint of malice. "What the hell are we to gain from the trip? What's the purpose?"

"We've reached a point in the case where I believe we must go backward in time before we can move forward."

"You're talking in riddles again," said Coldmoon, draining his brandy. "We're equal partners now— remember?"

Pendergast leaned forward. "Here is why we must make this journey, *partner*." He went on to speak in a low voice, in short sentences. Coldmoon, listening, swore first in Lakota, then in English—and then remained quiet until Pendergast sat back once again.

"Okay, Kemosabe," he said after a silence, rolling his eyes. "That's some crazy shit. But I've been with you long enough not to dismiss it out of hand. I'll ride shotgun with you. On two conditions. First: if there's any blowback from this little field trip, you'll take one for the team."

"Agreed."

"And second—Oregon isn't all that far away from Colorado. I can't promise you that, once I'm out west, I won't get a hankering to head for Denver. Where my real job is waiting."

"I'll take that chance."

"In that case, I'd better start packing." And Coldmoon stood up.

"Armstrong?"

At the sound of his first name, Coldmoon glanced back. "Yeah?"

"*Pilámaya*."

"No problem." And Coldmoon vanished into the hotel.

43

For Coldmoon, the next twelve hours passed in a blur. There was some frantic packing; then an Uber to the Savannah/Hilton Head airport; then a bumpy but mercifully short ride in a prop plane to Atlanta—and then they were moving briskly through the big airport, Pendergast's badge perpetually clearing the way, and onto the flight to Portland with minutes to spare. Once again in the air, Coldmoon—against his better judgment—ordered two vodka tonics. He woke up in Oregon with a headache, and followed Pendergast to an airport rental agency. He took the passenger seat while Pendergast got behind the wheel of a Jeep Wrangler. Coldmoon took notice of how rare this arrangement was: Pendergast behind the wheel, playing chauffeur. He realized the senior agent had mapped everything out in advance, handling logistics effortlessly, batting aside impediments.

At four o'clock in the morning, as they were driving north out of Portland in a drizzling rain, Coldmoon fell asleep again.

He woke up, cramped and sore, to a leaden sky. He checked his watch, compensating for the time change, and found it was six in the morning, local time. Pendergast was guiding the vehicle up a twisty road that hugged the side of a mountain. Coldmoon sat up and wiped the drizzle away from the window as best he could. Outside he could see a wild landscape: mountain after mountain, many with their peaks cloaked by lowering clouds. The forest was endless, Sitka spruce, western white pine, mountain hemlock, and a dozen other shaggy specimens he couldn't identify. At least, he thought, they were in the west. He cracked the window and breathed deep of the fresh mountain air. He was heartily sick of the east.

Pendergast, not taking his eyes off the road, offered him a large insulated cup of black coffee. Mumbling his thanks, Coldmoon took it, figuring that Pendergast must have stopped for gas while he was asleep. It tasted about like he expected, but at least it was lukewarm.

They rode in silence for another twenty minutes, weaving through a labyrinth of hills and low mountains. The road was narrow and potholed. Only two or three cars went by the other way. Now and then they passed a house or a trailer huddled at the end of dirt driveways; once they passed a lake and a small dairy farm carved out of the forest; but otherwise there was only mist, and looming mountains, and an unrelieved dark green.

Pendergast turned off whatever road they'd been on and started north on a road with a sign marking it as State Route 21. As they continued, Coldmoon felt the coffee warming his insides, and he found a feeling of claustrophobia stealing over him. He'd grown up

in the Dakotas, where trees such as these were rare
enough to have individual names. But he'd seen a lot
of the world since then. During the last two cases with
Pendergast alone, he'd experienced the deep snows of
Maine, the beaches of Miami, and the swampy bayous
of the Everglades. But those places felt different.
Here…here there were too many damn trees. And
they grew thickly, leaning over the vehicle so it was
like traveling in a tunnel. Where the hell were they?
Coldmoon pulled out his cell phone and tried to fire
up the GPS, but there was no signal. On impulse, he
reached into the glove compartment and retrieved the
Washington-Oregon map he found inside. He turned
it this way and that, looking for Route 21. He saw
Mount St. Helens—Christ, he hoped they weren't
headed that way—but the roads were like strands of
vermicelli scattered here and there randomly across
the folded paper, and he couldn't find Route 21. At
last, he gave up.

Pendergast pulled the vehicle off the road and into
a small parking lot with a wooden sign that read GOAT
MOUNTAIN TRAILHEAD. He glanced at Coldmoon.

"Where are we?" Coldmoon asked.

"Washington State. Roughly twenty miles north of
the Mount Adams Wilderness."

Coldmoon digested this a moment. "Great. Wonderful. And that is…where?"

"Close to the man I told you about, the one we
came all this way to see. Dr. Zephraim Quincy."

"Anybody who lives out in this wilderness doesn't
need to *be* a doctor. He should *get* a doctor."

In response, the FBI agent continued north on 21.
In about two miles they passed a small, battered road
sign that read WALUPT LAKE, and Pendergast slowed

again. Blinking against the mist, Coldmoon could make out the lake: its water almost black, surrounded by deep forest among the omnipresent mountains. On the far side, beyond a stand of trees, was a small farm, with a shed and a barn and just enough flat acreage to grow something. Beyond, the mountains rose again.

Pendergast remained still for a moment. Then, reaching into the back seat, he brought out a padded duffel he'd brought along. To Coldmoon's surprise, he pulled out a DSLR camera body. Coldmoon knew something about fine cameras, and he noticed the senior agent was holding the latest Leica S3. Reaching into the duffel once more, Pendergast pulled out a lens: an aspheric Leica Summicron-S, naturally. That piece of glass alone had to go for eight or nine grand— if you could find one.

"Couldn't you have found a more expensive camera?" he asked. "What's wrong with your cell phone, anyway?"

"For my purposes, quality is key. Now, please be silent: I want to achieve just the right degree of bokeh."

"Are you trying to win a photography award?"

"Only indirectly. My primary aim is to produce a maximal amount of nostalgia."

Pendergast fitted the lens to the camera, aimed it at the farm across the lake, took his time focusing, and then shot several careful exposures at various focal lengths. Then he put the camera back into its duffel, crossed a bridge over one end of the lake, killed the engine, and let the car coast off the highway and down the grade onto the approach to the farm. They came to a stop behind the barn. Pendergast got out— quietly—and Coldmoon did the same. They eased their doors shut, Coldmoon taking his cues from Pendergast.

Beyond the barn stood an old two-story farmhouse. It had been handsome once, in a colonial "five over four with a door" style that seemed out of place here, with a variety of sheds and other outbuildings attached to its flanks. But time had been unkind to it: the outbuildings had fallen into disrepair, and the house itself hadn't been painted in at least a decade. A few of the shutters on the second story were leaning away from their windows.

The entire place was cloaked in the silence of early morning, mist rising from the lake beyond the farmstead.

Pendergast motioned, and they crept into the barn. In the gloom, Coldmoon could make out various machinery, most of which was unfamiliar to him. There was also a hayloft and what looked like cow stalls and a milking apparatus, long abandoned.

"So what're we looking for in here?"

"What's the term? Fishing expedition. This will be our only chance to investigate."

But there appeared to be nothing of interest. They exited the open barn door on the far side of the structure. Pendergast stopped a moment, pausing to take in the surroundings. Then he approached the farmhouse, Coldmoon at his side. Together they mounted the steps, and Coldmoon instinctively put his back to one side of the door while Pendergast rang the bell.

There was no response. Pendergast rang again; rapped loudly; rang a third time. Finally, Coldmoon heard a stirring within. A minute later the front door opened partway, revealing an old man dressed in long johns, who—with his white hair and beard—would have resembled Father Christmas if he weren't so thin. In one hand he held a Remington 870, muzzle pointed at the floor.

"What's all the ruckus?" he asked. "You sick?"

"We're quite well, thank you," Pendergast replied.

"Then what the hell are you disturbing me for at seven in the morning?" The man's eyes had an almost mischievous sparkle, but the barrel of the shotgun lifted about twenty degrees toward the horizontal.

Pendergast had his ID and shield out while the weapon was still in motion. "We'd like to ask you just a couple of questions, Dr. Quincy."

The old man considered this. Then he shrugged and stepped back from the door. Quickly, Pendergast stepped in, followed by Coldmoon. The man led them down a short hallway and into a room that once was probably a consultation office, full of old magazines and some medieval-looking medical diagrams hanging on the walls. While everything was old, it was spotless and organized. There was a desk, an examining table, two chairs. Quincy slipped behind the desk and gestured for the agents to sit.

"I'd offer you coffee, but it's too damned early," the man said, moving a stack of medical journals aside to clear his desktop. Something in his economy of movement made Coldmoon realize that, though the man was old, he must have been virile, even formidable, in his prime.

"We appreciate your letting us in," Pendergast said.

"You mentioned you had a couple of questions," Dr. Quincy said. "I'm going to hold you to that."

Pendergast gestured as if to say this was fair enough. "You offered medical assistance when we rang the door, I believe. Are you still practicing?"

The man laughed. "Now, how should I answer that to an officer of the law?"

"If I weren't an officer of the law, and I came here with a caddis fly hook stuck in my thumb, what would you do?"

The man considered this. "Well, seeing as only locals ever come by here, I'd extract the hook, stitch the thumb up if necessary, apply some Betadine, and—since my surgical license expired fifteen years ago—tell the patient to be more careful with his fly fishing."

He laughed, and Pendergast gave a slight smile in return. "That's a shrewd answer, Doctor, and I didn't hear a word of it. Besides, my interest lies more in your memories than it does in the present."

"Is that a fact?" said the old man. "And why would two FBI agents have any interest in my memories?"

"Because we have a lot of threads, and we're hoping you could help us braid them together. Now, I do know something of your background—please tell me if I'm mistaken about anything. Fifty years or so ago, you were enrolled at the University of Washington School of Medicine—the only medical school in the state at that time."

The man nodded silently.

"Your family ran the farm here: raspberries, dairy products, apples, and turkeys. Your mother had died while you were in college and, with you as the only child, your father looked after the farm while you went to medical school. Correct so far?"

"If it's my biography you're writing, add a heroic war record and a moon landing while you're at it," the old man said. But, Coldmoon noticed, the humor did not dispel the fact that when Pendergast began asking questions, the doctor had become guarded.

"Heroic isn't actually too far from the truth," Pendergast continued. "Because when your father was injured in a farming accident and could no longer do the work, you came home. The farm was heavily mortgaged, and with your medical school bills on top of that, it was impossible for you to continue your studies."

Dr. Quincy said nothing.

"You did all you could. But your father's injury meant that you had to give up medicine to manage the farm." Pendergast paused. "Everything still accurate?"

"You're telling more than you're asking," the doctor said, "and that's more than a 'couple of questions' already. Get to the point."

"What I'm curious about, Doctor, is how you went from such dire straits—dropping out of med school, managing the farm alone, trying to keep it all afloat—to finishing your medical degree and residency in orthopedic surgery, hiring someone to help around the farm, paying off the mortgage, and turning this place into a going enterprise for almost forty years, even while maintaining a successful surgical practice in Tacoma."

"You're the biographer," the doctor said. "I guess you'll just have to figure it out."

"Biographers can't work without sources. I can give you a few more specifics, if that will help. We're not interested, precisely, in your good fortune. But we are interested in someone you were acquainted with many years ago. Someone who, like you, appreciated poetry. Someone whose initials are, or should I say *were*, A.R."

The old man abruptly twitched, as if administered

a galvanic shock. Coldmoon could only admire how quickly he mastered it.

"We're not here to arrest you—or the woman in question. What I propose is a simple exchange of information. I imagine you can guess what I want to know. And I *know* you must be eager—despite yourself—to hear the information I can offer about A.R. in return."

The old man remained silent, but Coldmoon could see the wheels turning in his head.

"Information," the doctor finally repeated.

"Precisely."

The doctor went silent again for several moments. Then: "What do you want to know, exactly, about this person?"

"The more light you can shed, the better."

"I'm not going to do that," Quincy said, his voice low and harsh. "I made a promise, and I won't go back on it—no matter how many years have passed."

This time, it was Pendergast who remained silent.

Finally, the doctor shifted in his chair. "This person you mention. Is she...still alive?"

Pendergast bowed his head in assent.

Coldmoon could see a succession of conflicting emotions cross the doctor's face before he again mastered himself.

"And where might she be?"

At this, Pendergast smiled. "How about that exchange of information?"

After a long silence, the doctor said: "I made a promise."

Pendergast rose. "Well then, I fear we have nothing more to speak about. Agent Coldmoon? Let us go."

"Hold on!"

Pendergast paused and turned. In a softer, kinder voice, he said, "Doctor, I truly appreciate the promise you made. But we're speaking of events that happened half a century ago. You—and the lady—are, quite frankly, nearing the close of life. If there's any hope of your ever learning who she is now, or where she is—this is it."

The doctor said, "You first."

Pendergast gazed at him steadily, then said: "She owns a hotel in Savannah, Georgia. And she has no possession she treasures more than the book you gave her."

At this the doctor flushed and passed a trembling hand over his white hair.

Pendergast quoted, *"To me, you'll always be 'that great social nomad, who prowls on the confines of a docile, frightened order.'"*

The effect of this was even more profound. The doctor struggled to maintain his composure. *"She* showed it to you?"

"Not intentionally." Then, very gently, Pendergast said, "And now, Doctor, it's your turn."

The doctor removed a cotton handkerchief, mopped his face and tucked it back into his pocket.

"I found her by the side of the lake. She had had...a terrible fall."

"You saved her life?"

He nodded. "I took her in, fixed her up, nursed her back to health."

"What kind of injury?"

"A compound displaced fracture of the right femur."

"The lady still has a limp."

"I fixed her up as well as anyone could under the, ah, circumstances."

"You were in love with her?"

Coming out of the blue, this question surprised Coldmoon almost as much as it did the doctor. But it had the desired effect; on the heels of a sustained assault, the old man's defenses cracked under this unexpected blow. He sank back in his chair with an almost indistinct nod. "We loved each other. Very much."

"But she left. Why?"

He shook his head.

"Let me help you: She was in trouble, she was an outlaw, she had committed a serious crime. To protect you and herself, she had to leave, establish a new identity. And so she disappeared from your life."

He nodded.

"What was her crime?"

A long silence ensued. "She'd stolen something."

"It must have been quite valuable."

"I suppose. But the big crime was not stealing it, but *how* she stole it."

"What was it?"

"Some sort of computer, or device, in a briefcase. She said it was going to make her fortune."

"What did it do?"

"She never explained, except in veiled hints. Something about time."

"Time?"

"She made an odd comment about the flow of time. That's all I know."

"How did she steal this item?"

"I'm sorry, but that's the question I'm not going to answer—the one at the heart of my promise. If I told you, the FBI would come down on both of us like a ton of bricks. We'd go to prison for sure."

Pendergast sighed. "In that case, I have nothing further to ask." And he signaled to Coldmoon that it was time to leave.

"Hold on!" the doctor said again as Pendergast prepared to rise. "You haven't told me her new name."

Pendergast looked at him. "And you haven't told me her old one."

The man frowned, sitting up again, pugnacity flaring in his rheumy eyes.

"Now it's your turn to go first," said Pendergast.

Quincy's white knuckles gripped his chair. Coldmoon could see him struggling. "Alicia Rime," he finally said.

"Her name now is Felicity Winthrop Frost. The hotel she owns in Savannah is called the Chandler House. An excellent establishment. And she is a most formidable woman, if a bit frail—and quite lonely."

After a moment, Quincy nodded. "No doubt."

Pendergast rose, followed by Coldmoon. He began to turn toward the door. Then he stopped. "One other thing," he said. "Is it possible she used this mysterious instrument you mentioned to pay off your mortgage and cover your medical school tuition?"

"I've got no idea," Quincy said. "I've said too much already. I think it's time for you to leave—right now."

That was it. Coldmoon followed Pendergast out of the farmhouse, down the steps, and back to the waiting vehicle. And the whole time, Dr. Quincy stood on the steps in his long underwear, silent and motionless, a look of infinite sorrow on his lined face.

44

Gannon heard a voice raised in complaint, as she'd known she would eventually, from the end of the hall where Betts was reviewing the daily rushes. She already had a good idea of what he was going to say, but she'd learned it was better to let him mansplain "his" ideas to her rather than come up with them independently and try to sell them to him.

"Gannon?" she heard. "*Gannon!* You around?"

She headed down the hall and into the editing room. Moller was in the chair next to Betts, a dour presence.

"Come in," Betts said, gesturing. "Take a look."

She came in and stood behind them. On the computer screen was the last of the footage from the previous day.

"This is great," Betts said. "Love your angles. You really nailed it."

Gannon couldn't help but blush. Normally, Betts was stingy with his compliments.

"Moller, you look good, too. Right? I hope you're happy."

Moller bowed his head in grave affirmation. He never looked happy, but that, Gannon realized, was part of his shtick.

"But here's the thing," Betts went on. "We've got all this footage of Moller, the crazy mob scene, the press—all great stuff. But you know what we don't have?"

She knew perfectly well, but she said, "No."

"We don't have creepy footage in a lonely cemetery. We need atmospherics. And we need to see Moller all alone, checking out some haunted place. We can't get that in broad daylight with a big crowd around. You know what I mean?"

"I agree."

"Good. Now look at this, here." He pressed a button and some of Pavel's Steadicam footage started rolling on the screen, showing the cops working the crime scene among unkempt tombs.

He paused the video. "There. You see, behind them, back through all that overgrowth? I was there. You can just barely see it, but there's more graves. And a mausoleum, with a door partway open. Hard to tell, but it looks like it's coming off its hinges. Maybe we can get in, film inside."

"I see that."

"Good. That's where we need to shoot. We'll bring some lights with filters, a fog machine, do it up good. See if we can't register some more evil, I mean *real* evil, like the vampire himself—if you get my drift."

Moller's dour look deepened. "But that area of overgrown tombs is not where the young man was abducted. It is not where I registered a strong supernatural presence."

"That doesn't matter. I mean, it *does* matter—but this is a cemetery, for Chrissakes. There're ghosts all around, right? And we need to get some good B-roll in the abandoned cemetery, after dark. That's the perfect spot to do it. Gannon here will get the fogger going, generate some mist. With low, raking lighting, it's going to look super. Right, Gannon?"

"Absolutely."

"What do you say, Gerhard?"

"I am willing to try. When do you plan to make this excursion?"

"When? As soon as the sun sets, of course."

45

As they drove away from the farm and into the inky maze of mountains, Coldmoon turned to Pendergast. "That was interesting."

"What I found most curious was the injury," said Pendergast.

"Broken leg? Why is that?"

"Think about it. What was she doing way out there, in the middle of nowhere, all alone, with a broken leg?"

"Maybe she fell off a mountain."

"Perhaps. Perhaps not..." Pendergast slowed the car at a fork—again, unmarked—and after a moment chose the left-hand route. "What was your opinion of the fellow?"

"A lost soul. Eighty-plus years old and the poor guy's still pining for that woman, never gotten over her. She must've been quite the firecracker in her day."

They drove on in silence before turning onto Route 141—another backwoods road, but at least one that seemed more traveled. Half an hour later, they merged onto I-84 in the direction of Portland. Coldmoon felt himself relax at the wide expanse of highway ahead, and the dark forbidding mountains beginning to recede in the rearview mirror.

"So," Coldmoon said. "I'm still not clear how you found that guy, to be honest, or what it has to do with the murders."

"I explained as little as possible back in Savannah, because I wanted you to be a check on any assumptions or hasty conclusions I might have made. I knew that Frost had found her new identity in this region of Washington State—in the cemetery in Puyallup. Given that the book Constance examined appeared to be a parting gift from her lover, it seemed a safe assumption that she'd lived in the area—and that was when I realized Berry Patch was not just some private trysting spot, but a town. Or, given its minuscule population, what is known in Washington State as a 'populated place.'"

"I didn't see any town at all."

"A scattering of houses and a post office. Population eighty-five."

"Sounds like something out of *Li'l Abner*," Coldmoon said.

"The small population was, for me at least, a blessing: there proved to be only one resident with the initials Z.Q."

"So. You think the old guy is going to look her up?"

"I imagine a titanic struggle is going on in his mind about that very question."

"But that doesn't really answer my basic question: how does this connect to the murders? You didn't shed much light on that back in Savannah, either."

"Consider the following facts: Frost was the person

most intimate with Ellerby; they had an altercation two days before he was murdered; she has refused to help the police; there is gossip in the hotel—admittedly absurd—about her being a vampire; she may not be as weak as she seems; the inscription in the book suggests she once committed a crime; and finally, there's the fact that she assumed a stolen identity. While none of this is dispositive, my intuition tells me she must be connected to the murders in some way."

"And are you any closer to figuring that way out?"

Pendergast said nothing.

"So where to now? I see we're not heading back to the airport."

"Just one more stop, my friend," said Pendergast, putting on his turn signal and preparing to exit the freeway. "I promise you, we'll soon be boarding our flight back to Atlanta, in time for a late dinner at our hotel."

They headed for the off-ramp to some little town on the outskirts of Portland called Corbett. "So what are we doing here?" Coldmoon asked.

"The postmaster who serviced Berry Patch in the early seventies has been dead for twenty years. His wife helped him until he retired. She then remarried, was widowed a second time, and now lives at the Riverview Retirement Home here." He paused. "I'm confident that Berry Patch—like other secluded hamlets, Spoon River included—thrives, or at least thrived, on local gossip."

The Riverview Retirement Home was set high on a ridge, just off a switchback of Corbett Hill Road. From the outside, the place resembled an elementary school—Coldmoon had an extremely low opinion of "rest homes"—but it had a good view of the Columbia River, and inside it was neat and bright. Each resident, it seemed, had a private room. Faith Matheny, the twice-widowed assistant postmistress, was ninety years old and suffered from DLB—dementia with Lewy bodies—which usually presented (so Pendergast informed him) with slower memory loss than Alzheimer's. The old woman claimed to remember nothing of interest after the day of her second marriage. But Pendergast was so charming, and so persuasive, that soon he had her telling so many tales of life in Berry Patch that Coldmoon had trouble keeping track of it all.

The woman did recall Quincy with fondness. He was a fine, handsome young doctor, had a practice in Tacoma but returned most weekends to the farm. He was especially liked because every year, Quincy and his father, who raised turkeys on their farm, would donate birds for and preside over a grand Thanksgiving dinner for all eighty-five residents of Berry Patch, held in the Presbyterian church activities room. Then she frowned. Except that one year, when he didn't show up. Very odd. People said it was because his father was sick in the hospital.

And what year was that? Pendergast asked.

Nineteen seventy-one, she remembered. She was sure, because that was the same year a storm pushed a tree down on the schoolhouse and the Dotsons' mare drowned in Walupt Creek.

Pendergast was as good as his word: within another hour they were taking their first-class seats in a flight that would get them back to Atlanta by seven PM. Pendergast had been quiet during the drive from Corbett to Portland International, which was fine with Cold-moon, who was in no mood for conversation. As the flight attendants closed the doors and went through their preflight routine, Coldmoon felt Pendergast lay a hand lightly on his arm.

"Armstrong," he said, "I plan to spend the flight in meditation. I'd appreciate it if you would make sure I'm not disturbed."

"Sure. I hope to catch forty winks myself." Cold-moon could guess the odd mental exercise Pendergast meant by "meditation"—he'd seen him at it once before, in a snowbound hotel in Maine. He turned away, then sensed Pendergast was still looking at him.

"There's something I would like to share with you," Pendergast said. "It might help shed additional light on this excursion if you search the internet for a certain D. B. Cooper. I think you'll find his story makes interesting reading."

"D. B. Cooper?" The name was familiar to Cold-moon, but he wasn't sure why.

"Yes. The name he actually went by was Dan Cooper, but in their reporting the press mistakenly called him D. B. Cooper. That's the moniker that has persisted over time."

"How much time?"

"Since the day before Thanksgiving of 1971, as a matter of fact." Pendergast leaned back in his seat, crossing his arms over his chest like an Egyptian mummy, and closed his eyes.

46

THE CAMPAIGN BUS EASED through the police barricades blocking Drayton Street. Seeing this, Senator Buford Drayton felt a rush of pride in his historic family. The Draytons went all the way back to the Founding Fathers, and a Drayton had signed the Articles of Confederation. The Draytons had played an important role in the War of Northern Aggression as well. No wonder Savannah had named a street after them. That was one reason he'd chosen Forsyth Park for the kick-off rally of his re-election campaign: to remind voters of his family's patriotic service to the country, and those among its ranks who had fought for the cause—to which there was a splendid monument in Forsyth Park.

The bus came to a halt with a hiss of brakes. Senator Drayton exited his private wood-paneled sitting room in the rear of the bus. He found his chief of staff, communications chief, and campaign chief seated around a table in the main section of the bus, talking strategy. They all rose when he came out.

"I want to personally review the setup," he said.

"Yes, Senator," replied the campaign chief.

An advance man helped the senator down the steps. He stood at the edge of the park and looked around. People were already gathering along East Park Avenue: big crowds of followers, many wearing the signature blue-and-red cap of his campaign with its STAY WITH DRAYTON slogan, many carrying placards with the same message, dressed in red, white, and blue. He heard their distant roar, and it gladdened his heart.

He looked at his watch. Five thirty PM. The rally was scheduled to begin at eight, but as usual he'd actually start at nine: he'd learned that, for political rallies at least, the anticipation of the wait—with supporters chattering excitedly among themselves— brought their energy to a fever pitch. The weather report said scattered thunderstorms, but only a 20 percent chance. The sky was mostly clear; things were looking good.

Across the great lawn, at the foot of the Civil War monument to the Confederate dead, a stage had been set up and draped in bunting. On the vast expanse in front, thousands of chairs were being placed, with plenty of open lawn behind and on either side for the overflow crowd. Drayton began strolling toward the stage.

As he walked, he noticed the chairs were not being arranged as he would have liked.

"Hey, you!" He veered from his route toward a heavyset man who appeared to be a supervisor.

The man turned toward him with an annoyed expression, saw who it was, and changed his look right fast.

"Look here," said Drayton, "are you the one in charge of this?"

"Of setting up the chairs, yes, Senator."

"Then what do you mean by arranging ragged lines such as all these?"

"I'm sorry, Senator."

"Straighten them up. I want them to look crisp and even—not wandering all over like a line of recruits on the first day of boot camp."

He laughed and looked around at his staff, and they all laughed, too.

"Get them nice and straight."

"Yes, Senator, right away."

The supervisor nodded and went off, yelling and gesturing at the workers who were unfolding and setting up the chairs. Drayton watched as they started adjusting them. Hell, if they'd set them up right the first time they wouldn't have to do it again.

He continued to the stage and mounted the steps. A podium, draped in more bunting, stood in the middle, with a row of twenty-one flags forming a backdrop. Above were two giant screens that would project Drayton's tanned and smiling face to the distant parts of the crowd. Now they displayed a still picture of Drayton, gesticulating from the Senate floor, with the tag line *Georgia, Stay with Drayton*.

The engineers were still setting up the last touches of the sound system—two towers of Voice of the Theatre speakers, powerful enough for a rock concert—taping down cables snaking every which way. On the far side, a police sergeant was talking to a group of about thirty cops, apparently issuing assignments.

Drayton turned to his chief of staff. "Where's the commander?"

"You mean Delaplane?" the chief said. "I haven't seen her."

Drayton descended the steps on the other side of the stage and went over to the sergeant, who broke off his talk.

"Welcome, Senator," he said. "Looks like it's going to be a big evening."

"Well, maybe," said Drayton. "Where's your commander?"

"She's not here."

"I can *see* she's not here, Sergeant—" He peered at the man's ID. "Sergeant Adair. What I want to know is, *why* isn't she here?"

"I believe she's tied up with that case, but we've got everything under control, I can assure you."

"I am *not* assured. The top person should be here, supervising. This is the most important security concern in the entire city of Savannah right now. So why the hell isn't she here?"

"Senator, I can inquire if you wish."

"Yes, I *wish*. Jesus."

Sergeant Adair took out his radio and called headquarters. Drayton could hear the dispatcher telling the sergeant that Delaplane was not available.

"Ma'am," said the sergeant, "Senator Drayton is here and wants to, ah, know why she's not supervising the event in person."

After listening to some more back-and-forth, Drayton started to lose his temper. "I want to talk to her personally," he told Adair. "Hand me the damn radio."

The sergeant, his face growing red, spoke to the dispatcher. Drayton took the radio. "This is Senator Drayton. I want to speak to the commander, *now*."

After a long moment, he was finally put through.

"Commander? I'm wondering why you're not here in person, supervising security for the rally. Don't you realize there are people out there threatening to protest and maybe even cause violence? I've got almost half a million dollars invested in this rally."

"Senator, let me assure you, we've got over a hundred officers working security, we've set up portable scans at six entry points—we've got everything under control."

Drayton listened impatiently to the commander's cool voice. "How do you know that if you're not here? I want you *here*, do you understand?"

There was a short silence. "All right, then, I'll be down in about half an hour to review security measures personally. But I assure you again, there's no cause for concern."

"Commander, I can't imagine what's more important than security for the largest political rally in Savannah in years."

"I will be there, Senator. But to your point, I just might mention we have a rather involved homicide investigation in progress—one that you've taken a personal interest in."

"Yes, and whose fault is it that it hasn't been solved?"

The commander signed off and Drayton handed the radio to the sergeant. He turned to his chief of staff. "I thought you had this under control."

"Yes, sir. It will be, sir."

"Christ, what a bunch of numb-nuts. Let's get back to the bus. Makeup's supposed to be here by now, and I've got to start getting ready."

Drayton climbed back on the bus just as the makeup artist arrived with her two assistants and gear.

"Come aboard," Drayton called, "and let's get the show on the road."

They set up a portable makeup chair and table, and Drayton settled down with care and plucked at the creases of his pants to keep them crisp. He leaned his head back against the headrest. "Pay particular attention to my nose and under my eyes," he told the makeup artist. "Cover up those veins. There are going to be cameras from every angle, and hot lights, so make sure it's able to last a couple of hours."

"Of course, Senator."

He closed his eyes and let the woman work over his face, covering up the varicose veins, the dark circles under his eyes, painting and whisking and brushing away his wrinkles and liver spots.

As she worked, he tried to relax and focus on the speech ahead, instead of thinking about that ass-clown running against him, who the polls indicated was creeping ahead. This rally would nip that in the bud. In his mind's eye, he could already hear the roar of approval, see the sea of shining faces and waving placards, the band playing as he walked out on the stage. That moment was always one of the biggest thrills of his life.

47

I<small>T WAS</small> 7:30 <small>PM WHEN</small> Constance was summoned to Pendergast's bedroom, accessible through a common door that joined their two suites. It was ascetic and clean, as his sleeping chambers always were: no doubt he'd asked the staff to remove items of furniture or decoration he deemed objectionable.

"Constance?" Pendergast said. "In here, if you please."

The voice came from an open door on the far side of the bedroom. Constance knew Pendergast had taken this suite for himself specifically because it contained this extra room—a space originally intended, according to hotel legend, as a sniper's nest from which to pick off approaching Yankees. She crossed the bedroom and entered it curiously.

Pendergast had turned it into a sort of private war room. The walls were of the darkest ocher, and there was only a single, narrow window—lending credence to the sniper story. The room was small and piled with books: volumes on local history, astrophysics, the supernatural beliefs of Eastern Europe, and a dozen other subjects that seemed to have no common thread among them. There were also maps of Savannah pinned to the walls, both old and new, with several locations marked with highlighter. When and how Pendergast had amassed all this, she had no idea.

But it was Pendergast himself who gave her the greater shock. His eyes were red-rimmed, and his skin even paler than usual. He was tense and appeared excited. He sat at a desk, a vintage Emeralite lamp throwing an absinthe-colored pool of light over the clutter of books and maps. Despite the room's disorder, the desk itself held only a bottle of Lagavulin, a half-full glass, and a pill container. This, along with his demeanor, disturbed Constance.

"Please have a seat," he told her.

She sat down opposite him.

Pendergast leaned in toward her. "I hope you'll forgive me, dearest Constance, if I seem brusque. There is a need to move quickly. I've put many pieces of the puzzle together, but several are conjectural and others don't fit properly. This is where I need your help. If I'm right, only Frost can supply the answers—and only you are in a position to get those answers from her."

"She might not be up yet. She normally rises at ten PM."

"You may have to rouse her. You've forged a bond with the old woman; you're her confidante."

"I would hardly call myself a confidante."

"But you do feel a certain kinship with her, correct?"

"You could call it that."

"And she feels the same for you?"

Constance nodded. Then she hesitated a moment—

Pendergast's entire frame was radiating eagerness, impatience. And yet she had to speak. "Aloysius, 'kinship'...that's only part of it."

"What do you mean?"

"She knows I'm...not what I seem."

"So you told me."

"She told me my eyes were like hers—except even *more* aged. Sitting there, speaking to her...I could see myself on that sofa, surrounded by dusty books, writing in journals nobody would read." Suddenly, she leaned forward across the table. "Aloysius, the truth is *I've already been that woman*. All those decades Dr. Leng prolonged my life artificially, kept me in that mansion, *I was Felicity Frost*...imprisoned in a young body instead of an old one. And now that Leng's dead, and I'm aging at a normal rate..." She stopped, sat back abruptly. "Am I doomed to live through that twice? I'm *already* superannuated. Don't you see?"

"Constance, I *do* see. And I could tell you I understand. But nobody, nobody could fully appreciate what it's like to be blessed—cursed—with a life like yours. The terrible things you've witnessed, the years you endured alone...those are burdens you never asked to bear. And, alas, burdens only you can truly understand."

Constance sat back, looking at him silently.

"But you've told me, whispered to me, of so much. I know your history almost as well as you do. Your life is not that of Miss Frost. You have me now."

"I have you," she echoed distantly.

Pendergast began to speak. "Constance, I don't know how to—"

"*You* may not," she interrupted. "But I do. So let's get back to the reason you asked me here."

"My dear Constance—"

"You need my help again. What are these answers you mentioned that only I can ask her?"

Pendergast hesitated, then—looking into her eyes—left his sentence unfinished. Instead, he reached into his jacket pocket and removed a folded sheet of what looked like airline stationery. "Four questions."

Constance began to unfold the sheet, but Pendergast put a hand on hers. "She may lie at first—after all, she's spent most of her lifetime lying. But she must be made to understand that what she's been doing all these years now threatens to destroy Savannah. If necessary, show her these." And, reaching into his jacket, he pulled out some beautifully composed photographs of a farm by the edge of a lake.

"How bucolic," she said. Then she unfolded the sheet he'd given her. She read it once, twice, before looking up in disbelief. "These questions...they're mad. Are you—?"

"I know how they seem," he interrupted. "But if I'm right, Frost won't think them mad at all." Reaching forward and taking her other hand, he spoke quietly, urgently, for several minutes. The surprise on Constance's face deepened—then turned slowly to astonishment. Her guardian, quite obviously, was in the throes of some all-consuming puzzle; the hands that gripped hers were icy cold.

"Be gentle, if you can," he said. "But these questions must be asked *with authority*—and you cannot leave her rooms until you're sure she has told you the truth."

"That hardly seems like a recipe for fostering a relationship," Constance said.

"This is more important than any relationship!"

These angry, impatient words seemed to burst out of him. Then Pendergast looked away, and—for the first time in her memory—he flushed deeply.

When he did not release her hand, she detached it herself, then stood immediately. "I'll do what I can."

"I can ask no more," he replied after a pause. "Except to promise you that—"

Without waiting to hear the rest, Constance turned and left the small room. A moment later, her heels could be heard crossing the marble floor of the suite's foyer; then a door opened and shut, and only silence remained.

48

WELLSTONE SAT IN HIS car in the last of the gloaming, outside the three-story brick warehouse that Betts and his crew had leased the top floor of. He had found himself driving there, with no plan in mind, no goal, just a simmering anger mixed with feelings of frustration and humiliation. The son of a bitch had gotten the better of him at every turn: not because he was smarter, but because he had the sort of low cunning of a natural-born bully.

The warehouse was a charming old building—as far as warehouses went—in an old part of Savannah about half a dozen blocks from the Ye Sleepe. How nice for Betts that he could afford both sleeping quarters and a studio setup. It aggravated Wellstone to think of Betts getting this level of financing, or for that matter any financing at all. It was a sad commentary on how gullible people were—the ignorance, lack of education, and credulity that allowed a cynical fraudster like Betts to rake in the bucks.

Thinking about Betts brought to mind the feel of

soufflé sauce sliding down his neck, and the memory offered up a fresh surge of outrage. If he'd gotten his hands on the SD cards with the fake, preloaded images, that would have finished Betts forever and exposed Moller as the charlatan he was. It was almost unbelievable, how those three would-be demons Moller Bluetoothed to the press had gone viral. If he'd been able to expose them as fakes, showing those SD cards of creepy images *before* they had been superimposed on freshly taken photos, that would have gotten him on every morning show in America.

He shouldn't have been surprised that Fayette would screw up. Of course she would. He was annoyed at himself for thinking otherwise. But then, his own plan to access Moller's camera—so carefully thought out—had failed as well. He couldn't imagine how another opportunity would arise. He was out of options.

His thoughts were interrupted by some people coming out of the building. Among them were Betts and Moller. They got into one of two white rental vans parked in front—no Ubers this time. Maybe they were going somewhere to shoot. Seeing Betts and Moller and their self-satisfied faces only sharpened his feelings of shame and anger. Those SD cards were his ticket, and they were so close—Moller was toting his briefcase—that Wellstone could practically touch them. Was he falling into that journalistic trap of becoming personally involved in the story?

Another group of people came out, among them that cute DP, everyone toting camera equipment. The muscle-bound bastard who had pushed him in the restaurant loaded it in the back of a second van and slammed the doors. They all piled inside, laughing and talking.

Wellstone's curiosity went up a notch. They were going on a shoot. But at this time of night? Why the hurry? Nothing like a new murder had happened ... at least, not that he knew of.

Almost without thinking, he started the car. The vans went off in a screech. A moment later, Wellstone's car eased away from the curb and began to trail them.

49

Wellstone followed the two vans through the narrow streets of Savannah, negotiating a snarling mass of detours and police barricades caused by some political rally, until at last all three vehicles were moving freely along Skidaway Road. He realized they must be heading to the cemetery, and sure enough, within minutes the vans took the turn onto Bonaventure Road and pulled into the parking lot at the cemetery welcome center. Wellstone drove past the stone gates, then parked on a nearby side street. He grabbed his Canon with its 200mm telephoto lens and walked back to the cemetery entrance. The vans had left the parking lot and were inside the cemetery now, heading slowly down one of the graveled lanes. They disappeared among the oaks, but Wellstone wasn't concerned: he was certain they were heading to the same place as before—the site of the boy's abduction.

It was a pleasant evening in the cemetery, the dying light throwing long shadows over the silent tombs.

But Wellstone was in no mood to enjoy the peace. This was his last chance. He was going to bird-dog those bastards, Betts and Moller, until he had proof of fraud.

The cemetery was large, and it was close to half a mile to where he finally spotted the vans: parked where he expected at the far end of a lane, in the old part of the cemetery. He approached cautiously. As far as he could tell, there were no tourists or other visitors. The place was deserted. Normally it closed at sunset, but it looked like Betts had obtained permission to film past then.

Moving closer, he saw there was no one in or near the vans. The crime-scene tape had been taken down from the area, and this corner of the cemetery had been restored to its former desuetude and abandonment. So where were they? He located the tomb of the angel with upraised arm, where the abduction had occurred—but there was no one there, either.

He paused to listen. And now, in the gathering silence, he heard faint voices coming from the overgrown area beyond the angel. He moved closer. Crouching and peering from behind a tomb, he realized the group had penetrated the abandoned section of the cemetery. Keeping out of sight, he worked his way closer until he had a clear view of the crew. They were busily setting up lights and a generator near an old mausoleum, overgrown with vines, door partly open. The generator fired up. And there was Moller, the charlatan: suitcase open, black velvet spread over the ground, laying out his bogus equipment.

Wellstone settled down behind a large tombstone, camera in hand, and waited with anticipation. Since they thought they were alone, they might feel freer to engage in open fakery. The 200mm f/2 telephoto lens on his Canon R5 would be able to capture almost anything, even in low light. And there was always the chance they might have some other plan in mind that would, even temporarily, leave Moller's camera exposed. If he had the chance, this time he'd just take the damn thing and run—later he could work out any necessary excuses.

The golden light disappeared from the upper tree branches and the cemetery filled with twilight. Now they began filming. It was obviously just B-roll at first, establishing shots among the gravestones. Moller was still messing around with his equipment. Betts and the muscleman were pushing on the door of the mausoleum, trying to get it to open farther. He watched as they tapped on the hinges with hammers and tried to force it using a crowbar—a disgraceful violation of the privacy of the dead. Their faint curses echoed through the tombs. But the door refused to be forced.

Having no success, the two of them went deeper into the abandoned area while the rest of the crew remained behind, shooting B-roll. Rising, camera in hand, Wellstone followed the pair at a cautious distance. He looped around, then drew closer as it became easier to stay hidden in the thick brush. Here the tombs were even older and unkempt, many listing or broken. Looming through the vegetation ahead, he could now see a semiruined mausoleum, incongruously large. As he crept closer, he saw that it was constructed in the Gothic style, surrounded by a wrought iron fence of spikes, gate open. The bronze door that once shut up the mausoleum lay on the ground, leaving a gaping rectangle of darkness in its place. The mausoleum had been neglected even by the standards of this decayed region of the cemetery: its granite construction was cracked, streaked with damp and covered with splotches of lichen. Ivy climbed up its face. High on either side, the mausoleum had windows that, instead of glass, were covered by a grillwork of bronze. Marble urns had once decorated the pediments on either side of the door, but they had fallen and were scattered about the ground in pieces.

Wellstone watched as Betts and the muscleman ducked through the hanging vines and went inside the mausoleum. For a few minutes, he could see their flashlights flicking around. Then they came out, looking pleased, and began walking back to where the crew was filming. Wellstone followed at a distance.

The B-roll shooting was apparently finished. He could hear Betts talking enthusiastically about the location they'd just found, giving orders to break everything down and move it to the new site.

With remarkable efficiency, the crew disassembled and carried everything deeper into the cemetery, Betts leading the way. Reaching the old mausoleum, they fired up the generator and began setting up once again, hanging lights on tripods and shouting back and forth as twilight gave way to purple darkness. The lights snapped on, casting dramatic shadows. The muscleman set up two odd-looking machines on either side of the shooting area, obscured behind tombstones. Wellstone wondered what they were for—until they both began to spew fog. The mist drifted through the air in sheets and ribbons, looking remarkably realistic, and in the raking lights it blossomed like a lamp lit from within, creating an effect both spooky and dramatic.

Wellstone took pictures of all of this, and a few

short snippets of video as well, documenting the transformation of an ordinary, if creepy, abandoned cemetery into something out of a horror film. While this wasn't yet proof of fraud, it certainly gave a sense of phony manipulation. So far, so good.

And now the crew started setting up a shot with Moller. The DP issued a stream of orders about the lighting and fog machines, while Betts and Moller went over some scene they were about to shoot, the director showing the fraudster where to stand, where to walk, what to do.

Now the scene was ready. Moller pulled out the silver dowsing wand. He began prowling the area as the cameras rolled, holding out the wand with shaky arms while the mists swirled about him. The wand seemed to pull him insistently toward the open door of the mausoleum as if possessed. *"There is something evil here!"* He could hear Moller's expostulations. *"Sehr teuflisch! Evil, evil! In the crypt!"*

Almost trembling with glee, Wellstone got the whole thing on video, making sure to show the lights, the fog machine, Betts's hand directions, the orders of the DP. Although Moller made a show of remaining independent, it was nevertheless staged—all staged. He then set up his wooden camera and took some photos, no doubt fakes like the previous ones. At this point, Wellstone realized that he might not even need the camera's SD cards: this footage would be sufficient to expose what a sham the whole thing was. This might be the very story he needed, dropped right in his lap. His excitement and interest mounted when he realized that they were going to do a second take, and a third, shooting the same scene multiple times. If that wasn't a demonstration of fraud, what could be?

After the third take, Betts seemed satisfied. Instead of packing up, he ordered the crew around, setting up another shot. This one, it seemed, was going to take place inside the mausoleum. The DP and crew moved the lights near the tomb's outside wall, high up on their tripods, so that they shone through the grillwork windows, illuminating the interior of the crypt.

Wellstone shifted his position to get a better view. The lighting, coming through the grillwork, cast a patchwork of crazy shadows inside. Very effective. He took more photos and video clips while they set everything up.

Now the second shoot began. Moller allowed his wand to lead him into the mausoleum. This was accompanied by a lot of jerking and trembling. Pausing inside the door, Moller proclaimed *Evil! Evil!* in his deep voice, the silver wand jumping in his grasp. They did four takes—but of course, in the hands of a good film editor, it would look seamless and convincing. That didn't matter: Wellstone had the goods, the smoking gun. He was capturing a record of bogus paranormal sausage being made. This wouldn't just be a cap to his book, he realized. This footage could expose, on television and in the lecture hall, just how these phonies worked. More than that: it could itself make a fine documentary about paranormal fraud.

He wondered if Betts would appreciate *that* irony.

Now they broke down the set a third time, moving their shoot deeper within the mausoleum. Unspooling power cables from the generator, they brought the lights inside. A fogger was moved up to the door, pumping mist into the yawning cavity. Night had fallen: a black night, the moon hidden behind clouds. A chill wind began to blow. Wellstone wondered how they were all going to fit into the little stone temple. But when the lights inside grew fainter, he realized with surprise that the mausoleum must have a second level, with a passageway going down to a larger space below. This must be why Betts had been so pleased: it was like a ready-made set for his sham production.

When the entire crew was inside, Wellstone moved swiftly up through the trees, pressing himself against the rear wall of the mausoleum. Obviously, this was where the biggest fraud of all would take place: where Moller and his bogus equipment would film the fake vampire, or whatever other images he'd prepared for this evening's work.

Standing on tiptoe at one of the windows, looking in at an awkward angle, he began shooting video of what was going on inside.

50

COLDMOON AWOKE FROM A nightmare involving large trees, toboggans, and lumberjacks in plaid work shirts chasing him with axes. A hand was gently shaking his shoulder. He came partially awake—Christ, he was tired—but was pleased to find it had been only a dream. The figure silhouetted in golden light, gently prodding him with soft fingers, was extremely attractive. Perhaps he could dive from one kind of dream into a very different one.

But the silhouette wouldn't let him alone, and with a groan and a mumbled curse, Coldmoon became fully conscious. In the gloom, he could see that the sylphlike figure waking him was Constance Greene.

"Yes?" he croaked.

"Pendergast needs you," came the contralto voice. "Both of us."

Coldmoon checked his watch. "Now? I just finished two cross-country flights for the guy."

"Get dressed, please, and come down to the hotel's library."

Coldmoon sat up, then flopped back down again with another groan.

"If you're there in five minutes," Constance said, "and sufficiently presentable, I'll get you some *pejúta sápa*."

"The way I like it prepared?"

"For God's sake, no." She turned with a rustle of expensive silk and left his room.

It was ten minutes later that Coldmoon—now dressed and fully awake—stepped into the library of the Chandler House: a narrow room overlooking Taylor Street. The room held wall-to-wall bookcases, with a few tables and several comfortable reading chairs. In one corner sat Pendergast and Constance. They had pulled a sofa and two armchairs away from the other furniture in a kind of defensive posture. Coldmoon walked over and sat down. As promised, there was a large pitcher of coffee and some cups with saucers. Without speaking, Coldmoon poured himself a cup and sipped suspiciously. He put the cup down on the table between them and sat back.

Pendergast, so drawn and pale he might have been a candidate for Moller's monster-diagnosing equipment, sat across from him. "I'm going to tell you both a story," he said.

"Oh, goody," Coldmoon replied sarcastically. He had looked up D. B. Cooper on Wikipedia and been as entertained as Pendergast promised, yet he'd been unable to figure out how that celebrated cold case could be linked to the current killings—although he could see a number of possible links to their trip west.

"Both of you know different pieces of the story," Pendergast went on. "Neither of you knows it all. Our trip west answered half of it. The other half belongs to Constance. I tasked her with a most difficult undertaking…and she has followed through."

"What was that?" Coldmoon asked.

"Asking the proprietress of the Chandler House four questions."

Four questions? Coldmoon glanced at Constance. She was sitting on the sofa between Pendergast and Coldmoon, utterly still and—apparently—emotionless. Coldmoon knew from personal experience this might be a bad sign, and he discreetly edged his chair away from the couch.

"I'll tell the story, as reconstructed with the help of Constance, as efficiently as possible. Time is of the essence." Pendergast drew in a breath. "A little over fifty years ago, a young woman named Alicia Rime was employed as an airframe designer at the Boeing aerospace complex in Portland, Oregon. She was a brilliant young engineer, and she had been moved from the company's headquarters in Chicago to the advanced operations facility. This was a secret location, not unlike Lockheed's 'Skunk Works,' where employees worked to develop new technologies. Beginning in 1970, important steps were being taken toward fly-by-wire systems, as well as novel approaches for improving safety. At that time, Rime was the only female engineer at Boeing.

"Soon, Rime began to learn that the more senior engineers in her department were poaching her work and taking credit for it themselves. Given her lack of seniority, and—alas—the fact that she was a woman, management circled the wagons and turned a blind eye to what was happening. And it wasn't long before

Rime's excitement turned to disenchantment, then bitterness.

"At this point, she gravitated toward an older engineer working in advanced operations. He had been a rising star in earlier years, but—as his ideas became perceived as more and more impracticable, even bizarre—his work was disparaged or, worse, dismissed. By the time Rime met him, such treatment had driven him to work alone, not sharing with the others. He was a widower, with no family to speak of. He'd been laughed at one too many times, and now he kept his projects secret, locked in a safe when he went home for the night.

"Not surprisingly, the old man and Alicia Rime, the two outcasts of the department, forged a friendship. Eventually the older man began to share the secret of his work with her.

"His idea had been to develop hardware and software that could model human behavior. He took a dazzlingly unconventional approach, using a computer language of his own invention, far more advanced than LISP. His goal was to predict pilot behavior using AI. If a computer could predict, even a minute in advance, what a pilot might do given a set of circumstances, it would be an extremely powerful tool in avoiding pilot error.

"Alas, his efforts to create predictive AI ended in failure. The world is ruled by chaos, and human behavior is too complex."

Pendergast allowed this observation to settle over the small group before he continued.

"But this scientist was a true genius, and he was not yet ready to admit defeat. After abandoning AI as a tool, he hit upon another idea—an insight based on the

Schrödinger's cat effect and the many-worlds theory of the physicist Hugh Everett, proposed in 1957."

"What the hell does a cat have to do with anything?" Coldmoon interrupted.

"Never mind the cat. The many-worlds theory is a phenomenon of quantum mechanics, which says that all possible worlds are physically realized in countless universes parallel to our own."

"I've no idea what you're talking about."

"I'm not surprised. The important thing is that our elderly engineer succeeded in building a device that employed quantum effects to predict the future."

Coldmoon shook his head. "I'm going back to bed," he announced.

"Don't be so hasty; I think you'll find the rest of the story worth your time. That engineer's machine used quantum mechanics in a very original, very *practical* way. Most physicists spend their time speculating and theorizing; he actually *built* something."

"That can see into the future," Coldmoon said. "Of course he did."

"*Modicae fidei!*" Constance said, annoyed. "Be quiet, and maybe you'll learn something."

A short, awkward silence ensued. Chastened, Coldmoon poured himself another cup of coffee and, as requested, kept his thoughts to himself.

Pendergast tented his fingers. "The many-worlds interpretation states that we live within a multiverse: a place in which *all possible outcomes* of any action are occurring simultaneously. Schrödinger's cat is alive in one world and dead in another."

"There's that cat again," said Coldmoon.

"Or to be more prosaic: In our own universe, we are here speaking calmly among ourselves. In a different but parallel universe, you got up and did indeed go back to bed. In yet another, the ceiling is rotten and has just fallen down on our heads. And so on, ad infinitum."

He stopped, as if expecting another protest from Coldmoon. When none came, he glanced at Constance. Then he continued.

"Events in universes parallel to ours don't always change that dramatically. Physicists believe the universes *most like ours* are those which run *closest to us* in the quantum stream of time. According to brane theory, these universes are layered next to each other, like membranes, in higher dimensional space. So close that they sometimes touch, and thus open a window or portal between the two.

"Our elderly engineer managed, using the principles I've just described, to create a machine that could open that window and peer through it into another universe, very close to ours, except running at a slightly different timeline. The machine doesn't see into our future. It's looking into a universe almost identical to ours, *one minute ahead*."

"This is crazy," said Coldmoon.

"I assure you this is well-established physics that many, if not most, physicists believe in."

"So what good is it to look one minute in the future?" Coldmoon asked.

"It makes all the difference, as you shall see."

Coldmoon fell silent, and Pendergast went on. "So: Our elderly scientist built a prototype machine. That extra minute of predictive time would be enough to warn a pilot of catastrophic events. Lightning, extreme turbulence, engine failure. However, the engineer was tired of being laughed at by his colleagues. He needed to make a dramatic demonstration of its power, one that anyone could appreciate. That would be stock trading on Wall Street. It would display where a stock price would be, one minute ahead. It doesn't take a rocket scientist to figure out the value of such a device.

"The old man confided in Alicia Rime. He told her he was going to bring his device—which was small enough to fit into a briefcase—to the Seattle head-quarters, where he could demonstrate it to the CEO and board of Boeing at a retreat the weekend after Thanksgiving.

"Rime thought it was a crime for Boeing to get a device like that, especially after the way she, and the engineer, had been treated by them. She tried to con-vince the engineer to keep the machine for himself and not give it to Boeing. She suggested the two of them could quit their jobs and use the machine to make money. But he was adamant: it belonged to Boeing, he had developed it on their time, and so forth. They had a bitter falling-out. She'd come to hate Boeing and—though she had no rights to it—saw the machine as her ticket out. But her elderly acquaintance never gave her the opportunity to examine the device or even get a look at the plans, and by now they were estranged. And he kept the device, and plans, in his safe at all times, or on his person.

"She knew he was planning to take a flight from Portland to Seattle: Northwest Orient 305, carrying the briefcase with the device. She also knew the type of jet that flew that route was a Boeing 727-100. This is a critical pivot in our story, because she had an intimate knowledge of that aircraft as well. For example, its three engines were mounted unusually high on the rear fuselage. It was able to fly at a lower altitude and lower speed without stalling than any other commercial jet. But particularly important, and virtually unique to the 727-100, was the airplane's aft airstair, and the ability of this stair to be lowered during flight—from a control in the rear that nobody in the cockpit could override. This ability was so secret that it was even kept from many of the crews that flew commercial flights. However, it was not a secret to the engineers at Boeing.

"The board retreat in Seattle was scheduled for November twenty-seventh, 1971—the Saturday after Thanksgiving. The previous Tuesday, Rime contrived to have an altercation with her manager over credit he'd taken for some of her blueprints. As a result, she was told to clear out her desk by the end of the day, which she did, and left. Nobody ever saw her again as Alicia Rime…except the farmer-cum-doctor we met in the backwoods of Washington."

"How in the world have you figured all this out?" Coldmoon asked.

"The four questions, as you shall see." Pendergast shifted in his chair, leaning on his elbows and looking at Coldmoon. "Still thinking of going back to bed now, partner?"

51

Gannon finished setting up the lighting and positioning her two camera operators in opposite corners of the mausoleum, where they wouldn't accidentally film each other. As she looked around, she felt a certain thrill. The interior couldn't have been better if a Hollywood set designer had created it. The two side walls were lined with marble crypts, each with a door carved with a name and dates, and various short epitaphs in Latin or English. Some doors had been shattered by vandals or age. Several crypts even had bones spilling out of them, and an actual human skull sat on the floor, staring upward, its jaw agape as if in a frozen scream. A skeletal arm hung out of another crypt, with shreds of tendons adhering to the bone, dressed in a decayed sleeve of silk and lace. A gold ring decorated a bony finger. It was a director's dream. But at the same time it made her uneasy, thinking that these remains had once been people, that this was not just the plaster and paint of a movie set. Why wasn't there somebody taking care of old vaults like this, before they deteriorated into such a frightful state?

The central area of the crypt was open, and it led to a broad doorway in the rear. The doors that had once hung there had been made of wood. They had evidently rotted and then been smashed and torn off their hinges by vandals, pieces scattered about. Beyond, a staircase led down to a second level, with walls of cut stone blocks and a vaulted stone ceiling, prickled with tiny stalactites of lime, some dripping water. In the reflected lights, she could see more crypts down there, also smashed up by vandals. She shuddered.

Pulling her gaze from the doorway, she turned to Gregor. "Move the fogger over there," she said. Gregor, a big muscled guy she truly hated, did everything she asked, at least—but only reluctantly and with grudging slowness. Sure enough, with a scowl, he picked up the fog machine. "Where, exactly, do you want it?" he asked in a tone of aggrievement, as if her request had been too vague for him to follow.

"Right in that corner, where it's out of sight," she said. She had never been on a set that didn't have at least one asshole. She never allowed herself to be provoked, even by sexist jerks. This set had more than its share of pricks, but it was balanced by the fun of being in Savannah and the efficiency of Betts and the talent of Moller, both of whom knew exactly what they were doing—fakery or not.

"Gregor," she said, "set a Lume Cube up against that back wall, low, about three feet off the ground."

Wordlessly he carried the light over, hooked it to a cable, and turned it on. Gannon eyed it critically. It cast light from below, which gave everything a creepy Lon Chaney look: effective if not overdone.

Betts had been going over Moller's moves in the next scene. Now, with cameras rolling, Moller came in through the mausoleum door—there was a background spot behind him, raking through the mist—his silver dowsing rod twitching.

"*Evil*," he pronounced in a stentorian tone. Then: "*There is great evil here…*"

His voice dropped to a near whisper at the final words. Once again: effective. She glanced over; her camera operators were nailing it, as usual.

"One, do a slow pan of the crypts," she murmured into the headset.

Craig did the pan, lingering on the skeleton's arm and the skull on the floor. Beautiful.

"Two, close-up on face."

Pavel zoomed his Steadicam in on Moller's face, which was twitching, the eyes wide and staring. The wand continued to tremble, and then, slowly, began to point downward—toward the doorway and descending stairs.

"*Down*," said Moller in a tremulous whisper. "*Down.*"

52

OVER THE LAST SEVERAL minutes of Pendergast's recitation, as the pieces came together in his mind with what he had read about D. B. Cooper, Coldmoon had grown both more fascinated—and more incredulous.

"So you're saying this Alicia Rime is D. B. Cooper," Coldmoon said. "The skyjacker who was never found, whose crime was never solved."

"Bravo!" Pendergast turned to his ward. "Shall we fortify the man with a wee dram of Lagavulin?"

"Why not?"

Coldmoon noticed that, beyond a lack of emotion, Constance seemed to be projecting an unusual iciness—toward him and Pendergast both. He gratefully took the generous measure of scotch Pendergast handed him. Pendergast then poured a glass for Constance and one for himself.

Pendergast shifted once again, making himself more comfortable. "Perhaps you can pick up the thread now, Agent Coldmoon, and tell *us* where it leads."

Coldmoon was tempted to decline, feeling slightly patronized. But the story was so outrageous and intriguing, and the pieces were starting to come together so quickly, that he couldn't help himself. "Okay, let's see. Rime got herself fired from Boeing so her later disappearance wouldn't cause suspicion. She booked a seat on the same flight, disguised as a man, so the old scientist wouldn't recognize her. And to throw off the later investigation. She used the name Dan Cooper."

"Correct," Pendergast said. "In those days, it was easy to book a flight in a fake name."

"It was Wednesday, the day before Thanksgiving. Once in the air, he—I mean, she—showed a stewardess an attaché case containing a phony bomb, then a note demanding two hundred thousand dollars. The idea was to make it look like a straightforward hijacking, to divert attention from what she was really after. She asked for two full sets of civilian parachutes, primary and reserve."

Pendergast nodded. "That was to make sure the authorities didn't sabotage the chutes—and asking for a second chute implied she might take a hostage along."

"Right. So when the plane landed in Seattle, she collected a ransom of two hundred thousand dollars and the parachutes and ordered everyone off the flight. But she *didn't* allow them to get their hand luggage."

"Precisely," said Pendergast.

"Let's see..." Coldmoon thought back to the files he'd read. "Cooper demanded the pilot take her to Mexico City, with a refueling stop in Reno. That would route the plane over a vast, remote forested landscape at night. She ordered everyone into the cockpit, where they couldn't see what she was doing. Then she opened the luggage compartments and took the briefcase she wanted."

"Yes," said Pendergast. "And it was noted later that many of the overhead luggage bins had been opened and their contents scattered, with items missing. She no doubt lowered the aft stairs and tossed some luggage out, again to confuse things and cover up her real target."

"Right. So she took the briefcase and jumped." Coldmoon shook his head. "Imagine jumping into a storm at night like that. Woman or man—doing that took serious stones."

Pendergast sipped the Lagavulin. "The D. B. Cooper case was one of the longest unsolved cases in FBI history. It wasn't closed until a few years ago, in fact, with no solution. Various landing areas were suggested, countless suspects developed, questioned, and abandoned. Endless computer and physical simulations were run, taking into account different surface velocities, wind speeds, altitudes—but none ever turned up a body or the money. Years later, a rotten packet of that ransom money was found in a sandbar in the Columbia River. That led many to believe he was dead."

He looked at Coldmoon. "If you were in Cooper's shoes…what would you have done after jumping off that plane?"

Coldmoon considered this for a moment. "The ransom money couldn't have been spent. That's what tripped up the Lindbergh kidnappers. He, I mean she, would have known the FBI microfilmed or marked all the bills before giving them to her. So she tossed the money into the wind, to make it look like she'd died in the fall." He paused. "Next, I would have free-fallen as long as I dared, so their calculations of where I landed—along with the dusting of money—would throw off any searchers. And less chance of anyone spotting the chute."

Pendergast spoke as Coldmoon took another sip of his Lagavulin. "That's exactly what happened—with one exception. Something went wrong with the chute, and she sustained a violent impact."

"But she didn't die," Coldmoon said. "Obviously. Because Dr. Quincy saved her life."

"Precisely," Pendergast said. "And now, for this final part of the story, we should turn to Constance. Because she got it straight from the source."

"That interview," Constance said after a brief pause, "was probably the final exchange I will ever have with Felicity Frost."

"You mean Alicia Rime," said Coldmoon. "Alias D. B. Cooper."

Pendergast nodded. "That was the first question I had Constance ask Frost: *Are you D. B. Cooper?* As I'd hoped, it threw her so off guard that it was easier to get answers to the other three questions. Constance?"

She spoke quietly but quickly, as if dealing with something she wished to be rid of as fast as possible. "Miss Frost—Alicia—knew a great deal about avionics. She knew that the hijacking would precipitate a massive manhunt. The time of her jump and the location of the plane would not be known for certain, in the days before GPS. She jumped out into a moonless, stormy night, landing somewhere in the vast forests of southern Washington and northern Oregon, a huge and almost impossible area to search. The air force jets that had been scrambled to follow the 727 didn't see her jump.

"She told me she opened the main chute and began to dump the money, but the money got caught in the canopy, deflating it. She cut that chute free and deployed the reserve. And this was her one mistake: she hadn't noticed that the reserve was a training chute, not meant for actual use. Normally, such chutes are loosely stitched closed. This was something she'd never thought to check on. And now, she was rapidly approaching the ground without a deployed parachute.

"She had the presence of mind to slash the stitching away and free the training chute. Luckily, she carried a knife and the chute had a functioning ripcord. The chute opened successfully, but she was still moving at a high speed when she hit the water."

"Water?" Coldmoon asked.

"Yes. She landed just upriver of Walupt Creek falls. The current carried her over the falls and into Walupt Lake—near Berry Patch. Roused by the cold water, she managed to swim to shore, despite the fractured leg. She passed out on the pebble beach. And that's where she was discovered in the morning by a young farmer. The briefcase she had stolen was still strapped to her body with parachute line."

"And that young farmer was Zephraim Quincy," Coldmoon said.

Constance nodded. "That morning, he hadn't yet heard about the skyjacking. He was living alone in the house. His father was in an assisted-care facility with a serious head injury, from which he would eventually die. Quincy was struggling to keep the farm going. Alicia didn't tell him anything at first, except she categorically refused to be taken to the hospital. He carried her back to his clinic and was able to reduce her fracture, splint and plaster her leg. The paper that morning didn't carry the news of the hijacking—it had happened too late the prior evening. So he cared for her that day, evening, and night. That, by the way, is why he never showed up at the traditional Berry Patch Thanksgiving dinner. The next morning, when the paper landed on his porch, he saw the headline and the sketch of D. B. Cooper above the fold. He realized that the woman he rescued, oddly wearing male clothing, must be Cooper.

"Five minutes later, when he walked into his clinic, he was carrying the newspaper. As he began to dress her wounds, he mentioned that he had alerted the sheriff and asked if there was anything she wanted to tell him before he arrived. She then told him everything—or almost everything. She especially emphasized that she hadn't hurt anyone and that the bomb was a fake. She begged and pleaded with him not to turn her in, to call off the sheriff.

"By this time, I suspect the young farmer was already in love—a case of love at first sight. He was moved by her plea. He hadn't really called the sheriff—that was just a test to see her reaction. So he kept her there in the farmhouse, caring for her and nursing her back to health. She, in turn, fell in love with him. For a few months they were happy, in their farm tucked away in the wilderness, like Tristan and Isolde in the forest of Morrois. No one knew she was there. But, of course, it was too good to be true, and for obvious reasons it couldn't last. The searches were getting closer and FBI agents visited Quincy's farm several times. D. B. Cooper was now on the FBI's Ten

Most Wanted list and over two hundred agents were working the case. She couldn't hide forever.

"By spring, Alicia was well enough to travel. She knew that if she didn't leave Quincy then, she never would. So she wrote him a note of thanks, planning to place it on the kitchen table early one morning and avoid a difficult scene. To her surprise, however, Quincy already suspected her plans: he'd awoken before sunrise and prepared her not only breakfast but a backpack full of supplies—enough to get her out of the state and beyond any danger of being apprehended. He gave her what little cash he had. He also tucked into that backpack their favorite book, inscribed to her. She had already researched a way to get a new identity and she knew exactly what to do. After leaving the farm, she headed for a large cemetery not far away—in Puyallup—and found a grave of a girl with her approximate birthdate. She assumed that identity."

"It's clear that Quincy loved her daring and courage," said Pendergast. "He even admired the fact she was a rebel, an outlaw, as evidenced by the inscription: '*that great social nomad, who prowls on the confines of a docile, frightened order*.'"

"How did you get her to tell you all this?" Coldmoon asked.

"It was Aloysius's second question that really broke her down, got her talking. *Did you hijack the plane in order to steal the suitcase with the device?* She responded in the affirmative."

She let this sink in a moment before continuing. "Now under the new name of Felicity Frost, she traveled to the Midwest. The year was 1972. At some point after leaving the farm, she managed to get the scientist's machine working. Her plan—in the short term, at least—was to make enough money to achieve independence. The future could wait. Using the device, she learned how to focus it a minute into the future and began making modest spot trades on a variety of Big Board stocks. As she grew more proficient, she began trading in options and was able to make larger profits. And though she never grew greedy, within a year she'd earned enough to pay off the mortgage on Quincy's farm, and to send funds to the University of Washington Medical School paying the rest of his tuition—anonymously, of course."

Coldmoon didn't need to ask whether the two had ever corresponded again—the hunger in Dr. Quincy's eyes for any crumb of information about the woman made it clear they never had.

53

WELLSTONE, HIS CAMERA PRESSED against the grille, shot video of the whole sorry scene: the smoke machines, the shenanigans with the dowsing rod, the phony photographing with the box camera, the orders from Betts between each take—*Do this, Don't do that*. It sickened him a little to see how disrespectful all this was to the dead. He noticed there was actually a skull lying on the floor. That had been someone's mother or father, for heaven's sake, not some prop. But he'd make sure this desecration would be just another nail in the coffin for Betts's reputation.

The viewpoint he had wasn't optimal, so he snuck around to the front of the mausoleum and, staying low and in darkness, filmed through the open door. The door he was crouching next to was bronze, and he noticed that its heavy hinges had been broken by force, and recently, as the metal was shiny and fresh in places. He briefly wondered who had done it and why: pulling off that door must have been no mean feat. Then he shrugged and returned his attention to the fake horror show.

From this vantage point, he could now see there was another staircase, leading down to a lower level. He wondered what an elaborate tomb like this would be doing at the far end of the cemetery, so utterly neglected and forgotten. It must have once been an important Savannah family, no doubt now extinct. He would have to find out something about their history. That would be part of the story, part of the outrage. He squinted and looked through the long lens, trying to read the last names on the crypt doors. He could just make them out, with an inscription below.

HEWITT HUNNICUTT III

B. 1810

D. 1910

THUS SAYS THE LORD GOD TO THESE BONES:
"SURELY I WILL CAUSE BREATH TO ENTER INTO
YOU, AND YOU SHALL LIVE. "

He captured that on video, too.

They had finished filming in the outer chamber of the tomb, and he waited as Betts and Gannon gave orders for the breaking down and moving of equipment to the lower level. He was almost seen when someone emerged to spool out more cable from the generator. But it was an overcast night, and he managed to retreat into the darkness in time. He shivered, feeling a chilly wind picking up, stirring the invisible leaves above his head, the whispery sound rising and falling, almost like the breathing of ghosts. Why would a tomb have two levels, anyway? He re-called an H. P. Lovecraft story in which a fellow was working in a sub-basement, or something, and broke through the floor into a passage that had been carved up *from below*...

He put this out of his head. Now even he, the skeptic, was getting spooked.

There was a break in the action, and he took the opportunity to switch out the SD card in his camera, which was almost full.

All the lights, smoke machines, everything was now being moved down the stairs to the lower level. He waited, watching from the darkness, until they had vacated the upper chamber. As risky as it was, he realized he would have to get inside the tomb if he wanted to continue filming. The big event was evidently going to occur on the lower level, and that was something he couldn't miss. It occurred to him that, if he was caught, the first thing they would do would be to confiscate his camera's memory card. He plucked the full SD card from his pocket and hid it in his shoe.

At the opportune moment, when everyone's attention was occupied, he ducked through the doorway into the mausoleum itself, crossed the upper chamber, and pressed himself against the wall next to the stairs that went deeper into the tomb. He could hear Betts's voice coming up from below, telling Moller how they were going to work the next shot.

Crouching, practically on his belly, Wellstone crept into the doorway, edging the human skull aside so he could peer down the stairs. A humid, unpleasant smell rose up—not surprising, considering what was stored down there.

He raised his camera to his eye and once again began shooting.

54

Iᴛ ᴡᴀѕ ᴛʜᴇ ᴄʀᴀᴢɪᴇѕᴛ thing, Gannon thought as she surveyed the lower level of the tomb. It had originally been a rather small room, not unlike the crypt above, lined with marble. The walls and ceiling were built from blocks of carved stone, damp and slimy with age. If anything, the crypts down here seemed even older than the ones in the upper chamber. The vandals had really gone to town: many of the crypts were smashed open, pieces of marble and bones strewn everywhere, along with rotten bits of clothing, shriveled ladies' button-up boots with bones still inside, a pair of eyeglasses, and a mummified head swathed in gleaming long blond hair done up in braids, with two rotten ribbons.

But even more than that, it was what lay beyond that really struck her. Someone had torn down the back wall of the crypt, exposing an earthen passageway that—against all reason—went on into darkness, like a tunnel. It wasn't a well-finished tunnel, either; it looked more like something picked or clawed out of the earth. Roots dangled down from above, and the floor was a sea of mud. Deep in the tunnel, she made out what appeared to be faint lights—like the glow of fireflies, only stationary. What the hell was that—some sort of glowing fungus?

The more she looked, the more inexplicable this find seemed to be. No mere vandals would have taken the time and effort to dig so long a passage, or one that tunneled so deep. Was it some sort of unfinished construction site, the crude first step toward enlarging the mausoleum to accommodate more dead? That hardly seemed likely. Besides, if someone had dug this tunnel, where had the earth been put?

"This is messed up," Craig, the primary camera operator, muttered into the headset. "We shouldn't be down here."

Gannon didn't answer. She could feel his nervousness. More than that: she shared it. Even macho-man Gregor was subdued and sweating. The air was close and foul.

"Gannon! You awake? Let's get these lights set up."

She looked up as Betts came over.

"This place is a gold mine," Betts told her. "That tunnel over there, for example—it's like a gift dropped into our laps. If I dug the thing myself, I couldn't have made it look better. Worse, I mean. Anyway, here's the plan: Moller's going to move from the bottom of the stairs, over there; pick his way through all these bones and stuff; and head for the opening to that tunnel. I want some shots of all this stuff on the floor—especially, oh shit, is that some girl's head? What a find. Get a good close-up. Think you can handle that?"

"Sure." She swallowed. "Listen, I'm a little concerned."

"About what?"

"This doesn't feel right. I mean, is it even legal for us to be in here? Look at all these bones. Somebody trashed this place. *Desecrated* it. We can hardly move around without stepping on bones."

Betts glared at her, then tilted his head back and laughed. "O-*ho*! This is a fine place to find your conscience, in the middle of a shoot a hundred feet deep into a tomb."

"Have you considered that what we're doing might be illegal?"

"Of course I've considered it! Look, we didn't break in. The door was open. The cemetery is a public venue. We have permission to be here. Even if we didn't, we're a documentary news team. We have a first amendment right to follow a news story, even onto private property."

"But this isn't really a news story."

"Are you kidding? Moller's going to find something down here. Something newsworthy. This is the first time I've seen the guy actually look excited." He pointed toward the ragged mouth of the tunnel. "He says the source of the evil turbulence is down there, and when we reach it, he's going to photograph it with that special camera of his." He grasped her shoulder. "Gannon, this is no time to get cold feet. In for a penny, in for a pound. Am I right?"

"Right." And he *was* right—sort of. This wasn't like her. She'd shot footage at car accidents, fires, suicides, murder scenes, and she'd never flinched. But this...this was different. The bones, the tunnel, and the awful smell that clung to everything had spooked her.

She took a deep breath and went back to work,

briskly telling Gregor where to put the lights, repositioning the fog machine, working out her exposures. Gregor was unusually cooperative and subdued, and she could see that he was genuinely spooked. This, if nothing else, was a refreshing change. Maybe he should be scared more often. The only one who seemed unaffected, in fact, was Pavel, the Steadicam operator. He looked, as always, as if he was on the verge of falling asleep. Staring at his heavy-lidded, drooping eyes helped to calm her down—if only a little.

55

The rest of the story can be quickly summarized," Constance said. "She didn't tell me how she spent the two decades between her Midwest sojourn and coming to Savannah, but by the time she arrived here, she was wealthy. She told me she liked the idea of rescuing a historic building and restoring it into an upscale hotel. On a visit to Savannah she fell in love with the city and found the right building. She bought the abandoned factory and rebirthed it as the Chandler House. It would be a place where she could indulge in her love of books, paintings, and music. She became an imperious and eccentric proprietress, brilliant and commanding. She continued to make profitable trades but never let herself become seduced by the machine. She realized that it would be dangerous to push the technology further, even as computing power vastly increased over the years. She made just enough money to live well and have all she wanted, but not beyond. She naturally kept the device secret."

"Who could you trust with it?" Coldmoon mused.

"Precisely the conundrum," said Constance. "So the years passed. And passed. And passed. Eventually, she felt age beginning to creep up on her."

She fell silent for a moment, and the moment lengthened. Confused, Coldmoon looked from Constance to Pendergast and back again.

"More and more," she resumed, "she began turning to Patrick Ellerby, her hotel manager, for help. He had started as assistant manager, a handsome and somewhat roguish fellow. Exactly how the two became so close is something Frost refused to discuss. It's clear she felt a genuine affection for him. I think to some degree he served as a replacement for Dr. Quincy: empathetic, a little awkward perhaps, independent, fond of poetry and mathematics. But unlike Quincy, Ellerby wasn't an honorable man. He saw in Frost a route to a comfortable existence for himself. Perhaps he began to work upon her in the mode of *The Aspern Papers*, ingratiating himself, romancing her, gaining her trust. In time, she shared her deepest secret with him: the machine she had secretly set up in the basement, and just as importantly, the physics behind how it operated. This is, essentially, the same information she gave me in response to our third question: *How can this machine see into the future?* And this provided a lot of the science underpinning what Aloysius has just explained, along with—"

Abruptly, Constance paused again.

"Are you all right, my dear?" Pendergast asked after a moment.

"I'm fine." She took a breath. "As I was saying, eventually Frost turned over the operation of the device to Ellerby, since she was increasingly confined to her fifth-floor rooms."

At this she turned to Pendergast. "Tell the rest, please."

Pendergast shifted position. "Here, a new element enters the picture. Ellerby studied the device and the schematics that came with it, and he apparently realized—with advances in computational hardware, software, and a deeper knowledge of quantum mechanics and brane cosmology—that the device, now almost fifty years old, could be made more powerful. Much more powerful. And he had the mathematical and computer skills to, ah, 'goose' it, as the saying goes. Ellerby was confident that by increasing the machine's power, he could look not one minute into the future, but thirty minutes, maybe even an hour. That's enough to make billions.

"Of course, he tried to conceal these ambitions from Frost—but she was too shrewd a judge of character not to have understood what he was up to. As the financial logs and computer forensics show, he suddenly began to make money—vast amounts of money. Two hundred million dollars in three weeks. All perfectly legal and aboveboard. Because, you see, there are no laws against using a time machine to play the market. It was around this point that Frost took the extraordinary step of leaving her rooms and investigating the basement—where she found Ellerby doing the one thing she'd expressly forbidden. This led to their infamous argument, which was overheard by half the staff. But in her elderly state, she could do nothing to stop him."

"So you're saying Ellerby found a way to increase the machine's power," Coldmoon asked, "to poke a bigger hole in that parallel universe?"

Pendergast nodded. "Your analogy to poking a

hole is apt. Because that's where Ellerby's story ends—and our murder inquiry begins. And that is where my fourth and last question comes into play."

"Which was?" Coldmoon asked.

"*Was Ellerby's death connected to the device in the suitcase?*" Pendergast replied. "But here we move into more speculative territory that Frost refused to explain to Constance. But it stands to reason that the 'hole' Ellerby poked became larger and larger as the machine grew more powerful; Ellerby made more and more money on the market...and then it happened."

"It?" Coldmoon repeated.

"The hole grew big enough for..." He paused and fixed both of them with glittering eyes. "Something to come through it."

"*Something?* What do you mean? From where?"

"From the other side."

He rose. "But I think the time for explanation is over. It's time to see this for ourselves." He glanced toward Constance. "If you'd lead the way, please?"

56

LYING PRONE AT THE top of the steps leading to the tomb's lower level, Wellstone shot clip after clip with his camera, trying not to fill up his second—and last—SD card. Damn, he should have brought more…but then, he'd had no idea he would strike gold like this. And gold was exactly what it was: that last bit, with Betts reassuring the DP and squashing her objections—that little conversation alone was going to hang Betts. There were so many things wrong with this: paranormal fraud, trespassing, and a disgusting lack of respect for the dead. He could even hear footsteps from below crunching the bones from time to time as they dragged power cables back and forth and set up the lights and fog machine.

But what the hell happened in here? he wondered as he waited, camera at the ready. This went beyond mere vandalism. Somebody—more than one person, probably—had gone to a lot of trouble and effort to break up these crypts, haul out the remains, and scatter them around. That wasn't the work of idle, drunken teenagers. It seemed more like a deliberate attempt to desecrate the resting place of the Hunnicutt family.

Now, down below, they began shooting again. The lighting in the lower level raked into the artificial fog, creating a glowing mist, low-lying and swirly, as Moller continued his charade with the silver wand and obsidian glass. He also had his phony camera out again. Christ, Wellstone wished he'd managed to get his hands on that. But he reminded himself that now, the point was moot: the footage, stills, and audio he'd captured in the last half hour would sink Betts deeper than the Mariana Trench.

A movement of air, foul as if it had emerged from the throat of a ghoul, was drifting up from below. What were they disturbing down there that would exude such a nasty smell? The eddies from below continued, making the atmosphere around him even closer than it already was. It felt almost viscous. Unbidden, images came to Wellstone's mind: rotting bodies, decaying crypts, the suppurating flesh of the dead exhaling corpse gas. He tried breathing through his mouth.

Now, it seemed, Moller's bullshit device was leading them toward something inside the slimy mouth of that strange tunnel Wellstone could just make out at the far end of the lower level. And Betts, it seemed, wanted to set up his next shot inside it.

But, Wellstone saw, the crew had finally had enough. There was reluctance—even resistance—to this suggestion. The muscleman spoke up, and Wellstone could hear his words, echoing and distorted within the enclosed space. He didn't want to go into the tunnel. It was ankle-deep with mud. You could hardly breathe down here. As it was, they'd only be able to fit the Steadicam inside. The DP was backing him up, saying it was dangerous to drag cables through an area with so much water.

Betts argued with them, cajoled them, sweet-talked them. Moller, for his part, remained silent, his equipment at the ready. Gannon continued arguing, saying it was risky; that they shouldn't be down there, returning to her earlier concern that this could land them in serious trouble.

It didn't seem that Betts was making any headway. Wellstone moved back a little from the steps, preparing to get out of the mausoleum fast if there was a mutiny.

Betts turned to Moller to draw him into the argument.

Wellstone strained to hear the notes of Moller's deep, German-accented voice rising up from below. He advocated entering the tunnel. That, after all, was where the source of evil was. The indications were clear, and his instruments were in agreement. This was what they had come to find; this was what they were risking everything to achieve...and if they turned back now, it would all be thrown away, a huge opportunity missed.

Betts rounded on the muscleman and accused him of being a pussy. They could make do on their own, he said disdainfully; the Steadicam had its own light, and Betts himself could carry the other equipment. If she wished, Gannon could hang back at the opening to the tunnel with the others; Betts and Moller would go ahead, with just the Steadicam.

The DP reluctantly agreed to this.

As they broke down the current set and everyone moved to the rear of the lower level of the tomb, where the mouth of the tunnel lay, Wellstone saw yet another opportunity and seized it. He began creeping down the slimy steps, one at a time, keeping out of sight by pressing himself against the darkness of the far wall. The air grew closer and more vile with every step he took.

Near the base of the steps, he found a hiding spot behind a crypt that had been shattered to pieces, the remains of its huge lid leaning out into the stairway. He knelt behind the lid and peered through the viewfinder of his camera. It was a perfect vantage point. From here, he could see everything, shoot everything, his powerful telephoto bringing the action ever so close.

57

At the appointed hour, Senator Drayton climbed down from his bus, which had been driven onto the lawn and parked behind the Confederate monument. With aides before and behind him and his wife at his side, he walked around to the front, mounted the stairs, and strode onto the temporary stage, just as the band struck up "Battle Hymn of the Republic." He checked the chunky Rolex Presidential on his wrist: nine o'clock precisely. A roar greeted his ears: a medley of clapping, horns, whistles, and noisemakers. He drank it in for a moment, then raised both arms, flashing the victory sign with each hand. The people seated on the great lawn rose up in their thousands as if with one mind, cheering, while the crowds standing in the rear and to either side went equally wild.

He smiled and waved as the noise went on and on, the seconds stretching into minutes. He felt that indescribable thrill course through him: a feeling better than sex, better than a shot of the finest bourbon—the electricity of victory, of admiration, of *power*. How could he lose with this outpouring of support? His pathetic opponent could never pull together a crowd like this, even before Drayton's hackers and disinformation wonks had gone to work on him.

The only obstacle in his path to re-election was this damned murder investigation. Pickett, his old "friend," had really failed him, assigning that asshole FBI agent and his sidekick to the case. They hadn't done jack shit, and—as if to rub his face in it—they'd gone off to Washington State the night before, after he'd given them specific instructions...and a specific warning. And that Commander Delaplane was no better, just spinning her wheels, a waste of space if ever there was one.

He waved as the cheering continued. If everything was going well, then why did he feel this tickle of apprehension? Because he not only wanted to win this election; he *needed* to. The new Jekyll Island sewage treatment plant was going out for bids, and there was a lot of money to be made in kickbacks. Not kickbacks, he reminded himself—*legal* campaign contributions, made by those bidding on the work. *Kickback* was practically a moribund concept—thanks to the Supreme Court, it was 100 percent legal for those who wanted to give in return for "constituent service"—as long as there was no quid pro quo. And there would never be a quid pro quo, because nobody had to say or write anything. It was all just understood, in the secret, unspoken language of politics. But even unspoken, it was as old as the hills: you scratch my back, I scratch yours.

His mind drifted back to that rogue FBI agent, Pendergast, and his partner, Coldmoon. Especially Coldmoon. After re-election, with Pickett out of the way, he was going to make a special project out of that sucker. He was going to bring the full power of his office down on that smartass, insect or not. Coldmoon would be sorry he ever shot off his smart mouth. Drayton would send him packing to the nearest reservation. And he would deal with Pendergast, too, put that southern undertaker of an agent out to pasture in Alaska or North Dakota, where he would freeze his ass off for the rest of his career.

These thoughts ran through his mind as he continued waving at the crowd. God, he hoped those sons of bitches in the press area were getting this. *Invincible*, that was the word that now came to mind. His people loved him.

The cheering finally trailed off as the governor of Georgia took the podium to introduce him. The man heaped on the honors and praises, one fine phrase after another rolling off his tongue. It was a perfect speech, short, elegant, and to the point—and then the governor yielded the podium to him.

The cheering began all over again as he waited, waved a little, waited some more, waved again, and finally cleared his throat to signal the beginning of his speech. He heard, in the far distance, some catcalls and jeers, but they were faint. He'd made it clear to his advance team that those bastards were to be kept well at bay, and none too gently, either.

"My fellow Georgians," he began, the towers of speakers echoing his voice back from the buildings surrounding the park. "Now is the time of decision. Now is the time of firmness. Now is the time of…" He went on and on, reading his speech from the teleprompter, although he'd practiced it so many times he had it memorized. He paused at particularly well-turned points to allow more cheering and applause, the audience obliging every time.

This was fine. So very, very fine. His enemies and detractors could eat shit and die—with support like this, there was no way he was going to lose this election.

58

As they left the library, Coldmoon felt a slight buzz from the Lagavulin—or was it from the mind-bending concept of a machine that had, somehow, opened a hole in the universe? The idea was absurd, impossible...but since he'd first partnered with Pendergast, the absurd and impossible seemed to have grown commonplace. The world according to Pendergast, he realized, was a far stranger place than he'd ever imagined.

As they entered the foyer of the hotel, Coldmoon noticed a television blaring in a lounge area. On its screen was Drayton, standing live on an elevated stage, thrusting his finger into the air and bellowing to a roaring crowd.

"Look at that *wasichu*," snorted Coldmoon as they passed. And then he halted. "Hold on a minute."

"That so many of you have braved the crime wave to come out tonight is a testament to your courage and conviction—"

Now Pendergast and Constance paused.

"—*I have been dismayed by the FBI's inability to solve these crimes, but I can assure you in my role as senator—*"

"Hey," Coldmoon said. "He's talking about us."

"—*In the face of their ineffectiveness, I am bringing all state and local resources to bear in catching the monstrous criminal or criminals behind these savage killings—*"

"He's blaming us, the jackoff!"

"Not just us, my dear friend, but ADC Pickett, who it seems has been shielding us from the senator's wrath all this time—and whose career will suffer for it."

After listening a moment longer, Pendergast and Constance continued on, and Coldmoon hurried after them. There was nobody behind the desk, and they slipped past toward the offices beyond.

"What are we going to do about it?" Coldmoon asked.

"Does the FBI involve itself in politics?" asked Pendergast as they reached the door to the cellar.

"It's not supposed to."

"You have your answer."

The door to the basement was locked. Pendergast slipped a little tool out of his pocket, and with a brief twist of his wrist, the door swung open.

They descended into the gloom. At the bottom of the stairs, Pendergast paused to remove his jacket. "You might want to check your sidearm, Agent Coldmoon."

"Right."

Pendergast took the Les Baer from his shoulder holster, ejected the magazine, checked it, palmed it back in. Coldmoon wasn't sure why this precaution was necessary just to examine a machine in the basement, but he made sure his Browning had a round in the chamber. He noticed that Constance, not to be outdone, had slid her stiletto out of one sleeve: a vicious little device, he thought as he watched the thin, wicked blade spring out at lightning speed. She knew how to use it, too; he'd seen some demonstrations that he'd just as soon forget. Noticing his stare, she gave him a wry wink, then slid the blade home.

"This way," she said, taking the lead. She led them past Ellerby's trading office and deeper into the basement, heading away from the central corridor and making for an area that was roped off and marked STRUCTURALLY UNSOUND.

"One way to deter attention," drawled Pendergast as they passed by it.

Just as it was growing too dark to see well, Constance touched a light switch and some naked bulbs came on ahead, casting baleful shadows. There was a strange, almost industrial smell in the air, Coldmoon noticed, like burnt rubber. Dead insects crunched under their feet as they walked. Constance led them past a double row of old storerooms, wooden doors splitting from dry rot.

"Did Miss Frost give you such precise directions, or are you just a modern-day Natty Bumppo?" Coldmoon asked.

"I prefer the moniker of 'Deerslayer,' thank you," Constance retorted.

Ahead, their path was blocked by a shabby door. Constance opened it to reveal a large storeroom. It was, or appeared to be, a graveyard of old hotel furniture. Most everything was covered in moldering sheets, tears here and there exposing the bones of discarded armoires and bedposts. Constance led them through the cluttered space, which ended in a large wardrobe pushed up against the far wall. Constance tried the wardrobe's doors. They were locked.

"Aloysius?" she said, stepping back.

Once again, Pendergast applied his lock-picking set. The doors swung open obediently, revealing rows of old clothes.

"Perhaps our friend Ellerby was a fan of C. S. Lewis?" asked Pendergast drily.

Constance stepped in and, sweeping aside the hangers, revealed a half-height panel. "If so, here's Narnia." She drew it back, exposing a dark hole.

"I'll go first," said Pendergast.

He ducked through, and they followed. A moment of blackness, and then Pendergast switched on a light to reveal a modestly sized room, more than half taken up by a machine that sat against the rear wall. Coldmoon stared at it, unsure what to think. *Machine* didn't do it justice, nor did *contraption*. He'd never seen anything like it. It appeared to be a fusion of two large pieces of apparatus, wired together. The first was a device with a dazzling array of finely machined brass gears, wheels, knobs, dials, chain belts, and springs, almost like the inner workings of a gigantic clock. This was connected via thick bundles of wires to an untidy rack of computer equipment—motherboards, disk drives, keyboards, and monitors, bolted into place in a seemingly haphazard way. Two brilliantly polished stainless steel wands with copper bulbs attached protruded from opposite ends of the machine and pointed to each other at ninety-degree angles.

"How...how do you turn that baby on?" Coldmoon asked. "I don't see any switch."

Pendergast moved toward it gingerly and examined the fantastical device in silence, moving from one end to the other, peering at it with glittering eyes. He took out a penlight and began probing its innards.

Coldmoon breathed in deeply, then forced himself to look away and examine the rest of the room. There was a small metal table on the wall opposite the machine, with a chair and a cheap lamp. Sitting on the table was an ordinary laptop, next to a disorganized stack of papers and a notebook. A nearby wastebasket was filled to overflowing with balled-up paper.

The room itself was half-ruined. A brick wall to the left of the machine had a large hole bashed through it, broken bricks strewn about as if hit with a wrecking ball. Beyond, a black hole yawned. Several deep grooves raked the wall surrounding the opening, and it was splattered with what appeared to be the same strange lubricant or grease that they'd found on the bodies of the bloodless dead. The floor was littered with debris—wires, tubes, broken glass, plastic. And it was covered with more dead insects, most heavily in the spot under the single lightbulb hanging from the ceiling. They weren't moths, as Coldmoon initially thought. Perhaps they were dragonflies. But as he looked closer, he saw this, too, was incorrect: although the dead insects had wings like dragonflies', these were attached to bodies that more closely resembled hornets'.

Coldmoon walked over to the broken wall. Beyond lay what appeared to be an old coal tunnel. Lumps of coal were still scattered on the stone floor amid puddles of water, and the walls and ceiling were whitened with lime.

A faint whisper of fabric, and Coldmoon realized that Constance was now standing beside him. "I imagine this is how the creature escaped the building."

Coldmoon blinked once, twice. "Creature?"

"Yes. The one plaguing Savannah."

"This is just too strange."

She turned her violet eyes on him and quoted. "'Not only is the universe stranger than we suppose, it is stranger than we *can* suppose.'"

"And whose deathless pearl of wisdom was that?"

"Heisenberg, some say."

"You mean the guy in *Breaking Bad*?"

Constance issued a low, mirthless laugh.

Coldmoon stared at the machine, shaking his head. "That's the most insane-looking thing I've ever seen."

"I imagine," Constance replied, "that the true insanity will start once Aloysius determines how to turn it on."

As if on cue, a honeyed voice rang out. "I do believe I've found the switch."

59

Pavel seemed willing to go into the back tunnel in the tomb with Betts and Moller. Gannon gave him the go-ahead, hugely relieved that she didn't have to follow. She set up lights at the entrance to the tunnel, but they didn't penetrate the darkness beyond very well, because the tunnel took a gradual turn to the right. She decided it didn't matter: the Steadicam had a light on it and that would be enough for Pavel to get his footage. The main thing was that she wanted them to hurry up and get the footage and then get the hell out. She hoped to God that Moller wasn't going to linger.

Through her monitor, she watched what Pavel was shooting. Moller was walking forward slowly, in the front, by himself. He had laid aside the dowsing stick and was now proceeding with the Percipience Camera alone, ready to take pictures of the spiritual turbulence. The uneven clay walls of the tunnel, scored and scarred as if by a rake, flashed in and out of sight as they were caught by the Steadicam's illumination. It occurred to her that it looked like a gigantic burrow. This was unbelievably dramatic and frightening—even terrifying. *She* was frightened. At the same time, she told herself this was killer footage. Betts and Moller and their producers were going to make a fortune, and it would surely drive her own career forward, even into feature film territory. Being a director of horror movies had been her life's ambition ever since she saw the gorgeous original version of *The Haunting* as a little girl.

She was a little sorry Pavel was using the Steadicam; it didn't quite offer the handheld effect she thought would be perfect. But it was too late to change now. If Betts insisted on a second take, she'd swap out the Steadicam for Craig's shoulder rig—but this was one scene she prayed would get done in a single take. She was encouraged to see that Betts and Moller were up to their ankles in mud, and she doubted if even those two would want to do it again. Moller should just take his damn pictures of spectral disturbances or whatever and then they could get the hell out. God, she was looking forward to getting a breath of fresh air; it was like being under a foul, moist blanket. The smell of burnt rubber was now being overlaid with the stink of a locker room...or something even worse.

She shook this away and focused on her harness monitor. What the hell were those little glowing spots?

"Two, see if you can zoom in on some of those glowing spots when you get closer," she said into the headset.

"No problemo," came the answer.

Moller proceeded slowly down the tunnel, his shoes making an audible sucking sound with every step. He stopped, raised his camera, took a picture, and another. Then he continued with great care, raising each foot and placing it ahead. As he made the gradual turn in the tunnel, a sprinkling of the glowing splotches came into view.

"Pavel, tighten on those spots, please," she said.

The camera zoomed in on the cluster.

"What the hell is that?" Gannon said, more to herself than anyone else. They looked like dripping blobs of goo, or maybe fungal growths, a sort of dirty greenish color, grading to a blue in the interior.

Pavel had just finished getting some good, close footage of the nasty sludge, or whatever it was, when there came a grunt of surprise from Moller. The Steadicam swung around and Gannon could see Moller raising his camera to photograph ahead into the murky darkness. Gannon could see something in front of him, a looming shape. For a moment she was horrified, and then she realized it must be some awful trick Betts had set up in advance: two large, slitted, bloodred eyes, glowing in the dark. What the fuck? No wonder Betts had been so eager to go down the tunnel, to encounter this mockup or dummy. This was too much. He should have warned them. Boss or not, she was going to have his balls for breakfast.

The eyes blinked—double sets of lids, the inner horizontal, the outer vertical. The dim crimson orbs vanished, then reappeared. With a sound like the rustling of dead leaves, the eyes approached.

"What the fuck?" Pavel said. The Steadicam swung on its mount, then grew level again, as he began to back up.

Even from her position at the mouth of the tunnel, Gannon felt a movement of warm, stinking air across her face. A sound followed, a wheezing hiss like a torn bellows being compressed. A shape materialized into the light of the camera.

Gannon stared in her monitor. No way was this some mechanical contraption rigged up by Betts. This was real.

Pavel continued to back up, slowly, one step at a time.

"Jesus," murmured Gannon. "Oh, *Jesus*..."

She could see, through the monitor, that Moller was still standing a few paces ahead, frozen in place. But it lasted only a second. Moller spun around, dropping the camera, an expression of unadulterated horror on his face, his eyes literally protruding from his skull. He opened his mouth and a scream tore through the mephitic air; a hideous, gargling, wet scream as he tried to run, the muck tripping him up. He went down out of the camera's field of vision, the great dark thing covering his back. Betts, ten feet behind Moller, whirled in an effort to get away—but he, too, lost his balance in the mud, falling forward while grunting like a terrified sow. Pavel also turned and ran, the Steadicam swinging wildly on its harness.

With a gasp of fear, Gannon stumbled backward, trying frantically to unbuckle the monitor from its harness, desperate to rid herself of the deadweight. Everyone around her was scrambling to get away, dumping their equipment, and turning to flee—as a great gust of dank, oily air issued from the mouth of the tunnel and a huge shape came beating out, rushing toward them, demon wings spreading like a cape, voices screaming in terror and agony.

60

WELLSTONE, HIDING BEHIND THE crypt at the entrance to the tomb's lower level, was growing concerned. Moller and Betts, followed by a camera operator, had entered the tunnel, but because it seemed to both descend and make a turn, they were soon out of sight. There was no way he could get closer without revealing himself, so he had to be content with filming the crew that was left behind. That included the DP, who had refused to go in the tunnel—and no wonder, considering the foul mud that puddled its floor and the stench it emitted. But that was no impediment to Betts and Moller; they were like bloodhounds on a scent.

It looked like he wasn't going to be able to record the final act of whatever it was Moller had planned. It clearly involved the phony camera, which Moller had been clutching as he went in. Wellstone already had enough footage to prove this was all a staged bit of hocus-pocus. But missing the chance to record the finale was annoying.

As he watched the three disappear around the curve

of the tunnel, he paused, finger on the shutter release. Even if he wanted to document more, his second memory card was just about maxed out. As he crouched in his hiding place, he felt a mixture of emotions— excitement, disbelief, and fear. No: *fear* was too strong a word. He was growing uneasy. And no wonder. He couldn't wait to get the hell out of this dark and desecrated vault. Maybe he already had enough footage. It wouldn't be a disaster to get caught now, and possibly searched or even abused by that muscle-bound goon. Although, he had to admit, the guy was looking pretty sweaty and nervous at the moment. It was always the tough guys who cracked first.

He heard a muffled sound from the tunnel, like a wheezing bagpipe. He quickly readied his camera: maybe he'd get a chance for a decent shot after all. The noise was quickly followed by another, much louder— a scream and a powerful beating sound that shook the tomb. What was going on? But then his fear, which had spiked, settled as he understood: Moller's show was beginning. He heard another scream. Now the DP at the mouth of the tunnel was backing up in fear. Suddenly, she turned and tore off her monitor and harness, while the rest of the crew scattered to a chorus of shouts and screams, running pell-mell for the steps.

What the *hell*?

At that moment a dark shape exploded out of the tunnel mouth with a great rush of foul air, so large that its leathery wings scraped the walls. It lit upon the scrambling muscleman, grabbing him and forcing him to the floor of the tomb with an unfolding of those monstrous wings.

Wellstone couldn't move, couldn't breathe; he felt exactly as if he were in a nightmare, his limbs paralyzed, his body frozen. The creature's huge, rugose body was topped with a tiny head, which looked like a mosquito's, with bulbous compound eyes. A tube covered in bristles protruded outward from the head, sliding in and out, its point stabbing spasmodically this way and that.

The creature held the muscleman in place with crablike, hairy pincers attached to bristly pads. The roving tube—spasming in and out—homed in on a spot on the man's leg. Suddenly, it buried itself deep in the man's upper thigh. As his awful screeching echoed through the tomb, there was a wet sucking sound, deep and rhythmic. The creature's wings settled down over the body, covering it like a blanket, and the screaming abruptly ceased.

Seconds later—although time no longer mattered to Wellstone—the sucking noise stopped and the creature was up again, leaving the desiccated remains of the muscleman behind. With a burst of speed, it snatched another member of the crew, ripping her in two pieces as easily as twisting a loaf of bread, blood and viscera spewing out like a bursting tomato.

Wellstone's vision grew obscured. After a moment, he realized it was his own hand, held out protectively before his face. Some atavistic impulse took over, his muscles relaxed, and he sank down behind the broken crypt, curling up like a fetus, trying to make no noise, motionless, his body on autopilot. He heard the screams, the heavy beating of those awful wings, the sounds of tearing meat, of alien suction; he smelled the humid, burning-rubber stench of rushing wind as it passed over him.

And then the beating faded; the sounds died away; there was silence. And absolute darkness.

Time passed.

Then Wellstone found that he was crawling on his hands and knees in the darkness, tears running from his eyes and snot from his nose. He encountered something wet and sticky and, with no guidance from himself, his body slipped around it. One hand found a worn stone step and, unbidden, his body pulled itself closer: up the step, then the next, then the next. A faint gleam of light now was visible above, and his body moved toward it.

Reaching the top, he saw a room and, past it, the open door of the mausoleum. The light he'd seen was beyond the ruined doors. He crawled toward the light, advancing one knee, then one hand, then one knee, moving slowly and without thought.

Finally he passed through the door. The light was on his right, shining brightly, and a machine to his left was pushing out a stream of fog. He could hear the thrum of a generator.

There was a woman here. Sitting cross-legged on the ground. A blond woman, splattered in blood, with her head buried in her hands. She looked up at him as he emerged from the tomb, her face a perfect blank. The blood on her face looked like ghastly red freckles.

She looked at him for a while, then she lowered her head into her hands again.

Now Wellstone's body decided it could crawl no more. It was as if his agency had departed. He lay down next to the woman and curled up, once again in a fetal position, covering his head with his hands. Vaguely, he sensed that he was waiting, but for what, or whom, he could not say... any more than he could, or would, say anything else—ever again.

61

Terry O'Herlihy pushed Deuce off his lap, got up from his living room couch, walked through the doorway into the kitchen, and opened the refrigerator. After a brief inspection, he took out a diet iced tea, unscrewed the lid, and walked back to the couch. With a sigh, he flopped down, his form fitting easily into the depression in the springs in front of the TV. A moment later, Deuce jumped back up. Deuce was a black Pomeranian, his wife's pride and joy. It was his job to take Deuce for his nightly walk, and the way people snickered at his leading a toy lapdog by the leash made him feel like a prison punk.

He took a sip of iced tea, muttered a curse, then screwed the top back on. A humid breeze came through the open windows, stirring the embroidered lace curtains, and he held the bottle to his temple. The window air-conditioning unit had broken two days before, and his social security check wouldn't be coming until next week. If the damn stuff wasn't fit to drink, it could at least cool him off a little.

He glanced around the dimly lit room: at the shabby dining room table, the shabby hooked rug, the photos of family members in carefully dusted but yellowing frames. Forty-two years at the tool and die factory, five days a week, waiting to retire—and now he was retired, all right. Good and retired.

His wandering gaze fell on the ashtray atop the coffee table. Molly had wiped it so clean that it almost sparkled in the dark room. She was a tidy woman, but this was something that had nothing to do with tidiness; she didn't want ash, or butts, or anything in the room that would put his mind to smoking.

Same with the liquor. One at a time, she'd thrown out his bottles of rye, stuffing knickknacks in the places they'd been. The shelf in the kitchen that once held booze was now piled with dishes. She'd found the bottle he kept in the basement, too—made a big production out of disposing of that one. She was a stone bloodhound, that woman.

"Shit-fire," he muttered, putting the iced tea down with a bang. Why couldn't the woman stop dogging him? He'd spent his whole life working. What was wrong with a pack of smokes and a half-pint? Well, all right then, a pint? He felt fine; he didn't care what the doctors at Memorial said. It wasn't like he was stepping out on the battle-ax or something. A man deserved his little pleasures.

The fact was, he did have something stashed away for a rainy day—a carton of Kools and a couple bottles of Old Overholt Bonded—somewhere Molly would never find them. Just knowing they were there made him feel better.

He raised one cheek off the sofa and busted ass. Deuce pricked up his ears and looked at him reproachfully. "Come on, boy," he said a little guiltily, rising from the couch again with a grunt and reaching for the dog's leash. "Let's get this over with."

Stepping outside, he found the night air was cooler than the house, but only a little. He paused. The clouds were clearing from the night sky. The Avondale district of east Savannah was quiet, but in the distance he could make out lights and hear some kind of racket: that senator was in town again, making a nuisance of himself.

He gave the leash a yank and headed east on Louisiana Avenue. His route never varied: a few blocks down New Jersey, a block west on New York, and then a couple more back up Ohio Avenue and home. It was a short run: five minutes, as long as Deuce didn't get too busy sniffing some other dog's mess.

As he made the turn onto New Jersey Avenue, he saw the Deloach boys sitting on their front porch in the dark. A strong smell of weed drifted toward him, followed by some whispering, giggling, and then finally, a falsetto voice: "Nice hamster you got there, Mr. O'Herlihy."

Peckerwoods. He ignored them and picked up his pace a little, forcing Deuce into a trot.

He should start taking a cigarette with him on these walks. That would make it enjoyable, at least. Take tonight, for instance: Molly would be down at New Jerusalem until at least ten, planning for the upcoming game night and silent auction. But no: she'd smell it on his breath when she came home.

He could see the intersection with New York Avenue ahead. Deuce stopped to investigate a big-ass turd, but Terry was in no mood and yanked him away.

"No fun tonight, boy." At this rate, he'd make it home in a hot minute.

The wind shifted, and suddenly he heard more noise. But this wasn't coming from downtown: it seemed to be coming from the direction of the cemetery. And it wasn't cheering and clapping: it sounded more like screams.

As he stared curiously in that direction, he saw a dark cloud rise up into the heavy sky. But clouds didn't rise like that. And clouds didn't have wings.

Deuce began squeaking and barking hysterically, jerking on the leash. But Terry didn't notice. He was staring at the thing in the sky.

Skeletal wings beating slowly, it rose up, glowing a pale blue in the ghostly light of the moon. Even from this distance, he could see it had a body like a dry leather sack. As Terry watched, it hovered briefly, then—flap, flap—it glided over the Placentia Canal. It circled the industrial area hard by the cemetery, its hideous little head moving this way and that as if searching for something. And then, quite abruptly, it veered away and shot off like an arrow.

It was headed for downtown.

Terry watched until it vanished in the smoky late-spring night. Even when it was gone, he remained still for a moment. Then he shuffled around and made his way—slowly, stiff-legged—through people's backyards and driveways in a beeline for his own house. The moment he opened the door, Deuce shot inside and burrowed under the couch. Still, Terry paid him no heed. He headed past the living room, down a hallway, and into the spare bedroom. In the back of the closet, he found the loose panel of veneer and reached into the space behind it. He felt around, grabbed the carton of cigarettes, and pulled it out. But he tossed it aside, reached in again, and found a bottle of Old Overholt. Ignoring the cigarettes, he made his way back to the living room couch, sat down, and—cracking open the bottle—began sipping slowly and meditatively as the distant sounds of the night began to change.

62

Pᴇɴᴅᴇʀɢᴀsᴛ ʜᴀᴅ ᴛᴀᴋᴇɴ ᴛʜᴇ notebook off the work-table and was consulting it. Now he held it in his left hand, open for reference, while with his right he gently grasped a lever that rested on two metal supports. Beside it was a large meter with a black dial.

"That doesn't look like an on switch to me," said Coldmoon.

"It's called a knife switch. Primitive, and it will easily electrocute the careless user." He consulted the note-book again. "It would be advisable if you both stepped back. I believe that whatever is going to manifest itself will do so in the space you're currently occupying—where those two giant electrodes are pointing." And he indicated the polished steel wands, each topped with a small copper globe.

Coldmoon hastily stepped back, followed by Constance.

"This"—Pendergast indicated a dial on the face of the machine, with two hand-drawn tick marks labeled *I* and *II*—"would seem to indicate a choice of power levels. We shall start with the lower of the two."

"Are you sure about this?" Coldmoon asked.

"Not entirely." Pendergast gingerly swung the knife switch over to the opposite bracket. There was a loud spark when it made contact, and then a low vibration began. Pendergast stepped back and joined them at the far wall, and together they watched the machine warm up. A computer monitor winked into life, and various data began scrolling up several windows.

Coldmoon felt his heart pounding. He didn't think it was a good idea to just turn the damn machine on like that. But he had no alternate suggestion to make. And besides, there was no point—there never was— in arguing with Pendergast.

The vibration gradually intensified, until Coldmoon could almost feel it in his gut. The needle on the dial beside the switch began to quiver. A curious warmth seeped into the room, like the glow from an infrared lamp. And then, a flicker of light raced from one copper globe to the other. Another flicker danced from globe to globe. And then, a third arc of light appeared—but this time, it stopped midtransit, hovering at the intersection where the two steel rods pointed. He stared. The flicker began to slowly expand, and it looked to Coldmoon almost as if the very air between the copper globes had become visible: shiny, silvery, gossamer veils, rippling in a strengthening wind. And then the shimmering effect began to fade, and as it subsided, the air cleared and—in its place—a scene came into focus: a nocturnal image of a crowded city square, lit up and bustling with people and cars, and hemmed in on all sides by skyscrapers.

With a start Coldmoon recognized it. "Hey, isn't that New York?"

"So it would appear," Pendergast murmured.

It was as if a window to a distant place had opened before them. But its edges were vague and indistinct, composed of ever-shifting, rainbow-hued light. Coldmoon swallowed. The window—the portal—danced and flickered in the center of the room. It was impossible...and yet, there it was before him.

"That's Times Square," Constance said, "looking south toward the New York Times Building, and from a significant height." She paused. "I would guess the vantage point is somewhere on West Forty-Sixth Street—probably the Marriott Marquis hotel."

"I believe you're right," Pendergast said.

It was a dazzling view of the brightly illuminated square, festooned with huge screens mounted on the surrounding buildings, all glowing with advertising and logos and news images. Near the bottom of the Times Tower ran the traditional news "zipper" and, below that, a stock ticker, with stock prices running continuously along a chyron. It was a lively evening, the square swarming with tourists and theatergoers. And sound—Coldmoon could faintly make out the sounds of Times Square filtering through the portal: horns honking, the murmur and shouts of the crowds, a police whistle, the calls of buskers and hawkers. And an equally faint scent wafted out, as well: the smell of the city, of auto exhaust and pavement and burnt pretzels and shish kebab on a warm May night.

Coldmoon stared. It was too realistic to be a television screen, no matter how high the resolution; it was—again, there was no better comparison—like looking through an open window. His eye drifted over the view in wonder, then focused once more on the Times building and its iconic stack of giant screens, including temperature, date, and time.

Date and time. "That's Times Square right now," he said, astonished.

After a short silence, Constance said, "No, it isn't."

"What do you mean?"

"That isn't Times Square—at least *our* Times Square. And it's not now, either."

"The hell it's not. The date and time are posted right up on those screens. See? Nine eleven PM."

Constance slipped out a cell phone and showed its screen to Coldmoon. "It's nine *ten*. The Times Square we're looking at is one minute in the future."

Coldmoon stared back and forth from her phone to the image. The time on the large screen within the portal changed to 9:12. As it did, Constance's cell phone changed to 9:11.

"This is the secret to Ellerby's trading," Pendergast said. "And Frost's before that. As you can see, the stock ticker is streaming the price of various stocks—one minute in the future. And only the stocks of major companies are displayed, which explains why Ellerby restricted his trading to Dow Jones Industrials."

Coldmoon stared at the ticker. Stock symbols and numbers were indeed scrolling past on an endless ribbon, the symbols and numbers just so much gibberish to him. "Um, one minute? That doesn't seem like much of an advantage."

"It's enough to make a modest profit, especially during a volatile market," said Pendergast. "Which is what Miss Frost had been doing these many years: eking out small but steady gains. But when Ellerby took over the operation, he wasn't satisfied with small profits. Once he figured out how the machine worked, he was able to build an improved version using updated technology." He waved a hand at the device.

"As you can see, this is not Frost's modest briefcase machine, but a far more powerful one, capable of seeing deeper into the future."

Coldmoon could only shake his head again.

Pendergast held up the journal. "If I understand Ellerby's notes, the Roman numeral II on that dial is the second power setting. That increases the power beyond what Frost, and her friend at Boeing, intended, allowing the device to penetrate into a parallel universe running about an hour in the future. But recall, what we're seeing isn't *our* future. It's a window into parallel universes exactly like ours, whether one minute or one hour ahead. Knowing what stock prices would be in an hour, and trading on that information, would allow one to make millions. *Hundreds* of millions."

"So why are we looking at this view and not something else?" he asked.

"Frost explained that to me," said Constance. "Shortly after she got the original machine fully functional, she went to Times Square, entered a building on the north end of the intersection, ascended to a height that allowed a good vantage point, and aimed the machine out a window and down Broadway. She focused it, or rather tuned it, to this very scene. After that, wherever she took the machine, she could always use it to observe the parallel Times Square from that same vantage point. As long as the stock ticker ran the current stock prices, and as long as she didn't focus the machine elsewhere, she could trade on that information."

"This is too crazy," Coldmoon muttered. "I'm having a hard time wrapping my mind around it."

"Please do wrap your mind around it," said

Pendergast, "because I intend to increase the power to the higher level."

"Why?" Coldmoon asked.

"Because that's what Ellerby did."

Coldmoon glanced at Constance; she had turned toward Pendergast, an odd expression on her face.

"I really don't think that's a good idea," Coldmoon continued. "We should call in the FBI Evidence Response Team, have them pack this baby up and take it back to Quantico, where it can be examined in a state-of-the-art lab."

Pendergast raised an eyebrow. "You'd prefer to let our beloved *government* get their hands on it? Do you really have that much confidence in our political leaders to use this in a wise and beneficent way?"

"Oh." Coldmoon paused. "I hadn't thought of that."

"We must do this ourselves," Pendergast said as he placed his hand on the dial. "I'm convinced this device is key to whoever—or whatever—is plaguing Savannah. If we're going to understand it—and confront it—we need more information first."

And he began slowly turning the dial farther.

63

As Pendergast increased the power, it looked to Coldmoon as if someone had abruptly heaved a stone into still water. The mirror-clear view of Times Square wavered and grew suddenly distorted. The vibration in the room increased, causing an odd, slightly nauseous feeling in Coldmoon's gut—something below the range of hearing but not below the body's ability to sense it.

Now the portal flickered and shimmered, images passing by almost more quickly than he could make out: tremendously accelerated in time-lapse, twisting and tangled up in ever-shifting shapes like knots, folding and refolding over each other. Coldmoon saw many Times Squares flash past in the blink of an eye—but he also saw, or thought he saw, bizarre astronomical images of stars and galaxies and nebulae, whirling alien landscapes and twisted black holes, all in furious succession.

Pendergast's fingers stopped at the dial's second and last setting. The churning visions settled and the image of Times Square stabilized once again, like a pond returning to a quiescent state. It was still night and everything looked as before. Only now, Coldmoon noted, the time on the Times building read 10:15—an hour into the future.

The portal itself also seemed different. The shimmering edges of the image were heavier now, creating the effect of looking at this Times Square through a glimmering tunnel. And in those tunnel walls, Coldmoon could barely discern the flitting about of grotesque, otherworldly shapes. The smell of burnt rubber, which had never gone away, now intensified as a stream of warm, humid air issued from the portal.

With a sudden movement, one of the dragonfly-things, and then a second, zoomed in from the edges of the tunnel. They approached the portal, stopped, then wriggled through with effort, as if emerging from a cocoon.

"Stay back, please," Pendergast said, stretching out an arm in warning. They watched as the two insects buzzed the room: the same creatures Coldmoon had seen dead on the ground, with gossamer wings and fat abdomens carrying vicious stingers. The two spiraled upward toward the naked lightbulb in the ceiling, diving at it, hitting it again and again until their wings were broken and they fluttered to the floor. At the same time, several more insects squeezed out of the portal's membrane and flew at the lightbulb, circling and ticking on it incessantly before tangling with each other.

"It would appear," said Pendergast drily, "the higher setting allows creatures to pass through. And not from a familiar Times Square universe, either." He paused. "It seems there are other universes in there, quite different from ours."

Coldmoon watched the insects grappling, stinging each other frantically as they fell to the ground, tumbling around in a death embrace.

"Only small creatures," said Constance quickly. "Frost explained this. Those parallel universes are stacked like membranes on each other. Their edges are visible as you look down the tunnel. She called it a manifold space. It's from this space that the tiny insects emerge."

Pendergast frowned. "Frost knew of this?"

"She was speculating," said Constance.

Coldmoon saw the portal deteriorate. Its interface began to grow unstable, flickering in and out. The foul odor increased, along with the sounds from the other side: a strange scrabbling noise that raised the hairs on his neck.

"I think we've seen enough," Pendergast said, stepping up to turn down the power.

"Wait," Coldmoon cried out. "Do you see that?" He pointed at the biggest screen on the Times building, still visible in the unstable light. It was flashing BREAKING NEWS. Then the screen dissolved into what was apparently a live video feed, taken from a news helicopter: a city in flames, people running terrified through the streets, dead bodies strewn everywhere.

"That's Savannah!" cried Coldmoon. "My God, what's happening?"

Swinging into view of the camera came a beast out of nightmare: a giant bat with a distended body, a wicked mosquito-like head swiveling this way and that, its dripping proboscis spasming in and out. And on cue, the news ticker began streaming: HUNDREDS DEAD IN BRUTAL ATTACK ON SAVANNAH GA, MILITARY MOBILIZED...

64

Seconds after the newsfeed flashed across the portal, with Pendergast's and Coldmoon's attention riveted on the scene of disaster unfolding on the Times Square screen, Constance ducked out of the room, exiting through the concealing closet and out into the basement. She'd had a revelation and was already thinking beyond the devastation that was being wreaked—*would be* wreaked—on Savannah.

She took the stairs up into the lobby, and then still farther up, three more flights. Making her way quickly down the hallway, she reached the closed door that led up to Frost's penthouse. This time it was locked. Pulling a hairpin from a pocket of her dress, she picked the lock, then ran up the stairs. The door at the top of the landing was locked, too; Constance shook the knob and then, in a sudden display of rage, violently kicked it—once, twice—and it flew open, banging loudly against the doorstop.

The interior of the apartment was even darker

than usual, lit only by a few Tiffany lamps. Along the room's far side, the shutters over the French doors had been pulled up, exposing the balcony and the twinkling rooftops beyond. The *byōbu* screens had been pulled back, giving the rooms a spectacular view of Savannah. The moonlight, punctuated by scudding clouds, threw dappled shadows over the bookcases, sculptures, and furniture.

She glanced around quickly. Frost was just visible, sitting on the same sofa as during their previous conversation, the pearl-handled cane resting by her side. She was wearing an elegant kimono-style dressing gown in crimson silk, and beneath it a white silk blouse. There was an open bottle of wine on the tea table, and a single glass, half-full.

The book she never seemed to be without was on her lap, and she was making a notation in it. Now Frost put volume and pen aside. "That was rude," she said. "However, at least you spared me the trouble of having to open the door. I'm afraid this old corpus of mine is acting up more than usual this evening."

This was said in the same droll tone the woman had used before. Constance nevertheless detected a quaver in the old lady's voice: an undercurrent of fear. Breathing hard, she stepped forward.

"Join me in a glass of Giacomo Conterno. Since your last visit, I've been doing some rooting around in my collections."

"There's no time for wine or chitchat," Constance said.

"My, my, you do seem a trifle overexcited."

"You lied to me."

"I never lied to you."

Constance cut her off with a gesture. "At the very

least, you left out something important. Something Ellerby did."

Instead of answering, Miss Frost raised her glass. But her hand was trembling so much that she put the glass down without sipping.

"I've seen the machine," Constance continued. "In use. Both at the first setting...*and* the second. No doubt you saw that yourself when you surprised Ellerby in the basement. But there's more to it, isn't there?"

Hearing this, Frost remained silent.

In an instant, Constance stood over the proprietress. "No excuses," she said. "No remonstrances. You're too old for those to matter, anyway...Miss Rime."

Hearing herself addressed by her true name, Frost's pallid eyes widened.

"You robbed an old man of his life's work. And now you've let Ellerby turn his invention into a nightmare. Intentional or not, you still have to answer for it. So you will tell me what you've been withholding... beginning with whether Ellerby experimented with any settings *past those marked on the dial*."

The world-weary façade dropped from Frost's face.

"The time for lying is past. Savannah's on the verge of destruction—we saw it in the machine. Tell me everything you know, everything you *suspect*, now."

"It's the many-worlds hypothesis I mentioned," Frost said immediately. "Patrick was greedy. He souped up the machine to see an hour ahead. But to do that, the portal has to traverse many more universes— some quite unlike ours. And the chance grows that the portal would not simply cross those worlds, but... intersect with them. Open a door to them."

When she fell silent, Constance heard, filtering up from below, what sounded like shouts and screams:

faint through the closed windows but distinctly audible. "Do you hear that?"

"Sounds like typical Savannah drunkenness," said Frost.

"It isn't. We're out of time. Answer my question: if Ellerby pushed the machine farther than level two, *what would happen?*"

But even as Frost began to protest, a tremendous crash sounded outside. The eyes of the two women met. They both moved to the French doors overlooking Savannah. Constance flung them open and stepped out onto the balcony, stiletto in hand. A yellow light played over her face as she stared eastward, toward the sound of tumult and chaos. Frost stepped out on the balcony beside Constance. As the two gazed down across the city, Frost instinctively raised a hand to her mouth—but it did little to muffle the cry of horror that came involuntarily to her lips.

65

Commander Alanna Delaplane stood at the southern end of Forsyth Park, flanked by two lieutenants, observing the rally. So far it had gone off without a hitch. She could see the senator on his platform, high above the crowd, his voice booming out from the speaker towers. Behind him were two gigantic screens displaying and amplifying his speech as he stabbed the air with his finger and pumped his fist, the crowd roaring its approval and waving placards and flags.

Delaplane privately believed Drayton was a first-class jackass, one of those politicians who gave a lot of lip service to supporting law enforcement but, in fact, was always first to cut funding. But she'd never breathe a word of her personal views to her colleagues. Nobody knew her politics and that was just fine with her.

The protesters the senator had been worried about turned out to be half a dozen dispirited young people waving signs and shouting, unable to make their voices heard over the boom of the speakers and the roars of the crowd. She wondered how a guy like Drayton could generate a turnout this big and enthusiastic. There was something about him a certain type of person loved, it seemed. She just couldn't see it.

Her radio hissed, then emitted a screech, followed by a torrent of unintelligible shouting.

"Officer," she said, "take a deep breath and identify yourself."

"Officer Warner, ten thirty-three! Got a…flying…a crazy thing flying…attacking…*What the—?*"

There was so much background noise the words disappeared into the roar. "What is the nature of your situation?" Delaplane yelled. The officer had sounded incoherent, panic-stricken.

There was a burst of static, and then the transmission was cut off.

Now the radios of all the cops around her were suddenly abuzz with hysterical chatter. As she tried to get through the jammed emergency frequency, she heard sirens to the east. And something else: a chorus of car alarms and faint screams.

She pressed transmit. "Dispatch, dispatch, Delaplane here. What's going on?"

"Avondale, east Savannah, multiple reports of assaults. Something, uh, flying, assaulting people."

"What are you talking about?"

As the dispatcher spoke—and none of it made any sense—Delaplane could hear a sound in the air, a clamor rolling in from the disturbance to the east and rapidly getting louder. She turned and looked over the tops of the oaks lining Drayton Street. Now she could see an orange light in the sky, and a rising column of smoke—a fire.

She focused on her radio, but the dispatcher was

making no sense, just broadcasting a 10-33 over and over. The officers around her seemed uncertain what to do, looking to her for direction.

Delaplane rounded on them. "Okay, you heard it. We got a situation in east Savannah. Something big, a ten thirty-three, all officers respond. Now. Let's—"

Drayton's voice faltered midholler. The crowd stirred, suddenly silent, uneasy. The eastern sky was reddening fast and the night was now filling with the sounds of car alarms and sirens. The booming voice from the speakers stopped and she glanced over at the stage. Drayton was staring eastward, mouth agape. And then she saw what he was staring at: a dark shape, backlit by the reddish sky, flapping its wings slowly, almost lazily, as it approached. She stood transfixed as her mind tried to make sense of it. A bird of prey? No: it was too large, too far away. Some sort of flying contraption? It was dark and yet shimmery at the same time. It glided over the tops of the buildings, which seemed to reflect off its underside. Christ, it was the size of a small plane.

The deep silence that had fallen over the crowd was cut by a single thin scream—and then all hell broke loose. The massive shape came straight for the gathering, gliding in as if attracted by the noise, light, and multitude. It passed over the stage, abruptly illuminated from below by the floodlights. Now she could see it in detail, but that was of little help: it was like nothing she'd ever seen in her life. A mosquito head with huge bug eyes and an oily feeding tube was affixed to a monstrous, batlike body the color of liver. The wings were webbed with engorged blood vessels, and from its belly hung two rows of hairy, withered dugs. After passing over the stage, it banked and came back around, pumping its wings with a sound like tearing silk, gliding in low, each thrust sending a wash of foul, humid air over the terrified, stampeding crowd. Delaplane saw the greasy proboscis thrusting out, like a dog's nose scenting the air, the compound eyes swiveling this way and that.

In a flash, the gathering had been transformed into a pandemonium beyond all belief. The thousands of rallygoers ran from the platform like a massive wave, with an inchoate roar of terror, scrambling every which way, falling and being trampled, chairs clattering and overturning, shoes coming loose, people clawing up the backs of others as they tried to escape— and on the stage, high above, was Drayton, his face on the giant screens slack-jawed, jowls quivering, as the creature swooped in. Delaplane saw a flash of savage talons close like a steel trap around Drayton's torso, and then he was yanked upward, the creature rising into the air with a beating of its leathery wings, with Drayton twisting and writhing like a fish torn from the water by an eagle, a single shrill scream echoing down from above.

The senator's security detail—the few who hadn't fled—pulled their weapons and, crouching on the stage, opened fire on the thing as it rose. Delaplane pulled her own Glock, the cops around her following suit, but the thing was beating upward and out of range—and she held her fire; the chances of hitting the senator were too great. Besides, it seemed the barrage of gunfire from the others wasn't hurting it, just making it mad. As she watched, it reared its mosquito head back and plunged the sharp end of its dripping, tube-shaped labrum into the senator's body. Drayton's keening voice was abruptly silenced—followed immediately by the wet, gurgling sound of a thick milkshake being sucked up with a straw.

She pulled her radio again. "Commander Delaplane, in Forsyth Park. We need SWAT, we need National Guard, we need heavy weapons, we need full mobilization. Now! *Now!*"

And just at that moment, the panicked, mindless crowd reached the police staging position, surging over them like a human tsunami, and Delaplane felt the glancing impact of a burly man with a shaved head, and she staggered backward as the crowd streamed by.

66

FOLLOWING PENDERGAST, COLDMOON SPRINTED up the basement stairs and into the lobby. The normally sedate space was quickly filling with a crush of panicked people streaming in from outside, seeking shelter. Some were sobbing with fear, others hysterical, a few drunk. As they pushed their way through the flow, Coldmoon wondered where the hell Constance had gone to when she'd slipped out of the room like a cat. God knew what that bloodthirsty woman was going to do.

Once they were outside, the situation was even more chaotic. To the south, in the direction of the political rally, he could see a monstrous flying creature circling like a buzzard, its outline shimmering with an otherworldly gleam, a strange glowing cross, almost like a scar, on its left wing. Something—a body—was gripped in its claws. Pulling his firearm, Pendergast ran toward it, against the crowd, and Coldmoon struggled to keep up. The air was filled with the din of screaming, sirens, and sporadic gunfire. The sidewalks and streets were packed with panicked people trying desperately to get away, to get anywhere, as long as it offered refuge from the creature.

As he watched in awe and horror, the monster flung away the corpse in its talons, which went tumbling off into the darkness, and then swooped down on the terrified crowd still in the park, to a chorus of screams and a scattered volley of weaponry. It rose again, beating its wings, with several fresh writhing people in its talons, wings shimmering.

Coldmoon stared at the fearful thing, trying to keep moving, trying to make sense of what he was seeing. This was not Wakinyan, the Thunderer, the sky spirit his grandmother had told him of. Nor was it Unktehi, the huge horned serpent that had troubled his childhood dreams. No: this was some terrible amalgam, a foul obscenity, a battle-scarred monster that had no place on Earth or in mythology.

No place on Earth…

"Keep up!" Pendergast barked as they struggled toward the park, while the thing whirled overhead, tormented by gunfire as a bull might be by fleas. It dropped once in a while to scoop up more people, ripping them apart in midair, flinging the pieces away and then diving again, in a fury of bloodlust.

Pendergast dodged and weaved through the flow of people like a cat, Coldmoon in his wake. "We have to get closer to it," he said. "And gain some altitude." Then, suddenly, he pointed. "The church!"

Coldmoon heard a crash ahead and saw the amplifier towers toppling over in a shower of sparks and sizzling arcs of electricity. A moment later, flames licked up from the giant wooden stage, swiftly growing into a conflagration. The fire seemed to excite the creature, driving it almost to madness: it circled around, wings brushing the fire and scattering burning lumber, and made a loop above Whitaker Street, wingtips clipping trees and striking the façades along the park, sending glass and bricks crashing into the crowded street. A car, crushed by a falling tree, burst into flames.

The fabric of the Whitaker Street Methodist Church loomed up, its steeple outlined against the fire. They ran up the front steps. The oak doors of the church were closed and locked, terrified people huddling in the portal. Pendergast snaked his way through them, went for the lock on the door, and in a moment had it open.

As people streamed into the sanctuary, Pendergast veered off toward one side. They paused to catch their breath and take stock. Coldmoon could see the orange light of the burning grandstand flickering through stained-glass windows.

"This way," Pendergast said.

He had found a stairway behind a door, and they began climbing, taking the stairs two at a time. In a moment they came out in the choir loft, facing a wall of organ pipes. But Pendergast was already making for a locked door in one corner; a quick twist of his wrist and it flew open, revealing an old iron staircase spiraling up into darkness.

Round and round the tower they climbed, until they were stopped by a ceiling with a trapdoor. Pendergast slammed it open with his shoulder and climbed into a small square room surrounded on all sides by louvers. Countless small bells hung suspended by ropes from horizontal beams: the church's carillon. But Pendergast, paying no attention to these, pushed his way through the louvers, triggering a din of tinkling bells, and came out on a small walkway that surrounded the steeple. Coldmoon could see they were above the tree-tops. The monster, still circling, was coming around in a long, lazy loop that would take it directly past the church.

"Higher," said Pendergast. He swung up, grasping a rusty iron ladder fastened directly to the outside slope of the steeple itself.

"Wait!" cried Coldmoon. "Don't you realize this is hopeless?"

Pendergast paused ever so briefly.

"We already know what's going to happen!" Coldmoon shouted. "We *saw* it!"

"*Nothing* is certain!" Pendergast replied fiercely, and began climbing.

67

CONSTANCE STARED OUT OVER the rooftops to see, circling above Forsyth Park, a creature out of a nightmare. Leathery wings spanning several dozen feet or more sprang from a swollen, hairy abdomen, itself festooned with two rows of greasy, foot-long paps. Protruding above the wings was a head that looked like a hellish mix of horsefly and mosquito: compound eyes gleaming in the reflected light, wicked proboscis slithering in and out from its maw. Big as it was, the head was still horribly small in comparison to the distended body, and it gleamed like the chitinous exoskeleton of an ant. As Constance stared, the beast seemed to go in and out of focus—once, twice—its silhouette flickering like a bad video.

She had seen this effect before: when looking through the portal.

Even as she watched in horror mingled with fascination, the thing swooped down toward the park and, talons furrowing up divots from the ground, snatched up two individuals. Rising again, it squeezed them between its claws like grapes and let the remains drop away.

Constance spun around. Miss Frost was standing beside her, one hand over her mouth, horror-struck.

"I imagine this is your work," she said coldly. "Yours and Ellerby's."

"No—"

"Ellerby pushed the machine too far, didn't he?"

The old woman stared.

"You went into the basement. You confronted him. You knew he'd built a new machine. And you knew what it might do."

"I *didn't* know—" Frost said breathlessly, backing up against the French doors.

"But you guessed." Constance advanced on her. "You could have stopped him. You could have destroyed the machine."

"He threatened me—"

"You didn't stop him because you *loved* him."

Frost had no answer.

"When Ellerby was killed, you could have said something. Maybe this"—she flung back an arm—"could have been prevented. But you were in denial. You stayed up here, playing the piano and drinking absinthe, while that demon out of the Old Testament killed, and killed again. And now those deaths, and *this* destruction, are on you."

"No, no," the old woman croaked. "Please, I didn't know. I'll do anything—"

"Maybe you can redeem yourself," said Constance.

The old lady gulped for air. "How—?"

"Help me kill it. You said you had a collection of weapons. Show me."

After another shuddering breath, Frost took tight

hold of her cane and stepped inside from the balcony.
She led the way into the library. One wall held display
cases of objects of unusual industrial design. Frost
hurried up to the adjacent wall and touched the plate
of a light switch, which opened to reveal a large brass
drawer pull, fastened vertically.

"You do it," Frost said, stepping aside. "It takes
strength I no longer have."

Constance grasped the handle and pulled. With
a creak, a large section of the wall swung away on
hidden hinges. Beyond she could see a row of narrow
metal doors, all closed, spaced perhaps four feet apart,
marked with labels.

Frost pointed with her cane. "Third door on
the left."

Constance opened the door and turned on the light.
Arranged on shelves she saw a veritable museum
of weaponry. Along the left wall were derringers,
dueling pistols, ancient six-guns, and—ironically—
a Les Baer 1911 Heavyweight. And on the wall to
her right were two long guns, including an ancient
Henry .44 rimfire lever-action. Beside these rifles was
an automatic weapon with a drum magazine and—
beneath it—a worn wooden case with black stenciling
on one end.

"I helped bring that thing to life," Frost said. "I
have a duty to destroy it."

"What about ammunition?"

She pointed to the weapon with a drum magazine,
resting on two rubber-covered hooks. "This Thompson tommy gun has a full magazine." She glanced
back at Constance. "I suppose you've never handled a
machine gun?"

"Not one that small."

Frost began to laugh, then faltered when Constance did not smile.

"And that?" Constance pointed to the wooden crate.

"A recoilless M1 'stovepipe' bazooka."

Removing the wooden lid and flinging away a covering of straw, Constance saw a metal tube, about the length of a bassoon but with a wider mouth, painted in camouflage. A handgrip was attached to its belly. Nestled against it were shells with fins. Constance lifted it out.

"No," Frost said. "That one is suicide. Those old solid-propellant rockets become unstable over time. The ones in that crate are only ten years younger than I am."

"Very well." Putting it back, Constance picked up the tommy gun and swiftly examined it. There were two lollipop-style toggle switches set just above the left side of the wooden grip. Constance swiveled the rear switch from "safe" to "fire" and the front switch from "single" to "full." Then she reached for the charging handle on the right side of the receiver and, with a firm yank, pulled it all the way back.

"I guess you weren't kidding," Frost said.

At that moment, the lights flickered, then went out.

Carrying the gun, Constance ran out of the storage vault, through the library, and to the balcony. It was brighter outside, the city painted with flames from a dozen fires. She paused, shocked anew at the sight of the creature and the destruction and death it was wreaking. It was closer than where she'd first seen it, gliding over the park, approaching the hotel.

She knew the drum magazine carried a hundred rounds, which seemed adequate to bring down the creature. It was not an accurate weapon, better at spraying bullets at close range than hitting anything distant.

She waited. The monster was making long, low circles over the city, dipping down and killing as it went—getting closer to her with each turn. Now and then, she could see the impact of bullets against it; they dimpled the chitinous exterior, and occasionally penetrated it, but none appeared to do serious damage.

She raised the weapon, brought the notch and post of the sights into alignment, and watched it, waiting. It approached and banked, exposing its underbelly—and she fired a burst. The submachine gun bucked in her hands, the rounds rattling around inside the drum. She saw her fire was dropping too early and she corrected. With her second burst, she saw shimmering gouts of blue stitching their way along the thing's underbelly, and she knew she'd connected.

With an unearthly screech the creature veered around and came arrowing straight for her, its leathery wings cutting through the air. As it approached, she stood her ground, firing short bursts. Although most of the rounds hit home, and they had clearly done some damage, their main effect seemed to be enraging it further.

Still it came on, screeching, directly at her. Constance held her ground, firing. At that moment she heard a whoosh and a tongue of smoke like a tracer bullet spiraled toward the creature, striking one wing with a massive explosion, spraying phosphorescent flesh and blood. The creature squealed and dove away.

Frost was standing at the other end of the balcony, bazooka on her shoulder, its business end resting on the parapet.

"I thought you said that was too dangerous to use," Constance called out.

"Less dangerous than that hell-spawn," Frost replied.

It was rising up into view again, shrieking its desire for revenge, compound eyes shining like ghastly reflectors. There was now a small, ragged tear in one wing, caused perhaps by the bazooka. Constance aimed, let off the final burst from her magazine.

And then, suddenly, Constance was knocked down by an explosion, the Thompson skittering away and off the edge of the balcony. She sat up, her ears ringing, as a roiling cloud of smoke rose up, revealing Frost, lying crumpled near blown-out French doors. The bazooka lay across her, its tube petaled and afire.

It was all too obvious what had happened.

The beast had veered off. Constance took the opportunity and rushed over, scooped up Frost, carried her inside, and placed her on a sofa. The old woman's crimson Japanese nightgown was now soaked with blood. There came a shuddering crash from outside as the creature rammed the building, all the windows shattering and throwing glass across the carpets, the entire structure shaking.

At the noise, Frost's eyes fluttered open. They came into focus, swiveled toward Constance. And then the mortally wounded woman raised one arm and—with a faint crook of the index finger—beckoned her nearer.

The creature rammed the building a second time, plaster falling and cracks running across the walls and ceiling. A chandelier fell with a crash.

Constance knelt. The woman gripped her forearm

with surprising strength, staring into her eyes. Her lips moved, but no sound came.

"How," Constance asked, "can we kill it? It seems almost impervious."

"It must be...super..."

"What?"

"Superposition," she gasped. "It...exists in both worlds. But it can be harmed...far more easily in its own."

The old woman's hand went limp and slid off hers, falling to the floor.

Constance heard the creature's scream of rage and saw it heading once again for the balcony. She sprinted for the door as another crash sounded, this one massive, apocalyptic: the beast was beating its wings against the building, clawing at it, shaking it to its foundations. Constance flung open the door to the staircase and fled down it as another blow came; there was a crackle of splintering wood and grinding brick; and then, with a roar of collapse, everything came down around her and there was only darkness.

68

Cursing, Coldmoon followed Pendergast up the outside pitch of the steeple, grasping one rung after another. He wasn't normally afraid of heights, but the ladder was badly corroded and he could feel it shifting and groaning under their combined weight. Everything looked so tiny below: the people like ants, their screams faraway...except here, at eye level, the monster itself was enormous, terrifying: flapping and gliding, its bug eyes rotating, that horrible mouth tube sucking in and out. As it passed by, it left in its wake a foul reek of burnt rubber, its talons dripping with gore and tattered clothing.

As it glided northward toward their hotel, Cold-moon, clinging desperately to the railing, could hear the stuttering sound of an automatic weapon, tiny bursts of flame stitching themselves along the under-belly of the beast. This was followed by a muffled roar, the brute screaming in pain as it was struck by a more powerful blast.

They kept climbing until they were just below the

top, above the treetops with a clear line of fire in all directions. Looking northward, Coldmoon could see the beast attacking a building, beating its huge wings against it, circling up and dashing itself once more against the structure, screaming all the while. Bricks, broken pieces of wood, and glass flew into the air before falling back into a widening cloud of dust. It swerved off and, with a hideous screech, resumed its circling rampage.

"Jesus," Coldmoon muttered, more to himself than to Pendergast. It looked like that thing had just taken out the upper floor of their hotel.

The beast began circling toward them again.

"Get ready!" Pendergast cried, wrapping an arm around a rung of the ladder while he pulled out his 1911. Coldmoon did the same, bracing himself, Browning in one hand. There was a sharp snapping sound as one of the attachments to the steeple ladder broke off with a green puff of oxidation. This was followed by another snap. The ladder began to sway.

He couldn't think of that now. He had to focus on the creature.

It was closing in on the church. Up close it seemed more alien than ever, almost like a projection, with a semitransparent shimmer moving in waves across its dark leathery hide, looking almost like the exoskeleton of an insect.

Coldmoon took a bead as he tried to control his breathing, his pounding heart. As the monster glided past, not fifteen feet from them, he fired one round after another, evenly and carefully, aiming at the creature's center of mass. He could hear, directly above him, Pendergast's measured firing as the agent emptied his mag.

The beast was hit. It twisted in midair, emitting a dreadful screech at the upper frequency of audibility, like talons on a blackboard—and came back around, flying straight at them.

"Down!" Pendergast cried.

Coldmoon needed no encouragement. He holstered his Browning and half climbed, half slid down the rungs, the creature closing in. With a judder of metal, the rotten ladder snapped free from a row of fastenings and swung out into space. Coldmoon lost his footing, grabbing desperately at a rung with only his hands as he dangled in limbo, swaying a hundred feet above the ground, bodies and cars below like so many tiny toys...but then it swung back, picking up momentum, and Coldmoon managed to get his feet back on the bottom rung as the ladder slammed against the steep roof. He jumped desperately for the narrow balcony below and fell heavily onto it. It swung wildly away once again with Pendergast still clinging to it. Grasping the parapet, Coldmoon reached out and pulled the senior agent onto the walkway. The two dove into the carillon nest just as the ladder peeled away entirely—and the creature struck the steeple.

There was a shuddering crash and the entire structure jarred sideways with a mighty cracking of wooden beams and a cascade of slate shingles as the top began to shear off.

Coldmoon dove through the open trapdoor, tumbled partway down the spiral staircase before recovering his footing, then continued down at top speed, Pendergast behind him. The staircase crackled like fireworks as its wood frame shattered, showering them with splinters. They reached the bottom just as the entire tower tore away, plummeting into the crowded street with a thunderous roar, sending up a great plume of dust.

Coldmoon and Pendergast emerged into the nave just as the creature came back to hit the church broadside. It thrashed against the windows, beating out the stained glass and showering everyone inside. The crowd surged toward the doors, panicking to get out amid the rain of glass and falling beams. Pendergast grabbed an old woman and led her out the back door, Coldmoon following with a child, emerging into a small churchyard in the back, while the creature abandoned the church and flew off, resuming its circling of destruction.

In the churchyard, they paused to recover their breath—and their wits.

"We need heavier weapons," Pendergast said as he ejected an empty mag and slapped in a fresh one. "These do minimal damage."

Coldmoon checked his Browning. "Listen to me. That heavy weaponry won't arrive in time. We know how this is going to end; we *saw* the future— Savannah in ruins, this church burned to the ground." He looked into Pendergast's eyes and saw real despair.

Pendergast reached out and grasped his shoulder. "There is one thing."

"What?" Coldmoon cried.

"Maybe the future can be changed."

Coldmoon stared at his partner. There was a new look in his eyes.

"How?"

"Don't follow me," Pendergast said. And then he was gone without another word.

Coldmoon turned. The creature was coming around once again, bloody talons extended, ripping into the crowd of fleeing people.

He had four rounds left. He braced himself, holding the Browning with both hands, and aimed as the monster swept toward him.

69

IN THE SHELTER OF the old war monument, Commander Delaplane had set up a makeshift emergency command center, commandeering Senator Drayton's campaign bus to do so. He was gone—gone for good—and his people had all fled. But the bus was exactly what she needed, fitted out with a police scanner, radio, fast internet, and several flat-panel television screens tuned to news channels. It also had an independent source of power, necessary now that pockets of the city had been plunged into darkness.

What she was witnessing was incredible, unfathomable—and so she'd tried to push the disbelieving part of her mind away for the time being and concentrate on the tasks at hand. The grandstand had gone up like a bonfire and was still burning furiously. The park was now mostly clear of people, at least those still alive and mobile; left behind was a vast scene of horror, with the wounded crying out in pain and the dead left trampled in grotesque positions on the grass and surrounding walkways. Yellow beams from portable torches or flashlights winked here and there. Some EMTs had arrived and were struggling to do basic triage, but they had few ambulances or equipment.

The problem was, people couldn't escape the historic city center except on foot. The narrow streets leading away were jammed with abandoned cars, blocks and blocks of them, many ablaze. Most of the EMTs and fire crews were unable to get through. In addition to the hordes of tourists in town, thousands of people had been bused in for the rally—those very buses parked on side streets causing blockages of their own. People were desperate to take shelter somewhere, anywhere. Her radio crackled with reports of restaurants and hotel lobbies flooding with humanity. And the hellish creature was flying around in a fury, killing indiscriminately, bashing into buildings, and knocking down power poles and streetlights.

She and her officers were desperately trying to get an orderly evacuation underway, but the scene was proving too chaotic. She'd never seen anything like it. Many people, including some of her own officers, were literally losing their minds.

A news helicopter had appeared with a camera crew, flying along the southern end of the historic district. She could see the simulcast on one of her television screens in the bus. They certainly had stones—or were just plain stupid. When the monster spotted the chopper, it went straight for it as it might a rival, talons extended. Grabbing a shotgun from the weapon cache, she ran outside the bus just in time to see the chopper spiral down from the sky, crashing just beyond Martin Luther King Jr. Boulevard. A ball of fire rose up over the rooftops, enveloping the West Broad Library in smoke and flame.

Delaplane stood outside the bus, shouting largely ineffectual commands into her radio. The monster, having knocked the helicopter from the sky, was now cruising the length of Whitaker Street, flying low. She heard an eruption of gunfire from the direction of the Methodist church. Two people were clinging to a ladder bolted to the steeple, firing at the brute. From this distance she couldn't be sure, but it looked like the two FBI agents. Christ, they were brave. The monster, annoyed by the gunfire, swooped back around, smashing the steeple with its wings and sending it toppling into the street. Then it clawed at the church's façade, violently flapping its wings in a fury. Many people had taken refuge in the church, and now they came streaming out like ants from a burning log.

She got back on the radio. "Where the hell is the National Guard?" she screamed. "We need more firepower!"

The hopeless dispatcher said the guard couldn't get through; the streets were jammed.

"Have them get out of the damned vehicles and hoof it!" She paused. "Put me through directly!"

A few seconds later, a Guardsman from Operations got on the line. What she wanted wasn't possible, he said; it was against protocol to abandon their backup firearms, ammo, and equipment in the vehicles.

"Fly them in on choppers, then!"

The man told her that Black Hawks, loaded with troops and missiles, were being scrambled and would be in the air in fifteen minutes.

The eerily calm voice infuriated her. "Fifteen minutes?" she said, hoarse from yelling. "I want them now! And where the hell are those MRAPs you said were on their way?"

They were, she was told, trying to clear passageways from the interstate through to West Gaston Street and from the Truman Parkway through East President to Bay, but both routes were blocked by deserted vehicles and were taking time to clear.

"Bring troops up the river, then!"

They were working on that, she was told, but it wasn't a simple thing, and—

With a curse, Delaplane cut off the transmission, holstered the radio, and turned to the officers who had responded to her call. Only twelve. But they were all good men and women—and they were awaiting her orders.

"Listen up!" she said as she looked down the line. "The National Guard's on its way. But we can't wait. Until they get through, we've got to take this bitch down ourselves. You all ready?"

There was a ripple of silent nods.

"That's what I like to hear!" She raised the shotgun, ratcheted a shell into the chamber. "*Lock and load!*"

70

Pendergast raced down Whitaker Street through a hurricane of chaos. Ignoring the shrieks of the creature circling above, he navigated among the half-burnt vehicles until he saw the bulk of the Chandler House ahead and to the left, through the smoke.

The upper floor of the building was wrecked, and the structure looked unstable, with great cracks running down the façade. Pendergast entered to find the lobby empty and lightless, a pall of dust hanging in the fetid air, the structure still groaning and settling from the damage. Reaching into his jacket, he pulled out a small Fenix flashlight from his suit pocket and switched it on. Moving quickly, he made his way to the service door and descended into the basement, then raced down the long corridor past the off-limits sign, into the graveyard of hotel furniture. It was much quieter down here, the clamor above almost inaudible; much louder were the occasional creaks of the hotel's old timbers, complaining of the recent assault. Pendergast reached the large wardrobe in the far wall and threw open the door, entering the secret room. A phrase of Constance's echoed in his mind: *Those parallel universes are stacked like membranes on each other.* Constance was holding something back...and now he thought he knew what it was.

Once in Ellerby's lab, he turned on the light, relieved to see the hotel's backup power was working. Everything appeared as he and Coldmoon had left it. He saw that the device was off, the knife switch open, the dial twisted all the way counterclockwise.

Thank God Constance had not gotten here before him. He was certain she realized what he now did.

He checked his weapon: a round in the chamber and a spare mag. He threw the knife switch to activate it, turned the power switch to the first position, and waited while it hummed to life. When the portal appeared between the two poles—shimmering, streaming with light—he moved the switch to the second position. Turning back to the portal, he filled his lungs with air, took one hesitating step, then abruptly walked into it.

There was a crackle of lightning; blue arcs of electricity shot out of the portal, and he felt himself thrown backward and onto the floor.

Slowly, he stood up again, gathering his wits. What had gone wrong? He'd seen plenty of insects come through the portal. The beast had clearly come through the portal. Why couldn't he make a reverse journey?

As he went back over his thoughts of the evening, his own words returned to him. *The "hole" Ellerby poked became larger and larger as the machine grew more powerful; Ellerby made more and more money on the market...and then it happened. The hole grew big enough for something to come through it. Something from the other side.*

But Ellerby had been using the machine at the higher setting for weeks already, looking an hour into the future. The creature had not come through the portal until recently; the last time, in fact, that Ellerby fired the machine into life...

And then he understood. Ellerby, possessed by greed or curiosity, had decided to push the machine farther, past its second setting...and in doing so, created a portal wide enough for something much larger than insects...

He glanced quickly down at the dial that controlled the main power. Grasping the knob, Pendergast rapidly twisted it past the II mark.

The hum of the machine rose almost to a scream. The portal brightened, its edges beginning to flicker with a furious intensity. The view of Times Square, which had just stabilized across the portal, now faded into a shimmering tunnel, with the Square itself attenuated to a small image at the far end. *Those parallel universes are visible as you look down the tunnel.*

Pendergast extended his hand. This time, he was able to pierce the membrane. But he pulled his hand back instinctively when he felt a crawling sensation.

Once again, he took a deep breath. Then, without allowing himself time to think any further, he tensed and strode into the portal.

71

D ELAPLANE LED HER OFFICERS across the park and toward the beast, which was now battering down another church, this one on Drayton Street. Seeing its furious assault on a Christian icon just made her more certain this was a creature from hell itself. She wondered if she might be witnessing the Apocalypse— with this the beast of destruction, the dark angel of the bottomless pit as described in Revelation. But whether it was the end or not, she still had a duty to carry out. She'd always been a believer, tried to live as a Christian, and whatever happened to her, God would sort things out. Right now, she had a responsibility to fulfill—to protect the people and kill that bitch monster.

She led her officers past the burning platform and to the north end of the park, where the brute was now flying up from the ruins of the church. With a screech it banked north toward the river, and she thought for a moment that perhaps it might just fly off. But no such luck: it came back around, huge wings flapping as it gained speed. It was heading in straight and low, following a path that would take it along Drayton Street. As it swung lower, its wings clipped a power pole, sending it down in a shower of sparks.

Delaplane turned to her crew. "Spread out and take cover among the cars. We'll unload as it flies past."

Drayton Street was packed with abandoned cars, in the roadway and up on the sidewalks. Her officers fanned out among them, crouching behind vehicles and taking aim as the creature came beating its way up the street, fast and low, backwash from its wings thrashing the trees on either side.

"Wait for my signal," Delaplane cried. She didn't want any panicked firing before it came into range.

It glided still lower. The stench of burning rubber filled her nostrils. She could see it closely now, its bug head swiveling this way and that, its proboscis, like a big-bore hypodermic, trembling and twitching. The entire thing was shimmering with a faint blue light, as if electrified, and at times it seemed almost transparent, more a hologram than something solid. But the death and destruction it was wreaking were real enough.

She felt the roaring in her ears as the beast closed in. "*Fire!*" she screamed, and they unloaded as it swept over. The thing reacted violently to the rain of lead, twisting and issuing an unholy screech. It thrashed its wings, tangled momentarily in a great oak, then tore off a heavy tree limb as it reversed flight and plunged down, talons extended like steel traps. The cops kept up their fire as the enraged creature scrabbled among the cars, bashing, crushing, and overturning them as it tried to get at her officers. She watched in horror as it sank its talons into one of them, Sergeant Rollo, rising into the air as it literally tore the man into pieces, then flinging the gobbets away and coming back to seize another.

While the firing seemed to enrage the creature, it didn't appear to be doing any significant damage. As she watched, it briefly flickered in and out of focus.

Delaplane kept up a steady fire until her ammo ran out; she ejected the magazine, pulled the spare from her service belt, and rammed it home.

Now rage took over. She stood up and, holding the Glock in both hands, silhouetted by the grandstand burning furiously behind her, fired again and again as she cursed and damned the creature to hell, firing until her spare magazine was empty. The creature came at her, its compound eyes glowing; she flung away the gun and yanked out her ASP baton, pouring more curses upon the beast's approaching head as she telescoped the baton to full length and waited to swing it, preparing for what was likely to be her first and only blow.

72

A REVOLVING TUNNEL OF light surrounded Pendergast, at the end of which was the view of Times
Square. It was like being inside a child's kaleidoscope
tube: ever turning, ever changing, disorienting and
dizzying. The tunnel was a slice or hole bored through
stacked layers of light; he surmised the layers were the
edges of parallel universes punched through in order
to reach the one at the end. They were constantly shifting, moving, folding and refolding upon themselves,
advancing and retreating. And through these folds
he could see glimpses of *worlds*: of strange landscapes
and endless seas, parched deserts and mountains that
pierced the skies, erupting volcanoes and blue glaciers.
At first, his skin felt as if it was burning and yet freez-
ing at the same time. This feeling receded, replaced by
a tingling sensation. The feeling grew stronger, until
it was as if countless tiny fire ants were crawling over
every inch of his skin.

He ignored it; ignored, in fact, everything but
the critical task at hand: watching and waiting for

the moment when the world he sought came into view.

He took another step, and another: his feet sank into the opalescent surface beneath him, swallowing him up to his ankles before launching him forward with a vertiginous sensation of negative gravity. The air around him suddenly filled with coruscating streams of tiny, almost microscopic particles, glittering like gold dust as they moved in undulating, ever-changing patterns.

All the while, Pendergast watched and waited as the worlds beyond the tunnel of light flickered in and out, one after another, diaphanous as dreams.

Then he saw the universe he wanted—and plunged into it.

First, there was intense blackness, replaced by a brilliant white. Pendergast found himself lying on the ground, unable to remember for a moment where he was, what had happened, or even who he was. The feeling of disorientation quickly passed and he climbed to his feet, scanning the landscape around him. He might have been unconscious for a minute, or for an hour; it was impossible to be sure. His watch—a manual-wind Philippe Dufour—had not fared well in the journey: both the minute and small second hands had apparently spun so quickly that they melted into the guilloche of the dial. As he turned around, examining his surroundings, he nearly lost his footing. Regaining his balance, he realized that the gravity in this place was less than that of Earth—significantly less.

He was standing on what could have been a plain of salt, except for the fact that it was blinding white—and smooth as silk. He took a short step forward, shielding his eyes. As his foot met the ground again, a small cloud of crystals—like glittering snowflakes—rose up and fell back. The sky was salmon pink, grading upward into black. Wisps of strangely shaped clouds seemed to crawl, rather than drift, across. Gingerly, he took a breath: the air had an unpleasant, oleaginous texture, and it smelled strongly of burnt rubber.

He was standing in what appeared to be a shallow volcanic crater. The walls of the crater were dead black, rising abruptly from the white floor. Above its jagged rim, a sun hung low in the sky, smaller than Earth's and a dusky red. Next to and just above it stood another sun, smaller still, this one greenish-blue: a double star system. And above it all was a black empyrean, torn by tongues of livid lightning, as if a tremendous battle filled the sky: but there was no thunder, and the bolts of energy did not wink out immediately, but rather dispersed outward slowly, morphing into tangled shapes like drops of ink on blotting paper. Dotting the plains around him were crystallized pillars of salt, twisted back upon themselves like corkscrews. They reminded him of Lot's wife. Here and there the pitiless white of the salt bed was relieved by the green forms of spiky bushes. Except they weren't bushes at all, but some sort of animal, moving slowly, hunching along like inchworms.

He shook his head, trying to clear his mind. A few hundred yards away, he saw movement: a pack of animals had spotted him and were loping over. He drew his Les Baer and gave it a quick examination to make sure it had survived the journey intact. The approaching animals had insectoid heads, not un-like the monstrous thing in Savannah, with bulbous compound eyes and tubelike mouthparts, covered in a leathery brown skin that pulsated with engorged vessels. They spread out like a pack of wolves and began closing in.

Pendergast realized he was being hunted.

He hoped they were intelligent animals: intelligent enough, at least, to be afraid of him. He let them trot close enough to come into range, and then flicked on his laser sights, carefully centered the dot on the chest of the leader, and squeezed off a round. The animal bucked backward in a spray of blood, tumbling up into the air and spinning lazily end over end, leaving a twisted contrail of crimson behind it in the low gravity.

That the creature could be shot was, at least, a reassuring development.

The other creatures immediately bolted, tearing off at tremendous speed and vanishing over the rim of the crater. He went over and looked down at the dead animal, which had hit the ground about ten yards away—the blood on this planet was even redder than his, he thought grimly. He turned the grotesque beast over with his toe. It had eight legs: that would account for the rippling way in which it moved. It looked more *insecta* than *animalia*. Perhaps, in the alternate universe, this was a world where insects had evolved into the niches occupied by mammals on Earth.

As if on cue, he felt, more than heard, a vibration; and moments later a vast cloud of insects came streaming over the horizon, millions of them, forming weird, ever-shifting shapes as they flew, until they almost blotted out the sky above him. Just as quickly they passed, surging toward the far side of the crater—but not before several had dropped to the ground around Pendergast's feet. Kneeling, he saw they were identical to those he'd seen flying out of the portal.

As he glanced back at the receding cloud, forming and unforming, he spotted a creature flying along the serrated rim of the crater. Huge leathery wings; insectoid head; hairy, swinging dugs…quickly, he pulled a compact Leica monocular from his suit pocket, but he was too late. The creature had dropped down below the rim and disappeared.

Still, he was certain it was of the same species that was at this moment reducing Savannah to a charred ruin in his own universe. Maybe even the actual doppelgänger.

He scanned the sky for others, but it was empty.

In his disorientation and surprise, he'd almost forgotten that time was of the essence. The rim was a half mile away, but in the lower gravity he might be able to get there quickly. He tried running and soon discovered that if he bounded ahead, almost hopping like a kangaroo, he could move rapidly. It took him only a few minutes to reach the spot where the white surface met the black, crusted lava base of the crater rim. He began climbing the slopes, jagged with lava and sliding cinders. But once again, low gravity came to his aid, and he found that as long as he was careful where he landed, he could move up the slope in a series of jumps. He avoided the prickly walking things, which on closer look appeared to be part insect, part plant. In another minute he approached the ridgeline, then crept to the top and peered over the edge.

There, in a rugged landscape of solidified lava a thousand yards below him, was a smooth bowl of red sand: a nest. Along its edges squatted half a dozen of the beasts, wings folded like bats. In the center moved a swollen, bloated creature with shriveled vestigial wings, at least three times the size of the others. It was sitting on what appeared to be the cells of a honeycomb, except—as Pendergast noted when he glassed it with his Leica—the chambers were not six-sided, but octagonal. In every cell, Pendergast could see greasy, wriggling yellow larvae, segmented with wart-like tubercules and thick bristles. Their heads were tiny, ending in sharp, reedlike siphons that stuck straight upward. The puffy creature—perhaps the queen?—was squirting a thick treacle-colored liquid down into each quivering tube, like a mother bird dropping worms into the gaping mouths of her young.

Moving the monocular away from this grotesque sight and glassing the surrounding creatures, Pendergast saw that one of the farthest from the queen had exactly the same scar of a cross on its left wing as did the brute in Savannah. This must be it: the double of the creature attacking Savannah; the one he had come to kill.

Having been a big game hunter in past years, he knew what he had to do. This was going to be a classic big-game-style stalk. But armed with only a handgun, he would have to get close—very close. And he would have to find a way to draw it away from the others: whether he could kill one such creature was debatable, but he had no chance at all against the entire hive.

He returned the monocular to his pocket, tested the direction of the wind with a damp finger, and then began creeping over the ridge.

73

THE WIND, AT LEAST, was in his favor, blowing from the direction of the nest. He didn't know if the creatures could pick up the scent of a human, but he would not take the chance.

He felt the intense pressure of time. For every minute he spent hunting the beast in this world, people were being killed in his. His watch was useless, but he knew at least half an hour had passed since he'd witnessed the smoking destruction of Savannah on the Times Square news screen. In another thirty minutes, the Savannah he'd seen would have become reality. With this in mind, he redoubled his pace.

Below and to his right, the crater rim graded into hundreds of steep splatter cones—dead volcanic formations created by lava blowing out of a vent. Here and there he could see smoking fumaroles dotting a rough lava plain. This plain offered the best approach to the nest: But there remained the difficult, if not impossible, task of drawing the one creature away from the rest.

Pendergast moved along the slope with exceeding caution, descending into the valley of the cones. The smoke and steam pouring from the fumaroles provided an excellent screen, allowing him to move from one to the next without being observed. The air stank of burnt rubber and sulfur. He moved forward as swiftly as he dared through the forest of outcroppings until he had reached its end. Taking cover behind the cone closest to the nest, he decided to chance climbing it in order to get a better view.

The cone was steep, but the rough lava that formed it offered many hand- and footholds, and he was able to ascend quickly in the lower gravity. At the top was an opening, a narrow chimney of frozen lava about three feet in diameter, a lava pipe or tube in its center widening as it arrowed down into darkness. The cone appeared to be dead, with no smoke or steam rising from it.

He peered over the top. From this vantage point, he had a clear view of the nest, about two hundred yards away. Two hundred yards was, under normal circumstances, the absolute limit of his weapon's range. He couldn't get any closer—there was no cover of any sort—and the beasts were sitting around the edges of the nest, looking this way and that, on habitual alert.

He paused to consider the effect of lower gravity and thinner air on the aiming and distance of his 1911. A round would travel farther and have less drop and wind deflection. With the weapon's seven-plus-one capacity, and a spare mag with another seven, he had fourteen shots to take down the creature and, if absolutely necessary, its nest mates. Those were not good odds.

He briefly considered the possibility that, if he killed the queen, the rest might die. But that was not the case with similar creatures on Earth: kill a queen termite, or bee, and the colony simply bred a new one.

Pendergast wondered how acute their hearing was. Although he couldn't see anything that looked like ears, he was confident they could make out sounds, given the cries the creature emitted back in Savannah.

He didn't have much time to work out the problem. He picked up a small rock and threw it far to his right, then quickly peered over the rim with his monocular to observe the effect.

The rock made a small clattering noise about fifty yards away. The effect was dramatic: the brutes suddenly straightened up, their insect heads whipping around in the direction of the sound, bug eyes staring, mouth tubes twitching.

It seemed that their hearing was quite keen indeed.

He noted movement in the distance, coming in over the crater rim. He froze as a shape appeared in the sky. It was much bigger than the others, truly gigantic. He glassed it as it circled for a landing at the nest: it was brawny as well as massive, with a head twice as big as the queen's, its wicked proboscis slick with grease, the veins in its taloned legs bulging and flexing as it settled in, folding its wings and making soft noises to its nest mates.

This was obviously the male.

Pendergast cursed himself for not realizing sooner the others were all females. Now he'd have to contend with this monster as well. Despite having sworn off hunting, he bitterly missed his Holland & Holland .500/465 royal double rifle, powerful enough to take down anything.

Such wishful thinking was useless, however, and he put it aside. There was the question of behavior to consider. In some species, the male was the main defender of the herd; in bees and some other social insects, however, the females were. He wondered what the case was with these brutes.

He tossed another stone.

The creatures all went on high alert again, but it was the male who spread his wings and flew up to investigate, gliding over and circling the area where the stone had fallen, looking around with its compound eyes. Pendergast made himself as invisible as possible behind the edge of the lava cone. The male, satisfied nothing was amiss, returned to the nest.

Now Pendergast understood: to have any hope of targeting the female, he would have to kill the male first.

The next question was where to place the shot. If the thing even had a heart, guessing its location would be too risky, given its size and alien physiology—and besides, if it was truly like a mosquito, it might have three hearts, as mosquitoes did.

That left a head shot as the preferred method of attack. A great pity the head was so small in relation to the body: the alignment would have to be perfect.

Pendergast tossed another rock, carefully calculating its distance and location, then braced himself, Les Baer at the ready. With a rattle, the rock hit the ground not far from the base of the cone.

At this, the male's head jerked up again, then the thing took off with a screech, more alert than before. It swooped over the area where the rock had fallen, eyes swiveling on short eyestalks, peering everywhere.

Its return route, Pendergast hoped, would take it close to the cone.

The beast circled a few times, finally satisfying itself there was no threat. As it turned to fly back to the nest, Pendergast waited—gauging the perfect moment—then stood up and cried out, waving his arms.

The thing swerved in midair, locked eyes, and flew straight at him—aligning itself exactly as Pendergast had hoped. He raised his weapon, waited a beat. As it closed in on him, he saw the beast was even more brutally ugly than he'd believed: puckered skin like a rhinoceros, covered with greasy bristles and webbed with bulging veins like pipes.

He squeezed the trigger twice, a double tap into the head, the Les Baer bucking fiercely. As the beast gave a roar of fury, Pendergast threw himself down and it came careening past the cone, talons rasping the lava above his head. To his dismay it flapped back around, flying lopsided, one of its eyes hanging from a torn stalk. Its syringe-like proboscis was quivering, shooting in and out, and Pendergast was so close that he could make out rows of needlelike teeth within it.

He fired two more shots as the creature came back at him, both directly into the good eye. The eye exploded like a watermelon hit by a sledgehammer. He threw himself down, but this time he couldn't escape the raking talons, one of which tore into his left shoulder, ripping it open and tumbling him partway down the steep slope.

With a gasp of pain, Pendergast reached out with his other arm, grasping a handhold in the rough lava and arresting his slide, while the huge creature thrashed about, tearing at the air with its claws in a blind fury before crashing to the ground in a shower of gore.

All six of the other creatures had now left the queen and taken off, coming for him. There was no way he could fight all six at once. As the blood bubbled from the wound in his shoulder, Pendergast grasped the Les Baer in both hands and—carefully, deliberately— aimed at the flabby, pulsating abdomen of the queen, and squeezed off a round. The creature was two hundred yards away but presented a big target—and the round hit home.

A squeal like that of a stuck pig burst from its mouth; it arched its back and threw its tiny head up, whipping it back and forth with a high-pitched keen- ing and squealing. The effect was as Pendergast had hoped: the six beasts broke off their flight and whirled back to protect their queen. He glanced back at the male: it was sprawled at the base of the lava cone, gasping and clawing, blood and thick fluid pouring from its exploded eyes.

That monstrous brute, at least, no longer presented a threat.

Meanwhile, the wounded queen continued to squeak and squeal. To Pendergast, listening, it sounded less and less like animalistic cries of pain and rage, and more like—language.

Abruptly, the six creatures broke off their flight to the queen and turned back toward him. They separated as they flew and approached more quickly than before, creating difficult targets. Suddenly, as if on cue, they turned and converged on him from six directions at once, in a spiraling pattern that made a fatal shot exponentially more difficult.

Pendergast realized that he had underestimated their intelligence and ability to strategize—perhaps fatally so.

As they closed in, talons extended, he realized there just might be a way out. A moment before they converged, he swung down the inner wall of the cone, into the lava pipe, and then clambered down the chimney, bracing his feet on either side of the walls, doing his best not to fall into the abyss below. Once he was wedged between the walls of the tube, he grasped the Les Baer with his good hand and aimed straight over his head.

The first creature landed and immediately jammed its head into the hole, the glittering spear of its mouthpiece stabbing down like a striking snake and grazing his shoulder. It made a sucking sound even as he fired straight up into its head. It fell back and a second beast jammed its head in, proboscis thrusting, and then a third, spraying grease and fluid on him even as he fired point blank into their nightmare faces, the tubes slashing around him, sucking and stabbing, sticking him when he wasn't quick enough. He soon emptied the first mag and slammed home the second, firing whenever a creature appeared.

And then all went silent.

Had he killed them all? He checked his magazine and found he had three rounds left. He felt the warm blood running down his arm and dripping from his fingertips. He was running out of time in more ways than one.

Bracing himself, legs on either side of the lava tube, he tried to pull himself up, only to be seized by a wave of dizziness. Judging from the amount of blood on his shirt and arm, he guessed the claw of the male must have damaged or even severed his subclavian artery. In addition, his upper body had suffered a number of shallow stab wounds. He was rapidly becoming hypotensive; the bleeding had to be stopped immediately.

Still straddling the yawning chasm, feeling his strength ebb away, he holstered the gun and worked his jacket off, doing his best to ignore the pain. He bit down on the cuff of his shirt and tore off the sleeve, then used it to tie a crude tourniquet under and around his arm, knotting it above his clavicle to provide pressure. He would lose consciousness soon, and if he did so in this lava chimney, he would fall to his death. He had to get out—now.

With the last of his strength, he struggled up and out, then lay back on the steep cone, digging in his heels to keep from sliding down the slope. At the base of the cone, he counted five dying creatures in addition to the big male, heads blasted open by his gunfire, one or two still twitching and keening.

Where was the sixth?

The question was answered by a scream as the last of the brood—he could see the scarred cross on its wing, along with a fresh tear—came for him like a meteor, straight out of the sun. Still on his back, Pendergast yanked out the Les Baer and, with hardly the strength to raise his arm, fired the last three rounds into it even as it came down on him, talons grating the lava with a rasping noise. It slumped to one side, then collapsed, lying athwart Pendergast's body. He could feel the noisome heat, the wings and dugs throbbing and twitching. He tried to push the thing off, but it was too heavy, and he was too weak.

Fight over, Pendergast lay pinned on his back, staring up at the alien sky with its two suns, unable to move. He was a mile or more from the portal, and there was no way he could get the creature off him and stand up, let alone walk the distance back. Blackness encroached on the corners of his vision as he began to lose consciousness. Slowly, the strange world closed in on him.

Rescue was impossible; nobody knew where he was, let alone how to reach him. His last thought, as darkness folded around him, was a resigned sadness that he had to die here all alone, with no one to grieve, on an unknown and alien world.

74

Coldmoon, standing amid stalled and burning cars on Drayton Street, had long ago emptied the spare he carried for his Browning Hi-Power. Now he was out of ammo and the monster was still wreaking havoc, circling and diving, tearing apart anything that moved—people, terrified dogs, pigeons, cars. Most of the crowd had managed to get off the streets and take refuge inside buildings, but the thing, seemingly enraged to the point of madness, had begun attacking the buildings themselves, tearing away at the façades with its talons, its terrible wings beating: Wakinyan, the Thunderer.

The power was out everywhere, the scene lit only by fires, with the exception of buildings equipped with their own generators. The city was rapidly becoming what Coldmoon had seen some forty minutes earlier on the giant news screens in Times Square: a burning ruin.

He knew in his heart there was no way to change the flow of time; if he had truly seen the future, then everything they were doing now was futile. Pendergast had, characteristically, vanished— off on some desperate gambit, probably—but even he couldn't change what was predestined. Coldmoon felt enraged at his own powerlessness. Where was the National Guard, the military, the SWAT teams? What was taking them so long? It might be too late for Savannah, but the beast that was pounding it into ruin was still very much alive. Alternate universe or not, there had to be some way to destroy it—there *had* to be…

He heard gunfire directed at the monster. It seemed to be coming from the direction of Gaston Street. There must still be some pockets of resistance, maybe cops. He could join up with them and, if he was lucky, might even find some extra ammo. He jogged toward the sound, weaving among the cars.

As he approached the corner of Whitaker and Gaston, he saw Commander Delaplane with about half a dozen of her officers. They had taken cover among some wrecked buses and were firing at the maddened creature swooping and circling above. He ran over and crouched next to Delaplane. She was a mess: muddy, uniform askew, bleeding freely from a long gash in her left forearm. A telescoping baton lay beside her, twisted crazily out of shape like a coat hanger.

"What happened to you?" he asked, nodding at her arm.

"Close encounter."

"You all right?"

"Now that I'm back here by our ammo dump, I am."

She gestured in the direction of a canvas-covered object near the rear of one bus. Coldmoon scurried over to it, keeping low; he filled both mags with 9mm rounds.

"Where the hell are the troops?" he asked, coming back around.

"*We're* the troops."

"What about the National Guard?"

She paused to fire a shot, then ducked back down. "They're 'mobilizing.' Say they can't get through, can't bring in additional choppers because that thing's already torn two of them out of the air, so they're bringing in MRAPs and tanks. But even those need to clear a path."

"It's been forty minutes!"

"The longest damn forty minutes in history."

Reacting to their fire, the thing came around and raked the top off the closest bus with its talons, rocking the vehicle and scattering metal and plastic everywhere. It angled in again, gliding low, and suddenly there was a high-pitched scream close at hand as it snatched up a female police officer crouching next to them. The beast rose sharply upward, beating its great wings as the cop screamed and fired until the brute pierced her with its gore-encrusted sucker tube.

"Mother*fucker*!" cried Delaplane. She leapt up and backed away from the bus to get a better field of fire, emptying her weapon into the creature in a display of almost insane courage.

The thing flung the husk of the officer away and swooped down once more, this time aiming directly at Delaplane, talons extended. Coldmoon crouched and readied his weapon, even though he knew it was futile as it came in at Delaplane, claws extended. She was a goner. He cried out in frustrated rage, unable to avert his eyes.

And then something strange happened. The thing seemed to flicker in and out like a bad television image shot through with snow. There was a loud crackle of electricity; arcs of lightning shot up from each of the beast's wings, meeting over its head in a burst of ionization. Breaking off its attack, it rose up, seemingly confused, mounting higher and higher. Its bluish metallic glow grew stronger as the thing emitted a stutter of agony. It began to twist and thrash, bellowing, its crackling blue aura flickering and intensifying...and then it seemed to come apart in midair, the flesh separating from its bones and falling away in streamers of light, the entire beast coming down, slowly at first and then faster, as it fell apart, turning into a shower of bones, which tumbled down and landed on the grass of the park—shiny metallic bones, along with a horrible little skull with yawning eye sockets and a metal feeding tube. Everything came to rest on the grass, smoking; and then even the bones began to flicker and crackle with sparks and crumble to glowing dust before finally winking out of existence completely. In a moment nothing was left but scorched grass, drifting smoke, and the oily stench of burnt rubber.

"What did I just see?" said Delaplane softly, lowering her weapon.

"I have no idea," said Coldmoon.

A hush fell as the cops around them began to rise from their places of cover, staring with shock and wonder as the smoke dissipated.

"The fucker just..." Delaplane began, then fell silent a moment. "It just did a Wicked Witch on us."

At that moment, Coldmoon heard a crash, and a massive army bulldozer appeared on Gaston, ramming stalled and smoking cars aside. As it moved into the park, it was followed by a line of tanks and MRAPs full of troops.

"And here comes the cavalry," said Delaplane acidly. "Right on time."

75

THE SOUND OF EXCITED humanity. People running, shouting, yelling; knocking over or trampling each other in a rush. Horses rearing in their harnesses, breaking free of carts and plunging into the milling throng. Omnibuses stuck in intersections, unable to move, as the crowds flowed like maddened lemmings around them. Loud explosions; smoke drifting through the air...And, above all the chaos, a thousand feet over the roofs of the tenements and brownstones, a long shape glided into view: on and on it emerged from the concealing clouds, as if its sleek bulk had no end, moving with silent purpose...

Abruptly, Constance opened her eyes. Around her was pitch darkness. As full consciousness returned, she realized the vision was not a dream, but a memory—of the day she'd witnessed the *Graf Zeppelin* make its maiden voyage across the Atlantic, passing over New York City on its way to the landing spot in Lakehurst. The crowds had not been screaming in terror, but rather cheering and lighting fireworks. And she was not in bed: she was buried in the rubble of what had previously been the top floor of the Chandler House.

She lay in the darkness for a moment, giving herself time to remember. She had fought the creature from the balcony, Frost's weapon had misfired, Constance had carried her inside—and as she died, Frost whispered something to Constance. And then the beast had thrown its weight against the roof of the hotel, the ceiling had caved in, and all had gone black. As she came fully awake, she realized it was oddly quiet.

As Frost's final words came back to her, Constance sat up. Spots danced in the darkness before her eyes. With effort, she freed her arms from a broken timber that lay across her leg and carefully felt along her ribs, shoulders, and spine. Everything hurt. But nothing, it seemed, was broken. She pushed more debris away, then rose, coughing at the clouds of brick dust. She took an unsteady step, then another, feeling her way through a ruined tangle of furniture, joists, and plaster. A wall brought her progress to a halt. Using her hands, she felt along it until she found a doorknob. With an effort, she pulled the door partway open, and—seeing a faint red light beyond—stepped through.

But she was not on the landing at the top of the narrow stairs. Rather, she was in a partially collapsed hallway, lit only by emergency exits. Her eyes, long used to darkness, adjusted. She was on the hotel's fourth floor, surrounded by the rubble from above. *Frost.* She was gone now—in more ways than one. But nevertheless, Constance realized what she had to do. She walked down the hall. Reaching the staircase, she descended to the lobby, then to the basement. How long had she been unconscious? It was silent outside; the beast was no longer screaming.

She went down the basement corridor, through the

wardrobe, and into the room with the machine. To her surprise, the light was on and it was running at high power, the whole room vibrating, the dial turned past II. As she stared into the portal, she saw that the image had changed. The view of Times Square an hour into the future was gone, replaced by a tunnel of coruscating light, the distant endpoint now just a muddy, swirling pool, as if it had been recently disturbed.

She looked at her watch. More than forty-five minutes had passed since they had first seen the destruction of Savannah through this portal. There wasn't much time left...if there was any time at all. Savannah was already becoming the burning ruin they had seen on the news screens.

But that was not her concern: not now. She stared into the portal. The image at the far end of the tunnel was beginning to clear. And at last, she could once again see Times Square: distant, attenuated.

She recognized it immediately, intimately—but it was not the Times Square of the present, but rather its predecessor, Longacre Square. The wide square was paved with dirty cobblestones. Iron hitching posts for horse carts ran parallel to the pavements. There were no automobiles to be seen. Police with nightsticks, wearing helmets resembling Prussian *pickelhauben*, directed traffic of horse-drawn carriages and drays.

It was like a scene from a snow globe: a glimpse from her childhood long, long ago.

She recalled again what the dying Frost had told her. *But of course.*

She was wasting time. Without a second thought, she lunged through the portal.

76

It was like being scooped up in a curling wave. She was whirled about, bands of light and dark whipping past her, until she managed to stabilize herself on a spongy surface of light. She was deep in the tunnel. At its end was the place from her childhood: not minutes, not an hour, but more than a century back in time. The walls of parallel universes around her turned endlessly as she passed by, like leaves from a magic book, each page opening into some strange world of wonder—or terror.

The beast that was savaging Savannah came from one of these worlds. But which? She watched as the layers turned, folding and overlapping. And then she saw an insect—a dragonfly, with the deformed head of a mosquito—wriggle out from one of the folds. Recognizing it, she forced her way in.

A moment of blankness, and she found herself lying on her back, surrounded by a plain of pure, unrelieved white. She struggled to her feet, instinctually grasping her stiletto. She glanced around, head still aching as she took in the otherworldly landscape: the brilliant plain, the black walls of a crater in the distance, the two suns and pink-to-black sky.

Her eyes fell on the strange, powdery white ground. In it she saw a disturbance, like a faint snow angel, and beyond, a set of footprints leading away.

She knelt to examine the marks more closely. There was a clear handprint, and the impressions of shoes. *Pendergast*.

So the thing she'd dreaded had happened. He'd made the same deductive leap that she had and come through the portal. Perhaps he'd even succeeded, if the silence she'd heard from outside the hotel was any indication. Had the monster vanished? Had he managed to kill it here, in its own universe?

Whatever the case, the tracks led in only one direction. They did not return.

She began to follow them, heart pounding, stiletto in hand. She moved as rapidly as possible, ignoring the pain, bounding along in the low gravity. At one point, she saw a pack of hyena-like creatures with insect heads, but at the sight of her they immediately fled.

Pendergast's trail led straight to the base of a ridge formed out of black frozen lava. As she followed the track, just before reaching the lava, Constance heard a rumbling sound and felt the ground vibrate. Suddenly the surface of the plain to her right bulged upward and fractured, snowy powder dancing into the air from the disturbance.

She halted.

The cracks widened and then a head appeared: a shiny beetle skull with black eyes and long, curved mandibles that clacked as they moved. It stared at her, then began to slide out, exposing a long oily body with a cluster of eggs adhering to its belly.

Constance held her ground.

The creature continued to slither up and out of the ground until its entire body was exposed, coiling and recoiling around itself, snapping its hairy mandibles. It approached her slowly, cautiously, a brute at least five feet in length. But its intent was obvious: it was a predator, and she was prey.

Still Constance remained motionless. She sensed that to retreat, to give even an inch, would be fatal.

"Stay back!" she warned, holding out her stiletto.

The creature drew itself up, coiling ever tighter as its bug eyes stared at her.

She stared back. It was impossible to get close enough to stab it—the mandibles were each a foot long and capable of crushing her.

She flipped the knife around, and—grasping its blade between thumb and forefinger—aimed, then threw it as hard as she could.

It struck the creature square in the left eye, which immediately split open with a nasty wet sound, spewing green jelly. With a high-pitched hiss and a frantic clacking, the beast stabbed its tail into the plain and dug itself back into the ground, disappearing into a cloud of white powder, leaving behind a viscous, quivering pool of jelly—and her knife.

"Bitch," Constance muttered as she picked up the stiletto and wiped it off.

Quickly, she made her way to the base of the lava ridge and climbed. Gaining its summit and peering over the upper edge, she saw a bizarre sight. Inside a nest of reddish sand set amid the lava beds, a gigantic white maggot was mewling and wriggling, waving its tiny black head back and forth as it sat on a brood comb of squirming grubs. It was bleeding from a wound.

It looked like a gunshot wound, with an entrance and exit.

Her eye was drawn to a scene of violence a few hundred yards away. A cluster of lava cones crowded an area of black basalt. Circling the cone nearest the nest were half a dozen dead creatures like the one ravaging Savannah. They were lying amid puddles of blood and gore, their insectoid heads shot to pieces. One of the creatures lay apart from the others, slumped on the side of the cone, wings broken and crooked. There was something under it—a human body.

With a cry, Constance bounded down the ridge, falling in her haste and scraping herself on the sharp lava, then rising and running on. Reaching the base of the gore-covered cone, she rushed over to the spot.

The foul creature had fallen across Pendergast. He lay unmoving, eyes half-open slits.

"Aloysius!" she cried, lifting his head. She pressed a finger into the side of his neck but could feel no pulse. Blood had drenched the rocks below him.

She had to get the brute off him. She grabbed it by its snout and broken wing and pulled.

It didn't move.

She seized the wing in both hands and yanked downhill, letting gravity help her. It shifted no more than a few inches.

She got on the uphill side of it and, taking a prone position on the sharp lava bed, placed her feet against the creature's body and pushed with every fiber she could muster.

Now at last it rolled partway off. A second push got it off him entirely.

Rising again, she rushed to examine his injury. The left side of his body was covered in blood, and a crude tourniquet had been tied around the shoulder and knotted beneath the armpit. The tourniquet had loosened and blood was oozing out. She quickly retied it, then pressed her palms over what she could see was a deep shoulder wound. She felt his neck again, trying to steady her hand and calm her mind, and thought she could detect a faint pulse.

Grasping his arms, she hauled him to a sitting position, then—with a supreme effort—draped him over her shoulders and attempted to stand. He seemed frighteningly light until she realized it must be due to the low gravity, not blood loss.

She staggered down the cone and set off at the fastest pace she could manage, Pendergast draped over her back and shoulders, his blood soon soaking her own clothes. If he was bleeding, she thought, his heart must still be beating—however feebly.

Aloysius Pendergast felt disconnected, disembodied. He had a strange vision of a broad plain stretching endlessly beneath an alien sky. At times, he seemed to be walking across it; other times he was floating. Slowly, as awareness returned, he realized that the floating sensation was, in fact, someone bearing him on her shoulders. Then he was walking again, or so it seemed, Constance's voice whispering urgently in his ear, her arm propping him up. That was followed by a sudden falling sensation, along with coruscating lights and a tingle that stirred the hairs of his arms. It all ended abruptly as he landed on a hard floor. He felt himself being dragged—in darkness now—and then he heard a sudden rush of voices.

"He's close to exsanguination!"

"Hypotensive," cried a man's voice. "Give me a hypo and epinephrine. And we've got to expand this guy's blood volume. Set an IV with unmatched O negative and run it full open."

Pendergast felt very far away indeed from the rush of activity around him. Two vague shapes materialized in his field of vision, and he felt his shirt being cut away and something being done to his shoulder. Behind them stood another form—a frightful woman drenched in blood, and it took a moment for him to realize it was Constance, covered from head to toe in red. He tried to speak, to ask if she was hurt, but found he was slipping back into darkness.

"Miss?" he heard a concerned voice ask. "Are you hurt, too?"

"His blood, not mine," came the curt reply.

Now darkness—an internal darkness—was rising once again. Before it claimed him completely, he heard one final exchange.

"Is...is he going to survive?"

"Yes. He's going to make it."

77

In the Chatham County office complex, Agent Coldmoon sat at a conference table with four others: Commander Delaplane, Detective Sheldrake, Dr. McDuffie, and Agent Pendergast. His partner had recovered his normal pale complexion, and aside from the trussed up arm Coldmoon had seen earlier, now hidden by his suit, he appeared his usual unreadable, enigmatic self. But Coldmoon knew he was still very weak—and how very close he had come to death.

The conference room occupied a corner of the building's sixth floor and boasted large windows. Gazing out of them, Coldmoon could see, to the west, the morning sun shining over a tranquil landscape of industrial buildings, modest neighborhoods, and the ribbon of I-16 heading toward Macon. The view to the south, however, could not be more different. It looked like the ruins of some city during World War II after the Luftwaffe had finished bombing it.

A week had passed since the giant *capúŋka*—he could think of no better word for it than "mosquito"— had terrorized and laid waste to swaths of downtown Savannah…and then suddenly died. He assumed it had died; all he knew for certain was that it had vanished in an explosion of smoke and light that would have made the magician David Copperfield proud, leaving behind wrecked buildings, scorched cars, and casualties.

The lack of any remnant of the thing that caused the devastation had made the subsequent investigation of the disaster all that much more intense…and ultimately ludicrous. An enormous number of military units, CDC teams in biosuits, DHS teams, and countless other mysterious investigators from agencies he didn't know, and didn't want to know, had descended on the city. They were too late to do anything about the carnage, but were zealously gathering vast amounts of evidence, including scorched grass, broken brick, shattered glass, and all the cell phone footage and pictures they could find. Large areas of town were still roped off. Vans and trailers with strange markings, or no markings at all, were arranged into makeshift villages of humming generators and blazing lights in the many town squares in the affected area.

In the beginning, there had been a brief effort to contain and spin what had taken place. But there were too many cell phones, too much news footage, and too many eyewitnesses of the beast and its horror. The authorities finally put out a vague statement that mentioned a "unique mutation event," promising a "full and thorough investigation" and a careful sweep for any other anomalous creatures.

For the people of Savannah, on the other hand, the catastrophe had precipitated a different response: in the aftermath, they were pulling together as never before to rebuild the ruined sections of downtown. As it turned out, the body count was lower than initially believed; most of the dead were members of Senator Drayton's advance team, rallygoers, and unlucky tourists who'd been in the wrong place at the wrong time. Some of the town's wealthiest residents were pitching in to fund the reconstruction, and that— along with disaster relief, and Savannans' ingrained pride in their beautiful city—would see not only the damaged structures rebuilt, but also several historic sites that had been long awaiting conservation.

None of this shed any light on what had really happened. Coldmoon knew a lot more than most, but under Pendergast's orders he'd kept his mouth shut. The two of them had been subjected to innumerable debriefings and meetings, of which this promised to be the last.

His thoughts were interrupted by Commander Delaplane, who slapped shut the folder that sat on the table before her. It had contained a list of the usual questions—What was the nature of the thing? Where did it come from? What happened to it?—which she'd been obliged, for the record, to ask one final time. Naturally, nobody had any idea, Pendergast least of all. It was with some relief that Delaplane pushed the folder away.

"Well, that's done," she said. "Sorry. I know we've been covering the same old ground."

"Quite all right," said Pendergast mildly.

Delaplane shook her head. "It's remarkable, really: a week has gone by, and reports are still coming in.

Just this morning, I heard that the entire team making that documentary had been killed in the, uh, apparent lair of the creature."

"All except for the cinematographer," Sheldrake added. "And she was so freaked out that she's only now beginning to describe what happened. Incoherently. And that journalist found with her—Wellstone, I think?—they say he's irrecoverably insane." He consulted a notebook. "Akinetic catatonia, precipitated by psychogenic trauma."

"Closer to home," Delaplane went on, "what happened to Felicity Frost was particularly tragic." She turned to Pendergast. "You got to know her, right?"

Pendergast shook his head. "That was Constance, my ward."

Hearing her name, Coldmoon had to stifle an involuntary twitch. Over the last few days, Constance had been acting even more strangely than usual. When he'd been battling the creature atop the church, was it really possible he'd caught a brief glimpse of her on the balcony of the hotel penthouse, shooting at the beast with a tommy gun? Of course it was: he'd seen her do stranger things than that. She was as crazy as she was beautiful. And brave. She'd been the one to go after Pendergast and drag his ass out of that damned machine.

He reminded himself he didn't know anything about that. He was done with Savannah. Back at the hotel—which, pending reconstruction, had been stabilized by heavy steel bracers, jack posts, and Lally columns—his bags were packed. He had a flight for Denver that afternoon, and no power on earth was going to stop him from getting on that plane.

Now Delaplane was looking nonplussed, and Coldmoon—tuning in to the conversation—heard Sheldrake congratulating her for the commendation on bravery she'd received.

"Thanks, Benny," she said. "Who knows—maybe I'll make chief after all...in twenty or thirty years."

"It might happen sooner than you imagine," Pendergast said. He shifted in his chair. "Ah, Assistant Director Pickett. Why don't you join us?"

Glancing toward the exit from the conference room, Coldmoon saw Pickett leaning against the doorframe. Just how long he'd been standing there, Coldmoon didn't know. But the man's presence seemed a signal for the meeting to adjourn, because everyone began gathering their things, nodding and shaking hands, and heading for the door. Coldmoon stood to join the exodus, only to see Pickett motioning for him and Pendergast to remain behind. They stood at the door in an awkward silence.

Pickett glanced over his shoulder, making sure the others had gone. Then he cleared his throat. "I, ah, understand you two went toe-to-toe with the late Senator Drayton on my behalf," he said. "You look...well?"

Pendergast nodded.

Pickett hesitated again, with an almost embarrassed expression on his face. "That means a lot to me. On both counts."

"And I am equally grateful," said Pendergast, "for the way you protected our investigation from the senator. I regret the impact on your career."

"Actually," Pickett said, "Senator Drayton didn't have the chance to follow through on his threats. He was more of a blowhard than a man of action."

So he's getting his promotion, after all, Coldmoon thought.

There was a silence as Pickett fixed Pendergast with a long and particular stare. "I'm sorry, but I'm going to ask you one more time," he said. "For the record, you understand."

"I understand."

Pickett took a breath. "So: you have no idea where that creature came from?"

"Absolutely none."

"Or what it was doing here?"

"I have no idea."

"And you don't know what happened to it?"

"I'm afraid not."

Pickett swiveled his gaze toward Coldmoon. "And you?"

Coldmoon shrugged. "No, sir."

"In other words," said Pickett, "you're both as ignorant as everybody else."

"Alas," said Pendergast, "I'm afraid this is one case I failed to solve."

The color rose in Pickett's face, and for a moment Coldmoon thought he was going to get angry. But then he smiled faintly. "Perhaps it's best to let sleeping dogs lie."

"A most wise stratagem," Pendergast said.

"It's a shame, though," said Pickett. "That your stellar record, and your partner's, might be darkened by this failure."

Shit. Coldmoon hadn't really thought of that. He couldn't wait to get to Denver and into a normal FBI routine investigating ordinary things like terrorism, organized crime, and serial killers.

"On the other hand," Pickett said, "solving the

D. B. Cooper hijacking is a tremendous coup. I believe that was the FBI's longest-running unsolved case. No doubt that will balance things out as far as your record is concerned." He took a breath. "I'm still a little confused how you managed to do that in the midst of all this, though."

"Serendipity," said Pendergast.

"As soon as we put the finishing touches on that case and wrap it up, we'll make the announcement. I imagine…" He paused. "There will be some sort of press conference and commendations for you both."

"We look forward to it."

Coldmoon began to feel better.

Pickett cast his gaze out the window over the wrecked landscape. "This case was just too crazy. Who could have predicted this?" He turned his scrutiny back to Pendergast. "Just so you don't think I'm an idiot, I know you know a lot more about this."

"As you said, sir, better to let sleeping dogs lie."

"Which leads to my final question. Is there any reason for concern—in your *opinion*, of course—that there might be any further threats of this kind?"

"I believe," Pendergast drawled, "that you can rest easy on that point."

With this, he fell silent. What he did not say, nevertheless, spoke volumes.

"Then that's all," Pickett said. "Thank you. Now, is there anything I can do for either of you?"

"You can allow Agent Coldmoon to catch his flight to Denver," Pendergast said. "And Constance and I would greatly appreciate spending tonight in our own beds, back in New York."

"There was one thing…" Pickett began.

Coldmoon felt his spine stiffen. For a terrible

moment, he thought they might be shanghaied once again...but after a moment Pickett shook his head and said, "Never mind." Without another word, he stepped to one side and let them pass out of the conference room and toward the waiting elevators.

78

As HE TURNED OFF MONTGOMERY and headed east on Taylor, Coldmoon almost had to restrain himself from pulling ahead of Pendergast's uncharacteristically slow and painful walk. The debriefing he'd been dreading most—the one with Pickett—had gone more smoothly than he could have hoped. Pickett was a smarter guy than Coldmoon had given him credit for. He'd been cleared to leave for Denver. His bags were packed. He'd even taken the precaution of ordering an Uber the night before, although Pendergast had offered to give him a lift with an FBI pool car. Truth was, he didn't want to broadcast the fact that he'd arranged to get to the airport three hours early. He couldn't take the chance of getting dragged at the last moment into some bizarre new assignment. You never knew with Pendergast.

He glanced at his watch: right on schedule. He'd pop into the hotel, grab his bags, and soon Savannah and Pendergast would be dwindling specks in the rearview mirror of his career.

As they walked along, he couldn't help but notice all the activity. Trucks were parked along the curbs, some with beds full of rubble being cleared by heavy machinery, while others were unloading lumber, bricks, and construction materials. Regular citizens were pitching in, shoveling debris into dumpsters and cleaning up. The inhabitants of Savannah, it seemed, having received no explanation for the attack visited upon them beyond a wash of crazy conspiracy theories, had decided to move on as quickly as possible.

Now up ahead, Coldmoon made out the ancient façade of the Chandler House. It still looked a fright: surrounded by scaffolding, numerous windows boarded up, and the ruined upper floor covered in a superstructure of pipe and plastic. Most of the staff had returned once the building was fully stabilized, to help direct renovations.

As they came through the lobby doors, Coldmoon caught a glimpse of Chatham Square and the cluster of trailers and temporary Quonset huts he'd privately dubbed Fedville. A car was idling at the curb outside the lobby, an Uber sign posted inside the driver's window.

Early, Coldmoon thought. *Good omen*.

As they mounted the wide main staircase, Pendergast turned to him. "I see you plan to leave for the airport immediately."

Did nothing escape Pendergast's notice? "Yes, well, I thought it'd be a good idea to get a jump on things."

"Given past experience, that's probably wise."

They turned off at the second-floor landing, walked a few steps down the corridor, then stopped at the door to Pendergast's suite. "Well, let's find Constance and say our goodbyes," Pendergast said. "We have a little something to give you."

"Will it take long?"

"Just as much time as it takes to pass from my hand to yours." Pendergast gave him a slim smile. "My precipitate friend, I dislike maudlin farewells as much as you do. It will be quick and painless."

Coldmoon grunted in return. This was, after all, what he wanted. Still, he realized he'd been hoping for the opportunity to say no to a glass of cognac or a final heart-to-heart. Chagrin turned to curiosity as he wondered what token of thanks Pendergast was going to give him. Hopefully it would be something negotiable at a bank.

The suite had been spared damage, and sunlight flooded the spacious, orderly rooms. The doors were all open, and as he walked into the parlor Coldmoon could see the two studies with attached private bedrooms, their armoire doors thrown open and luggage set upon the beds in the universal language of travelers about to check out. Pendergast had wandered off briefly, but now he returned.

"This is curious," Pendergast said. "Where is Constance?"

"Packing?" Coldmoon asked.

Pendergast shook his head. He headed to his own set of rooms, returning a moment later. He picked up the house phone.

"Maybe she's taking a final turn around the city," Coldmoon said. "For nostalgia's sake."

Pendergast ignored this sarcastic comment as he dialed. "She's been rather out of sorts the last few days."

A voice answered the phone—apparently, from the

front desk—and Pendergast made some brief inquiries. Nobody had seen Constance Greene. If she'd left the hotel while Pendergast was gone, the doorman would know, as there was a system now in place for checking people in and out of the building.

"Most curious," Pendergast said as he hung up. He began walking slowly back into Constance's rooms, and Coldmoon followed.

"What are your plans?" Coldmoon asked.

"I'm taking Constance on vacation—a true vacation this time." He paused in her study, looking around. Coldmoon did as well. Everything seemed as neat and orderly as he would have expected.

"I've arranged for a surprise," Pendergast went on as he moved into the bedroom. "We're going to Rome, where the Vatican has agreed to open its private libraries and catacombs. It should be..."

Outside, a city clock struck noon. And at the same moment, quite abruptly, Pendergast stopped midsentence.

Coldmoon glanced around the bedroom, wondering what could have caught the agent's eye. The closet doors were open, revealing a rack of expensive and tasteful clothes. His gaze moved to a small writing desk by the bed, on which sat a black handbag and Constance's cell phone.

"She can't be far," he said. "Her phone's here." He glanced toward the bed, where two slab-sided suitcases of monogrammed canvas lay, open and empty.

Coldmoon watched in surprise as Pendergast seized the lambskin bag and upended it on the table, dumping out the contents. He then began rooting through its zippered pockets.

"What's going on—?" Coldmoon began.

"It isn't here," Pendergast murmured.

"What isn't there?"

"Her stiletto."

"So?"

"She is never without it. Never."

"Even in the shower? I mean, not that you'd…look, her cell phone's here, and she wouldn't leave without that."

Pendergast, ignoring him, began sweeping through racks of hanging clothes, pulling open drawers with his good arm.

Coldmoon glanced surreptitiously at his watch. This was crazy. Constance never strayed far from Pendergast. She was probably in the library, lost in a book.

As he tried to think of some reason to excuse himself, he paused again. Pendergast had now moved toward the bed and the open, empty suitcases that lay upon it. Reaching for the larger of the two, he felt around its lid, where the brass zipper met the fastidiously stitched leather edging. As if by magic, a small enameled gold box appeared from a hiding place in the lid of the suitcase. Pendergast flipped it open. Lined in plush purple velvet, with a number of tiny compartments, it was empty.

Pendergast pushed the suitcase aside and hobbled toward the door.

"Wait!" Coldmoon said. "Pendergast—Aloysius—what's going on? I've got to leave!"

When Pendergast didn't answer, he hurried after him. "What the hell's gotten into you?"

"Her jewels," Pendergast said over his shoulder.

"What about them?"

"They're gone."

"Maybe they were stolen," Coldmoon said, but even as he spoke he knew this wasn't the case; nobody could have guessed that suitcase lid was hiding anything.

"What's so important about the jewelry?" Coldmoon asked.

"Not jewelry," Pendergast said. "Jewels. They mean more to her than…The cell phone left behind…the missing gown…" He was moving faster now: out the door of the suite, down the corridor toward the stairs. He hurried down them.

Animated by a terrible premonition, Pendergast broke into a limping run as he crossed the lobby—dangerously fast for a man who had recently suffered such a serious injury. Hurrying after him, Coldmoon felt the shadow of that same premonition fall over him…especially when Pendergast reached the door to the basement, flung it open, and disappeared down the stairs. Forgetting his flight and the Uber waiting outside, Coldmoon followed, his heart accelerating as he realized what their destination would be.

Even as they were making their way through the shadowy basement, Coldmoon began to hear an erratic ticking noise. Acrid smoke hung in the air ahead of them, heavy with the stench of melted plastic and burnt wiring. It only grew thicker as they passed the final obstacles and ducked into the secret room that held the machine.

When they reached it, the room was stifling hot and too full of smoke to see much of anything. Coughing, Coldmoon did his best to fan away the fumes. As the air cleared, the outlines of the machine emerged, a sooty pall still drifting up from the vents in its sides. The two steel wands protruding from its front panels were scorched and steaming. The computer screen was blank. The ticking, he realized, was the sound of a superheated machine as it cooled off.

His eye fell to the control knob. It had been twisted to its farthest clockwise extent: past the first mark, past the second mark, past even the setting Ellerby had used to inadvertently summon the creature. Someone had redlined the machine: whether to sabotage it so it could no longer be used, or simply to fulfill its purpose one last time, Coldmoon could not guess. It had been pushed far past its limits and was now little more than a hulk.

Pendergast, after a brief inspection, had gone to the nearby worktable and picked up a crisp, unmarked envelope. As Coldmoon watched, he tore it open with a trembling hand, plucked out the single sheet within, and read it. After a minute, his hand fell to his side, and the letter—released by nerveless fingers—fluttered to the ground.

"Pendergast?" Coldmoon asked.

Pendergast neither moved nor acknowledged his voice. Coldmoon knelt and picked up the letter. On it, a short message had been written in an elegant feminine hand.

I am going back to save my sister, Mary. I belong with her, anyway. This machine has given me that opportunity—and Miss Frost herself made it clear why I must take it. In her, I see my own lonely, loveless future. It is anything but pretty. And so I will return to my past—the destiny I was meant to have. I will make of it what I can—what I must. If I can't have you on my terms, I can't have you at all.

Goodbye, Aloysius. Thank you for everything—most particularly for not coming after me, even were it possible. That I could not endure; I'm sure you comprehend my meaning.

I love you.
Constance

79

It was just after ten in the morning when the bus from Atlanta pulled into the Greyhound terminal on West Oglethorpe Avenue. There was a hiss of air brakes, and the gleaming metal door slid open. One after another, the passengers descended the steps into bright sunlight. Last to emerge was a thin elderly man with a battered suitcase and a mackintosh that had seen more than its share of weather. He began to step down, then stopped, holding one hand up against the sun.

"Jesus H. Particular Christ!" he said in a pained voice.

The bus driver looked down with an amused but affectionate smile. The old man had ridden in the seat directly behind him, and they'd gotten to talking on the trip from Atlanta. "First time in Savannah?" he asked.

"First time east of the Mississippi," the old man replied.

"You don't say."

"Hell—first time south of the Mason-Dixon, too." He descended the last few steps, squinting, then waved goodbye to the driver. As the bus pulled away, the man set down his suitcase, shrugged out of his mackintosh with some effort, folded it carefully, and placed it on the suitcase. He wiped his brow with the back of a hand and looked around.

He hadn't known what to expect of Savannah. For a moment, he tried comparing it to the places he knew: Yakima, Olympia, Seattle. But there was no applicable frame of reference. There were no mountains in the distance. Everything was flat. The buildings looked old and decrepit. The sky didn't hold the continual threat of rain he'd lived with all his life. On the other hand, there was plenty of water around…in the form of humidity. He'd never imagined that a place could be so hot and so moist at the same time.

He asked for directions, then struck out, heading east on Oglethorpe. The streets were busy with traffic, the sidewalks teeming with pedestrians. More than one of the latter glanced with surprise at the old man with the Santa Claus beard. But he paid no attention: he'd been stared at before. After about ten minutes he stopped again, took off his plaid work shirt, and carefully rolled it up inside his mackintosh, which he snugged back under the handle of the suitcase. Now he was down to a T-shirt and faded coveralls, but it was a uniform that seemed to blend better with the locals. Opening a zipper and reaching into the case, he pulled out a waxed bucket hat, crumpled and shapeless, which he stretched and massaged until it fit upon his head. It was a Stetson he'd used to keep the rain off his pate for forty years; now maybe it would protect him from sunstroke.

The man turned south on Barnard and walked through a small area of grass and trees, bounded on all sides by buildings. This was more like it. At the far end was a plaque, telling him the domesticated little park was named Orleans Square. Ahead now, over the roofs of the city, many with scaffolding, he could see dust rising and hear the familiar noise of construction.

At the sight, and the sound, he felt his throat constrict involuntarily.

Living as he did away from civilization, he didn't make it a practice to read the paper or watch the news. What happened beyond his property line wasn't his business, and he'd grown sick of the steady drumbeat of depressing and irritating news about which he could do nothing. His bus trip had taken him first from Seattle to Chicago, and then Chicago to Atlanta, and in the Chicago bus station he'd caught a glimpse of screaming headlines about the Savannah disaster. He'd picked up some papers and read about how the city had suffered some kind of attack, fire and explosions—the stories were baffling—with numerous casualties. This had heightened his anxiety, which was already at a high level. But he reassured himself that above all, she was a survivor—and a most formidable woman.

A most formidable woman. And quite lonely.

He should have done this—found her and gone to her—years ago. But there was still time. Heart pounding, he quickened his pace down Barnard Street. There were cranes ahead, and scaffolding, and the heavy-duty contractors' vans and pickups. The noise of construction was growing ever louder, and scenes of considerable destruction began to present themselves.

Something bizarre and ruinous had happened here, with multiple damaged buildings, scorched trees and, here and there, the hulks of burned cars.

Another ten or so blocks and he reached Chatham Square. Taking a torn and soiled piece of paper from his pocket, he unfolded it and glanced at some scribbled directions. This was the place. The Chandler House stood along the far side of the park, on Gordon Street.

But when he raised his eyes and identified the building, his heart sank. The long, rambling structure was surrounded by newly erected chain-link construction fencing, the upper windows covered with plywood, scaffolding surrounding it. Through it, he could see on the top floor indications of fire damage and collapse.

Taking a firmer grip on the suitcase, he made his way across the square. Several buildings on the other three sides were being restored as well, but the old man paid no attention to them. He crossed Gordon Street, then stopped in front of the hotel's brick façade, barely visible behind the scaffolding. A local cop stood at the temporary construction gate guarding the hotel's front door. He walked up to him.

"Can I help you?" he asked.

The man, staring at the façade, said nothing.

"Sir, can I help you?" the cop repeated.

"I'm looking for Miss Frost," the man said.

"Miss Frost? You mean Felicity Frost?"

The old man nodded. "She...owns this building."

The cop ingested this for a moment. "What's your business with her?"

"I'm..." The man broke off, coughing, then cleared his throat. "I'm a relative."

"I see." A pause. "Sir, I'm sorry to inform you that Felicity Frost is deceased."

"*What?*" The man met the cop's sympathetic gaze.

"I'm very sorry," the cop said. "She was killed in the disaster. If you inquire at city hall, they can give you additional information." He gently pointed the way for him, giving directions.

The old man walked away, but he began to feel weak and even dizzy, as if in a dream. A strange veil of darkness crossed his eyes, and the medical part of his brain warned him: syncope, due to a sudden drop in blood pressure. Looking around, he saw a hydrant a few steps away; he walked over to it and sank down. Here, in the shade, it was cooler. *Deceased.* His brain simply couldn't process it.

The last thing he remembered was taking off his hat and placing it carefully in his lap.

A hand was grasping his shoulder, shaking him gently but firmly. And there was a voice calling out: distant at first, then more distinct. "Doctor? Dr. Quincy?"

The old man raised his head at the sound. A person was standing over him; someone with a vaguely familiar voice.

He blinked several times, clearing his vision. His hat was in his lap, and his suitcase lay between his legs, where he'd apparently dropped it.

And then everything came back to him.

He heard the voice, calling his name again, and this time Quincy was able to focus. It was that FBI agent—what was his name, Coldmoon?—who'd visited him at Berry Patch.

"My ass hurts," he said.

"I'm not surprised," the FBI agent said. "I think you've been sitting on that fireplug for an hour."

Quincy looked down. "Jesus."

"I first saw you fifteen minutes ago. Thought it best to leave you with your thoughts. But come on—let's get you to your feet. I'll bet you could use something to eat."

"I'm not hungry."

"Well, you won't say no to coffee, I'll bet." And retrieving his suitcase, the FBI agent helped him up, then began escorting him down the sidewalk.

Quincy fended off the helping hand. "Where's that meddlesome partner of yours?"

"He's occupied."

"Well, I want to talk to him. I want some goddamned answers."

"He isn't talking to anyone right now—even me."

They walked a few blocks, and the stiffness in Quincy's limbs eased. Coldmoon ushered him into a diner. A waitress was standing behind the register, checking the morning's tabs. When she looked up and saw Coldmoon, she frowned.

"You've got your nerve!" she said, glaring at him. "Coming back in here!"

"Nice to see you again, too," Coldmoon said placidly.

Even though the restaurant was almost empty, Quincy noticed that she guided the two of them to the back, to the table closest to the restrooms.

"Coffee please, doll," Coldmoon said.

"I'm not your 'doll.' And don't try to sweet-talk me." The waitress glanced at Coldmoon's western-style shirt with its mother-of-pearl buttons on the front pockets. "That's a nice blouse. Do they make one for men?"

"She doesn't like you very much," Quincy said as the waitress walked away.

"That's why I'm here."

Quincy rubbed his forehead wearily. He was going to have to deal with this revelation at some point, but not now. God, not now.

"See that fresh pot of coffee, over there?" Coldmoon said. "Now: see that other one beside it, almost empty, with scorch marks on its sides, that's probably been there since six AM?"

"Yes."

"I guarantee she'll give me what remains of the one pot, and pour you a fresh cup from the other."

Quincy, uncomprehending, looked at Coldmoon, wondering what the hell he was talking about.

"She was very brave, you know. You would have been proud of her. She fought to the end."

"Tell me," Quincy said simply.

And Coldmoon began talking. He spoke for a long time as Quincy listened. It was an amazing story, bizarre, convoluted, and at times incredible. But that was Alicia—nothing about her was ordinary. He heard about how she created a new identity, bought and restored the hotel, used the machine, what had happened between her and Ellerby, and then the crazy thing at the end. Some of it was so outrageous he was disinclined to believe it, except that Coldmoon was a grounded and rational FBI agent. In a strange way, he sensed that Coldmoon had known he was coming and had already thought through what he would tell him.

Finally, the agent fell silent, the story over. When he did, Quincy took in a deep, slow breath, like an astronaut testing the atmosphere on an unknown world. It was going to take him a while to process the story, make some sense out of it—if he ever would. Nevertheless, he felt an invisible weight had been lifted.

"There's something else," Coldmoon said. He rummaged in a small day pack, brought something out, and handed it to Quincy.

The old doctor took the thin package wrapped in paper. As he unwrapped it, an odor of smoke reached his nostrils. Inside was a copy of *Spoon River Anthology*, deeply charred along its lower edge. But even flame could not conceal the years of wear that the battered cover, the dog-eared pages, spoke of so clearly.

Without a word, he opened the cover and saw the inscription he'd written almost fifty years ago:

From Z.Q. to A.R.
To me, you'll always be "that great social
nomad, who prowls on the confines
of a docile, frightened order."
Berry Patch, 4/22/72

The sight of the inscription, the memories it brought back, overwhelmed him with emotion. And he saw, below the faded words, much fresher ones:

I was once a nomad. But over these many years
of wandering,
you were always, always, my lodestar.
"Thy firmness makes my circle just,
And makes me end where I begun."
—Alicia

Quincy realized he was gripping the book so tightly his hands were shaking. He relaxed his hold, fighting off the need to weep.

"I looked it up," Coldmoon said.

"John Donne," Quincy said, still looking at the inscription.

"Yeah."

They sat there in silence. Quincy held the book, caressing it faintly, as he might someone's hand. At last, he looked up. "So when do I get to see Pendergast?"

"Sorry. You won't."

A brief hesitation had preceded this. Quincy looked more closely at Coldmoon.

"Something's wrong, isn't it?" he asked. "Something happened to him."

"Doctors are perceptive," Coldmoon replied.

As another silence descended, the waitress refilled their coffee mugs. Quincy noticed she did indeed pour Coldmoon's coffee from a different pot, emptying the burnt dregs and sediment into his cup.

"You're right about that waitress," he said. "That looks awful."

"Not in the least. That's why I come here. She saves the best for me, and I tip her accordingly." Coldmoon took a gulp, then put down the cup with evident satisfaction. "So. What now?"

Quincy shrugged. "God knows. Life is strange. The years of loneliness, the sudden hope, and now this. I don't know. I guess I never thought about it…beyond getting here, I mean."

Coldmoon nodded. "My people have a saying: 'The journey is the destination.'"

"Liar. Ralph Waldo Emerson wrote that."

A brief pause. "Damn," Coldmoon muttered.

"Nice try, though."

Coldmoon glanced at his watch. "Look, I've got some time, the evening's free. Let's get you a hotel room for the night. And then maybe we can grab a beer."

"Let's grab that beer now. It's a goddamned swamp outside."

Coldmoon smiled again—faint but genuine. "I knew beneath that crusty exterior there was something about you I liked." And, rising, he drained his coffee, dropped a twenty on the table, then followed the old man as he made his way, slowly and painfully, toward the exit.

80

THE MORNING SUN, FILTERED through a heavy veil of dust and coal smoke, fell feebly across the wide avenue in the west-central section of Manhattan. But it was a different sun, and a different city.

The broad thoroughfare where Broadway crossed Seventh Avenue was made of dirt, its potholed surface packed so hard from an infinitude of horse hooves, wagons, and trolleys that it seemed almost as impermeable as cement, except along the muddy areas surrounding the grooves of the cable car tracks and the hitching posts sunk deep in manure.

The intersection was called Longacre, and would not be known as Times Square for another twenty-five years. It was the center of the "carriage trade," an outlying district of the rapidly growing city where horses were stabled and buggy makers toiled.

On this particular chilly morning, this broad intersection of avenues and streets was quiet save for the occasional pedestrian or horse cart passing by, and nobody paid much attention to the young woman with short dark hair—dressed in a purple gown of an unusual cut and fabric—who stepped out from an alleyway and looked around, squinting and wrinkling her nose.

Constance Greene paused, letting the initial flood of sensations sink in, careful not to betray any sign of the upswell of emotions that threatened to overwhelm her. The sights, noises, and odors unexpectedly brought back a thousand memories of her childhood, memories so distant that she scarcely knew she still retained them. The smell of the city hit her first and most viscerally: a complex mixture of earth, sweat, horse dung, coal smoke, urine, leather, fried meat, and the ammoniac tang of lye. Next were things she'd once taken for granted but that now looked strange— the telegraph poles, invariably listing; the gaslights on various corners; the numerous carriages, parked on or next to sidewalks; the ubiquitous shabbiness. Everything told of a city growing so fast that it could scarcely keep up with itself. One only had to gaze around at the hurried signage, the brick and brownstone buildings that looked slapped together, the accumulated filth that nobody seemed to notice, to realize this was true. Most strangely, the white-noise susurrus of modern Manhattan was missing: the growl of car traffic; the honking of taxis; the hum of compressors, turbines, HVAC systems; the underground rumble of subway trains. In its place was a relative quiet: hoofbeats of horses, shouts, calls, and laughter; the occasional crack of a whip; and, from a nearby saloon, the tinny, off-key strains of an upright piano. She had grown so used to seeing the boulevards of Manhattan as vertical steel canyons that it was hard to process this scene, where the tallest buildings, as far as the eye could see, were sun-soaked, no more than three or four stories.

After a few minutes, Constance took a deep breath. She knew where she was. Now she had to figure out *when* she was.

She looked north up the avenue, noting the ground that had just been broken for what she knew would become the American Horse Exchange. Then she turned south. Her gaze took in the nearest shopfronts: the New Washington Market; a dealer in imported marble; Klein's Fat Men's Shop; a purveyor of Gambetta snuff. She walked in their direction, careful to keep her pace unhurried and casual. The gown she had taken from her closet, while the most old-fashioned she owned, was far outside the mode of the time and might attract unwanted attention. And it was cold: she couldn't help shivering. But there was nothing she could do about that—for now. At least it looked costly.

She walked past an execrable restaurant, its entrance shabby and dusty, offering a choice of oxtail goulash, potted veal chop, or pigs' feet with kraut for five cents. Outside stood a busy newsboy with an armful of papers, his clear piping voice announcing the headline of the day. She passed slowly, staring, as he held one out hopefully.

She shook her head and walked on, but not before noting the date: Saturday, November 27, 1880.

November 1880. Her sister, Mary, eighteen years old, was currently living in the Girls' Lodging House on Delancey Street, being worked half to death in the Five Points Mission. And her brother, Joseph, would be completing his sentence on Blackwell's Island.

And a certain doctor had only recently begun his ghastly, murderous experiments.

She felt her heart quicken at the thought of them still alive. She might still be in time.

There remained two immediate pieces of business. She continued down Seventh Avenue at a brisker pace, passing a pawnbroker on Forty-Fifth Street, advertising itself as the Broadway Curiosity Shop, sporting not only "100,000 tools for all trades" but also diamonds and jewelry for purchase, sale, or exchange. Several locked glass cabinets, with casters mounted into wooden bases, stood outside the shop, containing rifles, shotguns, primitive box cameras, watches, and other items representative of the goods inside. She hesitated, then continued; this was not the kind of establishment she was looking for.

She found that place twelve blocks south, in a better part of town near Herald Square: an expensive-looking jeweler that specialized in diamonds. The street traffic and the crowds were thicker here. She stepped inside and strode up to the nearest counter.

A salesman faced her from the other side of the glass top. He was young, the sleeves of his white shirt held in place above his elbows by black armbands, and he sported a leather visor over his sun-freckled face. He looked Constance up and down as she entered, his expression somewhat confused as he tried to place her and her unusual dress in the social and class milieu of the time.

"May I help you, miss?" he asked, slightly accenting the last word.

"I'd like to see your manager," Constance replied.

The man was taken aback by her directness but tried quickly to cover it up. "And what business might you have with him?"

"A transaction that will be much to his benefit, and that requires someone of greater authority than yourself."

This answer, even more direct and delivered with imperious crispness, was still more surprising. The man hesitated and then vanished into a room in the back. A moment later an older man, around fifty, with snow-white hair, appeared. He had a friendly, though guarded, expression—Constance imagined he'd seen his share of grifters and robbers. A jeweler's loupe hung from around his neck.

"How may I be of assistance?" he said in a neutral tone but one nevertheless more approachable than that of his employee.

Constance reached into the pocket of her smock—feeling the reassuring heft of the stiletto as she did so—and brought out a felt pouch. "I'm interested in selling a diamond," she said.

"Very well," the man said, removing a velvet tray and placing it on the counter. "Let's have a—" He suddenly fell silent as Constance turned up the pouch and allowed the diamond inside to roll out onto the velvet. It was a most unusual vermilion color.

Using rubber tweezers, the man picked it up and examined it with the loupe. A long silence ensued. He placed it back down on the velvet. A look of suspicion had gathered on his face. "Where did you get this, young lady?"

"It's a family heirloom." Constance replied, her haughty tone daring him to accuse her of theft.

The man fell silent. Once again, his eyes moved between her and the diamond.

With a show of irritation, Constance picked up the vermilion gem. "Have you ever seen a stone of this coloration?"

"No," came the reply.

"In your profession, have you ever *heard* of one?"

"Red diamonds are the rarest," the man said.

"If such a stone had been stolen, it would be news, would it not? The stone has been in my family for generations. I wish to sell it quietly and anonymously. Now: do you think you can manage that, sir?"

Conflicting emotions crossed the man's face. "Ma'am, I—"

"In addition to its unique color, you will see that it is not only genuine, but of exceptional clarity, with a carat weight just over three-point-five. Please note also the impeccable radiant cut."

Fixing the loupe to his eye, the man looked carefully at the stone again. Constance counted the minutes as he examined it from every angle, weighed it, and even immersed it in oil. Finally he lowered the loupe.

"Five hundred dollars," he said.

Constance fixed her gaze on his. "Don't think you can take advantage of me because I'm a woman. That stone is unique—and worth far more."

The man hesitated. "Seven hundred."

Constance held out her hand for the stone.

"Eight hundred and fifty," he said. "I can't go any higher because...frankly, that's all the funds I have on hand." He paused. "Since you wish to remain anonymous, I might point out that I *am* taking a risk."

Constance worked out just how large that sum was in 1880. Workingmen earned less than two dollars a day, and a good house cost fifteen hundred dollars. While it still was far less than the diamond was worth, it would do—for now. "Very well," she said.

She waited as the man went into the back room. She heard a whispered conversation, and—slipping her hand into her pocket and grasping the stiletto—she made sure she had a clear path to the door. But a minute later, the manager appeared again. Wordlessly, he laid a stack of bills on the velvet tray and overturned a small bag of twenty-dollar gold pieces on the velvet for her to count. Constance flipped through the bills and counted out the coins. She nodded. He put the notes in an envelope and the coins back in the bag and gave them to her. She tucked both bag and envelope into the pocket of her dress, thanked him, and exited to the avenue.

A block away, she found a couturier that, in addition to tailored dresses, also sold prêt-à-porter outfits. An hour later she emerged again, with a shop's assistant holding a hatbox and two large bags in tow. Instead of the purple gown, Constance was now wearing an elegant bustle dress of peacock-blue silk and white ruffles, with a matching bonnet and heavy Eton jacket. As she walked briskly to the curb, the gazes she attracted were admiring rather than curious. Constance paused while the assistant flagged down a hansom cab.

The driver began to get down from his seat, but Constance opened the door herself and—putting a high-buttoned shoe on the running board—sprang up easily into the compartment.

The driver raised his eyebrows, then mounted his seat as the shop assistant put the bags and the hatbox inside the cab. "Where to, ma'am?" he asked as he drew in the reins.

"The Fifth Avenue Hotel," Constance said, proffering a dollar bill.

"Yes, *ma'am*," the driver said as he pocketed it. Without another word, he urged his horse forward, and within moments, the cab was lost in the ebb and flow of the noonday traffic.

Authors' Note

The story of Dan Cooper (aka D. B. Cooper) as recounted in the opening chapters is a true one and is presented here with only a few embellishments, demanded by the novel that it precedes. As of this writing, neither Dan Cooper nor his remains have ever been satisfactorily identified.

The authors wish to apologize for the actions and unpleasant nature of Senator Drayton, who is an entirely fictitious character. No such person has ever disgraced the beautiful and time-honored state of Georgia with his or her representation. Likewise, Armand Cobb is entirely a figment of the authors' imagination and has no basis in any person who works or has ever worked at the Owens-Thomas House.

And while we are apologizing, a thousand pardons to Savannah—which we both believe to be one of the most fascinating, welcoming, gracious, and end-lessly mysterious cities we have ever visited—for the attentions this novel subjects it to. We urge all readers interested in charming and historic places to visit Savannah, where we are confident the mosquitoes they encounter—if any—will be of ordinary size.

ABOUT THE AUTHORS

The thrillers of **DOUGLAS PRESTON** and **LINCOLN CHILD** "stand head and shoulders above their rivals" (*Publishers Weekly*). Preston and Child's *Relic* and *The Cabinet of Curiosities* were chosen by readers in a National Public Radio poll as being among the one hundred greatest thrillers ever written, and *Relic* was made into a number-one box office hit movie. They are coauthors of the famed Pendergast series, and their recent novels include *Bloodless*, *The Scorpion's Tail*, *Crooked River*, *Old Bones*, and *Verses for the Dead*. In addition to his novels, Preston writes about archaeology for the *New Yorker* and *Smithsonian* magazines. Child is a Florida resident and former book editor who has published seven novels of his own, including such bestsellers as *Full Wolf Moon* and *Deep Storm*.

Readers can sign up for The Pendergast File, a monthly "strangely entertaining note" from the authors, at their website, PrestonChild.com. The authors welcome visitors to their Facebook page, where they post regularly.